CESAR THE BRAVO

Cirsova Publishing
2025

First printing: 2025

ISBN:
Paperback: 978-1-960381-47-7
Hardcover: 978-1-960381-48-4
eBook: 978-1-960381-49-1

Bravo copyright 2011 Ken Lizzi. First published in *Pirates and Swashbucklers volume 1*, 2011.
The Fire Demon, Or Brava copyright 2015 Ken Lizzi. First published in *Swords and Sorcery Magazine*, 2015.
The Quarto Volume, Or Knowledge, Good and Evil copyright 2016 Ken Lizzi. First published in *Swords and Sorcery Magazine*, 2016.
The Bronze Helm copyright 2022 Ken Lizzi. First published in *Tales From the Magician's Skull*, 2022.
The Red Hat copyright 2024 Ken Lizzi. First published in *Cirsova Magazine* 2024.
Witch Hunt appears here for the first time.

Contents

Bravo 7

The Fire Demon, or Brava 29

The Quarto Volume, or Knowledge, Good and Evil.. 51

Witch Hunt 75

The Bronze Helm, or Unfinished Business 297

The Red Hat 323

Bravo

Resinous smoke cutting through the reek of the alley announced my target even before the flickering orange light of the torches. With my right hand, I slid the cinquedea free from its oiled sheath at the small of my back, and with my left, I drew the main gauche from its sheath at my hip. I had been right to leave the rapier behind; the street the alley debouched into was narrow, little wider than the alley through which I crabbed sideways. No room for fancy sword play. Hacking with the wide blade and stabbing with the short off-hand weapon was the most promising option.

Not that a fight was a particularly *promising* option: looked like a procession of the bastards. Torch bearers as van and rearguard. A couple of body servants armed with clubs. Even a pair of arquebusiers. The torch smoke had masked the odor of the smoldering slow match each had coiled about one wrist. Well, the torch smoke *and* the fetid stew of garbage and shit that the city always marinated in from these early days of summer until washed away by the winter rains.

In the center of the procession paced the primary object of my attention—and next to him, one more, one whose role I couldn't immediately decipher. Even in the dancing, crimson-hued shadows I noted a certain resemblance. He was bigger than the principal target, not taller—though both stood a hand's-breadth above my middle stature, but bigger, shoulders widened from physical labor in contrast to the pinched form of the principal target, from whose shoulders the Collegium robes draped shapelessly like linen from a tailor's lattice dummy. They shared in common a paunch, spelling prosperity.

Long odds or not, it was time to earn my fee. I composed myself, adopting my working demeanor. A professional does not lose his head. Each man there was simply an obstacle to be dealt with, already factored into the price of my services. I stepped into the midst of the procession, right behind the arquebusiers, the tip of one blade pressed against the small of each one's back. I didn't run them through. I'm not a hired throat-slitter. I'm a bravo, and that means these affairs and affrays must be handled with aplomb.

"Oblige me, lads, and set down your artillery," I said, prodding them each to suggest a certain urgency. There was, of course. At my back were a body servant, a torch bearer, the magus, and the unknown party in his weather-beaten jerkin that smelled faintly of salt. The back of my neck prickled at the exposure. But the two gunners dropped their hackbuts willingly enough and stepped away from the pointy threats at their spines with alacrity, and kept high stepping, each man scraping a shoulder against one of the buildings hemming in the street on each side, scraping off a layer of soot and grime from the stuccoed exteriors. In better light, I might have been able to ascertain the underlying wall color.

I spun. "Uh-uh," I said, pointing the cinquedea at the body servant who'd advanced, club raised, squeezing by his master at the expense of his livery—a swathe of purple doublet dangled from forearm to elbow where he'd scraped against the tenement to his left.

"That goes for you as well," I said, waggling the point of my parrying dagger at the unknown man who'd clapped a hand to the hilt of a heavy cutlass. He took a step forward, but at the restraining clutch of the magus's hand on his shoulder, he stopped and let his hand fall from the hilt.

"Now, Your Eminence, be so kind as to about-face and head home," I continued.

"Or else what?" he answered, appearing admirably unperturbed.

"Or else I start puncturing large, irreparable holes in your entourage," I said, twirling the tips of my blades illustratively.

"Oh, the prospect is highly unlikely," he said and tugged a charm, or hollow bauble, from the chain of office that hung from his dewlapped neck. It was egg-shaped, of some dull-gray substance, pot-metal or pewter perhaps, and about half the size of my fist—or was until it smashed like glass against the cobbles and began emitting a geyser of scarlet smoke.

The roiling fume concealed the magus from view, spiraling upward and seeming to thicken and grow substantial.

"Come," I heard the magus say, "our journey is compromised this night. Let's oblige our rash friend and return to the palazzo. If we delay our excursion until tomorrow, he'll no longer be able to trouble us."

I didn't like the certainty of his tone. And I didn't like the form solidifying from the smoke: nearly twice my height, broad enough to nearly fill the street, long muscular arms terminating in taloned hands the size of dinner plates, elongated head flanked by pointed ears and topped with broad, spiral horns, fanged mouth agape, yellow eyes burning with an internal fire that almost matched the glow of the brick red skin. That illumination was about the only positive aspect I could see, since the torchbearers hadn't needed to be instructed twice and had taken the light with them, fleeing in opposite directions, presumably to meet at the magus's palazzo.

"I will ease my thirst with your blood and dull my hunger with the marrow of your bones," said the demon with a voice like a mountain lion caught in a rock slide. He came for me.

It is at times like these, traditionally, that people wonder why they got into this situation. I needed to pay my tailor.

I was a valued customer, and on the exclusive list of those to whom he was willing to extend credit. But his patience was not infinite. The last month had been rather lean. My landlord was beginning to shadow me and tally up the value of my few belongings. And if I ever wished to frequent a tavern or coffee shop again, I'd need ready coin. But most immediately, I needed to square with Donatello. Not just any man with a pair of shears and a needle can do justice to my frame. Donatello is an artist.

I was leaning against a wall opposite Giacomo's wine shop, enviously watching patrons enter, when I observed two very dissimilar men watching from a few doors down the Course—the street that runs the length of Plenum within the walls from Fontana Square to the pagan Temple of Sighs. It's a colorful stroll for those with time to gawp and sight-see, but not here where it seems to hold its breath for the passage through the Orine district; the shops, tenements, and warehouses lining the Course here are squat, unadorned affairs, seldom stretching over two stories and of an almost uniform shade of muck gray, the result of centuries of accumulated filth and neglect. And the people—with notable exceptions—match the squalor.

One of the two I recognized from the neighborhood, a sodden wine-sack by the name of Belatus or Baltus. He was gesturing at me and talking rapidly. He held out a hand. Something glittered and transferred to his palm from the other man's fingers. The other man was a Member of the Collegium, obviously, despite his getup of plebeian attire: loose breeches and an unpadded, brown doublet. He appeared both too prosperous and—a conundrum, this—too much the ascetic. His clothing was new, stainless, without a tear. And the unassuming burgher attire that he doubtless supposed was humble wear stood out here where most wore either rags, like Baltus, or dressed flash—hose, codpiece, slashed doublet—like I did. Though few approached the quality of cut and fabric I sported.

The magus approached, Baltus scarpering off as if he feared his benefactor might demand a refund. I made an elegant leg, bowing slightly at the waist, sweeping my sheathed rapier up and back with my off hand in the manner of a courtier. "Your Excellency," I said, demonstrating that his disguise was no match for my perception.

He raised an admonishing hand. "Please, discretion.

11

You are the bravo, Cesar?"

"I have that honor, Your Excellency," I said, troweling it on thick.

"Again, I ask for discretion. I am here incognito. Is there someplace we can speak privately?"

"Perhaps a cup of wine?" I asked, gesturing at Giacomo's. A free drink put me ahead in the transaction even if this meeting was otherwise bootless.

The magus's disguise fooled no one. Giacomo ushered us to a secluded table without even being asked and brought a vintage substantially superior to any he'd ever served me before.

"My name is Massim," the magus said without preamble. "I represent Fienze and, unofficially, the Bottelo family, in the Collegium. I wish to hire the services of a bravo."

I savored the slight sweetness of the velvety wine. "I assume you know the distinction between a bravo and a street thug? I will not club a man over the head for you in a dark alley. And I'm no assassin." This was not, strictly speaking, entirely accurate. But I had limits.

"Good. I am looking for someone who can offer more finesse, more resourcefulness."

"You've bought the wine," I said, though in point of fact he'd yet to do so; best establish that responsibility up front. Some men of his station tend to abandon a bill without thought, used to subordinates picking up the tab. "The least I can do is hear you out."

"Councilor Petro died early last week. Meaning a Red Hat is open on the Inner Council. There is a man, a member of the Collegium, named Fellitore, who is maneuvering for the empty Seat. I do not want him to be elected."

"I told you I am not an assassin. When I kill a man, it is face-to-face and he has an opportunity to defend himself."

"I am not asking you to assassinate him. Please, let me continue. You need to understand that the politicking behind the closed doors of the College involves a certain amount of gold exchanging hands. Now, Fellitore's family, the Dallagio from Senna, have funds but are not wealthy enough to account for the sums that have recently filled the purses of the Electors. The Botteli are hard pressed to match these—donatives."

I saw it now. Massim was angling for the Red Hat himself, but his family was losing the bidding war against Fellitore's.

"I am informed by a reliable source," the magus continued, "that Fellitore will undertake some sort of nocturnal adventure tonight, connected somehow to the source of his funding. Now, I would love to learn that source, but more immediately I want this adventure disrupted. It is of greater urgency that the flow of gold be stopped than that I discover its origin. Is my need clear?"

"By 'reliable source' I assume you mean a spy in Fellitore's household." I wasn't trying to impress him with my cleverness, just filling the silence while I weighed the job. Disrupting a meeting, putting a scare into someone, or even just creating the fear of discovery seemed practicable. "What do you offer?"

Massim named a figure. He was serious about the job. I could pay off Donatello. I could get four months ahead on my rent, patronize any tavern I fancied. Or get two months ahead on my rent and have Donatello stitch together something new. I'm not a tall man, but I'm put together like a bull, or one of those tenacious fighting dogs; all chest and muscle. Domenico, my fencing master, frequently voices his incredulity at my ability to walk a straight line, let alone achieve any grace with a pass or a parry. So when a man like me finds a tailor who can do him justice, he's wise to commission what apparel he can afford.

"Consider me hired," I said. "What are the specifics of tonight's activities?"

Massim laid out what he knew of the route and possible constituents of Fellitore's entourage. Then he dug into an inner pocket and produced a stoppered glass bottle about a hand-high and three-fingers around. "Fellitore is a High-Magus. If he draws a familiar demon, open this phial and toss the contents into the air between you and the demon—once it approaches within a pace or two."

Suddenly the fee seemed much less generous.

The fee certainly appeared paltry as the demon rushed toward me, talons tracing parallel lines of sparks as they raked the buildings defining the street. The demon's mouth widened, thin lips drawing back from glittering spikes of teeth, the whole looking capable of engulfing my head. It was enough to curdle the blood in a man's veins, that enormity of horror. And terror is one of a demon's primary weapons—along with the arsenal of fang, claw, and muscle. But familiarity can blunt the edge of terror. Summoned demons, while not entirely commonplace, are an accepted reality. And if a man intends to thwart a High-Magus, he'd better be willing to face that reality. A timid man would never have embarked on the chancy life of a bravo, would never have willingly put himself in this position. I knew, or at least hoped I knew, what I was doing. I did not freeze. I did not soil my under-linen. Quite. I had, after all, come prepared.

I let the main gauche drop to clatter against the cobbles. I plucked the phial Massim had given me from my waistband. The trick was mastering anxiety, preventing myself from a panicked, premature hurling of the phial. The demon wasn't a great distance from me, but some quirk of imagination rendered its approach as slow as the last drop from an upended wine cup, though objectively it was as precipitous as an onrushing bull.

I waited.

Then, when its mouth looked as wide as an ale barrel, I smashed the little glass bottle on the cobbles between us.

The result was miraculous and immediate. A scintillant metallic cloud erupted, a billowing curtain springing up between us, similar in color to the shards of the shattered demonic prison littering the ground, though less leaden-hued, the fine particles taking on a reddish gleam from the demon's glowing hide. Motes settled on my skin and the hardened, leathery skin of the demon. It stopped as if it had slammed into a solid iron wall.

I felt nothing. I took a tentative step forward into the cloud, a million swirling particles dancing on air currents, showing no sign of dissipating. The demon bellowed—some reference to my mother's chosen profession and the legal status of my birth—and reached into the cloud, its talons cutting through linen and skin, slicing my left wrist to the bone. But it jerked its arm back like I would if I'd thrust mine into a fire.

I suppressed a yelp as pain flared, wincing as blood welled up, staining sleeve and cuff. Ruined.

Bastard! I pressed forward, short sword raised to strike. Now, the thing about demons is that while yes, they are tough, if one is manifested here sufficiently to harm a man, a man can harm it. Or kill it. It isn't an easy task, but if enough men can gang up on one—or if one man is lucky enough to be standing within a magical protective curtain—sheer volume and force of blows can bring one low, same as a wild boar or a plate-armored cavalier.

That's what I did, hacking and stabbing with an undisciplined fervor that would have brought a pained grimace to Domenico's face. Glancing blows sprang aside as if I'd struck an ox-hide sack full of horn shavings. Well-placed strikes, however, pierced the demon's rugged hide, producing sap-like driblets of orange-hued blood that quickly faded to a dull brown.

It tried to fight back, but the narrow street played to my advantage. It could only attack forward, through the cloud, and its attempts were pained, tentative, so I was able to dodge the jabbing, pawing blows, punishing each with a cut or thrust of my own. At last I wrapped both hands about the short, ivory-embossed grip of the cinquedea, ignoring the flare of pain as I forced my injured wrist into service, twisted about my hips ninety degrees like a woman about to beat a rug, and released, hacking deep into the demon's side.

It had enough. When I wrenched the blade free of the wound, it showed me its tail—stumpy, vestigial—and fled.

I'd won. The ruckus should have disturbed even this neighborhood. Fellitore would not dare a second excursion tonight, unwilling to risk discovery and uncertain of who or what else lay in wait for him. Time to report to Massim. But first...

I groped about the suddenly darkened street, feeling around for shards of the egg in which Fellitore had imprisoned the demon. I stuffed as many large pieces as I could find into the purse at my belt. I located my dropped parrying dagger as well and slipped it into the sheath belted beneath the purse. Then, eyes adjusting somewhat, I made my way from the lightless streets of the Portine quarter to the more salubrious, illuminated grounds of the Collegium.

A disheveled, wounded bravo attempting a nocturnal entrance to the walled city-within-a-city that is the Collegium would normally be the stuff of comic opera. But Massim had left instructions with the elaborately liveried guards at the north-west gate, and I was granted entry without fuss.

Like most of Plenum's Lords and Masters—temporal, spiritual, magical—Massim maintained apartments inside the Collegium walls and a private palazzo in Plenum proper. Massim was occupying his apartments during the Red Hat selection period to maximize his political efforts, unlike Fellitore whose funding venture apparently required a certain distance from the curious.

A servant guided me through a maze of hallways decorated with a richness and variety that defied my ability to catalog and retain discrete memories of. It all melded into a sensory blur, like the music and conversation in a boisterous tavern after the second or third bottle. The servant deposited me in a study where a drowsy Massim met me in a night cape, robe, and slippers—a matched outfit, finely tailored, I noted.

The magus's rooms were about what I'd expected: that is, of a kind to drive a lesser man to envy. I occupied a tiny, vermin-infested room that amplified rather than mitigated whatever weather condition prevailed outside. Massim could stroll from one luxurious chamber to another, each tastefully appointed. But I had studied neither theology nor demonology (assuming they were different academic disciplines). In fact, the only formal schooling I'd undertaken was—and continues to be—fencing. Perhaps there was a lesson there somewhere in the value of education. I don't know. Dame Fortune spins the wheel. The trick is to make the most of the resultant position. Everyone has a lord, right? That is the way of the world. No matter where the wheel places a man, there is always someone above him. I'm content. Mostly.

Massim sent the servant away to prepare coffee, and I could see the sleep in the magus's face replaced by anticipation. But I must give him credit; he mastered his curiosity and attended to my wound first.

Rolling aside a woven carpet, he revealed a protective circle inscribed in the travertine floor tiles. He bade me stand within, and he summoned a familiar spirit, an impish figure no more than a foot high, garbed as a physician and wearing a mask like a long-billed wading bird. Or perhaps that was its actual face. The creature inspected the gashes in my arm, emitted high pitched 'tsk

tsk' sounds and set to work cleaning, anointing, and binding. The pain faded rapidly. The shirt was still a loss, however.

"Now, Cesar, regale me," Massim said as we sat sipping coffee from sparrow-bone thin porcelain cups, familiar dismissed and carpet back in place.

I told the tale, heightening my own heroics by contrasting narrative details: elaborate description concerning all I'd seen, laconic minimalism regarding my actions.

"You say the unknown man at Fellitore's side appeared familiar," Massim said. "Can you describe him?"

"Well, he was of a height with Fellitore, indeed similar in coloring and feature. Perhaps I confused similarity with familiarity." It was odd talking with Massim; my speech pattern and lexicon shifted almost without volition from the street cant and crudities of the Orine district, or the histrionics I employed when working, to the formal cadence and grammar of Massim's station.

"That is intriguing. You may recall that Luca Fellitore had a brother, Bruno, reportedly killed by corsairs when his galley was lost fighting near Breac. If Bruno wasn't killed..."

"If he turned renegade..." I said. "Yes, I see it. Fellitore feeds his brother intelligence of shipping manifests, embarkation dates, destinations. And Bruno in return..."

"Funds Luca's candidacy through the proceeds of his piracy." Massim completed the circle. "Neatly done. But it is apparent now why he's operating with such secrecy. If the truth came to light, his campaign for a Red Hat would fail utterly. He'd be hard pressed even to maintain his chair in the Collegium." Massim stood and paced the room. "Fellitore is finished. But I cannot simply make an accusation. I need evidence. I need a revelation. Fellitore must be seen to fall on his own. I cannot be seen to trip him."

"You need Bruno," I said.

"Yes, Bruno will tell all, whether his head is still attached to his neck or not. But you will need to move quickly. When Fellitore learns of his demon's failure, that you still live, he'll try to smuggle Bruno out of the city immediately."

"I will need to move quickly?" I asked. We negotiated another fee in short order.

I employed a rather roundabout route to Fellitore's palazzo, going by way of the Orine district. I was putting some serious wear in the soles of my foot-gear this night. Plenum covers a series of hills and a pedestrian is nearly always ascending or descending. It's taxing. I still had a lot of walking ahead of me and it was getting on toward morning.

In my room, I pried up the loose floorboard and retrieved my rapier, the oiled blade secured in a simple leather-bound sheath about which I'd wrapped a baldric, leather also but lined with a swath of crimson cloth for a touch of flair. I also changed my shirt. Over the top of shirt and doublet, I donned a solid leather jerkin. I removed the thin metal plates lining strategically positioned pockets in the interior and curving about the high collar. Then, removing the fragments of the demon prison from my purse, I attempted to fashion makeshift replacements. For a metal that had shattered so easily it proved remarkably malleable, and I was able to flatten pieces out enough to fit inside the pockets. Assuming I survived this night to earn the additional fee, I intended to employ a smith or armorer to hammer the fragments out fine and layer them on top of the customary steel plates concealed in the jerkin and codpiece. I'm afraid my handiwork resulted in a lumpy and unappealing garment. But on occasion a man can forgo appearance for effectiveness. If absolutely required. Besides, it was still dark and the odds were slim of any of my acquaintances recognizing me in the paucity of illumination that rendered night time Plenum the haunt of thieves, the well-armed, and the desperate.

So, frequently adjusting the unaccustomed weight and fit of my homemade demon-proofing, I continued on to Fellitore's.

Bruno Fellitore had been a captain of a mercenary company before his disappearance. That suggested competence and intelligence. I knew the type, having served before as a sword-for-hire when times were particularly difficult. It felt unnatural to admit competence in an officer, but the work of mercenary companies weeded out the stupid and ineffectual mercilessly. If he'd survived capture and risen to a position of importance among the corsairs, he was likely also tough and ruthless. His willingness to turn renegade, forswear the Faith and pledge himself to the Heathen, showed an eye to the main chance. A formidable foe.

I'd not ever want to face the choices he had. The corsairs are a constant threat, not just an irritant. They not only harry shipping, they raid the coasts for slaves, even so bold as to stage an assault on Plenum's port town of Spina, not ten leagues beyond the city walls. The atrocities they commit are legendary, and the leading captains' names are used to frighten willful children.

Well, tonight I'd lessen their numbers by one.

Sabatine Hill, where Fellitore kept his residence, was better lit than most of Plenum, and private security patrols kept the human vermin in check. I used the shadows to full advantage, reaching the high wall encompassing his palazzo unnoticed. The wall was mortared rock, probably topped by broken glass and crockery. I shrugged off my jerkin as I prowled about the perimeter. Fellitore's palazzo abutted estates on either side, sharing walls. Torchlight made me a trifle nervous about clambering over on the front-gate face. I located an alley further down the avenue and crept through, getting muck on my shoes and getting hissed at by a cat for my troubles.

The back wasn't much better. Torches illuminated another row of villas across the street running behind Fellitore's. But the hill rose higher here, the torches set back from the road and higher up, and a stand of towering cypress trees and stone pines broke up the run of palazzos.

Finding a relatively shadowed spot, I tossed my jerkin up to lay across the top of the wall. I took a few steps back, then hurtled forward, leaping up to hook my forearms over the wall, trusting to the thickness of my jerkin to protect me from spiky bits. My feet clambered for purchase, and then I was over, dropping unscathed within the grounds of Fellitore's palazzo.

A second-floor window was open to allow in the night breezes. A decorative trellis allowed a precarious entry into the servants' wing, and from there to the master suite of rooms.

Noise and light let me know that the demon's return had upset Luca Fellitore's equanimity. He was getting ready to move his brother *now*, no doubt dreading the gauntleted fists of the Collegium Guard pounding on his door, demanding entry to inspect his palazzo for fugitives.

I heard servants calling back and forth—one bidden to fetch the hired arquebusiers again, the speaker leaving no doubt that he didn't care in what temperament they'd be upon waking. Another was to assemble torches, another to see to the Master's warm cloak. The clamor faded behind me as I stepped from utilitarian passages into halls painted with almost lifelike frescos of classical scenes. Spindly tables set at intervals supported objets d'art or vases of flowers.

I found the Brothers Fellitore in a large chamber, high-ceilinged, extending up through the second story to the roof. The ceiling featured a painting depicting a dozen or so chubby cherubs flitting about on diminutive wings, some draping an ermine-lined robe over the impressive physique of a figure who looked facially much like Luca Fellitore. Two more of the flying tykes were lowering a Red Hat onto his head while he looked down upon us with a smile of beatific benevolence.

The real Luca Fellitore stood at the far end of the room near a fireplace that was crackling away despite the warmth. Before him stood his brother. And closer to me, spinning to face me, was the wounded demon. A long, gilded table spanned the room lengthwise between us, but the demon paid it no heed, flipping over the massive, marble-topped weight without apparent effort and sprinting the overturned length, howling its eerie, growling shriek.

I'm sure the room held more wonders worth noting: carpets, embroidered chair cushions and settees—a crowd of juggling dwarfs for all I noticed. A pissed-off demon charging pell-mell straight at me occupied all of my attention.

I've mentioned before that I understand how that could freeze other men motionless, too terrified to move, nothing more than sheep facing the butcher's knife. But Massim hadn't hired other men. He'd hired the bravo Cesar. I drew my rapier. When he neared, I stamped forward, pushing off my front foot, then crossed over with my back foot, swinging wide to my right, sword extended across my body in a flèche that struck home deep into the wide gash I'd hacked into the demon's side earlier that night.

It wasn't an easy maneuver, and it wasn't free. The talons of his left hand scraped along the collar of my jerkin and would have ripped open my neck if not for the fragments of metal lumped within. As it was, the claw of the demon's thumb sliced vertically through the bottom half of my ear, and the claw of his small finger gouged a sliver from my collarbone.

But I'd hit something vital.

"Enough!" the demon said and the green and white marble tiles at its feet began to emit a pinkish glow.

"No," said Luca Fellitore. "I forbid you to depart." Turning sideways so I could observe both with flits of my eyes, I watched Luca step within a protective circle.

Opening the collar of his robe he displayed a necklace with a red pendant like a spike of ruby. He grasped the pendant and tugged the chain taut against his neck. "You have not been released. The bargain is unfulfilled. By blood pact, I command you."

But evidently the bargain did not require the demon's death and it felt I'd dealt it a mortal blow if it remained, for as Fellitore wrapped his fist about the ruby spike to enforce his will, his eyes sprang wide and his mouth gaped and he screamed, clapping his free hand to his side in the same spot I'd twice wounded his demon.

"Enough," the demon repeated and began to sink through the floor as if it were a cleverly machined platform on a theater stage. Luca snatched the chain from his neck and hurled it to the floor, a welting of red visible even from where I stood and wisps of smoke rising from his palm where he'd gripped the pendant.

"Enough," said Bruno Fellitore, joining the chorus. "Enough is right, brother. I can kill a man well enough with steel. All your mummery and conjuring is just..." he faltered, his sentence defeating him.

"Wasteful extravagance?" I suggested, offering the brothers a bright smile, though the tug of my facial muscles sent a jab of pain through my torn ear.

The corsair didn't reply. He snatched out his cutlass instead. A nasty, efficient butcher's tool, wide-bladed, slightly curved, but of fine workmanship, a rounded knob of some greenish stone serving as a solid pommel, good for bludgeoning at close quarters. We'd see if the cutlass was as efficient in a spacious chamber as it was on a crowded deck.

"You are a nuisance. A tool of one of Luca's rivals, likely." He rolled his shoulders and gave the air a few preliminary swipes, warming up. "It doesn't matter, tool. You won't be a nuisance much longer." He looked me in the eye to gauge the effect of whatever threat or braggadocio he was about to unlimber. "Red Arm leaves no nuisance alive."

Red Arm. Well, that threat was a pretty good one. Red Arm had been terrorizing the Central Sea for years now, since not long after Bruno disappeared, in fact. The appellation derived from a particularly gruesome anecdote from one of Red Arm's first piratical ventures. The captain of a small caravel had refused to yield. He and the remaining crew were assembled on deck before their captor. The corsair lopped off the recalcitrant captain's arm then used the severed limb as a bludgeon to beat the man to death. Then the crewman next to him. And the next. Stopping only when the arm was just a useless red mass of bone fragments, tendons, and rags of skin. Red Arm nailed the remains of the arm to the prow of his galley and left it there until it rotted off.

Bruno must have sensed he'd scored a touch. He advanced a pace.

"Wait," said Luca Fellitore to his brother. "Let's not discard a tool that might be of use to us. You, bravo, are indeed a nuisance, as Bruno said. But a paid nuisance, I surmise. Correct? Sent at the bidding of—let me guess. Federico? Massim? No need to answer; I can respect professional confidentiality. But if you are willing to earn another man's gold, why not earn mine? I could use a proven asset like you." He named a figure. Bruno's piracy must be lucrative: it was a very large figure.

I am not a good man. For pay, I do things some men might consider questionable, criminal. I'll goad a man into a duel if paid enough by his enemy. Might even kill him, sword-to-sword, if the money is good enough. But I have limits. Luca's offer helped me better define them. This man before me, this corsair, this bloody-handed pirate, was an evil bastard through-and-through. If I accepted Fellitore's blood-stained gold, reneged on my deal with Massim, I would be allying myself with Bruno, tacitly embracing his evil. No. I would not cross that line.

Besides the usual thrill I always experience before combat, I felt a tingle of what might have been virtuous anger. It disconcerted me a touch, but I rode it, let it guide my answer to the Brothers Fellitore. "I already have a job, Your Excellency," I told Luca, then said to his brother, "Bruno, I'm about bantered-out. Look, I'm just going to kill you now so I can get to sleep before sunrise."

He came at me then. The man could fight. My rapier fended off his cutlass in a sparking clash of steel. I riposted to keep him honest. He batted the jab aside and stamped forward, chopping. I retreated a half-step, left foot first, then a full step, right over left as he kept coming. I crouched abruptly, arm straightening into a stop thrust that he almost impaled himself on, but he twisted to a stop and hacked down, trying to snap my blade. I deflected the blow and flicked the point at his front leg. He jerked the leg back and we circled.

"Kill him and be done with it," said Luca. "Where are my arquebusiers?" he called out. "Can't we just put a bullet in this fellow?"

Neither Bruno nor I paid him any attention. We continued exchanging attacks, the air ringing with curses and the clash of blades. He feinted a cut at my eyes, then swept the blade low at my leading leg, aping the gambit I'd employed against him. I raised my right leg high, allowed the cutlass to pass beneath, then dropped the leg down allowing my own weight to carry me into a lunge. Before he could check his swing and recover to guard I passed my rapier through his heart. Breath rushed explosively from his chest. His eyes lost focus, glazed. He slid slowly off the blade and fell to the floor, trailing an arcing jet of blood that splattered down my front.

"Bruno is dead," I said. I wiped my blade clean on Bruno Fellitore's jacket and sheathed it. Then I fetched his cutlass from where it had fallen from his lifeless hand and used the butcher's blade to separate his head from his body. "And so is your chance for a Red Hat, Your Excellency."

I briefly considered sending Luca to join his brother. But no. He was an old, unarmed man. I had limits. And I'd been paid to do a job. A professional focused on the task at hand kept his head. I let Luca Fellitore keep his. And once I delivered his brother's to Massim, I could go home and get some sleep.

But before sleep, I really needed to change out of these blood-soaked clothes. My laundress will never forgive me.

The Fire Demon;
or,
Brava

I parried late, re-directing the thrust intended for my chest to the thigh of my leading leg. Watching the thin blade bow into a half-circle, I was grateful for the capped tip. It still hurt, though. I stepped back, saluted to acknowledge the touch, then reengaged.

A dark-ringletted head peeked through the doorway to the salle. Had I not been otherwise occupied fending off a flurry of assaults, searching for an opportunity to counter, I'd probably have noted the round inquisitiveness of that large-eyed ten-year-old girl-child's face. And the trace similarity of features she shared with my assailant. As it chanced, I was soon able to take in the entire picture of the moppet; Domenico landed a clean touch, signaling a halt. Perhaps the word 'touch' is insufficient. The little man connects with the power of a pike thrust. I was again thankful for the blunted foils and stiff leather fencing jacket.

"Watch the beat and subsequent thrust to prime, Cesar. Damn you, how many times must I remind you?" His verbal instruction was as gentle as his physical.

I gestured at the doorway beyond Domenico's shoulder. "Sorry, Maestro, but I was distracted."

He pivoted with that easy fencer's grace that I try to

emulate. Try and mostly fail. The lift and drop of his slim shoulders hinted at an exasperated sigh.

"Valentina, you know you are not to enter during classes," he said.

Ignoring his admonishment, she entered bouncing, floor-length skirt flouncing. She hurled herself into Domenico's arms as he crouched to receive her. Indulgent father: a hitherto hidden aspect of his personality.

"Watch, father. I have been practicing," she said after disentangling herself from his embrace. From some concealed pocket within her bodice she conjured a wickedly pointed bodkin. With a whip of her arm she flicked the little knife in a glittering whirl to strike one of the fencing mannikins in the center of its wooden torso.

Beaming pride was an incongruous expression on Domenico's long, sour face. "Very good, my lamb."

"Nicely done," I said. And it was. One does not expect a woman—let alone a girl—in Plenum to be plying sharp steel outside the confines of a kitchen.

"Oh, it is easy," she said with the nonchalance of the newly skilled. "I'll show you."

I cast an uncertain glance at Domenico.

"Only a fool fails to accept instruction when offered. One can learn lessons from anyone or anything, you shambling peacock." Domenico's tender, affirming approach to instruction is, I think, his greatest attribute.

After that, a half-hour course in knife throwing was inescapable. It might have continued longer but for an interruption from Anacleto, Domenico's manservant.

"Sir, some foreign visitors have arrived requesting to observe a demonstration." Anacleto appeared flustered.

My interest was piqued. He was a difficult man to ruffle. I shot a glance at Valentina. She was vibrating with curiosity, shaming the efforts of a dozen puppies.

"Of course, Anacleto," said Domenico. "Convey them to the salle. Valentina, please, off with you." There was a stubborn set to her lip and a fractional second of nascent rebellion that gave way to obedience, and she left us without even a petulant stomp. "Cesar, would you mind if we completed your lesson before an audience?"

"Next session provided at a discount?" I asked. A bravo of uncertain and intermittent income must seize—or manufacture—a bargain when he senses the opportunity.

"All right, you parasite, though I happen to know your purse still clinks when you walk."

Bargain complete, we awaited the spectators.

Foreign visitors? Anacleto possessed a gift for subtle misdirection. I had been expecting some northerners, or perhaps Ihbarian fencing students wanting to observe how the Plenum style compared to their sweeping, florid school of swordsmanship. Instead, a troop of Heathens strolled with an air of arrogant possessiveness into the broad, wood-floored salle. There were six of them, five in dun-colored robes and a sixth in dazzling, bleached-white wool. Two preceded the man in white and three brought up the rear. Each of the guards—for it seemed evident to me that was their function—gripped the haft of a square-bladed, spike-backed hatchet thrust head down through the wide leather belts that secured their ankle-length garments. All six were bearded. In contrast to the groomed facial topiary sported in Plenum, their beards were wild, tangled foliage. Topping off the look, each man wore the flat-crowned, boxy lambs-wool cap ordained by their outlandish beliefs.

Domenico and I shared a glance, eyebrows raised in synchronized quizzical arches. Unchoreographed, but, I felt, impressive. While we were not currently at open war with the Heathen, their presence was uncommon in Plenum, Throne of the Faith and site of the Collegium. What did their presence portend? And could I profit by it?

Domenico advanced to greet the party. One of the guards moved to intercept him.

"Welcome. I am Domenico. My man informs me you wish to observe a bout." I could not tell if Domenico was addressing the guard or the august personage who required five bodyguards. In any event, it was the guard who responded.

"The Most Revered Purifier, Alfassan, Second Shield of the Believers and Husband of Three requires a demonstration of your barbarian sword play." He delivered that mule train of titles with pride, a committed sycophant living in reflected glory.

Alfassan, his importance established to his satisfaction, stepped forward with a raised hand and a placatory smile to demonstrate he was at heart really one of us common fellows.

Or perhaps I read too much into the gesture.

"Please," he said, "as I hope to be considered a guest, let us do without honorifics. I am Alfassan. I am merely an aficionado of martial skills and wish, as you say, Domenico, to observe a bout."

And so, Domenico and I staged a show. The Heathens arranged themselves cross-legged around the salle, resting their backs against plastered brick walls. They were, as far as I could tell, utterly rapt as Domenico put me through my paces. I'm certain I earned my discount, since Domenico was nearly as sheathed in sweat as I was when we finally put up our foils.

Alfassan pounded the floor with his open palm in appreciation. "That was thrilling, masterful, all I could have hoped for," he said. "Thank you, Domenico, and thank you..."

"Cesar," I supplied, noting the frowns of his entourage when I failed to apply "revered sir," or "most holy sheep buggerer," or whatever was the appropriate groveling appendage.

"Allow me to show my gratitude." He gestured, and one of his men presented a fist-sized purse to Domenico. Yes, I definitely earned my discount. "And perhaps the two of you would care to share with me a flagon of wine."

Domenico and I were developing quite the arsenal of shared quizzical glances. Were not Heathens prohibited from consuming wine? Still, breaches of heretical religious doctrine concerned me no more than my own breaches of the True Faith's doctrine.

Domenico politely declined. I, however, am always happy to cadge a free drink and so accepted the offer.

"Then, Cesar, once you have cleansed yourself, perhaps you can lead us to your favorite wine shop."

Cleansed myself? Well, it had been some time since I had last risked a full immersion in water. As long as I didn't make a habit of it, the occasional bath couldn't hurt.

CESAR THE BRAVO

We probably received a number of bemused looks as we paraded to Giacomo's wine shop: I, though still dripping from my bath, the picture of a stylish bravo from the top of my feathered cap, past the length of my rapier, to the curled tips of my shoes, leading this passel of grim-visaged Heathens along the dust-covered bricks of the Course. A more upscale neighborhood or district further up the Course might have been appropriate. The Sabatine perhaps, or the Jacline. But I enjoyed a perverse delight at marching these glowering, self-important exotics among the filth-encrusted, fire-trap brick tenements of the Orine district, my impoverished neighborhood. Besides, Alfassan had requested my favorite wine shop.

Alfassan sat and drank with me. The others did not, instead standing cross-armed about the dim, low-ceilinged den of cut-rate iniquity that was Giacomo's, intimidating all but the bravest or drunkest patrons until the place was nearly emptied.

In silence, Giacomo brought a flagon and two fired-clay cups, as unnerved by the invasion of Heathens as his clientele.

"You wonder at my drinking, do you not?" asked Alfassan, an easy smile breaching his beard.

"I own a passing curiosity," I said.

"The Speaker did ordain an injunction against the consumption of intoxicants, it is true. However, the Mouth of the Divine also instructed—and the Speaker's instructions are complete in their perfection—that when transacting business with the Barbarian in furtherance of the Divinity's will, one may emulate the customs of the Barbarian even in contravention of the Dictates of

34

Purification."

"And you are transacting such business in Plenum?"

"I am, at the behest of the Anointed First Shield. There has been, you may be aware, some disagreement concerning the rightful possession of certain islands in the eastern extremities of what you call the Cradle Sea. My embassy is to entreat the Predicant to employ the influence of his office and of the Collegium on those secular governments that wrongly lay claim to lands that belong to the Believers. Thus, we hope to avert any need to assert our unquestioned rights more forcefully. If a few flagons assist my endeavors..." He tossed back a cup and refilled it.

He was a charming bastard. I almost liked him. And, as we paced each other cup-for-cup and story-for-story "almost" dwindled.

I was hailing Giacomo for a third flagon when I spotted a familiar face. Under a stained wooden table, peeking out between a pair of three-legged stools, crouched Valentina. The little spy! I rose to escort her back to Domenico's. Best deal with her puppy-dog infatuation—understandable though it was—right away.

She must have guessed my intention. She scuttled out from beneath her concealment and darted out the door before I managed two strides in her direction. By the time I reached the doorway, she had vanished.

I returned to the table to express my regrets and take my leave. Alfassan extended an invitation to meet him at the embassy—a modest shelter in the Sabatine district—and I left him to pay the fare. I had a fruitless search for a little girl to undertake.

The next day, I summoned the courage to visit Domenico. True, I wasn't culpable for his daughter's escapade, but if she hadn't returned home—or even if she had—his displeasure would inevitably fall on the object of her pursuit—me. Fairness, rationality be damned.

As it happened, I received a temporary reprieve. As I stepped into the daylight, adroitly hopping over the contents of an upended midden pot, I caught sight of Valentina. She was sucking on her lower lip, gazing across the street at the narrow, shadowed entrance to the dank tenement building where I rented my chamber—the rats and other assorted vermin paid naught, the miserable freeloaders. Her expression lightened when she caught sight of me and she bounded heedlessly across the street to meet me.

"Uncle Cesar, I was coming to see you," she said.

Uncle Cesar? "How delightful. Why don't you tell me why you came to visit while we walk back to your father's home?"

"Fine, but I have to tell you about the red jewel and the bad man, and father doesn't believe me." She reached up to clasp my hand and walked with me toward Domenico's, chattering non-stop.

I did not pay attention at first, grasping only at length that after scampering out of the tavern she'd decided to follow Alfassan. My attention heightened when she narrated sneaking into the palazzo that housed the embassy, describing it well enough that I recognized the very building. She wasn't just prattling.

"And then he went into this big room and I followed and hid behind a chair and he moved some furniture and drew on the floor and talked in some funny language and a big man made out of fire was there and he got a red jewel out of a pocket and the fire man went into the red jewel — *woosh* — and then he ate the red jewel, *gulp!* And then I ran home and told papa but he was mad and didn't believe me and sent me to bed with only a crust and three olives because I was bad and ran away and told lies. So this morning I snuck out to come see you and we can go fight the bad man before he kills the Predicant and burns the city like he told the fire man. See, I brought my bodkin."

So she had. I confiscated the weapon under the guise of respectful examination and tucked it under my sword belt. I offered only non-committal evasions to her repeated exhortations to stage an assault on the Heathen embassy. It wasn't long before I was able to deposit her in the care of her worried father. Domenico was too relieved to do more than shoot me a glare that promised a rather intense bout during our next lesson. The threat almost entirely escaped me. I was too occupied reviewing Valentina's story. Domenico had not given it any credence, but too many plausible details lent the account a validity I could not ignore. I altered my steps to take me to the Sabatine district.

Walking the hills of Plenum provides ample time to reflect. And sweat, which does tend to yellow the brilliance of my shirts. While lamenting the need to launder this outfit again, I realized that I hadn't dressed for work. My metal-reinforced leather jerkin still hung in that splintered, vertical coffin that my landlord unabashedly termed a wardrobe. I was walking into a potentially violent situation with nothing between my skin and sharpened steel but a layer of sweat-stained linen and my own skills with rapier and main gauche. And no one was paying me.

I risk laceration, perforation, or decapitation only for ready money. I'll goad some fool into a duel when properly recompensed by a cuckold. I'll insult the wife of an inconvenient business associate. I'll spill wine on a hot-headed political rival. I am willing, in short, to hazard my tender flesh in a fight if the compensation is sufficient. I'm skilled and experienced, true, and I overlook no advantage, but I recognize full well that when bare steel is employed in earnest, even a novice might receive a providential turn of Dame Fortune's wheel. I don't do this for a lark. I don't hazard my life on the whimsies of a young girl.

Do I?

Such comforting ruminations brought me through twisting alleyways and closely packed hostelries, manufactories, and shops to the open boulevards and shaded palazzos of the Sabatine district. Dust-covered brick—soon to turn to a morass of muck when the first autumn rains saturated the dirt and shit that clogged the byways and thoroughfares—gave way to swept, stone-paved promenades.

The Heathen embassy was hardly a 'modest shelter.' The walled enclosure spread across a large lot on the sunset side of the Sabatine Hill, upon the crest of which were silhouetted such sections of the ruins of the Ancients that had not yet been scavenged for building materials. Neighboring estates vied with the embassy for the elegance of their neo-classical décor, abounding with plinths, columns, statues, and pediments—though I noted that the nude and semi-nude sculptures fronting the entry gate to the embassy were draped with heavy, dark cloth.

I was struck with a certain admiration for Valentina. Not only had she trailed Alfassan all this distance, she had also the temerity to sneak into the compound behind him. I wondered how I was going to do the same. And if I really meant to. He had, after all, summoned a fire demon.

Now, in Plenum, demons were not exactly a novelty. Many members of the Collegium were Magi, and these Magi—our lords and masters—were skilled demonologists. I was familiar with their use of demons as tools of war, bodyguards, healers, even as domestics or skilled craftsmen. In the course of my career I've had my dealings with various of these familiar spirits and so was not frozen with fear at the prospect of encountering another. Still—demon. And a fire demon with—if Valentina's account was to be trusted—the capacity to raze the city. This was not something I was eager to face.

I tapped my fingers a brief tattoo on the pommel of my rapier, took a deep breath, and strode to the front gate. Lacking a plan, I'd have to rely on boldness before good sense regained its proper ascendency.

The gate was unlocked. In fact, the thick wooden panel was ajar. I pushed it open and followed close behind its swinging entry.

The sentry inside was not expecting callers. He was kneeling, almost prostrate, in the Heathen attitude of worship, a robed lump in my path. His head lifted as I neared and I recognized him as one of Alfassan's entourage.

I'd kept my hands a conspicuous distance from the hilts of my blades with the half-formed notion of claiming an invitation from Alfassan. But the praying sentry offered me no chance to employ the stratagem. He surged to his feet like an acrobatic bear and rushed me. He tugged the hatchet from his belt and hollered something in a tongue that modulated from guttural to ululating.

So much for subterfuge.

I didn't have time for my rapier to clear leather. My left hand reached back to where the grip of the main gauche rode at my left hip. My right hand I raised to intercept his wrist, halting the descent of the blocky little ax striving to bury itself in my skull.

I kept my brainpan intact, but the bodyguard rendered my hat both practically and aesthetically useless. I continued to hold death at bay with my right hand. My left brought the parrying dagger around in a tight arc to bury it knuckle guard deep in his ribcage.

He wheezed into my face a mixture of fetid breath and blood then slid off of the short blade, collapsing onto his back, eyes open and glazing.

I looked past the corpse to the house, expecting a sally of murderous Heathens from the front entrance. Nothing. Well, my play then. Leaving my violated hat where it lay, transferring the main gauche to my off hand and drawing my rapier, I sprinted across the paved courtyard to the door.

The door was a thick plank set within a squared-off lintel over which curved a purely decorative arch. It was closed but not, as a quick experiment proved, locked, leaving me suspicious if I were about to pass into a lurking gauntlet of hatchets. Still, I'd come this far.

I put my shoulder to the door and followed it in, just as I'd done with the gate. I was inside a large, square antechamber, evenly set with pilasters about the walls, providing illusory support to a high, coffered ceiling. Doors in the center of each wall granted egress. I discovered why I hadn't yet been set upon by the remaining guards: they were busy packing.

Four bearded, robed men looked up from their tasks at open trunks as I entered. As one they straightened, reaching for their little axes.

"Did Alfassan leave word he'd invited me to dine?" Yeah, not even I was convinced. And my red-stained dagger didn't help.

The four of them spread out, bellowed something unintelligible in inharmonious chorus, and came for me. My skin tightened, maybe trying to keep my bones from fleeing. But I was calm at the core, beneath a thick layer of fear.

I didn't wait for them to reach me. I feinted to the left, went right, relying on my one advantage: the reach of my rapier. The Heathen on the far right swept down his hatchet in a desperate attempt at a parry. He failed. The tip of the rapier grazed his descending forearm before sinking into his chest.

I was disengaging blade from flesh when the nearest guard plowed into me with his left shoulder, driving me back while he brought down his ax. The bell guard and forte of my main gauche caught him on the wrist, the blade's edge cutting him to the bone and deflecting the ax blow. Instead of splitting my skull, he shaved off a patch of hair over my forehead, shearing off skin with it.

We moved apart, the shock of our respective wounds instigating a reflexive retreat. Unfortunate reflex for him: close range was his friend, distance mine. He provided me room to ply my long blade, and I did, pinking him high up in the thigh, puncturing an artery. That put him out of the fight just as the remaining two arrived.

Blood from my scalp wound was seeping through my eyebrows, threatening my vision. Good, maybe I wouldn't be able to observe my own death. The cut began to sting. I blinked away blood. The pain, however, remained.

One hit me high, the other low, and we fell in a heap, with me absorbing the brunt of the impact with the floor. I was lucky the blow didn't empty my lungs. It was still a tenuous position, me supine, my two assailants struggling up to a posture that would allow them to deliver ax blows.

Just a day ago, Domenico had told me that lessons could come in any form. True enough. Domenico wasn't my first instructor in the combat arts. The sword wasn't my first skill. I'd grown up learning the rough-and-tumble of the street fight, brawling in the gutters with other urchins, gouging, biting, and kicking over a crust of bread or a scrap of gristly meat. That sort of early ingrained competence doesn't easily disappear.

It was a sharp, brutal affray, a desperate struggle flopping, bucking, and rolling across a bruising marble floor. I dropped my rapier as a hindrance. To my right, the man who'd hit me low was up on his knees, preparing to bring his hatchet smashing down. My right hand shot inside his robes. I clutched the hairy pair of brains within his smallclothes and squeezed. Squealing, he released the hatchet and both of his hands clutched my wrist.

To my left, the Heathen who'd hit me high was having a bit more trouble, tangled up in his robes. He punched awkwardly at my head, impeded by the sleeve trapped under his knee. He scrambled to his knees. His hatchet descended, a short-armed blow. I punched up with the main gauche, driving it up beneath his chin. The hatchet cut a shallow groove in the back of my shoulder, deprived of most of its force. The bodyguard toppled, a jet of blood appearing to propel him backwards.

The remaining assailant bore down on my wrist, driving his thumbs in deep until I loosened my grip. Fine, I didn't need him by the balls any longer. My red dripping short-blade did its work once more, leaving me master of the field.

I staggered, battered and bleeding, to my feet. Death of a thousand cuts here. It was going to take a lot of wine to deal with the pain.

The Heathen with the leg wound sat on the floor, back against a pilaster, both hands clamped down against the punctured artery.

I stooped to regain my rapier then placed the point against his forehead.

"Where is Alfassan?" I asked.

"Too late. He has gone to keep his appointment with the Predicant, whom he will purify with fire." He spat at me, but it was a feeble effort. His face was a pallid, bleached mask. He'd bleed out soon.

What was my move now? I left the dying Heathen to

his fate and poked thoughtfully about for valuables, going through the robes of the fallen while I pondered.

A door opened. A dozen of the household staff crowded behind. Probably not Heathens, but here I was, looting, surrounded by punctured corpses. As far as they were concerned, I was just an armed robber.

They gathered their courage and tentatively shuffled in. That was my signal. I tucked a couple meager purses beneath my sword belt and fled.

The Collegium, that city within a city, abuts the Jacline district, the cliff faces and swelling hills creating a vast pocket for it to nestle within. But the Collegium's frontage slopes toward the Cloatus River. That meant that my route led primarily downhill. Battered, uncertain of the severity of my injuries, I was grateful to be spared laboring upslope. Of course, the jarring descent of the steeper downhill passages sent waves of pain rolling from my heels to the crown of my bleeding head.

The sleeve of my shirt was torn and stained. A total loss. So I didn't scruple to tear it loose and wind it around my brow as a makeshift bandage. It would at least keep the blood from my eyes.

I hoped the purses I'd scavenged would pay my tailor for fresh clothes. Donatello is an artist and does not employ his needle cheaply. And he does not offer credit. At least not to me.

Such thoughts kept my mind off of the pain from my wounds and occupied my attention as I put on as much speed as my bruised frame allowed. My hope was that Alfassan was in no hurry and that I could catch him before he reached the Collegium gates. The guards would certainly not allow me through in my state. By the time I could convince anyone of the danger, Alfassan would have already loosed the demon.

I wish more of my hopes proved so well-founded. Alfassan wasn't rushing. I spotted him idling before me, approaching the Bridge of Virtues, the span leading across the Cloatus to the Fortalice of Peace. The Fortalice of Peace, hunkering on the opposite bank squat and drum-like, is the Predicant's retreat, and I use that term in both its recreational and defensive senses. From there, the Predicant could recover from such mentally taxing endeavors he actually performed while still keeping an eye on his seat across the Cloatus, or shut himself securely away if the Collegium itself should be sieged.

I summoned what additional speed I could muster. Alfassan was not far from the environs of the Collegium. Even now I could catch glimpses of sections of the wall through gaps in the treetops and among the ornate banking houses, permanent embassies, city government buildings, and other official structures that clustered near the true power of Plenum.

I wheezed up behind Alfassan just as he was passing the end of the gently arching bridge, the graceful granite depictions of Fidelity and Truth standing guard at the terminus of each balustrade. He heard me and spun about. Only a deaf man could have missed my unsteady lumbering with its punctuations of pained grunting and labored inhalation. I was tired and wounded, damn it. Stealth was not an option. I wasn't sure fighting was either.

The surprise he displayed upon seeing me was almost comic. And that surprise allowed me time to produce my sword. If I'd not been so fatigued, it might also have allowed me time to run him through. But, alas, no.

He stepped back a pace, and from beneath his robe he dragged a massive yataghan, a heavy implement of butchery, with a single-edged, slightly serpentine blade.

"Cesar," he said, a smile snapping shut the shocked gap in his beard, "how splendid to see you. You have perhaps been—ah—offering my men complimentary fencing lessons?"

"Not complimentary, no. They all paid." Perhaps I could cow him into surrender with my finely-honed talent for braggadocio.

Again, alas no.

"One more lesson, then, Cesar. Your last." The Heathen gripped the huge chopper in both hands and shifted to an open stance, right foot behind and at right angles to the left.

"Why, Alfassan?" I held up a hand to forestall an immediate reply or attack. "Not 'why kill the Predicant.' I can guess that. Why the lesson yesterday? Why the wine and conversation?"

He relaxed, still on guard, but not primed to strike. "Understand, Cesar, I am not returning from the Collegium alive. Whether I manage my audience with the Predicant or only manage to release the demon within the walls, the outcome for me is the same. I will perish in flame. But so will the Collegium. And in the ensuing conflagration so will much of Plenum. Yes?"

I nodded, not so much acknowledging his point as

inviting him to continue. I wondered how accurate his prediction truly was. The Collegium held the world's foremost demonologists. Certainly, they possessed the skill and knowledge to contain a single demon. Didn't they?

Alfassan took my cue and carried on. "A man with such foreknowledge of his own incipient demise has a certain license to indulge in final pleasures. I like witnessing skilled combat. I like wine and stimulating conversation. I enjoy the other activities that I allowed myself upon return to the palazzo.

"Now that I have, I hope, alleviated your curiosity, I will kill you before we attract an audience. It makes little difference; even at this remove from the walls, the demon will still engulf the city. But I would like to see this through as designed."

With that, he twitched back to full readiness with disturbing ease. He hiked the yataghan to shoulder height and charged. Any thought I might have held of leaving the defense of Plenum to others was rendered moot.

He fanned a zephyr above my head as I ducked. Even ducking hurt. I managed to pink him as he leapt back out of range, perforating him somewhere beneath the folds of his robe. In proper condition I would have...but I wasn't and so had to rely on what my abused frame could offer.

I tugged out the main gauche and summoned up a grin. "Lesson one," I said, displaying the reddened tip of my rapier. His fresh droplets glistened against the darkening varnish of his lackeys' blood.

"A touch," he acknowledged, and attacked again, a more cautious, probing assault directed at my leading leg.

My jarring parry sent ripples of pain through my arm.

Alfassan renewed his attack, applying more vigor with each blow. He began to drive me back, step-by-step. I would not be able to hold him off much longer.

He sensed his moment and hoisted the yataghan overhead, poised to messily bisect me.

Too soon. I stepped forward, crossing my blades scissor fashion and caught his cleaver just as it began to descend. A twist of my wrists and I guided the yataghan downwards, to my right. A flick with the parrying dagger and I cut deeply into Alfassan's right forearm. The yataghan grazed the edge of my calf before it clanged to the paving stones. Wonderful, not a piece of my outfit remained intact. Not much of my skin, either.

"Lesson two," I said.

His eyes wide with pain or rage—or both, probably both—Alfassan backpedaled.

"Thank you for the lesson, Cesar," he said when brought up short by the raised pavers lining the brink of the Cloatus rolling sluggishly a dozen feet below street level. "Not every endeavor will succeed as designed."

He spread his arms wide, cruciform, and began to chant, his guttural syllables entirely unintelligible to me.

The air warmed. A hint of sulfur wrinkled my nostrils. A waft of steam rose from Alfassan's robes where they bunched at his midsection.

He was calling forth the fire demon! Only a dozen paces from me, but he might as well have been a hundred. I could not limp close enough to shove my rapier through his chest before he completed his summoning.

A glow began to emanate from his eyes, then his

exposed skin. His chant took on a higher, more fervid note. The steaming grew more pervasive, and the air about him shimmered, the temperature even where I stood creeping from warm to uncomfortable to hot.

I took a painful step forward—a futile gesture was still a gesture. Then I stopped. I seemed to hear Domenico's voice in my head. "Even a small child can teach you something." And "You shambling peacock."

I remembered the bodkin tucked away at my belt. Releasing my rapier, I plucked free the little knife, recalling Valentina's lessons. I cocked back my arm, knife clutched between thumb and two fingers, sighted at my target whose glow was beginning to acquire an actinic quality, and threw.

The bodkin described three complete arcs before embedding itself in Alfassan's chest. The chanting stopped. But the heat continued to intensify, the glow reaching a near white-hot brilliance, forcing me to squint. Lines of red cracked through the luminescence, jets of flame bursting free. The demon was at hand.

Then Alfassan staggered. His heel caught the stone curbing, and he fell straight back, disappearing. A moment. A splash. Then a great pillar of steam boiled up with the hissing of a thousand angry cats, spreading into a canopy of heated water vapor.

Stooping like an arthritic old man, I recovered my rapier then gradually straightened and shuffled away. No way was I explaining this. I hoped the coin I'd scavenged from Alfassan's bodyguards would recompense the pain. And I hoped there was enough to purchase Valentina a new bodkin.

The Quarto Volume;

or,

Knowledge, Good and Evil

The smoldering slow-match puffed an acrid plume of smoke and sparks when it met the touch-hole. A pause. Then the arquebus leapt, driving my shoulder back before it, the forked support dropping into the churned mud of the battlefield. Whether or not I struck anyone with the tumbling lead ball, I never knew. The roil of smoke from the muzzle of my cumbersome gun joined with that of the two hundred others, generating a shifting, ephemeral curtain that masked the advance of the enemy. The reverberations of the gunfire hammered my ears like a rockslide at a marble quarry. I was unable to hear the thrumming release of a hundred arbalests sending heavy quarrels through the smoke, the crossbowmen supplementing the arquebus barrage.

The clamoring in my head eased enough to hear the ragged return volley. It was largely ineffectual. The bulky firearms are awkward to employ on the move. A ball harrowed through the mud a couple of feet to my left. A bellow that modulated from shock to pain came from nearby to my right. At least one ball had found a mark. No quarrels hummed by, the enemy perhaps disdaining the arbalest as superannuated technology.

The artificial fog concealing the advance shredded, and there they were. High boots over tight leggings. A few steel breastplates, but mostly padded brigantines and leather jerkins. A smattering of arched morion helmets. And, of more immediate interest, pikes, ranseurs, swords. Really not much to differentiate their lot from ours, though they tended to wear some sort of badge in a hue of blue while we sported red: a baldric, sash, spray of plumage, or some such. I didn't pay the details a great deal of attention, being far more concerned with weaponry than accessories. Roughly five hundred defenders were left after yesterday's set-to. About what the Captain had suggested in his pre-battle harangue. Behind the enemy, less than a mile distant and surrounded by a curtain wall, rose the castello, the target of this entire affair.

I let the arquebus fall and hauled free my cinqueada, then supplemented the short sword by filling my left hand with my main gauche. I'd left my rapier with the luggage train. The thin blade is more suited for single combat and urban engagements. Against armor, the sturdy blade of the cinqueada is more practical. I spared an envious glance at the katzbalger wielded by my immediate comrade-in-arms, one of the northern mercenaries serving in the condotta. The long, heavy blade of the katzbalger was just the thing for dealing with the oncoming thicket of polearms.

And then the assault crashed into us, and my

perception contracted to the immediate square footage before me. I batted aside a thrusting pike, the cinqueada scraping along the steel head before gouging a sliver from the shaft. I stepped forward, main gauche plunging across my body to dig into the leading wrist. The pikeman drew back, to be immediately replaced by another assailant who drove the hooked blade of a ranseur at my chest. Seemed a world away from the parry-and-riposte of the fencing salle back in Plenum, but the required moves were similar enough that I reacted instinctively. The chaos of the battle wasn't just another sparring session or even a duel, but I fell into the rhythm and focused concentration I was accustomed to, losing myself in the mayhem for I don't know how long. Whatever the length, I was sheened with perspiration, hair sweat-plastered to my scalp, when I felt the pressure begin to ease, the enemy beginning to draw back.

That was, of course, right when they sent a demon rampaging through our ranks.

I hadn't anticipated that. In my experience one expected a magus somehow involved in a summoning. And that meant a Member of the Collegium. To my knowledge, the Prefect whose domain we were intent on conquering was not a Member of the Collegium, nor had he ever been one. In fact, scuttlebutt was the Collegium had backed our expedition, tacitly, practically, and financially. So who had conjured the demon?

It was an interesting conundrum, the solution to which would have to wait. The shifting of the press, the wavering of weapons, the occasional fully-armored figure tossed bodily, all traced the demon's general heading. And I was right in the path.

The enemy had pulled back, clearing the way for the war-demon to handle the killing. I exchanged glances with a knot of comrades who'd come through the fighting together without serious wounds.

One of the northerners, a blond-bearded fellow standing a good head taller than me—in fact the very fellow whose katzbalger I'd envied—nodded. "Here he comes, Cesar." He knew my name. How did he do that? I'd been with the condotta a week and barely recalled the names of four or five of my fellows.

Again, the answer could wait. Blackened talons gripped the arm and shoulder of the soldier-for-hire immediately before me. With the sword in his free hand, the mercenary hacked desperately at the figure looming above him, then uttered a horrified shriek as his arm was wrenched completely free of his body.

The demon discarded both pieces and moved on to the next victims. He towered about eight feet tall, a thickly muscled form covered with a scaly hide like a viper's—if vipers grew to the size of oxen. And no snake's scales grew that thick. Teeth like inch-long steel spikes were bared in a ferocious display. This wasn't a creature that chewed its food, just shredded and swallowed. If demons ate. Yellow eyes glared at us beneath a thickly ridged brow.

I'd have been terrified if I hadn't dealt with similar situations a time or two before. In fact, the armor I was wearing was a souvenir of one such event. Well, not the armor itself—just a high-necked jerkin, really. But sewn into pockets covering the most vital areas were pieces of a peculiar metal hammered to conform to the pockets' dimensions. The metal had once been a prison or repository for a demon, and it retained certain protective or repelling properties.

So I wasn't terrified when I stepped up to face his assault. Not happy. Not bubbling with confidence. Just—not terrified.

He drove the talons of his right hand at my chest, intending to skewer me like a morsel of chicken breast on the tines of a fork. Absurdly ambitious, of course: I'm not a tall man, but I'm built like a stevedore, with a chest like a beer keg. His talons were nowhere near long enough to transfix me. They hurt though. While they failed to penetrate the thin plate sewn into the front of my jerkin, the force of the blow stopped me mid-stride and nearly drove the air from my lungs.

But the surprise stopped the demon short, as well. He visibly hesitated, not sure precisely why I wasn't spraying blood like a punctured wineskin. In that pause, I delivered a terrific backhand at the still extended right arm. A blow like that would have lopped off the limb of a man. I managed to dig the edge about an inch deep, just wedging it into the bone up to the blade's first fuller.

The demon snorted, pained, and drew back his arm, dragging me with him as I maintained my grip on the cinqueada. He raised me, dangling, to meet him at eye level.

"I am going to eat your face," he said. The statement was flatly matter-of-fact, despite being uttered in a voice like a millstone crushing broken glass. So maybe they did eat.

Distracted and hampered by my weight dragging

down his arm, he was unable to make good his threat before my fellows bore in, hacking away.

Even so, he still might have done for us all if a war-demon of our own hadn't been sent into the fray. Proof that the Collegium's backing was substantial. They'd not provided an Arch-magus, no white-bearded Primate vying for a Red Hat, but certainly no Catechumen either, not if he could conjure up a bruiser that size. An Adept or Deacon at the least.

That was enough for the enemy. Those who didn't surrender or scatter fled back to the castle.

The day was ours. Maybe I'd get paid soon.

When I'd scratched my mark, just over a week ago, next to a scrawl of symbols the recruiter insisted represented 'Cesar,' I'd received a single, shaved silver denarius. A token, but sufficient compensation to form a contract. Wages would not be paid up front. I, for one, was appalled by the cynicism displayed by this tacit affront to my honesty and rectitude.

The thing was, I could use a pile of money just now, but just as urgently I needed to remove my ass from Plenum. Signing on with a condotta fit my needs. I'd done it before when my fortunes ebbed to damp stone and gasping shore-fish. It wasn't ideal; I'm a city denizen and no bivouac-accustomed soldier. I dislike either giving or receiving orders. But a campaign offered egress from the city and the promise of loot. Both timely prospects.

Plenum had recently become a trifle unhealthy for me. As a bravo, I accept certain risks. Instigating duels, for a fee, at the behest of those reluctant to mix it up personally, presupposed the possibility of coming in second. That hadn't happened to me yet, though I carried enough scars to demonstrate the dangers of my profession. But in addition to the obvious physical hazard of sharpened steel, there were more insidious hazards: magistrates, bailiffs, and those with the money and influence to wield them—instead of a rapier—as a weapon.

I don't wish to rehash the incident. So, a simple summation: a certain candidate for a tribuneship had engaged me to pick a quarrel with his opponent for the open seat. That had gone well enough, first blood drawn publicly. However, instead of resulting in the defeated man's disgrace and withdrawal, he'd garnered public sympathy and overwhelmingly won the election. And immediately brought to bear upon me the weight of the civic authority of Plenum proper. Compared with that of the Collegium—the true power in Plenum and points beyond—such weight was relatively light, but still sufficient to crush a societal nonentity and marginal character such as myself.

Without coin to combat the Tribune with advocates in court (rather than drawn swords in an open courtyard), I'd yielded the field for the time being, abandoning the city a step ahead of the city watchmen prosecuting the arrest warrant.

And thus I signed on with the Condottiere, Captain Auquins. The Captain possessed a reputation as a winner, ruthless but punctilious. He'd been employed by the Aedile Claudio, who espoused some sort of claim— specious or otherwise—to the lands governed by the Prefect Orfeo, one of the petty Prefectures clustered north of Plenum, plentiful within a couple hundred miles, but less numerous as one neared lands claimed by northerners. The perpetually churning rumor mill of the condotta's mercenaries held that the Collegium backed the Aedile's cause, though how one of Plenum's money-shuffling bureaucrats rated a provincial Prefecture in the first place gave the rumor mill unlimited grist for speculation.

Still, the rumors had proven correct about the Collegium's backing. Its representative—cassock immaculate despite the mud—stood near the Captain and the Aedile, clearly integrated into the condotta's command structure. Captain Auquins stood atop a caisson, delivering his remarks in a resonant baritone. Several oxen roamed nearby, temporarily freed from their traces, grazing fruitlessly in the furrowed muck. Another caisson, and three bombards weighing down their gun carriages to the wheel hubs, hunkered nearby.

Off to one side humped two piles of corpses, theirs and ours, though it wasn't readily apparent which was which. It wasn't a sight I expected or wanted to get used to. In my line of work, I seldom generated corpses as a byproduct, let alone heaps of them. First blood usually sufficed. A matter of degree, I suppose. I had no claim to moral superiority over these hired soldiers. Paid fighters, the lot of us. Why we did it remained an open question. Different for each man, I guess. I wondered if seeing—and smelling—this harvest led them to the same proposition I was mulling: maybe I should have learned a different trade.

"You fought well today," the Condottiere was saying.

"The enemy is routed. Those not fled are cowering behind yon walls.

"I dispatched heralds to offer terms. The sad news is that they were rebuffed. The castello will not yield. The happy news: we now need not offer quarter. Once taken, it is yours to pillage."

He paused while the condotta broke out in a cheer. The wages of those of us who survived the campaign would pale compared to the potential spoils a vigorous looter could gain in an overrun town or an important fortification. Or even this modest outpost.

He waited until the exuberance subsided. "Yes. Take it, and it is yours. With a single exception. Within the keep, probably housed in the library, is a quarto volume. I will see hanged any man who damages or attempts to abscond with it. Aedile Claudio, our principal, will elaborate."

Auquins assisted the Aedile in hoisting his corpulent frame atop the caisson. "Thank you Captain Auquins. As the Captain said, there is a quarto volume, a certain book, approximately this big"—here he mimed a rectangle roughly the length of the distance from my elbow to the tips of my fingers and about two-thirds of that wide. "It will appear smaller and, likely, newer than the other books you might encounter. It will be furnished in silver and bound with silver banding. Take what else you wish. That quarto is mine."

Quarto volume. I knew the term. Reading isn't a skill a bravo from the gutters of Plenum is likely to possess. But I was not without friends. Domenico, my fencing master, could read. He even owned a second-hand instructional manual, an illustrated folio volume diagramming basic fencing technique. It was a prestigious possession; printing remains a novelty. Even I was aware that mechanically reproduced pages represented an improvement from hand-copied texts. And progress didn't stop there. The advances followed one after the other. Already folio volumes—massive, awkward things capable of performing emergency duty as dining tables—were being threatened with obsolescence by the recently introduced quarto volume. The cleverly folded sheets nested and stitched into signatures could be bound into more manageable volumes. They were the future of the printers' art. Until pushed aside by the next innovation.

Still, it hardly seemed worth all this fuss for a book. Even the sale of an entire library probably would not fetch enough to reimburse the Aedile (or whoever actually paid) for the cost of this expedition. It was enough to raise a degree of curiosity in a humble bravo as to the contents of said quarto volume. Also, certain muted regrets concerning a humble bravo's illiteracy.

Another reason soldiering is not for me: knee deep in gripping mud helping an ox team to drag a massive bombard into position is a miserable experience. I am never called on to do that as a free agent in the city. I could, however, see as easily as the most experienced soldier here why the big guns were necessary. There was a wall between the condotta and the castello. I could figure even more: while I am neither an artillerist nor a fortification engineer, I was fairly certain the bombards were going to get us past the obstacle in fairly short order. A glacis of earth and timber had been thrown up before the wall. It looked a recent effort and none too thorough. The turf was fresh, and sections of the supporting logs peeked through. The original towers, set at intervals along the wall to subject attackers to flanking arrow shot, had been newly resurfaced, a convex shell encasing the front face of each originally square bastion. I grasped the theory well enough: slanted surfaces to deflect cannonballs up and diminish their velocity, rounded walls to perform similar functions laterally. But it was an exercise in retrofitting, and an incomplete one at that. A fortification designed to truly withstand a modern artillery siege required more than this hasty patch job.

I might even have felt sorry for those inside were I not mud begrimed, splattered, and plastered. I had my doubts of any laundress being able to return this outfit to pristine condition. And I am fastidious about my attire, as is any self-respecting bravo. Yet another indication that the martial profession is not for me.

I had time to scrape off the worst of the muck while the gunners set up, sighted, and began firing their bombards. The first few salvos were exciting, all that flash and thunder. But after a while, it was just so much noise, interfering with naps, dicing, or conversation.

Things picked up again mid-afternoon when the cannonade finally breached a section of wall. It wasn't much, just a ragged gap about a yard wide, dribbling stone and mortar down the sharp slope of the battered glacis. Still, that was enough for Captain Auquins to call for an assault. Wisely not willing to lead a forlorn hope himself, he called for volunteers. The lack of enthusiastic response was a trifle awkward. But the Collegium's representative, a Deacon, we learned, by the name of Ambocello, gracefully eased the tension.

"Of course, Captain. I will happily provide you with a spearhead." So saying, and robes and vestments somehow still pristine, the lesser magus set to work with powders and with candles the hue of dried blood that emitted charnel odors. By the time each of the bombards had fired once more, a billow of multicolored smoke began to roil up from the center of the circle Ambocello had fashioned in the mud. The bestial, human-like form of a war-demon manifested within.

Volunteers were more plentiful now that they had this bulwark to mass behind. Not that I was among them. The van of the assault force was composed of the more heavily armored soldiers, primarily northern mercenaries with their heavy cuirasses and long, bludgeoning weapons. We more lightly-armed and armored would follow along behind to exploit the breach.

I cheered on the lead element. It couldn't hurt to appear gung-ho. The war-demon, raging and bellowing, outstripped the van as he sprinted for the wall. But the enemy had had sufficient time to prepare a defense—a defense that included a war-demon of their own, rising up to meet ours as he reached the gap.

They collided like bulls in rut competing for the herd. The shock sent a few more stones tumbling down the glacis. The demons grappled, growling, hurling insults and dire imprecations. They bounced each other off of the interior faces of the breach, each concussion showering down a load of stone blocks and filler.

From beyond the wall, I could hear defenders cheering

on their champion as we were ours. It lacked only a book-maker taking wagers to complete the prize fight atmosphere.

I'd lost track of which demon fought for which side when one lunged forward to sink his fangs into the other's throat. The afflicted demon released a shriek like a scalded cat and drove the talons of both hands into the ribcage of his assailant, hoisted him off his feet, and lurched forward, slamming both of them into one side of the breach. The impact visibly jarred each demon and seemed to knock the fight out of them. They slumped down into the mud, unmoving. Then, amidst a rising cloud of acrid smoke, both disappeared. They had each, it appeared, sustained too many injuries to remain.

A silence ensued. A pause fraught with disappointment and dismay. And then, having absorbed more structural damage than it could bear, the wall on either side of the breach collapsed in an avalanche of broken stone and rubble, leaving an open stretch two cart-lengths wide.

We needed no orders. Cheering, we stormed up the sloping glacis and poured through the gap.

The fight proved rather anticlimactic. The defenders were dispirited and demoralized. After a flurry of violence, most yielded, a few fleeing within the castello, the final redoubt.

Despite Captain Auquin's release, his troops for the most part did give quarter to those who surrendered. Most of the defenders were mercenaries as well, and a certain spirit of professional brotherhood pervaded.

Anyone else, of course, was fair game.

Prefect Orfeo was chief magistrate of the villages and freeholds within about twenty square miles of the castello. Many of the locals had fled within his walls upon learning of hostilities. Not all could fit within the castello and many were forced to rely upon the protection of the outer walls. Therefor, the situation was thus: the courtyard of the castello was the chicken coop; the unfortunate locals were the chickens; we were the foxes. It wasn't pretty.

After firing off a single round from my arquebus, I tangled with one of the few defenders who bothered to put up a fight. By the time I'd hacked off his sword hand, I was already late to the festival.

I retrieved my fouled arquebus and edged along the perimeter of the grounds, leaving clustered groups of the victors to their celebrations. It would have been a fine time for an organized troop to sally from the castello and counterattack. Probably would have driven us out handily despite our numerical advantage. But for the moment at least, they were still cowed and flustered. By the time discipline could be instilled, Captain Auquins would have the guns hauled through the breach, ready to batter down the castello, and he'd be bringing his men to heel.

Meantime, I could search for any ungleaned leavings.

Around the back of the keep, I glimpsed movement near a pile of refuse heaped near a burn-pit. The movement didn't recur, suggesting that someone was trying to hide from me.

I ambled that direction, not increasing my pace. I didn't want to flush the quarry. I skirted the mound of chicken bones, oyster shells, broken crockery, and other assorted detritus. The pit below still smoldered from the previous disposal.

There. A flash of limbs, long, unbound hair, skirts. A figure, a young woman scrambling to her feet to flee. I dropped the arquebus and had both arms wrapped around her waist within three strides. She thrashed, but only momentarily, then went limp with apparent resignation.

"Make it quick, please," she said. "Don't hurt me. I won't struggle."

All throughout the grounds, I could hear the cries of those who were struggling. I don't know, maybe long months in the field on campaign left the mercenaries hard up. I'm a cosmopolitan, a bravo of some repute. Companionship I can have when I've the itch without the use of force. And it hadn't been *that* long.

"Relax, girl. Get yourself cleaned up, dressed in a decent frock, share a flagon of wine with me—then maybe you'd have to worry about your virtue."

I loosened my grip and she turned to face me, perhaps taking in my disarming grin. She shrugged. "As you like," she said, sounding more apathetic than reassured.

"What's your name? Are you part of the household here?" I asked.

"Heloise. I work in the kitchen." It was the dull, flat voice of someone who knew and expected nothing better from life than a scullery maid's drudgery, punctuated by the occasional rape.

"Cesar," I said, completing the formalities. "You've been working for Orfeo for how long, Heloise?"

"The Prefect? Long as I can remember. My mother was a maid and a wet-nurse here."

"So you know the castello well?"

"Of course. It's my home."

"What would you think about helping me get in?"

An eyebrow hitched as calculations flashed beneath her unwashed mop of auburn hair. "What you want in for by yourself?" she asked.

"We're going to get in eventually," I said. "So I figure, get in first, grab the choicest cut of the pillage. Do you object? Do you hold some loyalty to Orfeo?"

"The Prefect's a good enough sort. He never ill-treated any of us." She was mulling it over, tugging at a grease-heavy lock. She shrugged.the "But I don't owe him no favors. Your lot is going to take over. One boss is as good as another, so I might as well have you look kindly on me."

Reasoned well enough, I thought, but it didn't display much in the way of initiative or imagination. This life was all she knew and so framed her conception of possibilities. It didn't occur to her that she could escape it, learn a new mode of existence.

"*I* will look kindly on you, especially if you can find me a way in near the library," I said, pouring all the charm I could muster into my rakish grin.

I couldn't decide if the expression on her face indicated incredulity or scorn. "I thought you wanted first crack at the prime loot. What do you want the library for?"

"I've heard rumors that's where Orfeo squirreled away some of the best swag." Close enough to the truth and this conversation had already dragged on long enough without me explaining the sought-after quarto volume.

She looked skeptical but said, "Right. Follow me, then."

"Wait." I handed her the arquebus. "This should be

sufficient token that you're with us. Hold it over your head so no one takes you for a threat. Five minutes after you get me into the castello go ask for Captain Auquins. Show him a way in, a different way if you have one. That's the best way for you to curry favor with the new landlords. Just make sure Aedile Claudio knows it was you who let us in, and you can move up from slops and onion chopping to sauces and chicken trussing."

An outbuilding housing a root cellar concealed a tunnel that connected with the lower vaults and foundations of the castello. Following Heloise's directions, I made my way to the top floor. It should have been perilous, if not impossible. The central keep was not large and was still generously supplied with defenders. But later additions and modernizing had increased the size and left behind narrow clandestine passages, employed primarily for discreet nocturnal visitations. Heloise had learned of these from her mother, who had, apparently, served in capacities supplementary to wet-nurse.

I emerged, appropriately enough, in a bedchamber. An open door on one side led to a music room, and through the doorway in the opposite side of the room opened the library. Straight across from the armoire from which I stepped, a stairway spiraled to the levels below. Up it echoed voices raised in various tones of resolution and despair. The Prefect's troops were still reforming and rediscovering their courage.

Crossing the bedchamber, I paused to liberate a fine amethyst set in a wide silver ring, a gold and ivory cloak pin, and a stray silver spoon. If I escaped with nothing else, these pieces constituted a substantial haul. Well, perhaps not the spoon. I would have rummaged through the wardrobe, but I doubted any of Orfeo's shirts would fit. And he seemed to have a particular fondness for red. Not a color I found flattering. Even if, by some chance, he matched my physique, the odds were his provincial tailor wasn't in the same class as Donatello, to whom I gave my exclusive sartorial custom. No, best not to compromise on fashion.

The library was a wonder, featuring two tall cases crammed with grand folios, obesely stuffed books straining their bindings, and loose sheets weighted down with bric-a-brac. I snaffled a couple of the more valuable—and portable—pieces. The room itself bent at right angles, another door at the far end leading to the music room. The floor was a game board of alternating travertine and green marble.

I ran my fingers along the spines of the collection, feeling the fine-grained leather, wondering what stories the books contained, what information they could impart. I felt a keen awareness of my limitations, and I didn't like it.

Then I saw the quarto volume.

It was conspicuous both for the flash of its silver chasing and for its size, a thick volume flanked by towering folios bound in severe black. I tilted it toward me and eased it off the shelf. It was heavier than I thought it would be, bound in a soft, buff-colored hide. Silver tipped each of the four corners of the cover. A cloth-of-silver ribbon poked up as a place marker. A band of silver, sewn into the cover, belted the book round, the clasp buckled, the buckle daubed with sealing wax for good measure. Tooled along the spine and across the front cover were symbols that I supposed spelled out the title.

The Aedile longed for this book. As did, from the evidence, the Collegium. What was so valuable about it? What was worth this expense and so many deaths?

I could not read. Breaking the seal would be a pointless exercise and only serve to direct the finger of suspicion at me upon delivering the quarto volume to Claudio. But somehow, I knew I was going to open the book anyway. And abruptly I was equally certain that I wasn't going to turn the book over to the Aedile. I'm fickle that way.

I set the quarto volume atop a lectern, the dimensions of which suggested it was constructed for folios. The quarto volume appeared diminutive on the expanse of the inclined surface. My fingers poised over the clasp. But there was never any real doubt. The sealing wax snapped cleanly as I thumbed loose the clasp, then hesitated.

I opened the book.

Dense print massed in formations, column and file, over the rough surface of the page. I thought for a moment that my eyes were tearing up, for the letters appeared to shift, then shimmer. I blinked. No, it wasn't my eyes, nor was it a manifestation on the page itself. A film rose, distorting the print beneath. The film coruscated, rippling into a haze that spread and condensed into a fumarole of reddening smoke.

A demon materialized before me. He was squat, hairless except for a fringe hedging the bony plate of his skull. He wore an artisan's apron slotted with loops and pockets out of which protruded dozens of tools. Muscular arms terminated in wide hands and long, agile fingers tipped by clipped talons.

"Shall I set up here?" he asked, his voice like an agitated hornets' nest. He didn't appear much interested in my answer for without delay he set to work fitting a stanchion into an angle iron—both pieces which he seemingly retrieved from some storehouse not visible or accessible to me—and riveted the assemblage to the travertine.

"What are you constructing?" I asked.

"A printing press, of course." Some sort of frame was in progress, assembled at an astonishing rate.

"And what will you print?"

"Copies of this quarto volume, of course," he said, snapping out the words as he affixed a horizontal crossbeam to the frame. Tetchiness is intimidating when expressed by a demon.

"Now that is fascinating. What—just from curiosity, mind—does this quarto volume contain?" Absent any compelling need to fight one, it is my policy to avoid antagonizing demons. Questions, unfortunately, seemed to increase this demon's native testiness. But I had to know.

"It is, inquisitive man, both a basic primer and a comprehensive treatise on theoretical and practical demonology."

A conveniently located chair beckoned. Seemed to me the best way to absorb this wallop was to flop down into it. I was dimly aware of the sound of conflict echoing up from the lower levels, but I did not yet heed it. For the moment, the demon's revelation crowded out all other considerations.

I began to comprehend the Collegium's true interest. Commerce with demons was practically a monopoly for its initiates, north of the Mother Sea at least. The east and south produced their own practitioners. What would it mean for our virtual overlords if the knowledge to summon these otherworldly entities was available to anyone with the ability to read and the aptitude to learn? No need for entry to the hermetic world of the Collegium, no binding commitment to its authority, regulations, and creed? For that matter, what would it mean to the rest of us? The Collegium—think what one might about arrogance and the corruption of power—at least provided a check on the proliferation of demons. Its Members—the assorted Deacons, Rectors, Councilors and what have you, all the way up the Predicant—may not all be scrupulous, altruistic, or wholly devoted to the True Faith. In fact, none of them might be. In my more cynical moments, I consider that likely, though some of them seem decent enough fellows. Yet even were they villains to the last man, their limited numbers prohibit blanket oppression. They seem more interested in internal squabbles and jockeying for power than in naked, iron-fisted domination. In the hands of the populace at large, those built in governors— numbers and political in-fighting—would disappear. What would an unscrupulous man do with access to such power, absent the strictures of expectations, learned ethical guidelines (even if honored more in the breach), peer oversight, pressure and vigilance?

The demon, unconcerned with my musings, was constructing racks upon which he assembled rows of moveable type in letter cases.

"Each book will be identical?" I asked.

"Discounting imperfections in the paper and idiosyncrasies in the individual matrices, essentially yes, down to the summons built into the seal."

I could sink no further into the chair, though I felt as if all support had been yanked from beneath me. What would numberless unscrupulous men do with access to such power? I asked, needing to confirm my conjecture, "Wait, so each quarto volume opened will summon a demon to print countless more, each capable of infinite reproduction?"

"Even so. Are there more questions you'd care to belabor me with?"

Which was worse: concentrated power or diffuse, unfettered power? Was it right that knowledge be restricted? Was it worse for perilous knowledge to be freely disseminated? It made my head hurt. How should I choose? Did I have that right? Why me? All I'd had to do was mind my own business, sneak out with the book, collect my reward, and I'd never have to face this dilemma.

The demon hoisted a ream of paper onto a shelf built into his press. From his unseen warehouse he wrangled a barrel sloshing with ink.

A tumult of conflict, the shouts and ringing clashes of arms, grew nearer. Still I sat, riveted by my internal conflict. I could imagine the chaos this proliferation of knowledge and power might unleash. And yet, I had a life as free as I could imagine. I instinctively shrank from anyone attempting to impose his will on me and dictate my actions. Yet another reason I made a piss-poor soldier.

Given my personal inclinations, how could I presume to circumscribe the options available to others? By deliberately eliminating a possibility wasn't I dictating their actions? I could not be certain what any individual might do with this information, could not presume the worst of every man.

No. I would not impose restraints. I would not act the censor.

Then the battle boiled up the stairwell into the bedchamber, taking the decision from my hands.

Captain Auquins fought at the head of the onslaught. Two of the remaining trio of defenders fell, pulled down to be swallowed up in the threshing swords of the condotta. That left only a single man, standing at the head of the stairs, defying the invading force. By the red sleeves blousing from beneath his steel breastplate, I hazarded he was Prefect Orfeo. He raised his sword, a rapier furnished with elaborate quillons and a finely etched blade. He saluted. Captain Auquins crossed blades with him. Once, twice. Then, with a deft upward thrust, the Condottiere took Orfeo beneath the chin and up into the brain pain.

I was uncertain if Auquins saw me, seated and perhaps concealed by angles of doorway and shelving. But he certainly saw the demon, busily slotting letters into slats. Auquins must be aware of the true purpose of his commission. He could see that the chance had passed of securing the quarto volume and sequestoring it deep in some dark vault beneath the Collegium. All that remained was damage control.

"Arquebusiers!" he ordered. "Grenadiers!"

It was, I deemed, time to make my exit. I slipped from

my chair and snaked into the music room. I hid behind a rack of lutes while troops lumbered up the stairs to assemble in ranks behind the Condottiere. When the flash and thunder of arquebuses and the concussion of exploding grenados commenced, I insinuated myself behind the head of the column.

I had, I thought later as I shuffled in turn down the stairs, spent enough time with the condotta. The loot I'd secured might be sufficient to buy my way out of trouble back in Plenum. I had connections, connections more inclined to be friendly upon receipt of funds. Perhaps while advocates and magistrates played through the farce, I might use the time to learn to read.

Behind me the quarto volume burned.

Witch Hunt

"There's a man I need to see with a sword run through his heart," the client told me.

Chapter 1

I was nursing a cup of watered plonk in Giacomo's Wine Shop when the client first assayed a furtive step inside.

I don't frequent Giacomo's Wine Shop for the quality of his vintages. Giacomo serves swill, reserving a bottle or two of Senna ruby for a discerning customer with a full purse who might stumble into the dive by accident. It isn't the ambience that attracts me, either. The dim light is its best quality. The scattering of flickering candles and battered lamps masks the filthy, unswept brick floor, the low ceiling, the ancient, hacked and splintering tables, and the unsavory clientele. Unfortunately, dim light can do nothing for the smells of unwashed flesh, spilled wine, spoiling meat, aging produce, and rancid lamp oil.

It certainly isn't the company that draws me to Giacomo's. The place caters to the dregs of the Orine district: cutpurses, ragpickers, unemployed day-laborers, back-alley bone breakers, and other assorted bums. And me: Cesar, dashing, debonair, bravo for hire.

Why then do I frequent Giacomo's Wine Shop? A fair question, simply answered: because it is cheap. I can make a shaved copper coin—a half-soldi—last most of the afternoon, if I'm not too thirsty. The grounds for my attraction to Giacomo's were likely shared by the rest of the afternoon tipplers. Scraping by, the lot of us.

Which was why I pegged the man in the doorway immediately for a potential client of mine rather than a patron of Giacomo's. He appeared too prosperous to set foot in the place. It could be he was lost, one of those monied unfortunates Giacomo would break out a bottle of Senna for. But his head was moving, as if he was searching through the dimness for someone rather than taking in the atmosphere of the wine shop and deciding whether or not he wanted to be there.

I got a good look at him while he scanned. My eyes had already had an hour or so to grow accustomed to the poor light. He was a man built to fill out crowd scenes in operas, everything about him mumbling the word "average." He rose to average height, didn't tip the scales above or below average weight. I'd be willing to bet a full scudo (assuming I had one) that, seen by the light of the candle dripping its wax onto my table, he'd display the average olive skin tone, and dark brown hair and eyes, shared by the bulk of my fellow citizens of Plenum. In short, nothing about him stood out. His attire suggested a middling-successful artisan or a merchant just breaking even; he wore a rust-red coat covering his doublet and most of his fawn-colored breeches. Boots matching the coat rose above mid-calf, nearly reaching the ties securing his breeches below his knees. Nothing elaborate, but not precisely cheap either. Considering the amount I've squandered over the years on the artistry of my tailor, Donatello, it's no surprise that I've picked up a working knowledge of the rough costs and value of men's fashion.

He worked up the nerve to enter, and, as I'd guessed,

wove through the tables in a more or less straight line toward mine. He didn't wear a sword, which eased his path, lessening any concern about the scabbard accidentally smacking a half-spifflicated low-life or spilling a drink—either eventuality likely to lead to unpleasantness.

He reached my table and paused. I waited a beat before raising my eyes from contemplating the sadly lowered volume of throat-scouring wine in the fired-clay cup. Sure enough, my candle revealed wavy dark brown hair, cut short, and dark eyes, little different than mine. There, however, the similarities ended. He was built to fit the standard mold. Not I. To the constant despair of Donatello, I'm built like a mastiff, low to the ground and all chest and shoulder. I ought to be a longshoreman or a stevedore rather than a bravo. I don't possess the classic, long-limbed, slender physique of a fencer. But, there you have it. Live with it. I do.

"Are you Cesar the Bravo?" he asked, pronouncing it correctly: "Chay-zar." Definitely a local, with no hint of accent.

I sat up straight, then leaned back, while maintaining eye contact. I cocked my head to one side. Studied insolence right up front helps establish the proper working relationship.

"Depends on who's asking," I said.

His wrist flicked and three silver pistras bounced and rattled on the stained and gouged surface of the table before coming to rest. "Three dead Urban Tribunes are asking," he said.

But the line sounded rehearsed, unnatural. Not a born

tough guy, this one. Play-acting the role, trying it on like a new coat.

Three pistras was nothing to disdain. Hardly a fortune, but it would get me current on my rent, even a month ahead. Not that living rough would be too much of a step down from the glorified closet of splintering wood and crumbling brick I called home.

Still, the rainy season was upon us, and a roof is a roof.

Despite my financial embarrassment, I let the coins lie. Eroded profiles of some Urban Tribune I couldn't name embossed the aged silver, a forgotten politician from generations past whose immortality faded further each time a thumb rubbed across his face.

Never snatch the money immediately. Never appear too eager.

"You're no Tribune, living or dead," I said. "Cough up a name if you want mine." I let a smile flicker across my face. "Fair is fair."

He paused, seemingly stumped by my recalcitrance. He'd come in with a detailed plan as to how this would go and was at a loss upon meeting the first check. I saw his Adam's apple bob as he swallowed. His eyes narrowed, and that seemed a sign that his resolution—the same resolve that had steeled him to step into this seedy establishment—had reasserted itself. He bent, pulled out the stool opposite me, sat down, and leaned forward, elbows on the table.

"Cesar, my name is Herbieto," he said. He paused, gathering himself before he continued. "There's a man I need to see with a sword run through his heart."

I picked up my cup and sipped, giving myself a

moment to digest that statement. I could use the work. Of that, there was no question. But I'm not a murderer for hire. You might feel the distinctions I make are overnice; that I concoct artificial, self-deluding differences to ease my conscience about what my job often entails—killing. Nonsense. I am a bravo. Not a thug, nor a midnight throat-slitter, nor a poisoner. I can often satisfy my clients with minimal violence, no more than first blood to conclude a point of honor. (Of course, my client hiring me to initiate a duel that the client should be engaging in himself might, by some calculations, be less than honorable. But that wasn't my concern.) I will insult a political or business rival, impugn the virtue of a man's wife, swagger about in an intimidating fashion outside the front door of a fashionable bistro. Whatever the client needs. My mere presence might serve; an embodiment of the threat of violence accompanying my client on an errand might dissuade an adversary from rash action. There is a measure of finesse, of flair, in the services I provide. Sometimes, yes, the ultimate result is that I end up killing someone. But it is always a fair fight, face-to-face, sword-to-sword. So, while I could use the pistras gleaming in the candlelight, I retained my professional standards.

"Well, Herbieto, you are right, I am Cesar." I set the cup back down. "But it sounds to me that what you're asking for doesn't require a bravo. If you want a man dead, why not hire an assassin?"

I gestured with my chin at a table in the corner farthest from the front door. A lone figure sat there, shadowed, keeping deliberately out of the circle of candlelight thrown by the single taper in the center of the table. Theatrically mysterious and sinister; that was Marteo.

"Marteo will take care of your problem," I said. "He's likely to charge a lot less than I will. Or, for even less, you could hire any number of the men in here to bash your problem over the head in a back alley. Thugs are a soldi-a-dozen."

Herbieto shook his head. His fingers found the coins on the table and he began shifting them about the table top, slipping the silver around knife gouges and clumps of congealed wax drippings. "No. No, no no. That would be too impersonal. I want someone who will face him, tell him at sword's length exactly why he's about to die. I want witnesses around to hear. I want him to die publicly disgraced, in a legitimate duel. I want to be there. Ideally, he'll see me, know for sure that I am responsible for his death."

Herbieto grew increasingly agitated as he spoke. He meant it. He might require a bit of time to work himself up to actually doing something, but he was a man of conviction.

I considered what was left in my wine cup; almost down to the dregs. I looked at the pistras Herbieto shuffled about the surface of the table. The silver tempted me. The blurred profiles of that long dead Urban Tribune called to me. But...

"Perhaps you do need a bravo. However, you're asking for a great deal. Certainly a lot more than three pistra's worth," I said. That was true enough. I added, "I've other jobs commissioned anyway." That was a lie. Herbieto couldn't prevent a brief smile at that. He could see at a glance that I had no other clients.

"This is merely a retainer," he said. "There will be more when the job is done."

Giacomo himself approached, his obsequious smile looking out of place on his usually glowering visage. Herbieto stood out from the regulars, his attire suggesting relative prosperity. He might thus be a prospect for a glass of Senna ruby, perhaps doubling Giacomo's profit for the day. I couldn't say for sure, not being privy to the price he pays for his inventory. Whatever, he'd come over himself instead of sending the wench who usually takes the orders, fills the cups, and delivers them while Giacomo performs the important function of sitting behind the bar and glowering.

"Sir, welcome to Giacomo's Wine Shop. I am Giacomo," Giacomo said, adding a flourish of his bar rag as he introduced himself. "What may I bring you? Might I recommend a glass of a particularly fine—"

Herbieto interrupted. "Bring two of whatever Cesar is drinking." He'd hardly glanced up at Giacomo's arrival and seemed to dismiss him from his attention with the same lack of interest.

"Bonfilia!" Giacomo bellowed, stalking away with his scowl back in place, summoning the tavern wench. I figured Giacomo had relegated Herbieto to the status of scum, along with the rest of us.

I reached out to tap a finger beside one of the pistras Herbieto was still toying with. "A retainer, you were saying?" I was pleased Herbieto had ordered two cups of wine. That saved me from facing an unpleasant decision: spending the last soldo in my purse on another cup here at Giacomo's, or stopping on my way home to buy a loaf of bread and a hunk of hard cheese in order to fill my belly with something more substantial than Giacomo's rotgut.

The former would ease a night in my rat trap apartment. The latter would make the morning more bearable. An empty purse, lack of prospects, and a heap of debt are easier to face without a hangover. A few years back, the choice would have been obvious—the wine. The hardships—the living hand-to-mouth, scrounging employment at the last moment—had seemed a lark. A drafty tenement apartment seemed romantic, the natural abode of a bravo making his way in Plenum upon the sharpness of his wits and his sword.

Nowadays it no longer felt so romantic to have a landlord pound on the warped wood of the ill-fitting door to an apartment that would start to feel cramped once the rat whelped her litter.

Nonetheless, I did not pick up the nearest coin. I waited.

While I waited, Tasso Longarm sauntered up to the table. Tasso was one of the toughs for hire I'd mentioned to Herbieto. He called himself a longshoreman. And in fact, on rare, far-spaced occasions, he did scrounge up some day labor away at Spina, a half-day's hike to the west, on the coast. Primarily, however, he earned what coin he could as a paid bonebreaker.

Tasso placed those long arms of his on the table, resting his weight on massive, scarred knuckles, and leaned forward. He looked like the world's most contented, happy ape. It must have been a constant disappointment for him, wanting to appear menacing and terrifying, but having his own goofy, apparently genial face undermining the effect.

"You," Tasso said to Herbieto, the words a low rumble, sounding as if they emanated from his chest rather than his mouth. "You have a problem, come see me instead of this little girly. He'll dance around it for a week before he does anything. I'll take care of it tonight, whatever it is, for half the price."

"All that talking must have made you thirsty, Tasso," I said. "Go on back to your table and have a drink." I kept my tone neutral, trying to avoid any hint of threat. Tasso doesn't frighten me, but he is a large, long-limbed brawler, with the hands and face of a man who has survived his share of scraps. Anyone can get lucky, and I'd just as soon not risk the chance of him getting one of those big mitts on me.

"What if I ain't thirsty, Cesar?" Tasso addressed himself to me this time. Herbieto edged to the rear of his stool, a man clearly in the throes of second-guessing himself.

My left hand dropped to my hip, where my rapier hung from the baldric. The smack of my palm on metal was clear and distinct. My fingers curled around the scabbard, and I pressed my thumb against the most immediately convenient section of the elaborate, curving geometry of quillons. I freed a half-inch of blade, with a scrape of metal on metal arising from where the ricasso met the locket of the scabbard.

"Lighten up, Cesar," Tasso said, a wide smile stretching his simian features. He pushed himself erect. "You can't blame a guy for trying to get some work."

I smiled back, let the rapier click back into the scabbard. "Better luck next time, Tasso," I said.

He grunted, then shuffled back to his table.

Herbieto scooted forward again. He watched Tasso's retreating back for a moment, then returned his attention to me. Resolve drove out second-guessing. He tapped the table, his finger in the vicinity of the coins. "As I was saying, Cesar, this is merely a retainer. I offer these three to secure your services. And to compensate you for having to neglect your other clients. Do the job, and there are twenty—no, twenty-seven more where this came from."

Thirty pistras? Thirty pistras could see me in more suitable accommodations, at least for a few months. It would allow me to resume my lessons at Domenico's salle. Honing the essential skill of my trade was critical. I'd been absent for far too long, unable to pay what the fencing master demanded for his harsh, but expert tutelage. Perhaps I could also pay what I owed Donatello. My shirts would not take much more laundering, and my doublet bore patches of mismatched fabric. Looking the part of a bravo often proved as valuable as a deft stop-thrust.

Nonetheless, I temporized. "Who has angered you so badly you want him dead? What did he do? No offense, but you don't strike me as the sort to attract enemies."

Herbieto's bland, nondescript features contorted, twisting into a furious grimace that rendered him almost unrecognizable, as if he'd donned the mask of another, more choleric man's face. The utter hatred expressed by his visage convinced me of his seriousness of purpose more than any words could. This deeply felt virulence explained how he'd pushed himself to step inside Giacomo's against all the dictates of common sense. For the moment, he appeared incapable of speech.

The appearance of Bonfilia provided him a reprieve, a

chance to gather himself. I drained the remains in my cup before accepting the full one Bonfilia offered me. She set another before Herbieto, scooped up the empty, and left without a word. She has a singleness of purpose, that one. Silent and quick. It deflects attention and limits the opportunity for hands to wander. Given the hands at offer in Giacomo's, I can't say I blame her.

Herbieto hid his face behind his wine cup, gulping down about half of it. Then he dissolved into a choking, coughing fit. "Gah! You drink this voluntarily?"

"Consider it training. Builds muscle and stamina."

The interlude allowed Herbieto a moment to gather himself. The rage had vanished, leaving behind Herbieto's placid, composed, blank canvas of a face. He cleared his throat, braved a cautious sip, then spoke.

"My father was an ambitious man. His millinery shop kept us sheltered, fed, and clothed."

Millinery? It required a moment, and I almost lost the thread of his remarks. Women's hats? Well, why not?

"There were only the three of us: father; mother; and myself," Herbieto was saying. "No siblings survived childhood. So, while the business did not produce a fortune, it provided well enough for us."

I tried not to let a trace of envy show. A childhood spent as the son of a merchant— even a struggling merchant— was something I could only dream of as a boy, fighting for scraps in Plenum's gutters with the other wild creatures before returning to the orphanage at night. I couldn't hold his relative good fortune against him. None of us choose the conditions of our birth and upbringing.

"This wasn't enough for my father. He was always

eager to speculate, invest every spare soldi in whatever schemes or investment opportunities came his way." Herbieto paused for another, longer drink. His palate seemed to be habituating itself. "So, when Prospector Vicenzu—as he called himself—dangled the lure, my father swallowed it whole."

"Prospector?" I asked. "Let me guess: a mining scam. Gold?"

Herbieto nodded. "My father left my mother to run the shop and brought me along with him. I was old enough to take over myself. But he wanted an extra pair of hands and a strong back for shoveling. I was obviously the better choice."

"How did Vicenzu run the con?" I wasn't a grifter. I did, however, make my living on what you might consider the wrong side of the street. I rubbed elbows with not only thugs and assassins, but also second-story men, confidence artists, tricksters, fences, counterfeiters, and cutpurses. I possessed some familiarity with the gambits conmen employed to fleece their marks.

"He seeded the ground. Grains and even a small nugget or two, buried. He'd bought up some parcels in the North, in the shadow of the mountains. Cold up there. No denying the beauty, but it is cold." Herbieto paused, staring into his cup as if seeing his memories therein. "He pointed out the sort of features he said were likely to contain gold, then let us poke around for a while. I remember being so excited when I turned over a spadeful and saw those yellow glints. My father was even more excited. He agreed to the price of the plot."

Herbieto drained the rest of his cup. He summoned

Bonfilia for a refill. Thirsty work, recounting a tragedy.

"Of course that was the only gold we ever found. My father wasn't easily discouraged. When surface spadework failed to produce anything, he began excavation into the hillside. He convinced himself that certain signs he'd gleaned from Vicenzu's instruction indicated a major lode somewhere inside the hill. We worked like Heathen galley-slaves. He never lost his enthusiasm, his belief that we were only a day away from striking it rich. Right up to the point he triggered the cave-in that killed him."

Bonfilia returned with reinforcements in time for Herbieto once again to take refuge in the wine. The events he recounted must have occurred decades in the past. Yet the memory remained fresh enough to unman this stolid merchant.

"I was outside the entrance, retrieving a new pick to replace one with a broken handle. I heard the rumbling, ran back up the slope into a cloud of dust and rubble. It took me an hour to clear away enough earth and rock to find even his arm. It took the rest of the day to dig his body free."

I said nothing. What could I say to allay an old grief? If I knew a magical, anodyne phrase, I'd have plenty of use for it. Who among us doesn't suffer an old grief?

"That was nearly twenty years ago," Herbieto said after a pause that lasted long enough for us each to need a refill. And he was still buying. He cleared his throat, then raised his gaze from his cup to look me directly in the eyes. "Yesterday, I saw Prospector Vicenzu pass in front of the millinery shop."

I asked the obvious question. "After twenty years, how could you be sure it was him?"

"I have seen him in my mind every day since my father died." That fierce look had returned. "It was him. Older, of course, and dressed as a city gentleman rather than as a rough prospector. But it was him."

"What did you do?"

"Nothing. Nothing for almost a minute. I couldn't move. I was stunned. By the time I recovered myself and ran out of the shop, I'd almost lost him in the street. I didn't, though. I could see his red hair beneath his bright green cap. Stiffened felt. Short brim, ostrich feather."

So he kept current with men's headgear as well.

I nodded. "You followed him."

"Yes. Once I'd forced myself out of the shop, it seemed my feet took me in pursuit. I couldn't think straight. If he'd still been close by when I got onto the street, I don't know what I would have done. Something unhinged and violent. Probably not *successfully* violent. The walking helped clear my head. We'd reached the end of the Vimine district, where it begins to merge with the Sabatine. I'd gotten close and was beginning to think straight enough to hold back, keep a cushion of people between us."

Herbieto stopped. He picked up his wine again, put it back down without sipping.

"Vicenzu entered a house. There's a neighborhood of houses in the shadow of the first rows of palazzos at the foot of the Sabatine Hill. Nice places, but not what you'd call villas. Still, I wouldn't mind living in one.

"There's a food stall on a corner where I could keep an eye on the house. I watched for a couple of hours. Good olives, and the bread is not bad. I don't advise the fish paste. I got to chatting with the server, and he told me that he'd seen Vicenzu a few times over the last week. That he meets with various people in and around those houses. Apparently, there is some turnover, the families who have lived there for generations are selling out.

"I had a lot of time to think. I didn't want to confront Vicenzu myself. He's probably a decade older than I am, but still looks fit. He's the sort of man who has practical experience fighting. I do not. What sort of justice would it be to challenge the man, only to die in the attempt? That wouldn't be justice. That would be stupidity."

Herbieto caught my eyes again. "I'm not a coward. At least, I don't think I'm a coward. It is only a question of recognizing my own limitations. Do you understand?"

"Only sensible to avoid a duel, Herbieto," I said. I'd had to reassure clients of their essential manhood before. I had the speech down pat. "It takes a special kind of foolishness to willingly put yourself in harm's way. Not being a fool doesn't make you a coward. It just makes you not a fool."

His eyes darted away, then back to mine. He wanted to, but he wasn't buying it. He still felt somehow lessened, a craven. There was little I could do about that, nor did I care to. Timidity was good for business. What work for a bravo if every man saw to his own fighting?

"Anyway," Herbieto said as he picked up his cup, the slightest tremble in his hand. "I ascertained that Vicenzu is around those houses nearly every day. After that, I made some inquiries concerning—gentlemen of your particular vocation. And here I am."

I rubbed a thumb against the satin facing of the baldric

crossing my chest while I considered. The smooth surface of the deep burgundy fabric had begun to develop rough spots. The leather backing below was sweat-stained and cracking.

I didn't want to accept this job. There remained too many unknowns. I would have to lay much of the groundwork myself, scout the target, evaluate his situation, status, associates, and allies before determining how best to issue a plausible, defensible challenge. Or *if* to issue a challenge. This Vicenzu might have influence, friends of wealth, contacts in the civic government of Plenum, or—even worse—in the Collegium. Not a straightforward assignment.

The three pistras on the tabletop still caught the candlelight. I couldn't deny that incentive was compelling. I was tired of the inability to replace an aging baldric when required. I was tired of patched doublets, of wearing over-laundered shirts. Of living in squalor. The best days of my youth were fading footprints behind me upon time's damp paving stones. Did I intend to spend the rest of my years this way?

I leaned forward and scooped up the coins.

"So, how close to the duel would you like to be?" I asked the client.

Chapter 2

The olives were good. Together with the bread and a cup of watered wine, they made for a tolerable breakfast. The boy running the food stall that morning told me his name was Betto. The stall itself operated as

"Madina's," named after Betto's grandmother, who still made a rare appearance at the place, serving a shift at the brick oven and behind the braziers.

Madina's food stall looked like little more than a sturdy shack, a linear building with an exaggerated front overhang. The interior held room for the cook to move around amidst the supplies, utensils, and cooking fires. A long counter running the length of the building separated cook from customer. The overhang sheltered a dozen stools for the clientele. I selected one that provided the best vantage point for observing the grouping of houses Herbieto had described the night before.

The city of Plenum sprawls over a series of hills, some genuinely precipitous, others gently swelling elevations scarcely worthy of the appellation. Most of the city's districts derive their names from one of these eminences. Where the districts meet and commingle in the valleys, the demarcation of one from another grows murky. So, while the food stall was certainly within the Vimine district, I was less sure where to place the neighborhood under surveillance. I could see the Sabatine rising beyond it, but the houses themselves had been constructed within the flat, level valley from which at least three hills were visible. A liminal zone existed in which buildings could not be clearly ascertained to belong to one district or another—except perhaps upon rolled parchments gathering dust in the storage room of some low-level urban cartographer working at the Aedile's office.

Surveillance is boring. The prospect of sitting my ass down for hours at a time doing nothing but watching and waiting was one of the reasons I'd been so reluctant to take on this job. I tried to engage Betto. I had to, really, for a few reasons. One was that he was my only immediate source of information. Another was that if I didn't befriend him, he wasn't going to tolerate my occupying a stool—valuable real estate in his business—for the bulk of the day. Yet another was that, when other customers were absent, he represented the only entertainment available. A thirteen-year-old boy may not provide the most stimulating conversation, but as I mentioned, surveillance is boring. You take what diversion you can get.

Intermittent rain pattered on the overhang. The braziers offered a welcome heat, and the smells of baking bread, sizzling meat, and fish paste provided a break from the ubiquitous smell of Plenum's streets. Those smells were, happily, less pronounced in a nicer area such as this. The reek of effluvia I was accustomed to in the Orine district was rarer here where interior drains led to underground cloaca. The locals didn't simply toss the contents of full shit-pots out the window. The visible excrement marring the cobbles of the street appeared to be equine in origin, not human. Thankfully little of that. Plenum hadn't developed as a horse-friendly city. The streets tended toward the narrow and the precipitous.

I'd figured Betto would be a prime source of information, seeing as he spent most of his day here. I suppose I should have realized that, stuck inside the kitchen of Madina's, Betto was not actually well-situated to observe what occurred outside. I gleaned from him that many of his customers were new, there to consider purchasing one of the houses recently up for sale.

"Why do you think they are all being sold now, Betto?"

I asked. I slid another half-soldo across the counter and pointed at the empty dish of olives by my elbow.

Betto produced one of those ambiguous shrugs a thirteen-year old seems to perfect. It could mean anything. But to that non-answer he appended "Most of my customers eat and go. I don't get a lot of conversationalists, like you, Cesar. But I overheard some talk. A lot of customers have been mentioning Hearth Demons."

I chewed on that for a while. That nugget of information could be an important clue. Hearth Demons. Plenum is no stranger to demons. The magi of the Collegium are the de facto lords and masters of Plenum primarily because they possess the aptitude and knowledge to summon and control demons. When you can do that, you pretty much get to run the show.

I've probably had more direct encounters with demons than most normal, magically ungifted people have. My particular profession has necessitated that I tackle a demon or two directly, or interact with them on a less adversarial footing. But for most of us regular folk, demons aren't quotidian. We see them, or the product of their doings, often enough, but at a remove. We seldom deal with them personally or on a familiar basis. The Collegium provides the intermediaries.

However, there is a persistent folk myth concerning Hearth Demons. Maybe there is an element of truth to it. More likely it is a result of collective wish-fulfillment, a common desire of us regular people to possess the benefits the magi seem to, calling up a demonic servant to cater to our whims. Whatever the source, the gist of the myth is that certain lucky abodes contain a demon bound to the place itself, and—most importantly—bound to serve the master of the house.

So, buy the house, get the demon.

I turned away from Betto and looked out over the neighborhood again, at the neat rows of aspirational villas. They were of a kind, with little obvious variation from outside. Two-storied, compact brick structures presenting little to the street but stout doors and narrow, grilled windows. Behind the street front would be two rear projecting wings and a tall, rear wall probably shared with a mirror image house on the other side. The snug courtyard bounded by the three wings and the rear wall would be the central feature, the pride of the householder, a miniature version of the enclosed pleasure gardens that the great palazzos climbing the Sabatine enjoyed.

The glimmer of a notion tried to coalesce into a concrete idea within my mind. But some essential element was missing.

I understood from Herbieto that Vicenzu was an accomplished grifter. Could he truly have the stones to pull off something on a grand scale here in Plenum? Right here in the shadow of the Sabatine Hill? What exactly was his scheme?

I munched at an olive, spat the pit into the street where it bounced and skittered to join some of its fellows in a hollow between cobblestones that was slowly filling with rainwater. I didn't like it, but Plenum needed the rains. After humid springs and baking summers, the streets grew foul. Unfortunately, these early rains only seemed to exacerbate the situation, revivifying smells that had grown dormant. And I didn't care for getting wet. The rain made the feather in my hat droop and ruined the drape of my sleeves.

The olive provided no insight, failed to crystallize my hunch. A puff of air at my back caught my attention, and I turned back to face the interior of Madina's. Betto was whisking a bar towel across the counter, fanning up little zephyrs in consequence. That towel never left him. When both his hands were occupied, it was draped over one shoulder. The rest of the time it was constantly in motion, like the tail of a fly-bedeviled horse, flicking here and there at real or imagined blemishes on the counter or the cooking area.

When I turned back again, Vicenzu had appeared.

He was striding westward along Escaline Way, a man with a purpose but no particular hurry, certain the world would wait for him. If he kept going, he'd eventually pass by Madina's. Assuming, however, his business took him to the cluster of houses I was watching, he'd turn to his left twenty yards or so prior to reaching Madina's where it squatted at the intersection of the Escaline and the crooked, nameless alley branching off northward.

I recognized Vicenzu from Herbieto's description. I did not question that this was the same man. "In his mid-forties, though still brisk and hale," Herbieto had said. "He could pass for younger, with that hair, red with the fire of youth. Tall and lean, with the face of a genial saint." Herbieto talked like that after his third—or was it fourth?—cup of wine. I'd appreciated it, seeing unexpected depths in a man who seemed dry bread at first appearance.

The orange flash of Vicenzu's hair shone from beneath

a narrow-brimmed bonnet of crushed red-velvet. The ostrich feather in the hat sagged in the rain. His doublet was dyed a dull bronze color, and the hose beneath were parti-colored, red and black. A rapier depended from the baldric slung across his shoulder. He seemed comfortable wearing it, not constantly readjusting it or fighting to keep the scabbard from tripping him up.

Finally getting sight of the target should have made me feel good. It didn't. Vicenzu wasn't alone.

I didn't mind the presence of the woman so much. Given other circumstances I'd have been pleased to see her, give her the thorough examination she deserved. At a guess, she was little more than twenty years old. She wore green, the square-bodice gown brushing the tips of shoes that couldn't hold up to much Plenum street travel. A small, elaborate hat offered little protection against the weather and revealed auburn tresses gradually losing the battle against rain to maintain their artificial curl.

What concerned me were the four men accompanying the pair. They weren't obtrusive about it. In fact, I'd wager most people wouldn't realize there was anything linking the four men, let alone connecting them to Vicenzu and the woman. But when you've had to keep an eye out for bodyguards as often as I have, you learn to spot them.

These were the men the thugs in Giacomo's Wine Shop aspired to be. These were competent men, the kind you could trust with a task more complicated than thumping someone over the head in a back alley. In a way, they each reminded me of Herbieto, with faces you'd not necessarily notice or remember, and dressed in a fashion that didn't draw attention. But there the resemblance ended. These were hard men, accustomed to violence. I was almost surprised I didn't recognize them. But Plenum is populous. I don't know everyone. And there was no reason Vicenzu couldn't have brought them in from out of town.

I supposed that whatever game Vicenzu was running precluded armed bodyguards looming nearby and intimidating the marks. The woman, however, did seem to be integral to the scheme. I, for one, was intrigued.

I reached behind me for another olive, not wanting to lose sight of Vicenzu and his team. I'd begun to find my curiosity piqued. What precisely was he up to? I felt I had an inkling of it, and the desire to find out how close I'd come tortured me. But I hadn't been hired to investigate. I'd been hired to provoke Vicenzu into a duel, then stick a sword through him.

How was I supposed to do that in the presence of four men whose job was to keep Vicenzu's skin unpunctured? And, for some reason, I felt reluctant to act the boor in front of this woman.

Complications. Always complications. It almost tempted me to keep Herbieto's retainer and get out of Plenum for a few months, maybe a year. The memory of the previous night in my apartment, however, provided compelling reasons to keep to the contract, earn the entire fee. The splintering floorboards made removing my boots for the night a dangerous proposition. Thin walls offered minimal protection from the increasing chill of the season. Even if the walls had been properly tucked and pointed brick instead of lath and plaster, the sagging, off-kilter old building left structural gaps that allowed in drafts from all sides that would have nullified the benefit. I'd suffered too many nights of the prime of my life to slip away in that single room, sweating most of the nights, shivering the rest. I needed out. I needed to complete this job.

Thirty pistras! Well, maybe. I had a hunch Herbieto was overstating what he could actually pay. Thirty pistras represented a substantial layout for a small shop such as Herbieto's. Looking back, he hadn't sounded certain when he'd mentioned the sum. Still, I was certain; certain he'd cough up some of it. The rest of it, I'd let him pay over time. And he would. An intimate acquaintance with the point of my rapier would convince him of where his best interest lay.

I wondered how much I'd have to earn to buy one of these houses Vicenzu was peddling. That was an idea. Not buying one, of course. I'd have to fall into a vat of pistras to be able to afford purchasing a house like that. But Vicenzu couldn't know the paucity of my finances. Perhaps I could approach as a potential buyer, a potential mark.

Could I pull it off? Did I appear prosperous enough to be taken seriously?

I considered. My customary fastidious attention to my attire would serve me well, were it not for my recent financial inability to maintain my standards. However, the rain might work to my advantage. It might obscure the patches on my doublet. And the doublet covered much of the frayed and yellowing shirt beneath. Everything I wore was originally of good quality. It might work.

Rising, I flipped another half-soldo onto the counter. Madina's provided a convenient spot, and Betto was a valuable source of information. Ingratiating myself with him was worth a bit of Herbieto's money. I'd have to start tracking expenses.

I angled my steps to intersect Vicenzu and the woman. I deliberately avoided glancing at his watchers. I couldn't see any upside in letting them know I was aware of them. The rain shifted from intermittent showers to steady drizzle as I approached.

Vicenzu neared one of the houses. The unassuming facade appeared no more appealing up close than it had from my vantage at Madina's. It was, however, clean, not marred by centuries of bird droppings, grease, soot, and various unnamable substances such as decorated most of the buildings in the Orine district. So, it looked pretty good to me, and hinted at nicer surprises within. The front door was an impressive slab of carved wood with a small rectangle of iron grillwork inset at eye-level. A heavy brass knocker in the shape of a grinning demon was hinged below the grill.

I found a puddle to splash a boot in as I neared and uttered a mild "Damn" to alert Vicenzu to my presence. Let his first impression of me be that of a clumsy, unobservant simpleton. Pity that meant the woman's first impression of me would be the same. Seeing her up close, I felt an urge to present the rakish Cesar instead, the real man rather than the guise I was adopting. But I did have a job to do.

The two turned at my graceless approach. Seeing him near at hand, I added another couple of years to my estimate of Vicenzu's age, but did not detract a whit from my evaluation of his competence. He showed no surprise, betrayed no nervousness or weakness. After the briefest examination—I couldn't be sure through the misty curtain of drizzle, but I thought I detected a slight, scornful lift of eyebrow—he broke out a welcoming smile.

"Savero the Builder?" Vicenzu asked. He gestured at the house behind him. "You are a trifle early for the appointment. I was about to open up the place."

I briefly thought about taking the opportunity Vicenzu offered to play this new role. But I discarded it almost immediately. If this Savero had an appointment then he was likely to show up at any time. And meanwhile I could be tripped up by any number of questions to which I did not know the answer. Better to not multiply my deceptions unnecessarily.

"Not Savero, sorry to disappoint," I said. "A builder, you say? A contractor, I presume. Certainly not a common laborer. If these places are within a laborer's budget, then I'll be disappointed."

Vicenzu produced a laugh, an easy, good-natured expression of mirth I'd have found genuine in anyone else. "Allow me to open up, and you'll see for yourself the level of quality I offer. And the bargain you'd be getting considering the resident...bonus." He squinted at me through a shifting veil of swirling mist and drizzle. "Assuming your budget exceeds that of a hod carrier or timber framer." He grinned to show he was making a joke instead of an indirect aspersion on my social and financial status. But I could see his uncertainty and decided to dispel it immediately, if possible.

"Cesar," I said, extending a hand, offering a wrist grip. "I import tinware. Discards and lightly damaged goods rejected by the contracted purchasers. It keeps me at Spina most of the time, but business has picked up to the extent that I'm considering a residence in Plenum."

I thought that a pretty good cover story for the spur of the moment. It did not make me sound too prosperous, was esoteric enough to discourage questions or any real curiosity, and the suggestion of an occupation that demanded significant time spent at the docks offered an excuse for any irregularities in my attire.

It seemed to satisfy Vicenzu, for he accepted my proffered hand and we clasped wrists. Then he turned to attend to the door, leaving me with my mind divided between two subjects. One: what had he meant by the phrase "resident bonus?" And two: the Woman. Vicenzu hadn't introduced her nor had she offered a name. So, for the moment, she remained "the Woman." The Woman made it difficult to concentrate on subject number one.

From the attention she paid me, I was at best an obstacle between her and the shelter from the rain offered by the locked house. The Cesar the Bravo charm had yet to exert its influence. Even in the rain, she looked worth the effort. Her face presented an appealing synthesis of contrasts: a delicacy of features and a firmness of countenance. Her large, hazel eyes seemed intended for a rounder, heavier visage rather than set above the high cheekbones of her triangular face.

I hadn't yet resolved on an opening gambit by the time Vicenzu's four minders arrived. They, apparently, hadn't taken me for Savero the Builder and descended upon me to ensure the safety of their principal. I could see three of them, the fourth I felt more than saw. My neck prickled.

My feet wanted to shift, turn to place my back against the wall. My hands longed to get ahold of my rapier, draw it free of the scabbard. It was all I could do to stand still and pretend I didn't notice them.

Vicenzu waved them off with a flick of his fingers he doubtless considered too subtle for his mark to notice. His mark certainly did notice, but I was still dissembling and, compared to the effort of failing to notice the four bruisers, it was simple to feign ignorance of the slight movement.

The bodyguards veered off without complaint or fuss. Smart, efficient. That concerned me more than did simple brute mass and an obvious propensity for violence. I concealed a relieved sigh as Vicenzu got to work on the clumsy iron lock securing the door. One look at that lock told me the house was unfurnished. The lock was too crude to keep out even a mediocre housebreaker from the Orine district. So, nothing to steal. What was this bonus Vicenzu mentioned?

With a bow and a flourish, I gestured to the Woman to precede me. I'm uncertain she noticed. I followed.

My career has led me into the abodes of the extremes of society. Considering the low end, my apartment is awful, true, but I've visited worse habitations. At the other extreme, my misadventures have taken me inside the palazzos of the great and powerful in Plenum, castellos of provincial officials, and even within the vast, luxurious halls of the Collegium itself. What struck me immediately upon stepping into the domicile Vicenzu was showing was its absolute ordinariness. That in itself was a marvel; none of it was ordinary to me, and yet it felt ordinary, the epitome of what a Plenum domicile should be. A sense of belonging enveloped me. I was at home.

The other aspect that struck me was how empty it was. We'd stepped into a linear entry hall, running off to either side, a blank wall directly ahead. While Vicenzu worked with a tinder box to light a lamp, I looked about me with what illumination the wet day outside allowed. The floor plan would be three rectangular boxes, divided into rooms and set about a courtyard. I didn't need the tour to know that. But these were empty boxes, stripped of furnishings. No rugs on the floor, no art on the walls, no tables, no chairs. And yet I saw little dust, suggesting the rooms had been recently denuded.

I couldn't guess Vicenzu's scheme. But he'd managed to acquire several adjacent properties and clear them of furniture in a short time. The sale of the furniture might have offset his initial investment, or it might be providing his immediate operating funds. Either way, I was dealing with a precise operator. It would behoove me to bear that in mind.

We passed through room after room, expansive or cozy as the function dictated. Some offered glimpses of the modest peristyle nestled within. Had I actually been the buyer I posed as, I believe I'd have been unimpressed. The building was entirely too basic, too much the exemplar of a style, lacking distinction. I, however, loved it. This was exactly what an Orine district gutter-urchin hopelessly aspired to. I kept that reaction to myself, remembering to sniff in appropriately disdainful or dismissive manners at each chamber or feature Vicenzu pointed out.

Vicenzu brought the tour to a halt in a small, windowless room. As with all the others, it was unfurnished. A small fireplace took up a portion of the back wall, ready to provide heat during the few months of cold that visited Plenum.

"Servant's room. The next few are exactly like this," he said, "suitable for servants or storage, depending upon how you run your household." He paused, tilting his head to give me an appraising look. A few large drops of water fell from the ostrich plume in his hat and splashed upon the brick floor. "I admit, Cesar, that I underestimated you. I assumed a man who spent most of his time in Spina would be dazzled by even the most modest of Plenum's villas. But you have shown me the error of making such assumptions, and I apologize. You obviously recognize the commonplace for what it is."

Here Vicenzu stopped. He offered a conspiratorial smile. "There is, however, something special about this place. Something I hadn't thought I'd need to reveal. But I can see I'm dealing with a discerning client."

I noted an absence, a movement of air currents. Exactly as if a woman in skirts had abruptly left her position behind and to my left. Vicenzu was gesticulating, drawing my attention to himself.

"I have an eye for a good thing, Cesar. I'm sure you do, too. You're down at the docks, you see a crate some other merchant deemed unacceptable. But you, Cesar, you perceive the possibilities, the value in that crate that escaped the dull eye of the merchant. It is the same with me.

"Take this place, for instance. It is a nice enough house. Solid, but hardly spectacular. What it does have, what I noticed that escaped all other potential buyers, was that this house possesses a resident familiar spirit, what is commonly referred to as a Hearth Demon."

Vicenzu was drawing this out, punctuating his prolixity with hand gestures. Wafting in from the hallway behind me, I caught a whiff of a scent I recognized. I'd smelled it all too often. The odor always varied, but inevitably involved musk, musty parchment, sulfur, and cinnamon. This time, the scent was faint, almost pleasant, the cinnamon predominating.

A whisking sound, as of something methodically moving across the floor, commenced from behind me. I turned around.

I wouldn't say I goggled. I'd half-expected something of the sort, and I was far from unaccustomed to demonic encounters, whether malign, benign, or disinterested. It was a squat creature, reaching no higher than my waist, though it massed enough, its smooth, almost glossy brown skin was taut with the roundness of belly, arms, and legs. It wore only an apron, the myriad pockets of which sprouted the implements of the house maid's trade. Its pudgy hands gripped a cutdown broom with which it busily swept the floor. Vicenzu's lamp lit up its cherubic smile, suggesting the demon's utter contentment with its chore.

Behind the demon, the Woman slipped into the small room, the chamber seeming even smaller with the four of us inside. She was brushing her hands against her skirts, the gesture probably intended to be surreptitious, but I caught it. I noticed the faintest hint of dust at her knees. Dust, or powder of some other sort. Chalk perhaps. Red and yellow chalk. The sort of thing that might be employed in sketching a quick summoning circle on a brick floor.

That was...unexpected. For more than one reason. At the same time, it solidified the vague theories about Vicenzu's scheme that had been floating around in the back of my mind and failing to land. The Hearth Demon tied to the house was bait-and-switch; Vicenzu's ploy to sell these properties at a markup. In fact, the Woman summoned the demon. Once money exchanged hands, the new buyer would never see the creature again. Or perhaps it would show up on an irregular basis until Vicenzu had finished selling off all the properties he'd purchased. I could only guess at the details.

It all fit with my half-formed guess regarding Vicenzu's game. What really surprised me was the Woman calling up the demons. Finding anyone outside the Collegium who could conjure and control demons was extraordinary. That it was a woman was unnerving.

The Collegium fostered a reputation as a paternalistic benefactor. It operated poor houses and hospitals. It oversaw our spiritual well-being, with the Predicant serving as the ultimate arbiter of right and wrong. But its primary concern was traffic with demons. And integral to that concern was ensuring that no one else infringed upon its monopoly. Only a magus could summon a demon. That was axiomatic. So, anyone displaying the capacity for the task must necessarily join the Collegium and become a magus. What happened to those men who refused?

And they were all men. I knew little of the women associated with the Collegium. On occasion, I'd see sisters of the Sorority outside an orphanage or hospital engaged upon some task requiring an excursion beyond the walls. But generally, they were cloistered away, unseen by the public as they attended to the good works that occupied them. I hadn't associated them before with demons. But who knew what occurred behind the walls of the facilities the Sorority managed? Not this impoverished bravo.

Could the sisters conjure demons? I now had a suggestion of the answer. But the woman here with Vicenzu clearly did not belong to the Sorority. That made her some sort of witch, I supposed. It took all of my vast reservoir of composure not to physically react as I absorbed each realization. I wanted to offer a polite nod to Vicenzu, turn on my heel, and bolt. But I had a job to do.

I summoned up a delighted smile. "A Hearth Demon," I said. I almost convinced myself of my enthusiasm. Then I reined it back, a merchant not wanting to reveal the extent of his interest. "Well, so it appears, at least."

"I assure you, Cesar, this is the genuine article," Vicenzu said. "Tied to the house, and dedicated to its cleanliness and maintenance. It would require at least an Arch-magus to banish it. Yours, with purchase of the house."

There have been times I've faced multiple opponents in combat. The number of factors you need to consider simultaneously when engaged with several people trying to kill you can be overwhelming. When faced with such circumstances, I've often fallen back upon instinct, allowing years of training to aid the mental processes that somehow occurred on a level I wasn't aware of, all the while battling for my life. But my preference is to retreat, to give myself time to think.

I felt something similar now, in the presence of a deluge of simultaneous realizations. Setting aside the interesting facts regarding Vicenzu's confidence game and the Woman's abilities, here I had my target right before me. His bodyguards were outside. The demon didn't appear to represent a threat. It puttered about, whisking its broom left and right as it maneuvered among us in the cramped quarters. The Woman was not obviously armed. I could simply run my sword through Vicenzu's heart and walk out. But that wasn't the job. And it fell outside the self-imposed bounds of my profession; it would constitute an assassination, not a duel. Besides, I'd forfeit the rest of my wages; Herbieto wanted to watch the fight, see me kill Vicenzu. He didn't want me to simply bring him the man's head.

What I needed to do was to establish legitimate grounds for a challenge. A public challenge. I couldn't merely insult the man here, with only the Woman as a witness. A demon's testimony carried no legal weight, certainly not this feeble-minded drudge's.

No, I had to get out of here. Find a place populated enough to both provide witnesses and reduce the odds of Vicenzu taking the expedient of setting his bodyguards on me once I worked my refined skill of getting under another man's skin.

What should be the nature of the affront? Abruptly, I had it, as the demon swept an invisible speck of dust from the brick between my feet. Like all the best lies, it built up from a foundation of truth. I'd be angered at Vicenzu's scheme. Call him out for attempting to gull me with a false Hearth Demon. He could not possibly allow such an assertion to pass unchallenged. Certainly not in public, or his entire game here would collapse. I could only imagine how much he'd invested up front. He'd not gladly walk away. It might ruin him.

Time to retreat, then. Get out of this house and into the public.

All this tumbled rapidly through my mind as I stood there, observing the Hearth Demon and the servant's room with what I hoped was the calculating mask of a potential home buyer. I had to speculate on that, never having made a purchase of anything more substantial than a sword.

"Intriguing," I said. "May I see the rest? I'd like a closer look at the courtyard."

Sometimes a gradual retreat is the safest. We toured the rest of the house, but I paid scant attention, my mind too busy planning.

The curtain of drizzle had lifted by the time Vicenzu extinguished the lamp and ushered me out the front door. The street had accumulated a few more pedestrians taking advantage of the break in the weather. Not enough for my business, however, and people on the move made for poor witnesses. At a glance, I was able to spot two of Vicenzu's minders. I imagined the other two were at hand, or taking advantage of Vicenzu's absence to deal with the personal business bodyguards often have to delay. See a man dancing from foot to foot while only a step or two from public facilities? There's a good chance he's a bodyguard keeping an eye on the important looking fellow nearby.

I didn't wait for Vicenzu to begin his sales pitch. "A cup of wine and a plate of something warm while we discuss terms?" I asked.

That took him off guard. He hadn't anticipated it would be so easy. "I'd like that. But I am still expecting Savero the Builder. I can't in good conscience wander off to some taverna. We could go back inside and talk, if you like."

"There's a food stall right over there," I said, and pointed at Madina's, barely visible from where we stood. I could make out an early lunch crowd beginning to gather. Ideal witnesses: congregated and bored. A public altercation would both entertain them and stick in their memories. "A deal should be celebrated with a drink. And you can watch for Savero the Builder from there, then give him the news he'll have to find another place to buy."

Cupidity won out. Vicenzu flashed an engaging smile. With that smile, his red hair, and the voluminous ostrich feather, the man belonged on the stage.

"I only recently breakfasted at Kertzel's. But how could I deny you anything, Cesar? Let's go."

He strode off toward Madina's, expecting the Woman and me to follow. I offered the Woman a smile. "Shall we?" I asked.

She ignored my gallantry and followed Vicenzu's footsteps.

I cast around again, pretending to take a final look at the house I was ostensibly purchasing, and located the third bodyguard. Then I followed as well, scripting the blistering obloquy I was about to deliver, calculating exactly what public abuse he'd be unable to ignore. The challenge must come from him. Vicenzu could spurn a challenge from me, could in fact use it to proffer a charge against me with the Questors. I'd fled summons from those magistrates before and had no desire to notify them of my renewed presence in Plenum. So, the right words and approach were essential.

The Woman was a dozen paces ahead of me, right on Vicenzu's heels, and I was closing the distance, splashing through the rainwater puddled among the cobblestones, when a black cloaked figure intercepted me, coming from behind and to my right. I felt the pressure of the blade point at my kidney.

"Someone would like a word, Cesar."

Chapter 3

There's a thrill that runs up the spine and a sudden chilling of the skin when you feel the pressure of a sharp point against your vitals. It is simultaneously invigorating and enervating. It has happened to me a number of times, but I can't say I'll ever get used to it. Nor would want to.

After the briefest of moments, I understood the prodding blade was a summons, not the sudden, bloody end of Cesar the Bravo. I nodded, kept my hands well away from my rapier, and said, "I keep regular hours at Giacomo's Wine Shop. Tell your principal he can drop in most days and find me there. Or, we can make an appointment."

The point dug in a fraction more. "Funny. Start walking. To your left."

Since my remarks hadn't got me immediately killed, I risked a glance over my shoulder. As I began walking. To my left.

The man pressing the dagger to my kidney wore livery beneath his black cloak, a parti-colored black and yellow affair that didn't tell much beyond the fact of his employer's evident wealth. I had already deduced that from the competence of the approach and the steadiness of the dagger hand; skilled work doesn't come cheap. The man kept close; I wouldn't be able to make a dash for it without getting six inches of steel into one of my valuable organs. He also maintained his positioning; I couldn't grab a wrist or arm to wrest the dagger away from him.

I caught a last glimpse of Vicenzu and the Woman as I moved away from them along Escaline Way. Both were looking at me, but were too far away for me to make out expressions. I could only assume they were not happy expressions. Whoever had sent the man with the knife at my back had truly dumped a cow flop in my soup tureen. My approach to Vicenzu was ruined. Might have cost me twenty-seven pistras. Or however much I would have ultimately squeezed out of Herbieto.

At the not-so-gentle direction of the liveried knife-man, I turned left again, off Escaline Way and, after a few minutes, began to ascend the Sabatine Hill. The modest houses of the sort I'd just toured gave way to the fine palazzos of Plenum's monied and powerful inhabitants. It was far from my first visit to these environs. Previous jobs had seen me here, on occasion even infiltrating one of the villas. Nice places, if you had the coin.

We turned at the end of a rank of shady cypress trees, climbed a flight of broad, deep steps, and entered the gated grounds of a villa. We'd reached high enough that the view would be worth a look. At least on a clear day, and if the viewer didn't have the threat of a blade shoved between his floating ribs if he stopped and turned around.

The villa backed against a shelf of the Sabatine Hill which continued to rise up, its flanks bearing increasingly opulent abodes the higher up one looked. I didn't look, instead taking in the yellow stucco facade of the house before me. The architect had, I supposed, been attempting elegance, but was constitutionally incapable of avoiding at least some ornamentation. A modest garden, wedged into the narrow space between the wall and the front of the house, showed careful grooming. Three or four statues — whether valuable relics of the Ancients or skillful replicas, I couldn't say — peeked from between topiary bushes or sheltered beneath spreading willows.

I must have paused during my examination. A sharp prod got me moving again, toward the front door. My patience with this jackass began to run thin.

We'd been expected. Another man in yellow and black livery opened the heavy oak door, its panels carved into decorative scenes. An extravagance of lamps illuminated a marble-floored entry hall. More statues lined either wall.

"Your sword, sir," the doorman said, holding out a hand.

An ungentle reminder at my back encouraged me to comply with the request. I removed my hat, eased the baldric from over my head, then handed both hat and scabbarded sword to the doorman.

"Mind these, would you," I said. "The hat could use a brushing." I gave the doorman my full attention, deliberately ignoring his fellow behind me.

The doorman took expression lessons from the statues. He remained stone-faced, pivoted on a heel, and left the hallway through a doorway to the left. Someone else replaced him, emerging from a matching doorway on the right.

I realized immediately I was dealing with a magus. Almost unquestionably an Arch-magus. A Primate, at least. He wore the black vestments of some Collegium office over a yellow doublet and black hose. I guessed that single outfit cost more than I'd spent on clothes over the last five years.

He wasn't an impressive specimen: his shoulders narrow, a potbelly bulging his doublet. But his graying, fashionably cut hair framed a face that retained a firm jaw despite the evident years of good living. He took me in with intense, dark eyes. He must have been a charismatic bastard in his prime. But at the moment, what I saw was a facade of confidence and determination. Habit, probably. Worry lay beneath that commanding, self-possessed expression.

What could worry a Collegium heavyweight to the extent he'd send out a servant to collect a bravo at knifepoint?

"Cesar the Bravo?" the magus asked. He didn't wait for a reply. "I am Primate Aldus Fenetto."

A Primate, then. One step below a Red Hat. A big shot, or close enough for the likes of a bravo such as myself. I'd have to keep sharp here if I wanted to keep my head where it belonged.

"To what do I owe the pleasure of this audience, Your Eminence?" I asked.

I think I made a creditable attempt at tamping down the sarcasm. Fenetto's frown—a temporary furrow between his eyebrows—suggested I might not have entirely succeeded.

"I'd like to offer you a job," he said, after a brief pause.

"As I was saying to your lackey, here," I said, jabbing a thumb over my shoulder at the jackass behind me, "I keep regular hours at Giacomo's Wine Shop."

A slight smile—half incredulous, half amused—crossed Fenetto's face. "Come with me, Cesar. I think you'll find my parlor a more comfortable place of business than your wine shop."

I didn't hesitate. I found nothing pleasurable about standing around in his marble foyer. And he was doubtless correct: pretty much any place other than my apartment would be more comfortable than Giacomo's Wine Shop. So I followed him back through the door he had come out of. The lackey with the knife kept pace close behind. Fenetto led through a room partially open to the elements and filled with plants I didn't recognize: lush, thick foliage and brilliant blossoms boasting complex, colorful shapes. There was a thick, earthy aroma in the place, and a sultry, humid quality to the air that belied the temperature outside; the warmth accomplished by some sort of hypocaust, perhaps, or maybe Fenetto employed a demon to periodically heat up the place. We passed out of that room into a hallway lined with more sculptures. An elaborate fresco decorated the ceiling. Brass-lined wall niches held lamps that lent the hallway a coppery glow. Several doors opened off the hallway. Fenetto led me to the doorway at the end.

"You can leave us, Klask," he said to the lackey. "I don't think our good bravo will attempt to strangle a Primate of the Collegium."

Fenetto's servants hadn't demanded my dagger: the long, parrying main gauche with its comforting expanse of hand guard. So strangling Fenetto wasn't my only homicidal option. But everyone there knew I was unlikely to institute violence against a man with demons at his beck and call. There was a good reason the Collegium was the de facto ruler of Plenum, not to mention most of the lands of the Faithful to boot.

Fenetto opened the door and walked into the room beyond. He wasn't the sort of man to usher a guest in before him. Or, perhaps—and I had to consider this more likely—he didn't consider me a guest. I followed him into a chamber that topped the rest of the villa's rooms as a showpiece of wealth and power.

A half-dozen paintings adorned walls plastered a pale gold color. I'm afraid I do not travel in the circles that would allow me to recognize the artists or the quality. But the paint appeared new and the style contemporary, with the figures rendered in a lifelike manner. A ceiling fresco, employing clever techniques of perspective, displayed Collegium magi supervising an exotic assortment of demons in completion of some task that I couldn't quite make out. It probably illustrated a mythic, literary, or scriptural reference I was unfamiliar with. Growing up in the gutters had done little to advance my education.

Shelves set between paintings held numerous books. Most were massive, hand-scribed tomes, but some were clearly printed volumes—smaller, more regularly bound.

I eyed those with some interest. A recent event had convinced me of the value of literacy. Pursuing that conviction, I had taken some tottering, baby-steps in the right direction, under the tutelage of my fencing master. His library contained a few battered, densely illustrated books teaching combat techniques, and he knew how to read them. He, and his young daughter, Valentina, had introduced me to the rudiments of reading. However, my lessons had ceased once my coin purse had withered to its current, desiccated condition. I hoped to resume both reading and fencing instruction once—if—I completed the job for Herbieto.

A desk—cluttered with books, scrolls, maps, candle holders containing stubby remnants of used tapers, and other, more mysterious examples of the type of esoteric bric-a-brac I associated with the magi—squatted in the center of the room. A window behind the desk rendered the candles currently unnecessary, its shutters open sufficiently to allow in light but not enough to provide a view of what lay beyond. I received only a suggestion of trees, hillside, and gray sky. Fenetto walked around the desk and sank into the chair behind it.

He gestured at me to sit. I glanced behind me, found an ornate, elaborately carved armchair with a plush, purple cushion waiting by the wall upon a carpet of the complexly patterned, geometrical sort woven by the Heathen. I dragged the high-backed chair toward the desk, the legs protesting loudly upon the marble floor once they cleared the carpet. A minor display of insolence; demonstrating to Fenetto that I wasn't utterly cowed, while not stepping so far beyond the bounds of propriety that I'd incur the wrath of an Arch-magus.

Fenetto frowned, but let my rearrangement of his furniture go otherwise without comment.

"I won't flatter—or frighten you—with the notion that you have a reputation in the Collegium, Cesar," Fenetto said without preamble. "You don't."

He may not have wished to frighten me, but I did experience a tightness in the pit of my stomach at his words. The less attention the Collegium paid to me, the happier I'd be. I wanted to believe him.

"But," Fenetto continued, "you have done work for one of the Councilors. Satisfactory work. I know Councilor Massim, and I know something of the job you performed for him."

"Oh? How is old Massim?" I asked, and crossed one booted leg over the other, tugging at the cuff as if dissatisfied with the fold. I did not like the fact that my name was on the lips of the high and mighty, but I wasn't about to reveal that fact before one of them. Nonchalance is an essential attitude for a bravo.

"Prospering. Politicking his way to influence among the Electors. It's possible, Cesar, that you will have, in some manner, played a role in choosing the next Predicant."

"I do what I can for the Faith," I said.

"Who could doubt your piety?" Fenetto asked.

The desert-dry sarcasm of the question almost made me like the man, Primate or not. I wondered if he was bucking for a Red Hat. Did his acerbic tone grate on the other magi? Did he require my help in furthering his political interests? I hoped not. I'd nearly gotten eviscerated by a demon the last time I meddled in the Collegium's internecine affairs.

The memory cooled my favorable inclination towards the man.

"Who indeed?" I replied. "After all, here I am, closeted with one the Faith's high representatives, obedient to a summons. Speaking of which, how may I assist your Eminence?"

"It would take a legion of demons to beat that insolence from you, wouldn't it, Cesar?" Fenetto released an amused snort. "Well, good. You'll need a bit of backbone."

Oh, would I? The Primate kept dropping phrases that lit the fires of my paranoid imagination and made my scrotum want to carry its burden up into my bowels to hide. I must have raised an eyebrow.

"Please, hold your questions, Cesar," Fenetto said. "It may take me a few minutes to provide you with all the information necessary for you to understand the task I wish you to undertake. I may not provide it in the tidy order that I would were I advocating some position or other before a committee of Councilors. This is a personal matter, not Collegium business. My rational faculties may be—disordered."

I had nothing to say to that, so I said it.

Fenetto cleared his throat, fumbled through the clutter on his desk, as though looking for a place to begin. He cleared his throat a second time, then got down to it.

"This is not easy for me, Cesar. I am a Primate of the Collegium, with a fair chance of earning my Red Hat and a seat on the Council. Certain social expectations accompany such a position. Blemishes upon one's past may limit one's prospects for further advancement."

Fenetto glanced away from me, ran through another

unnecessary clearing of his throat. "Would you care for some wine, Cesar? Perhaps a light collation?"

"Maybe later. How about you get on with it, Your Eminence?"

"Right. Yes. Well, to get closer to the heart of the matter, I have a daughter."

I shrugged.

"Yes, Cesar, I know. Half the Collegium have sired bastards. We are forbidden to marry, yet we remain all too human. If my fathering a child were all, I wouldn't have dispatched Klask to summon you. The problem—or, rather, one of the problems— is that my daughter, Maralla, was born with the Talent."

That straightened me up in the chair.

"Yes, Cesar. That makes the matter more complicated than simply another magus's by-blow to be overlooked." Fenetto drummed his fingers atop one of the books on his desk. "Are you sure you wouldn't care for some wine? I could use a cup."

What I wanted was for the man to get to the point. On the other hand, a magus of Fenetto's status in the Collegium would likely maintain an impressive wine cellar. Who was I to turn down the opportunity to sample his vintages?

"I'll join you for a drop or two, Your Eminence," I said.

Fenetto picked up a bell from the clutter on his desk and shook it vigorously. I heard nothing, though I could see the clapper slapping energetically about. One of the bookshelves to my left moved, swiveling soundlessly open upon oiled hinges. A demon—a hunchbacked creature reaching no more than five feet tall—glided in. It appeared roughly human, though with something of both ape and goat in its makeup. It wore Fenetto's livery, though its parti-colored doublet must have been slit in the back to allow for the two fluttering wings that emerged from between its shoulder blades. It didn't seem possible that wings so small and delicate could keep aloft such a heavy, misshapen creature. Then again, it was a demon. Or perhaps those little wings were merely intended to aid the demon's gliding, silent gait, not to send it soaring through the firmament.

"A bottle," Fenetto said. "The Cellian, I believe. And two goblets."

The demon shimmied noiselessly back the way it had come.

"You'll enjoy the Cellian, I think, Cesar. It comes from one of my estates in the north, from a south-east facing field that possesses an unusually high concentration of flint. Most of the buildings are faced with flint now, but we continue digging it up from the soil, with no end of the stuff in sight. My overseer insists the flint imparts unique qualities to the grapes."

I listened intently, tickled at hearing a magus—one of the high and mighty—doing the verbal equivalent of squirming in his seat. This was a man who truly did not want to discuss the subject for which he'd gone to all the effort to bring me here, and so was reduced to rambling.

The demon emerged again through the trick bookcase, bearing a tray upon which rested a fat-bellied bottle of dark green glass and two goblets of thick, amber glass resting upon silver stems. The demon set down the tray. It jabbed a claw into the wax plug in the bottle's neck, then slipped it free with a single, effortless tug. It poured two glasses, turned, then fluttered out, the bookcase swinging shut behind it.

Fenetto held up a goblet. I rose, took it from him, then sat, the wood of the chair creaking beneath me. A shaft of light caught the wine through the glass as I raised it, infusing the liquid with the rosy hue of sunset. I sipped. Whatever faults I might attribute to Fenetto, I couldn't fault his cellar. The wine carried hints of citrus and honey, leather and herbs. I drank again, this time deeply.

"Well," I said, after I'd drained half the goblet, "you probably should get around to explaining the problem of Maralla and her Talent, since you'll never get me more receptive than I am while drinking this."

"It is good, isn't it," Fenetto said, a proprietary smile brightening his face. But then the worry returned. "I'm wasting time, aren't I? Fine. Bear with me if it seems I am treating you like an ignorant child. But I can't expect you to be familiar with the internal politics of the Collegium, and I want you to understand the position I am in."

Fenetto took another sip. I matched him.

"Men gifted with the Talent are entrusted to the Collegium, usually as soon as the Talent manifests. This happens almost without exception. What family wouldn't want a son in the Collegium? There are rare instances of independent magi, usually found as court wizards in some distant, minor principality. Or you hear of recluses, hidden away in a dilapidated tower deep in the woods or high on some inaccessible snowy crag. We ignore such. They only enhance our prestige by their relative unimportance. But, the women, now. They present a problem."

Fenetto finished his goblet and reached for the bottle. I rose, extending my empty glass importunately. He obliged me.

Fortified, I sat down and sipped, waiting for Fenetto to pick up the thread of his discourse.

"Witches," Fenetto said after long moments he'd filled by drinking. "Women born with the Talent back in the days of the Ancients became witches. Influential voices in small communities. Occasionally troublesome in the larger polities. In the early days of the Collegium, we found witches a hindrance to our expansion of the Faith, to our mission of providing all-encompassing guidance to the Faithful. The solution, argued in Council and promulgated by an early Predicant, was the creation of the Sorority. The Collegium created a unified home for women born with the Talent. Their abilities could be harnessed, used to advance the Faith and the goals of the Collegium for the greater good."

Somehow the level of wine in our goblets had grown dangerously low. Fenetto paused to remedy the situation.

"But," I said, to prompt him, "if not every man with the Talent joins the Collegium, then it follows that not every woman does either."

Fenetto sighed. "And therein lies the problem. You see, while the rare independent magus presents no concern for the Collegium, the existence of witches does. The reputation of witches remains, a lingering remnant of the influence they wielded in the time of the Ancients. They offer an unacceptable alternative to what should be the universal authority of the Collegium. Because it is unacceptable, the Collegium refuses to accept it. Actively. There is a little-known department of the Collegium called the Venatores. The Venatores are tasked with tracking down and—dealing with—witches."

"Dealing with?" I asked.

"Ideally, the witches are inducted into the nearest house of the Sorority," Fenetto said.

"Ideally. Right."

"Yes, well, the Collegium does concern itself intimately with the Ideal."

"You serve wine this good, I suppose I can swallow a steaming load of sophistry along with it."

"Fine, Cesar," Fenetto said. "Those witches who resist are—with the sanction of the Predicant—killed."

I absorbed that while absorbing some more of the Cellian. But I savored the wine less than it deserved. I began to understand Fenetto's reluctance to discuss this. His loyalties dragged him in two separate directions.

"Let me guess," I said. "Maralla did not care for your suggestion that she join the Sorority."

Fenetto grimaced. "Therein lies another complication." He drank, deeply. When he came up, he said, "I haven't spoken to Maralla about this. In fact, I've never spoken to her. She doesn't know I am her father."

"Oh," I said. I began feeling distinctly out of my depth. What did Fenetto think a single, impoverished bravo could do that a magus, a Primate of the Collegium, could not accomplish? I figured he wanted some official distance. From what he'd told me, his position would be compromised if any of his political rivals discovered he was the father of a witch. He couldn't be seen to take an active role in shielding Maralla. And how could he do that anyway? Maralla had no idea he even existed. So, yes, he had a problem. But did he expect me to take on a shadowy arm of the Collegium, these Venatores? I'm a dangerous man with a sword, but I can't command demons. How could I possibly oppose the power of the Collegium?

I rose once again from my chair, snagged the bottle from atop Fenetto's desk, and brimmed my goblet.

"This is excellent wine," I said. "Let's call it fair recompense for kidnapping me. It isn't really. You disrupted the job I was on and cost me a substantial payday. But, we'll call it square, if you'll allow me to walk out of here and forget we ever had this conversation."

"I think, Cesar, that you underestimate yourself. You may think yourself unnoticed, but rumor of some of your exploits does circulate within certain echelons of the Collegium." Fenetto offered that with a slight smile, as though I should be pleased by the news, and apparently forgetting he'd already broached that subject. The Cellian *was* good wine, and heady. Then the smile disappeared and he fixed me with a concentrated, cold stare. "Worse, though, Cesar, is that you underestimate me. I am a father concerned for the life of his child. Do you think I won't do what is required to safeguard Maralla? Do you think I'll let you walk out of here without our having come to terms?"

I got a glimpse of the Fenetto that had risen through the ranks of the Collegium. My experience with the power struggles of the magi taught me that they did not play nice. So, I believed his implicit threat.

I set the bottle back atop the desk and resumed my seat.

Fenetto allowed me a couple of long swallows before he spoke again.

"I will not describe the lengths to which I have gone to protect Maralla," he said. "I have kept a watch over her since her birth. She was always a strong-willed child, but while her mother lived, and before her Talent manifested, I was not required to intervene. The last few years have proved taxing. But I have always succeeded in cleaning up any mess she made, kept her free of the Sorority, which she has shown no indication of wishing to enter. And I avoided any connection to myself, either from the aggrieved parties or from Maralla. But this time is different. Are you prepared to listen now, Cesar? Do you accept that you will be working for me?"

"It is an estimable wine," I said. I offered a rakish grin that—thanks to the influence of the estimable wine—was almost genuine. "Give me the details, then we'll talk price.

I'd hear him out. Once free of the villa, fleeing Plenum remained an option.

Fenetto nodded. He leaned back in his chair, goblet held close to his chest. "Maralla has recently involved herself in something that has attracted the attention of the Venatores. I do not have the specifics yet, but whatever it is, it has drawn the eye of Azeglio himself."

I raised an eyebrow. "Azeglio?" I asked. "Should I have heard of him?"

"He is the Questor General of the Venatores. I suppose there is no reason you should have heard of him. The existence of the Venatores is not common knowledge. Azeglio is a formidable man. He did not amount to much as a magus. I doubt he'd have risen above Catechumen.

But a man of ambition will find a way. And he found his way through the Venatores."

"So, the Questor General of the Venatores—this ambitious, formidable magus—has taken a personal interest in your daughter. Delightful. What exactly do you want me to do about it?"

"Simple, Cesar. I want you to protect Maralla from Azeglio and the rest of the Venatores." Fenetto raised his goblet, as if toasting an already accomplished victory. "Oh, and I want it done without Maralla knowing I exist."

"You're not the most encouraging of potential employers. You know that, Your Excellence?"

"How does one hundred pistras sound as encouragement?" Fenetto asked. "Ten now to cover any immediate expenses, the remainder when you've completed your task."

I considered that. I'd probably have to drop Herbieto as a client. But I suspected his purse was light anyway and doubted he'd be good for the coin he promised. A hundred pistras would more than compensate for whatever payment I might lose from him. Still, the Herbieto job seemed less likely to see my skin perforated by steel, or my flesh torn and devoured by demons. Vicenzu sported a pack of bodyguards, but he wasn't a magus commanding a force of dedicated witch hunters.

I temporized. "How would I even find your daughter? Where is Maralla? What does she look like?"

"You've already seen her, Cesar," Fenetto said, his eyes narrowing and crinkling at the corners with barely repressed humor. "You were following her when Klask arrived to collect you."

The Woman was Maralla? Well, how about that? The job became suddenly more attractive. Through a wine haze I caught a foggy vision of how I might be able to command two fees more or less simultaneously. Keeping an eye on Maralla would keep me close to Vicenzu, giving me another chance at wrangling a duel. And I'd already discovered that keeping an eye on the Woman was a pleasure in and of itself.

Plus, one hundred pistras! That would get me into reasonable accommodations and keep me in wine, clean shirts, and fencing lessons for a considerable time.

I gave Fenetto another appraisal, examining him for any familial resemblance to my still vivid recollection of Maralla. Maybe? Fenetto's mistress must have been stunning, because Maralla couldn't have received much of her looks from her father.

So, a hundred pistras and the opportunity—no, the obligation—to stay near Maralla. Perhaps engage her companionably.

"You've got yourself a bravo," I said, then drained the goblet.

Chapter 4

I had to concentrate on keeping my footing as I descended the Sabatine Hill. A burgeoning headache threatened by the time I reached the area where I'd lost Vicenzu and Maralla. I felt rather foolish standing there, as if they'd still be waiting for me. But there was the possibility they'd remain in the neighborhood, showing some other mark around the properties.

So I made my way back to Madina's, hoping a platter of bread, olives, and dried fish—washed down by a stoup of wine—might halt the headache in its tracks. And perhaps I might pick up the trail again.

The first part of the plan worked. I gave up about the time the sun began to settle behind the Jacline Hill. Plenum is no place to wander alone after dark, not even for a bravo. Unless he's getting paid or laid.

I was back early the next day to spend the morning— and some of the coin Fenetto had advanced—with Betto, sitting at what I figured was becoming my regular stool at Madina's. I'd spent a bit more of that coin the night before, paying a premium to my laundress to work overnight. So at least I had a clean shirt on, though it remained a bit damp. And my doublet and hat were freshly brushed. I hoped to make a better impression on Maralla this time around.

Vicenzu and Maralla, along with the four surreptitious bodyguards, appeared about the same time they'd arrived the day before. Someone awaited them next door to the house they'd shown me. I considered making my approach now. Volubly denouncing Vicenzu as a fraud and grifter in the presence of a mark might lead to the duel Herbieto was paying for. But it might also hamper my ability to attach myself to Maralla. Watching over her would be a lot simpler if she wanted to have me around.

Upon reflection I figured it best to stay put. Vicenzu, Maralla, and the mark all disappeared inside. The bodyguards dispersed. I watched, noting the sort of location each man felt to be the most discreet, which man stayed alert, and which took his ease. At the same time, I kept an eye out for anyone else watching the house. I had to place the Venatores at the top of my list of concerns; a secretive, dangerous organization threatening my charge. It was enough to twist any man's stomach, get the heart beating a trifle too fast, considering the sort of power and resources such an organization would possess.

At least I was getting paid well.

I was on another plate of olives accompanied by a strong, dry cheese, when the trio emerged. It must have gone well. The mark departed with every evidence of pleasure. Maralla's faux Hearth Demon seemed to have done the trick. Vicenzu and Maralla stood watching the potential home buyer walking away. Once the mark strolled safely from earshot, Vicenzu reached out to grasp both of Maralla's hands. She allowed it, though even from my distant vantage I noted a stiffness of posture. Vicenzu appeared to notice nothing, chattering away with broad movements of his fiery-haired head.

Then the pair began to saunter eastward along Escaline Way. I tossed coins on the countertop to settle the score with Betto. I glanced at the bodyguards. They began to move as well, though they maintained a distant overwatch, not closing in.

I still had no plan. But planting myself permanently on a stool at Madina's would get me nowhere. I had to stir things up somehow.

I moved. The cobbles were dry beneath my boot heels. Though the sky was overcast, no rain had fallen today. The street held more traffic, filled with people taking advantage of the break in the weather. I quickened my pace, closing the distance before Vicenzu and Maralla could disappear. I skirted a pair of students sharing an early bottle, already weaving about even this early in the day and taking up more than their share of the street. I dodged a group of laborers on their way to or from some job site, then put on a burst of speed that almost reached a jog.

"Vicenzu," I said, coming up behind the pair.

Vicenzu still wore the hat with the ostrich feather, though today he was attired in green and black. Maralla wore yellow, and wore it well. They both stopped and turned at my call.

Vicenzu cocked his head. I read surprise, alarm, and confusion in the expression that appeared momentarily on his face before being replaced with a politely questioning look. Of course, the expression I'd startled from him was so brief it might well have been a spasm of indigestion.

"Cesar the Importer," Vicenzu said, his tone neutral. "You'll pardon me if I note your behavior is a trifle...mercurial."

"Yes, cold feet, renewed interest," I said, flashing a broad smile. Vicenzu might be suspicious, but I figured he'd not willingly let a mark off the line once he'd set the hook. "That's how it must look. But you may have noticed someone with me. One of my employees, providing me with a piece of news I had to act on immediately. I apologize for such a precipitate, uncourteous departure, but if I hadn't returned to Spina by the evening, I would have lost a lucrative opportunity."

I kept my eyes primarily on Vicenzu, but couldn't help glancing at Maralla. So, this was a witch? It would be a shame to confine her within a Sorority. If she offered a typical example, I might make it my life's work to batter down the walls and release the sisters to mingle with the poor deprived men of the Faithful. It would be a public service. Her face showed no more expression than Vicenzu's other than a skeptical curl of the lip—a rather fine upper lip, not too thin, not overly plump.

"I take it you seized this lucrative opportunity, Cesar?" Vicenzu asked.

"Oh, yes. In fact, I think it might well benefit the both of us," I said. If I could get them to accompany me to some conspicuously public place, perhaps the Terrace Wine Garden overlooking the Laughing Fountain, I could begin to needle Vicenzu, get him to publicly challenge me. Running my sword through him would remove an obstacle standing between me and private conversation with Maralla. It wasn't ideal. Herbieto would not be able to observe this act of vengeance. And killing her partner before her eyes was a less than tactful approach to Maralla. But I was putting this together as I went. "Perhaps you and the lady would care to join me for a celebratory bottle at the Wine Garden? We could discuss the terms of purchase."

"Would you be buying this bottle, Cesar?" the Woman said. These were the first words Maralla spoke to me. Her voice possessed a cool, smooth quality that was somewhat marred by an undertone of skepticism.

"Of course," I said. "I am in funds." I gave her a dashing smile. I realize I do not present the archetypal picture of a bravo. I am not tall, lean, and rangy. I'm of less than average height and built more like a wrestler, heavy through the chest and shoulders. But I present myself well, dress as fashion dictates—when my purse allows—and I've kept most of my conventionally handsome features unmarked by evidence of violence. Most, I say; there is a bit of ear that I'll be missing the rest of my life.

The point is, I can flash the dashing smile with the best of them. Maralla, however, appeared unmoved.

"Or perhaps," Maralla said, "you'll excuse yourself after drinking a glass or two, then disappear as you did yesterday."

Vicenzu nodded. "The lady has refined instincts," he said. "Whatever game it is you are playing, Cesar, I don't care to join in."

"Now, Vicenzu," I said, "don't let yesterday's unfortunate incident stand between you and a tidy pile of coin."

Vicenzu shot glances over my left and right shoulder. "Enough. This man is wasting my time."

I sensed the presence of Vicenzu's bodyguards a moment before I felt their hands. I moved, lunging forward to break grips before they could take hold. I was only partially successful. One man grasped my right arm, while another clamped a hand down on my shoulder. I tore my left arm free of the closing fingers.

The two on my left tried again. The two on my right were no weaklings. But, as I've mentioned, I'm not the standard-issue, whip-cord lean bravo. I whirled, breaking free of the two on my right as the other two reached for me.

My wrenching and spinning took me a few steps from Vicenzu and Maralla. Heads turned in the street, as passers-by slowed to take in the action. The bodyguards reached for steel as they closed on me.

"No," Vicenzu said. "Public murder isn't a good look. No swords."

I heard grumbles of complaint as the bodyguards complied with an order they found distasteful. But they were professionals. Releasing sword hilts, they came at me to deliver a beating, fists clenched.

Vicenzu might be opposed to spilling blood in broad daylight upon the cobblestones of the Escaline. I, however, had no objection, especially given the four-to-one odds. My fingers curled around the hilt of my parrying dagger. The rapier was the wrong weapon for the distances involved, even if I thought I had the time to free it before the bodyguards got their hands on me.

As it happened, I didn't even have time to draw the main gauche. I'd cleared perhaps three inches of steel before the first of Vicenzu's hired guards got to me. He was a tall fellow, with a bent, oft-broken nose poised above a goatee that displayed as many patches of white hair as it did dark. He clamped one hand on my wrist while driving the other into the pit of my stomach.

It hurt, but I was prepared for it, and kept both my breath and my breakfast. I let go of my dagger with my left hand, letting the blade drop back into the sheath. With my right I returned the love tap, my gloved fist delivering a short hook into the aging bodyguard's ribs. He grunted, shifting away, but maintained his hold on my left wrist, trying to keep me in place for the second it would take the other three to get to me.

He succeeded. I twisted free just as the others closed in.

I've been in my share of brawls. They formed a common element of my childhood, raised in Plenum's gutters. A particularly unforgiving school, but instructive to those who survive. One of the fundamental lessons I learned is that against overwhelming numbers, and without a weapon, escape is the best option. Each of these men, individually, were tough, experienced fighters. But I figured I could handle any of them one-on-one. Four at once was too much to ask, even for Cesar the Bravo. All of them swarmed me in a whirlwind of fists and boots. I raised my hands, held close together, covering my eyes and cheekbones, and kept my elbows tucked in tight. Blows rained down. My hat was the first casualty, disappearing in the initial violent instant. A few kicks struck my shins and thighs. Fists glanced off the top of my head, slammed into my shoulders, deflected from my arms, and pounded my chest and back.

But even as the downpour of blows deluged me, I moved. I stomped a boot heel on an instep, and, as I felt the foot and the attached leg withdraw, I followed. I threw myself into a whirling spin that broke me free of the box through the one weakened wall. And I kept going, turning my stumbling spin into a run.

I didn't pay attention to direction for the first few strides, then looked up just in time to avoid colliding headfirst with a wall. I altered course, dodging a group of onlookers—I hope they'd enjoyed the show—and took off westward, down Escaline Way.

I could, I suppose, have turned around, drawn my rapier and main gauche, and attacked. With a sword in my hand, even against the four of them—or five, if Vicenzu had taken a hand—I figured my odds at about even. I am good with a sword. I should be: I've trained long enough and earned enough experience the hard way to be confident in my abilities. But a deadly battle in the street would help nothing but my pride. And given the blows I'd received, I couldn't be entirely sure of my condition. No, continuing the fight would have been stupid.

And so, beaten and humiliated in front of Maralla by Vicenzu's goons, I fled, tail between my legs. I fumed, my ears red from shame and anger as much as from the blows they'd received. Even if Herbieto couldn't pay the full amount he'd promised, I'd still do the job for him. It would be a pleasure to shove my sword through Vicenzu's heart.

The bastard owed me a hat.

Chapter 5

I licked my wounds at Giacomo's Wine Shop with the help of a flagon of throat-scouring red. Ideally, a bravo's life is one of action. But on occasion he needs to sit and think. This was one of those occasions.

I'd blown the opportunity to both attach myself to Maralla and instigate a duel with Vicenzu. Looking at the past in the dark surface of my wine, I could see that the opportunity had consisted primarily of wishful thinking. I've been able to accomplish much through audacity, bluff, and bull-headedness in my career, and perhaps I'd grown overly reliant on that approach.

My priority was clearly Maralla. That job paid more, for one thing. For another, keeping close to her should keep me in contact with Vicenzu. I could watch for my chance at earning Herbieto's payment. But in the meantime, I had to focus on keeping Maralla safe.

I knew where she was, of course. Fenetto had provided me with full details of her whereabouts. He'd filled me in on Maralla's background: her birth at the villa Fenetto had maintained for his mistress on a hilltop a half-day's journey to the east of Plenum; Maralla's happy childhood running—and later, riding her pony—through the olive trees and vineyards of the villa; her education under the tutelage of Sisters visiting the villa from the nearby Sorority; the death of her mother; Fenetto's scramble to invent a long-absent uncle who was the actual owner of the villa and who also tragically died shortly after his sister, willing the property to Maralla; Maralla's sale of the villa and her purchase of rooms in the city, in a fashionable section of the Lavernal district.

Fenetto was a doting father. His love of talking about his daughter was apparent from the wealth—the overwhelming, tedious wealth—of detail.

So finding Maralla again should be simple. I wouldn't need to cool my heels at Madina's again, eating olives and chatting with Betto. But finding Maralla was merely the beginning of the process. Watching over her presented the difficulty. How could I manage that all day, every day by myself? I could not. Simple as that. I would have to subcontract this job, or at least portions of it.

That decision required most of the flagon. Deciding on subcontractors required the rest.

"Bonfilia," I said to the hustling, overworked wench when she came by to gather my empty flagon and ask if I wanted another, "pour a cup for Tasso and another for Marteo." I let a few scudi clatter and scatter on the table. She nodded and scooped up the coins.

A few minutes later Tasso Longarm plopped himself down heavily on a stool across from me. He offered me his big, goofy grin.

"Thanks for the wine, Cesar. There some Holy Day I forgot about? Or do you got an arm you need broken?" Tasso twisted one of his hairy, sinewy arms and made a popping noise with his lips.

"Enjoy the drink, Tasso, and wait a minute. I don't want to tell the story twice," I said.

It required a bit more than a minute. Marteo took his time. I suppose he spent it trying to figure out how to make an appearance in a suitably brooding and dramatic fashion. Hard to do when you're expected, so I gave him points for effort when he slid onto the stool next to Tasso, produced a dagger, and drove its point into the scarred surface of the table.

"Do you wish to hire my services?" Marteo asked. He spoke to the quivering dagger, not meeting my eyes. Marteo embodied furtiveness, from his pinched, narrow shoulders to his darting eyes. He wore only black, always black, including a hooded black cloak that he usually wore with the hood raised, even indoors on the hottest days. There wasn't much to him; even I stand taller than Marteo, and one of my shirts would drape over his scrawny frame like a damp sheet hanging out to dry. But there is a fierceness in those shifting, black eyes, set in hollows beneath thick, black brows that suggest there is more to the man than a weasely little fellow trying too hard to appear dangerous.

"Well, that depends, Marteo," I said, "If you can be hired for something that leaves the subject alive, then yes."

"Maiming?" he asked. "Removing a tongue? Perhaps kidnapping?"

"I can snatch someone easier than this little rat can," Tasso said.

Marteo's dagger moved. In the dim light of Giacomo's it seemed almost magical how the blade disappeared from before Marteo to reappear, quivering once again, in the table top in front of Tasso.

"Take it easy, Marteo," Tasso said, sounding aggrieved rather than frightened. "I'm just saying a kidnapping is easier if you can carry the kidnapee. Unless it's a child, you'll have trouble lifting him. I won't." He plucked the dagger from the wood with two fingers and offered it, hilt first, to Marteo who accepted it with a shrug.

"So do you need two people kidnapped, Cesar?" Marteo asked. "One, perhaps, a child?"

"No one is getting kidnapped," I said. I pinched the bridge of my nose and closed my eyes for a moment. "Look, I'm working a job and I could use a little help. It will probably run all day, every day for a while and it would be nice to get a little sleep now and then. So I was hoping you two could take the occasional shift."

"Sure," said Tasso. "What are you paying?"

"What is the job?" asked Marteo at almost the same time.

I explained as much as I thought they ought to know, leaving out Maralla's Talent and the exact nature of the organization she needed protection from. That was a tricky bit of footwork, but not nearly as tricky as the financial negotiations. A hundred-pistra job would do me little good if subcontracting cost me the bulk of it. But, after some negotiation, they accepted one pistra a day, with a two pistra bonus if the work required any extraordinary violence.

I provided the location of Maralla's rooms and we established a watch schedule. After we sealed the arrangement with another cup of wine, I reconsidered the hours I'd committed myself to and realized I could use another pair of eyes. So the next morning I paid a visit to Domenico.

Domenico has been my fencing master for years. His salle on the edge of the Orine district has been as much a home to me as my squalid flat ever was. Certainly more commodious and comfortable. Welcoming, too, when I could pay what I owed for lessons.

The salle occupies most of the building on Testro Narrows. The exterior is primarily brick and stucco, though a substantial portion of the foundation is the stone block and concrete of the Ancients. A short, broad flight of stairs leads to a thick-paneled door of weathered oak, upon which is fastened a door knocker in the shape of crossed swords. Domenico's manservant, Anacleto, met me at the entrance after the fourth knock. His questioning eyebrow spoke eloquently.

"I can pay, Anacleto," I said. "Where is the Maestro?"

The interior, once past a plain, brick and wood-paneled foyer, is, if not opulent, then at least tasteful. Too simple, I suppose, to be considered elegant. A warren of rooms are walled with marble, plaster, or polished timber. The centerpiece is the expansive, cedar-floored fencing room with several mullioned windows placed high above to provide light ample enough to allow Domenico's students to observe each movement of point and edge.

"Wait here, please, Cesar," Anacleto said at the entry to the salle. "The Maestro is teaching."

The statement was unnecessary. I leaned against the doorway, crossed my arms across my chest, and watched as Domenico walked a novice student—some rich man's son—through the basic parries. I found that of mild interest: Domenico did not usually take beginners, leaving the inculcation of the rudiments to less gifted, more pedestrian instructors.

"Uncle Cesar!"

I turned. A year or two ago she would have bounced from the floor and flung herself at me. But Domenico's daughter, Valentina, was now—what, twelve? A new reserve or dignity weighed down her buoyancy. The joy remained in her voice, however. Valentina had—for whatever reason—always liked me. And I'd always liked her, the closest thing I had to family. She was—or had been—irrepressible. Too adventurous for her own good, though with a father like Domenico, she'd had the opportunity to develop the sort of skills that could see her through a spot of trouble. She still did not have the reach or strength to provide any real challenge to a grown swordsman, but she was pinpoint accurate with a throwing knife.

"Valentina, what a pleasure," I said. I offered her a courtier's bow and she giggled. She still wasn't too grown up to giggle.

We chatted for the remainder of the lesson, then she grabbed me by the hand and led me onto the familiar boards of the salle to see Domenico.

Domenico presented my contrast in many ways. Where I was bulky and muscular, he was lean; I the bulldog, he the cat. He rose to middling stature, little taller than I in truth, but the differing distributions of our body mass created an illusion of height when we stood together. He wore his padded leather fencing jacket, but it was more for show than any practical defensive use against his recent student. He required no plastron for protection against a tyro. He certainly hadn't worked up a sweat; his light brown curls displayed not a hint of dampness, though I detected a hint that either his forehead was growing or his hairline was receding. Well, if Valentina was growing older, I suppose her father must be as well. Thankfully such indignities would never happen to me. Right?

"Cesar," Domenico said, his tone carefully neutral.

"Maestro," I said.

Domenico raised an eyebrow. "Maestro? Are you a student again, Cesar? Of the fighting arts? Does this mean your purse is full once again?"

Several questions, each asking more than the surface implied. I'd not call him Maestro if I did not consider myself his pupil. Did I intend only to return to my lessons in sword, dagger, and grappling? I'd had occasion recently to regret my illiteracy. Having seen Domenico's lavishly illustrated manuals teaching fighting techniques, I'd approached him for reading lessons. We'd not advanced far before poverty forced me to drop all instruction. Did I also intend to re-engage with my enemy, the written word?

"I am ready to resume all lessons, Maestro," I said. "My purse is at the bursting point. In fact, I can offer you employment beyond teaching, with appropriate compensation."

That earned another raised eyebrow.

"I am a fencing master, Cesar, not a hired sword."

"I require your eyes and your time, Domenico," I said. "I do not anticipate any risk, though I'm willing to offer recompense for any unforeseen—unpleasantness." I mimed a brief cut-and-thrust passage to illustrate.

Domenico worked his chin between thumb and forefinger. "Attiring a young lady is an ever-increasing expense, Cesar, as an overdressed, preening rooster such as yourself can appreciate. Tell me about the job."

I ignored the familiar insult and told him about the job. I didn't really expect Domenico to accept. He'd been out of this sort of work since the birth of Valentina, shifting to earning his livelihood teaching violence instead of risking it. So I was mildly surprised when he agreed, accepting a late afternoon shift keeping an eye on Maralla.

I arranged times and dates for lessons, bade farewell to Valentina, then departed to relieve Tasso.

Chapter 6

Maralla occupied two rooms on the upper floor of a squat tower of creamy stone and decorative brickwork at the southern end of the Lavernal district, amidst a row of similar buildings. From her southwest windows, beneath the gentle slant of the dun-colored baked tiles of the roof, she could observe the lazy creep of the Cloatus as it bends south, flowing sluggishly away among the buff and gold hills of the hinterlands. From her eastern window I imagined she'd have a view of a wide swath of the city, from the genteel environs of the Broscine to the north to as far south as the Temple of Sighs, that tumbledown fane of the Ancients amidst an untended grove of cypress, wild grape, a variety of lilies, and other flowers beyond my capacity to name.

Tasso awaited me at a construction site that had been standing idle since the spring. Perhaps the owner had suffered financial reverses, or the builder had absconded with funds. Or perhaps some principal had died, tying up the project in lengthy probate proceedings. I didn't know. What I did know was that a partially completed second story offered a concealed and sheltered spot from which to observe the door to Maralla's building as well as her windows on two sides of it. The vantage wasn't close enough to see any detail, for which I found myself oddly gratified: neither Tasso nor Marteo could indulge any voyeuristic impulses. But one could see movement and get a good indication of the numbers inhabiting the rooms. The building site also offered decent lines of sight along the street upon which the door opened. Everyone approaching, or simply passing by, would be seen by whichever of us was on duty. At least, during the day. At night, anyone willing to eschew a torch or lantern could likely arrive unseen.

Tasso held out one broad, calloused hand as I ascended the incomplete stair, the mason having laid down his tools before his work reached from the street to the ground floor. Tasso wasn't offering to clasp hands; his cupped palm was a request for pay.

"Anything?" I asked. I retrieved a single pistra from the purse tucked beneath my doublet and securely tied to my belt.

"Hasn't left the house," Tasso said. "No late-night visitors." He squinted at the coin, grinned broadly, displaying a gap where one of his canine teeth ought to be. "Easy money, Cesar. Same time tonight?"

"If I don't wrap this all up by the end of Marteo's shift, yes," I said.

Tasso nodded and stifled a yawn. His long legs carried him over the missing stair, and he departed, back to whatever room it is he shared with his wife. I wondered, did he have children? Strange to think of Tasso as a father.

I took up my post, settling in to watch the two windows visible, periodically scanning the streets.

Surveillance, as I've mentioned, is boring. Absolutely nothing happens, until it does. If it ever does. I stood and watched. Or paced and watched. Or sat on an abandoned block of granite and watched. Heavy pewter clouds inched sluggishly by overhead. A steady drizzle commenced. I hadn't yet had the opportunity to purchase a new hat. I was thankful for the partially completed story above me, but the rain and the lack of a hat rekindled my animus toward Vicenzu and his bone breakers.

As if my anger summoned him, Vicenzu appeared, striding along the street, his red hair a beacon in the gray, wet air. He ascended the flight of stairs to the door of Maralla's building, and rapped on the door with the pommel of his dagger. The door opened—I couldn't see by who—then closed. A minute later Maralla appeared.

I tailed Vicenzu, Maralla, and the four bodyguards. Their destination came as no surprise, though of course I wasn't following them to see where they were going, only to keep an eye out for Azeglio and his Venatores. Whatever they looked like.

Madina's beckoned, and I spent a couple of quality hours with Betto. Frankly, the sparkle of Betto's conversation was beginning to pale. But the olives remained tasty. Vicenzu appeared ebullient when he bid farewell to the day's mark. He must have sold another one. I fantasized about snatching the hat from his head during the course of a duel, placing the ostrich-plumed topper on my own head, and only then driving my sword through his heart, coming up from a deep, low lunge after feinting his guard out of position.

I did not risk getting close enough to overhear much conversation as I followed them back. Vicenzu was gesticulating, Maralla shaking her head. Judging only from body language, there was little rancor in the disagreement. Perhaps Vicenzu was proposing dinner and Maralla was declining. I found myself hoping that was the case. Somehow I disliked the notion of any romantic entanglement between the two of them. Vicenzu and his entourage escorted Maralla back home, then left her. I resumed my observation post and suffered the petty pains of boredom until Marteo arrived to relieve me at sunset.

No sign of the Venatores. Perhaps they were less skilled than I'd been told. It would be nice to think so. So I distrusted the thought. Making my way back to the Orine district, moving at a good pace toward Giacomo's Wine Shop before twilight yielded to full dark, I reviewed Fenetto's description of Questor General Azeglio and worked on reestablishing a healthy respect for his powers and capabilities. A bravo should maintain a substantial self-regard, but there was no reason to grow cocksure rather than merely confident.

I was ensconced at my table, sipping a cup of wine and wishing it was even a fraction as good as what filled Fenetto's cellar, when Herbieto made an appearance.

He put his knuckles on the table and leaned his weight on them. Reflected candlelight placed red sparks in eyes recessed below frowning brows. The appearance of anger was incongruous, almost laughable upon such a bland face. He was like a growling puppy. This mask wasn't the visage of pure hate that he'd shown when discussing his father's death and Vicenzu.

"I see how you are spending my pistras, Cesar. Drinking swill instead of challenging Vicenzu." Heriberto's voice rose to a squeak and broke. He didn't seem comfortable with fury, and I wondered how much of it was real and how much was the assumed ire of a man who'd convinced himself that this is the emotion he ought to be experiencing.

"It is after dark, Herbieto. Vicenzu has gone home." I didn't know that. In fact I had no idea where Vicenzu lived. But I figured it for a reasonable guess. "I need to challenge him in public. Broad daylight would be best, unless there is some well-lit, crowded establishment he frequents at night, one that allows the likes of me in."

Herbieto's mouth worked. My unruffled response

wasn't what he'd imagined when he'd rehearsed this dressing down. I continued before he could decide on his next gambit.

"Sit down, Herbieto. Have a drink."

"A drink paid for with my money," he said, though he didn't sound convincingly indignant. "Have you even found Vicenzu yet?"

"Yes. Sit down, and I'll bring you up to date."

He vacillated for several seconds, then sat, by which time Bonfilia had arrived. I ordered two more cups. Herbieto seemed willing to wait for the wine before continuing his demands. That allowed me time to decide what to tell him. I couldn't very well explain that I was pushing aside his commission in order to undertake a more profitable venture. He needed to hear that I was making progress.

The wine arrived, and I drained the cup before me to make room for the new one.

"Well?" Herbieto asked, this time managing merely petulance.

"I have made contact with Vicenzu," I said. "I contrived to get under his skin. But he didn't bite. Instead, he set his boys on me. They pounded me pretty good before I got away, mostly the back of my head, my chest, and shoulders. The wine helps with the pain."

"Oh," Herbieto said. He picked up his wine cup, glanced at it for a moment as if it were an unfamiliar novelty, then drank. "I'm sorry. Are you all right?"

"I've had worse. The point is, I am aggravating him. Once I maneuver him into position, somewhere he can't sic his hounds on me without losing face, it should be simple enough to wring a challenge from him."

"Are you sure you will be able to find him again?"

"Oh yes. He is still running his confidence game. He also meets his accomplice to walk her to the houses. I tracked her to her rooms." That sounded competent and professional, as if I were diligently pursuing Herbieto's interests.

"Then I assume you will finish this soon," Herbieto said. "I have been neglecting my shop. It will be such a relief to get this business finished and off my mind."

He sounded like himself again, the anger gratefully dropped like an unwelcome burden. Herbieto visibly relaxed, comfortable now that he was once again trusting in me to fulfill my pledge.

I couldn't help myself. "Of course I'll finish this soon," I said. "I've got a play in mind for tomorrow."

Chapter 7

I didn't have a play in mind. Not then anyway. But I woke in the morning with a course of events neatly outlined. I must have been working it out in my sleep.

I had time to stop by Donatello's and purchase a new hat. I suppose Herbieto would be hurt if he'd known that I didn't ask him to supply my headgear. Herbieto probably had a sideline in men's toppers, something for the men in his shop to browse through while waiting for the women to decide on a purchase. But Donatello is an artist, a bona fide genius with cloth and shears. If buying the occasional accessory from him—a hat, for example—

keeps me in Donatello's good graces, it is worth the risk of snubbing a client. While there, I ordered a new doublet, a couple pairs of hose, and three new shirts, paying in advance as well as what I owed in arrears. Donatello has my measurements; they're probably written down somewhere, but I expect he's memorized them. Ours is a lengthy acquaintance.

With due consideration of the weather, I'd chosen an Ihbarian-influenced hat, with a somewhat broader brim and a low-peaked crown to shed rain, adorned with a rather smaller feather than I'd ordinarily have accepted. The hat was not simply a practical piece of seasonal attire, nor merely vanity; Vicenzu would have a harder time maintaining his honor if he allowed an affront from a stylishly attired man to go unchallenged.

The affront must occur in public, preferably before those of a certain social standing who would expect an insult to be met with a challenge. And I had a good notion of where that public place must be.

Vicenzu—probably to cement his bona fides as a man of wealth and social standing—had let drop during our first meeting that he'd eaten breakfast at Kertzel's. Plenum is a city of tradition and deep-rooted culture. Yet, perhaps paradoxically, at the same time it is driven by novelty and fads. At least among those with the luxury of time and money to lavish on fads. Kertzel's is one of the more recent enthusiasms: an establishment run by a northerner (or by someone posing as a northerner) serving pastries and strong tea for breakfast. A fashionably late breakfast, naturally, for the wealthy and indolent who don't have to rise early to begin the day's labors, who instead can lie abed late, after a night spent carousing.

There is an odd intersection between the life of the wealthy and the life of an impoverished bravo—I too often lie abed late, after a night spent carousing.

If Vicenzu made a habit of breakfasting at Kertzel's, I had him. It was an ideal stage on which I could present my play. I was sure I could prompt Vicenzu to say his lines. I'd had plenty of practice riling other men who were unaware they were playing a role. They gravitated naturally to the role of hero while I played the villain as broadly as my unwitting cast mate required. The spectators would enjoy Vicenzu and I creating an impromptu piece of theater, a bit of spice added to flaky, meat-filled pastries and fragrant teas. Vicenzu would have to respond, or be diminished in their eyes.

Kertzel's sat on a ledge cut into the Broscine Hill, about a twenty-minute stroll up Escaline Way from Maralla's place, eastward and a touch north. I guessed the proximity fit into Vicenzu's routine and perhaps recommended Kertzel's in the first place. Vicenzu could digest his breakfast while he ambled along the Escaline to collect his witch for the day's con game.

I couldn't imagine Vicenzu sharing his table with his bodyguards. He'd be unattended. Even if he was willing to accept a loss of face, he couldn't simply loose his guards on me.

Again.

No, I liked this plan. As I crossed the city, I liked it more and more. A break in the clouds offered a glimpse of blue sky above and a warming ray of sunshine, as if the heavens blessed my endeavor.

I neared Maralla's building, whistling and tapping out a rhythm against the hilt of my rapier. I figured I would stop by the lookout post, get a report from Marteo before I continued up the street to Kertzel's.

Marching the other way came a small parade of almost military aspect. I counted nine—eight identically attired with the ninth at their head. The eight wore doublets of a dark red, the hue of drying blood over hunter green hose. Six of them shouldered a short-hafted halberd, the two at the front carried swords. Blackened steel breastplates concealed most of the doublets of the halberd-armed men.

The leader of the troop was unarmored and dressed primarily in black. I noted that his doublet had been tailored to suggest the robes of the Collegium, and the turned back cuffs were the crimson of a Councilor's Red Hat. His own hat—a low-crowned, almost brimless number of pleated velvet—was darker, an oxblood red nearly matching the uniforms of his men. A white plume bobbed at its rear. A baldric matching the hat supported a rapier.

I couldn't quite make out his face. But the details I could see of both the man and his troopers matched the information Fenetto had provided. This was Questor General Azeglio leading a squad of his Venatores. That they were approaching the door of Maralla's building could not be mere coincidence. That must be their destination and she their target.

The beam of sunlight and the cloud break felt suddenly less cheering. My plan for Vicenzu dissipated like steam from a mug of Kertzel's tea. I'd been paid to protect Maralla from this very threat. But what precisely I was supposed to do about it was something I hadn't worked out.

Marteo doubtless watched from the abandoned construction site, concealed from the view of the Venatores. But I doubted I could rely upon him for any significant aid in a fight. He was an assassin, not a street brawler. I couldn't expect him to join me in a two-on-nine pitched battle. We'd both be slaughtered.

Yet I had a job to do, and I'd do it.

I'd slowed my pace immediately upon sighting the Venatores, though we were still closing, our combined speeds promising to bring me face-to-face with Azeglio by the front stoop of Maralla's building. I glanced around, taking in the surrounding cross streets and alleys, the doorways, low windows, and passers-by, desperate for inspiration.

I spotted a drying lump of horse dung near my boot, and bent to scoop it up in my gloved hand.

Azeglio had neared enough for me to see his face. He must have been born with that sneer on his face, he wore it so naturally. Some men of authority seem uncomfortable with it, uncertain or apologetic. Azeglio was not one of those. Every feature, from his thick black brows, down to his high-arched, long nose, to his neatly trimmed goatee (accenting a firm chin rather than disguising a weak one) betokened aristocratic hauteur.

I hated him at first sight.

"Hey, Venatores!" I called. I hucked the clump of crap at the parade, seeing three individual balls separate in flight as the missile arced toward the Venatores. "The witch isn't at home. And I'm not telling you where I stashed her."

I'm not sure all of them caught my words. Some of the Venatores were probably distracted by the horse shit splattering their uniforms.

But Azeglio heard me.

"Apprehend him," he said. Or rather, he snarled. The order carried an almost animalistic fury.

Azeglio stayed put. The others filed around him on either side, beginning to put on speed.

I spun on one heel and ran.

At least I'd diverted eight of the Venatores from Maralla. Azeglio by himself might represent the greatest danger. But I knew Marteo was watching. Perhaps he might slit the Questor General's throat. Or perhaps Maralla might summon up demons of greater power than those Azeglio could manage, looking out for her own ass better than I could.

But I figured it most likely that Azeglio would sit outside and wait patiently for his men to return with me, alive or dead. At the moment, I couldn't be bothered to devote much time to speculation. I'd done what I could. Now I had my own skin to worry about.

Plenum isn't a city built for running. The road surfaces are uneven and of varying materials. Cobbles are slick and rounded, notorious for turning ankles. And that is supposing a complete allotment of cobbles. The frequency of absent cobbles means that foot-catching cavities are commonplace. But I've had a lot of practice running. A lifetime primarily spent in Plenum, fleeing one scrape or another, has seen to that.

I scampered a dozen yards or so westward down the

Escaline, then cut south into an alley. Exposed brick, too newly laid to have accumulated more than a thin layer of grime, rose up on either side of me, blocking out the sun. A muck-filled channel ran down the center of the alley, and my boots splashed through filth as I ran.

I heard a voice behind calling for me to stop. I did not. Not until I could see the pool of sunshine showing the end of the alley. I eased to a stop—a sudden stop could lead to a slip or a stumble. Any misstep now might bear fatal consequences. I came to a halt at the end of the shadowed alley, turned, and drew my rapier and main gauche.

I doubted the Venatores had tried to send one or more of their number around to box me in. Even if they had, the layout of Plenum does not provide a neat grid of streets and buildings. It is instead a maze designed by blind rabbits. Straight lines are the exception rather than the rule. Any attempt to circle around behind me would probably result in a lost and confused Venatore. I'd been raised in the streets of this city and even I found myself disoriented on occasion.

Staying in the shade, with the relative dazzle of light at my back, and the constriction of the narrow alley hampering the Venatores' superior numbers, I figured this was the most advantageous spot to harass the enemy at the commencement of what promised to be a running fight.

"There he is!" cried the man in the lead. He was one of the two wearing a sword. Sergeants, I supposed. The sword hung from a baldric, but he held the scabbard in his left hand to keep the weapon from bouncing wildly as he ran, the same as I'd done. He slowed, reaching for the rapier hilt with his right hand.

I had time to observe his height—tall—and the pointed, neatly trimmed beard marred by a scar that prevented hair growth on the left side of his chin. He wore an oversized ring on the index finger of his gloved left hand. If not for the dimness of the alley, I'd have had the opportunity to catalog hair and eye color. I was set, and time seemed to stretch like a thread of honey from a spoon as my foemen closed the distance.

The men behind failed to recognize the need to reduce their pace. A chain of collisions occurred as those who didn't slow collided with those in front who had. The second sergeant barreled into the leading sergeant, sending him stumbling toward me.

I planted my back foot, sending my right forward, knee bending into a deep lunge, rapier extended. Assisted by his left hand dragging against the moist brick wall, the leading Venatore—Scar-beard—stumbled to a halt, swatting at my rapier with a wild parry that caught my foible with his forte.

Scar-beard leapt back as I straightened.

"Careful," he snarled over his shoulder. "You clumsy bastards nearly killed me."

"Come on," I said, "we'll get it right the second time."

The other sergeant squeezed in beside the first. There was just room for both of them to stand shoulder to shoulder. Facing me two on one wasn't a bad idea. But using a sword properly requires more than flailing about with one arm. Fencing demands the use of the entire body. Wedged in next to each other, neither of the Venatore sergeants had full use of his body.

I did.

I stomped forward, splattering filth, and lunged again, this time at the second sergeant. This one was shorter, on the verge of portly, and clean shaven. My point threatened his face, then dropped as he committed himself to a parry in quarte. I anticipated the slight resistance of blade entering flesh as my point drove toward his left thigh. But Scar-beard batted aside my steel at the last possible moment, and I only succeeded in tearing open the dark green fabric of Beardless's hose and scratching the skin beneath.

"Stupid bastard," Scar-beard said. He stepped back, uncorking the alley, leaving his compatriot to face me alone. "You want to fight him, go ahead." He placed a boot against Beardless's posterior and shoved, sending him toward me, sword arm flailing, eyes wide with terror.

Beardless tried to turn his erratic, whipping sword arm motion into a slash at my head. I brought up my main gauche as I stepped forward. I caught Beardless's rapier on the deep-bellied hand guard of the parrying dagger as I drove my own rapier point in just below his sternum, passing the blade entirely through his body.

Beardless grunted. His sword fell from his fingers, and he sagged forward. Blood frothed at his lips along with sounds that might have been intended as words. He raised both hands, clutching at me. He sagged, his weight dragging down my sword arm, and I could see over his shoulder Scar-beard moving in to take advantage of my position.

I leapt back, dragging my blade free from flesh that seemed unwilling to relinquish it.

Scar-beard snarled, impeded by Beardless sprawling between us. He turned his head, though not far enough that he couldn't keep an eye on me. "Move up," he said. "Baltos, Angelo. Baltos leads, Angelo keep close."

Scar-beard pointed his ringed finger at me. "Last chance to surrender," he said.

"I'm busy today," I said. "Can we schedule a surrender for tomorrow?"

He spat, adding droplets to the filthy rivulet running down the center of the alley. Then he eased back along one side of the wall, allowing two halberd-toting Venatores—presumably Angelo and Baltos—to move up.

The two came forward in a slow, disciplined manner, one right behind the other's shoulder, halberd extended far enough that I was facing two threats while only able—in theory—to engage with one.

I might be able to handle them individually. I could deflect the halberd with my main gauche, slip past the geometry of multitudinous points and sharp edges, then find a fleshy spot unprotected by steel breastplate. But that possibility seemed less inviting if slipping past one blade merely brought me into direct, fatal contact with the second, wielded over the shoulder of the leading Venatore.

Time to run.

The pool of sunshine behind me vanished as the clouds mended the sunbreak. A light drizzle began as I sprinted from the alley. I sheathed my weapons as I moved, with an ease only attainable through years of practice.

The sound of stomping, splashing boots pursued me. I turned to my right from the alley and pelted down the street. A wheeled cart piled with chestnuts and bearing a small, lit brazier at the front blocked half of the narrow street. The chestnut vender stood near the brazier, toasting nuts for a customer waiting in her doorway.

The fragrance of the roasting nuts smelled so good—especially after the dank odors of the alleyway—I almost felt sorry for what I did next.

I grabbed the handles of the cart, whirled it about and flipped it over behind me, scattering chestnuts and red-hot charcoal. I barely slowed, continuing down the street, listening to the profane protestations of the chestnut vendor and the startled, pained shouts of the Venatores navigating a minor avalanche of nuts, hot charcoal, and an overturned cart.

That gained me a few yards' lead. I poured on the speed, then cut to my left at the first opportunity. A street composed of a broad stairway— each step as long as a man, each riser a mere handbreadth—descended into a shallow valley. I hurtled down it, taking each stair at a stride, building up speed until I truly began to fear I was more of a danger to myself than were the pursuing Venatores.

The steepness of the street terminated in a cramped plaza centered on a decorative fountain and enclosed by adjoining—or connected—buildings of vine-covered, age-blackened brick. The street continued on past the plaza. The mouths of cross streets opened to my left and right, facing the fountain. The fountain was girded by a hip-high stone wall. Verdigrised bronze fish rose from within, spitting water toward the central figure: a siren atop a monstrous clamshell, the siren's weathered face bearing a bemused expression. The tail of one of the spouting fish projected to the edge of the wall. As I came stumbling into the plaza, arms windmilling while trying to keep to my feet and not sprawl headlong onto the cobbles, I reached out my left hand and briefly grasped the fishtail. I let go right as the hold threatened to wrench my arm from its socket and fling me sideways to the hard stones of the plaza. Instead, it slowed me and slewed me to the left, around the fountain. Hoping to shake my pursuers, I maintained the new direction, trying to regain speed as I made for the beckoning mouth of the street.

Calls from behind and above told me I'd not been fast enough. My new direction had not gone unobserved. The chase continued.

I passed beneath a curving brick arch that connected the buildings on either side of the street at the plaza's exit. I felt the drooping creepers festooning the arch brush the top of my hat.

The street I was now on dog-legged south then east. If a few alley mouths conveniently opened up along the eastward length, I could scamper down one before the Venatores even cleared the plaza, let alone the elbow of the dogleg.

No such luck. The street instead offered an unusually protracted stretch of linearity, unbroken by cross streets or alleys for a good fifty yards, before culminating at a street running to north and south.

Well, perhaps I could simply outrun the Venatores. I wasn't burdened by a breastplate and a heavy halberd. I'd slowed a trifle in my disappointment upon rounding the elbow of the dogleg. Now I sucked in a deep breath and picked up my heels, listening to the steady reverberation of bootheels on stone echoing from the walls of the buildings rising on either side of the street of disappointment.

I hadn't finished half the length of the street before I heard the hue and cry. I glanced behind me. Two of the Venatores had rounded the bend. Fast, long-legged bastards. I growled, re-focused, and really began to heel-and-toe it. These boots weren't made for extended bouts of running. I hoped I wasn't going to develop blisters.

The two fastest Venatores were closing, and their slower fellows had entered the straight run of the street by the time I reached the end and had to decide between north and south. I chose south, taking a swooping right-hand turn that brushed my shoulder up against the wall of an apothecary's dispensary. I'd entered a street devoted to shops and artisans, neat and attractive, the sort of location one hopes to encounter in Plenum but seldom does. Along with these ideal businesses came customers. I had to slow my pace as I dodged morning shoppers.

Perhaps the congestion would slow my pursuers. For a moment it seemed that way. Another glance over my shoulder showed no sign of Venatores. Only a selection of Plenum citizenry going about the day's business.

"Clear the street!" bellowed a familiar voice.

Shit.

Scar-beard's commanding voice, and a body of armed, uniformed men apparently ready to enforce the command, cleared the street before I'd regained more than a dozen or so yards of my lead. The Venatores came on. Another glance showed Scar-beard not more than a few paces behind the leading pair of Venatores.

The street before me curved slightly to the left and began to descend, leaving the stretch of silversmiths, lace tatters, and instrument makers behind. It curved again, rightward this time. As it bent back more or less directly due south, the descent steepened and I found myself picking up speed that had little to do with my own leg power. The street narrowed as it dropped, describing snakelike shallow curves to the left and right, though always trending south. Gaps began to appear between buildings on either side and the apparent age of the construction increased, the proportion of the work of the Ancients to more recent brickwork increasing. Then these were replaced by abandoned, roofless structures, ruins serving no purpose other than as sources of construction material.

One last wiggle of the street and it flattened out at the bottom of the hill. And I knew where it had taken me.

The sylvan grove appeared out of place in the city. But nonetheless, here it spread, untouched, near Plenum's southern limits. This was no park, no trimmed and tended pleasure garden. Cypress trees rose from tangled thickets bearing the fading colors of the dying flowers that had twined and twisted up during the spring and summer. Two vast shade trees and a number of smaller, gnarled olive and fruit trees vyed with the cypresses for space. And glimpsed amidst all the wild verdure squatted the gray stone and green marble of the Temple of Sighs.

Somewhere to my left, I knew, must lay the southern terminus of the Course, that vital traffic trunk that would take me back to the familiar squalor of the Orine district. I thought about continuing my flight, cutting sharply to the northwest along the Course. But I discarded the notion. I was getting tired of running and had little desire to head back uphill. Besides, my feet hurt.

The glade beckoned. Perhaps I could hide among the trees and bushes. People left the Temple of Sighs alone, preferring to forget that this remnant of the Ancients' pagan fallacy existed. The place possessed an unsavory reputation as an abode of untamed demons and a haunt of restless ghosts. Maybe the Venatores would spread out, search for me in the adjoining streets.

I had only seconds before the closest Venatores rounded the bend behind me. I left the street and plunged into the grove, bulling my way through shrubbery. The footing was treacherous as I left hard stone for squelching mud or ankle-grabbing underbrush. The ubiquitous smells of the city faded, or were masked by an increasing mélange of herbal scents largely unfamiliar to me. I dragged my leg by sheer brute force through a pair of grasping branches belonging to a ground hugging plant bedizened with shiny, chartreuse leaves that concealed those damned branches. Once through that snarl, I placed a tree trunk between me and my pursuers. Perhaps I'd lost them.

I heard again that voice I'd begun to hate—Scarbeard's. "He's in the Temple of Sighs. Get in after him."

Maybe I could carve out his tongue.

I moved further into the grove, ducking under a tree limb and skirting a thicket of tough, spiky-leaved shrubs bearing red berries. I nearly tripped over a fallen column so vine-wrapped I could barely make out the weathered fluting. A few columns remained standing atop their pedestals, the columns creating a gapped arc that presumably continued around in a complete circle. Beyond the columns, the crumbling walls of the Temple of Sighs greeted me. An entry that had long since lost its door—assuming it had ever had one—beckoned to my right. A marble pediment above the lintel bore a relief of a man's broad face, displaying a rather melancholy expression on its faded features. He seemed resigned, weary. But perhaps he'd appeared more dapper and cheerful before a thousand years of Plenum rain had done its work on him. That would be enough to get anyone down.

I darted through the entry, already hearing the thrashing sound of men wading through vegetation behind me as the Venatores entered the sacred grove. The Temple of Sighs must have been a wonder centuries ago. The crumbling walls—a half-dozen gaps providing ingresses in addition to the doorway—encompassed a space about thirty yards in diameter. Roofless now, it must once have been covered, the roof upheld by the ranks of columns that now stood or lay in disarray before me. Three of them still remained upright. The rest had tumbled. Some had fallen flat, breaking into sections. A pair here or there leaned against each other, the shafts providing mutual support against inevitable collapse. Others lay nearly vertical, held above the ground by the broken stump or the pedestal of a neighbor.

Rising in the center of the Temple stood the marble torso of a woman. Her head, arms, and most of one shoulder were missing. I guessed at one point she'd looked down at her worshipers from a height of twenty feet or so. The drape of her gown had weathered to a mere impression. One leg stood bare, a rounding of the knee still clear, hinting at the skill of the sculptor, dead for an age.

Vegetation had entirely overgrown the interior of the Temple of Sighs. The lengths and segments of columns rose from the verdure like the piles of a seaside pier. This sea was green, of all hues and shades. I wondered what the colors might be in spring. Then I returned to wondering how to save my own skin.

The height of the plant life varied, but looked to average about waist high, if you didn't include the occasional tree. Crossing this appeared a daunting task. Cutting through would ruin the edges of my blades. It would take hours with a whetstone to set that damage to rights.

But, perhaps I didn't have to cross.

The sound of pursuit neared: the grunts and profanity, the thrash of arms and legs breaking through branches. I had one idea, and I didn't have time to weigh it. Either I'd implement it or turn and fight.

With a grimace of dismay, I plucked the hat from my head, grasped the brim, then with a flick of my wrist sailed it across the Temple of Sighs. It landed—crown up, thankfully—atop a thicket growing beneath the point where two columns intersected, leaning against each other like a pair of lovers, or a pair of drunks. Or a pair of drunk lovers.

I drew my dagger, dropped to a crouch, and began to crawl through the brush. I took what routes the vegetation offered, squirming between shrubs, wriggling through larger areas around tree trunks, relatively free of clutching branches. Disturbed insects vied with sprigs of vegetation for the honor of jabbing me in the face, seeming to take direct aim at my eyes. Stubborn, stubby limb ends gouged my doublet; twigs, spiny leaves, and thorns tore at my shirt and hose. I was going to end up spending every pistra I earned on this job replacing my wardrobe.

When I heard the first of the Venatores enter the Temple I froze in place, my face halfway through a spider's web.

"He is in here somewhere," Scar-beard said. "Flush him out."

The sound of boots tromping shrubbery, legs thrashing through fronds and ungiving brush was followed by the *swish* and *thock* of halberd blades clearing paths through the growth.

Taking advantage of the noise to mask that of my own passage, I recommenced my crawl toward one of the gaps in the eastern curve of the temple wall.

"There he is," came an excited voice.

I froze again. Had they spotted my movement, a wake cut through the surface of the sea of greenery? Then I heard movement again, redoubled now, and clearly moving away from me. One of the Venatores had spotted my hat and they must have all been surging toward it, ready to slaughter me where I presumably was crouched hiding.

I moved again, less carefully now, absorbing scratches to the face, while my left shirt sleeve was reduced to tatters.

The rubble from the collapsed section of wall formed a ramp, already overgrown with vegetation. As the first Venatores descended upon my hapless hat, I crawled, still concealed, up to the lip of the gap. I pulled myself along my belly across the smooth, weathered stone and flopped over to the other side at the same time I heard the dismayed cries indicating the Venatores had discovered my deceit.

I grinned, stifling a chuckle, and began to rise to my feet. The sight of a Venatore pacing not a yard away stopped me. Scar-beard had left a man to patrol the exterior. Why couldn't my foes all be fools and drooling imbeciles?

Something, perhaps the jumble of angry voices from within the Temple of Sighs, drew the sentry's attention. He turned toward the gap in the wall. Toward me.

I drove upward from a crouch, springing upon the Venatore. He was able to produce no more than a startled grunt before I bore him to the ground, the haft of his halberd grinding into his throat. I clutched the shaft with both hands and drove down with all my weight and strength.

He tried to hold me off. He tried to call for help, but even if he'd had breath in his lungs, I was already closing his throat. The encounter lasted mere seconds, yet it seemed longer to me as I watched the desperation grow in his face. There came a crunch and a sickening gagging noise. The Venatore's eyes bulged, flicking wildly from side to side, before ceasing all movement, staring unseeing, straight up from within a face fallen slack.

I let the halberd drop. Killing a man is rarely a satisfying task. This one was worse than most. But I had no time for remorse or reflection. I took to my heels, dodging through the trees of the sacred grove, ears attuned for any sound of detection or pursuit.

Breaking free from the park, I found what I'd been striving for: the southern end of the Course. The Course ended its long, winding traverse of Plenum here, petering out in a patch of no-man's land, with the sacred grove of the Temple of Sighs occupying much of one side of the patch and a vast heap of rubble—the detritus of demolished buildings and sections of the ancient city wall—much of the rest. To the northwest, a few miles from this spot, near the beginning of the Course, the Orine district beckoned. Home. A change of clothes.

And Giacomo's Wine Shop. I needed a drink.

Dripping blood from a dozen scratches, my clothing shredded and daubed green and gray with mold and vegetal filth—and missing a hat—I commenced the jog back home while picking out insects who seemed no happier to be wriggling about within my clothing than I was to have them wriggling.

Chapter 8

Only vanity prevented me from going directly to Giacomo's. Instead, I pointed my boots toward my tailor's shop. Donatello looked askance at my shredded attire when I shuffled in to pick up the clothing he'd tailored for me. But he said nothing. So long as I continued destroying shirts, he'd have steady business stitching replacements. He did, however, go so far as to shake his head in exasperation as I snagged yet another hat from his stock.

Leaving Donatello's, I redirected my steps toward home. I sluiced a bucket over my head from the communal fountain nearest my building, though the steady rain accompanying my trip home had already gotten a good start on my ablutions. I tromped wearily up the creaking wooden steps, unlocked my creaking wooden door, then deposited my newly tailored clothes behind the creaking wooden door of my third-hand armoire.

I left the torn, dirtied, and bloodied clothes in a heap on the floor. I'd sort out what might be salvaged and what was only fit for rags tomorrow. I felt a little better in fresh attire. Not much, but a little. I'd rely on wine to get me further along that road. Sleep was probably what I needed, but it wasn't even noon yet. I'd only gotten out of bed a few hours ago. So an early lunch consisting primarily of cheap wine would have to do.

I considered donning my leather jack. This job had grown violent. A bit of thick leather between my skin and sharpened steel would be a comfort. The jack covered me from groin to neck, where a high collar rose to my chin. Strategic pockets within the leather allowed me to slide in metal plates covering a selection of vital organs. I had the metal plates still. I also had others of some material I believe to be metal, but couldn't swear to it. The stuff had once been in the form of a large, gray egg that contained a particularly vicious demon. I'd collected the material, figuring that if it could imprison a demon, it might also provide some protection against a demon's teeth and claws. And so it had proved, once I'd clumsily, but patiently, hammered the semi-malleable material into sections that fit—more or less smoothly—into the pockets of the leather jack.

For the moment I decided against wearing the armor. I was on my home ground, it was early in the day, and I had no reason to believe the Venatores had tracked me from the Temple of Sighs. I wanted a few quiet cups of wine at Giacomo's. Showing up accoutered for a battle would only invite questions. Besides, the awkward leather garment was neither comfortable nor stylish.

Giacomo squinted at me as I stepped inside. Not even the late morning brightened the gloom of the wine shop, beyond a stray sunbeam that had fought its way through the clouds, past the tall buildings of Plenum, and managed to sneak in beneath the low lintel of the wine shop's front door to illuminate about a square foot of the entry.

"You been trying to pet a lion?" Giacomo asked.

"Turns out they don't like to be kissed," I said. "Wine, Giacomo, not talk. And send over whatever you've got to eat."

As my eyes adjusted, I could see I wasn't the first customer. Giacomo caters to the early drinkers as well as the night owls. But the place was—from my perspective—unusually empty. That suited me. I wanted only a peaceful place to think and worry, and dull the ache of all the scratches and bruises.

The wine arrived first. Giacomo apparently watered it down for the morning crowd. I didn't complain; I could use a clear head.

I was halfway through the first cup before a girl I didn't recognize clattered a wood bowl onto the table. I spooned up a thick porridge of ground cornmeal mixed with chunks of sausage, garlic, and chopped broccoli rabe. It surprised me. I didn't think Giacomo's could manage anything more than day-old bread served with hunks of molding cheese and wrinkled olives.

So of course I wasn't allowed to finish the bowl. I'd scooped in only about four mouthfuls when Marteo skulked in. It wasn't yet noon, no skullduggery was afoot, yet Marteo skulked. He's probably furtive alone in his own room, slinking from shadow to shadow.

"Breakfast, Marteo?" I asked as he reached my table. "It's good."

"No time for food, Cesar," Marteo said. He placed his hands on the table and leaned forward, pitching his voice low. "Put your spoon down. You need to be listening, not chewing."

He had my attention.

"Is it Maralla?"

Marteo nodded.

I rose. "Did they grab her? Let's go." That had been my fear all the while I'd been sitting here, that the Venatores would troop back to Maralla's place and Azeglio would lead them into the building and nab Maralla. I'd been tempted to return, even before reaching my apartment, ragged and bloody. But having become familiar with the opposition, I had to accept the reality that I couldn't tackle them all alone. Not even with Marteo popping up here and there to slip a knife beneath a breastplate. All I could do was wait for the report, then figure out the next step. But right now, my immediate instinct was to take action, despite having no clear notion what that action should be.

"Sit down, Cesar. I said you need to listen." Marteo was practically hissing.

I sat down.

"After you led those soldiers on what I presume was an amusing chase," Marteo said, "I kept an eye on their captain. He was looking around. I suppose he wanted a place to sit. He found one—the steps leading up to our lookout."

So I wasn't the only one who had a bit of an adventure that morning. But lurking in a corner is what Marteo does, so his heart rate might not have elevated a single beat.

"I assume there is more," I said, reaching for what was left of my wine. I was happy to note my hand didn't shake.

"That man you described, the one Maralla is working with, came along. The captain summoned him over. Vicenzu sauntered over with his four bodyguards. After maybe five words from the captain, Vicenzu sent away his bodyguards. Then the two men talked. I listened."

I whistled. Azeglio met Vicenzu? "I don't think I want to hear it, but I know I need to. How badly have they complicated my life?"

"The captain seems to have been investigating the other fellow. Knew his name. He knew Vicenzu was running some scheme, buying up property cheaply, then somehow convincing buyers to purchase at above market rate. At least, that's what I gathered from the captain."

I nodded. "That's about right."

"Well, the captain threatened Vicenzu. Said he'd turn him in to the magistrates. See him chained to an oar. Vicenzu looked like he wanted to piss himself. But he's a real weasel. Get him in a trap and he's fierce and crafty. He figured the captain wanted something or he'd just have taken him without all the talk. He asked what the captain wanted."

Marteo stopped talking. He grabbed a stool and sat. "I think I'll eat something after all. It was a long shift, and all this talking is tiring."

I tapped my spoon impatiently against the table until the girl arrived to take Marteo's order. He sat silently after that, apparently waiting for food and wine to arrive before he continued his narration. But I'd no patience for it.

"Get on with it," I said. I may have actually growled.

Marteo offered a thin smile that in the gloom of Giacomo's offered only the suggestion of small, sharp teeth.

"Well," Marteo said, pausing long enough to demonstrate that he was continuing because he wanted to, not because he felt intimidated, "the captain explained exactly how Vicenzu convinced the marks to pay an exorbitant sum for the houses. He explained what Maralla is and who he is. You held out on me, Cesar."

I shrugged. "You didn't need to know. I only wanted your eyes, not your knives. Be honest, would you have agreed if I'd told you we were up against a clandestine branch of the Collegium?"

"I'm not afraid of the Venatores," Marteo said. "They die, same as everybody else."

The serving girl set down a cup of wine and a bowl of porridge. Marteo set to. He seemed disinclined to speak for the moment, so I joined in, shoveling in my cooling porridge and finishing my cup of sour, watered wine.

"So," Marteo said, after he'd finished about a third of his bowl, "the captain—or, rather, Questor General Azeglio—said that what he wanted was Maralla, that he couldn't give two rat farts what sort of scheme Vicenzu was running."

Marteo gulped down the rest of his cup, then picked up his spoon again. But he continued speaking instead of eating. "Vicenzu sounded more himself. Confident. He offered Azeglio a deal. Said he'd deliver her to Azeglio, with no fuss, no drama, no demons trying to rip out Azeglio's throat, if Azeglio let him finish his job first. He said he only had three more houses to sell, then he wouldn't require Maralla's services any longer."

I pushed aside my empty bowl. I lifted my cup to my lips only to remember it was empty. "What did Azeglio say?"

"He said yes. They had a deal. Vicenzu went inside Maralla's building. Azeglio sat on the stair until his men returned. Fewer of them than had left. Not bad work, Cesar, but I figure I could have accounted for more than two of them."

"I was trying to lead them away from Maralla, not rack up a body count," I said. It shouldn't irk me that the little assassin considered himself the martial superior to a veteran bravo and sometime mercenary such as myself. But it did.

I changed the subject, not wanting Marteo to see he'd gotten under my skin. "And then?"

"Nothing. The Venatores departed. Then a fellow by the name of Domenico arrived, told me he was my replacement. He took over, and I left about the same time as Vicenzu and Maralla. I thought about shadowing the bodyguards. Maybe take out one or two of them. But I thought you'd want to hear this news first."

He meant it, that part about killing a couple of the bodyguards. That wasn't braggadocio. Taking a human life was, for Marteo, a matter of indifference, to be undertaken casually if it seemed advantageous.

"You thought right, Marteo." I summoned the serving girl—got her name, Bienca—and ordered two more cups. "On me. You earned it."

Marteo flashed that toothy smile again. "Damn right, Cesar."

Chapter 9

I took my time returning to the watch post. Maralla would be working her part of the Hearth Demon scam. I had the leisure to stroll. Stroll and think.

Domenico had selected a spot that allowed him to keep an eye on the door of Maralla's building while keeping limber, stretching his legs in a deep lunge while remaining concealed from view. He nodded at me when I ascended the stairs.

I joined him in his limbering exercises. I'd been walking enough that my muscles wouldn't cramp from my morning's exertions. But taking advantage of an opportunity to maintain flexibility was always prudent in my line of work.

"Pronate your back foot more, Cesar," Domenico said, frowning.

Always the pedant, always the critic. Well, that's what I paid him for. That is, when I wasn't paying him to sit atop an unfinished building and spy on a witch.

I pronated my back foot more.

"I'll take over," I said.

"I still have another bell to go," Domenico said.

"Don't worry about it. I need to sit and think. I might as well do it here."

"What thoughts are drifting through that sluggish canal you call a mind, Cesar?"

"One is what sound an overpaid fencing master would make if he fell from a roof. The other is if I should inform our witch of her imminent betrayal by her partner and her subsequent capture by the Venatores."

Domenico grunted, conveying restrained surprise and interest with a single noise. Always efficient with his efforts, that one. He straightened smoothly from his lunge, pivoted, then lunged the opposite direction, hand extended as if gripping a rapier hilt. "That ought to keep you occupied. Do you wish to discuss it, argue the merits of each position?"

"Not really," I said. I summarized the events of the morning, then said, "I'll figure it out. Slowly, no doubt, what with my sluggish canal and all."

Domenico straightened up. He patted my left shoulder. Reassuringly, I thought. "Relax the shoulder. You're too tense for a smooth recovery."

With that, he left. Supercilious ass.

I still hadn't made up my mind when Maralla returned, escorted by Vicenzu. Vicenzu displayed no signs of discomfort or nervousness that I could see. He appeared his genial, flamboyant self as he doffed his plumed hat, bade her good day, and sauntered off, his bodyguards discreetly trailing him.

Maralla watched him go. Before she'd turned to the door, I'd made up my mind. I scampered down the stairs. She was at the door, fingers gripping the handle as my boots hit the cobbles of Escaline Way. I sprinted across the street.

"Maralla," I said, catching her attention as she was passing through the doorway.

She turned. I caught the moment of recognition.

"You," she said. "What do you want?"

She held her body stiff, the one arm visibly tense, prepared to slam the door in my face. She wore a tawny orange today. A less vibrant color than I had come to expect from her. Earrings of a leaden gray, adorned by a tracery of gold, dangled from her earlobes, peeking from behind the curls of hair that brushed her cheeks.

"I want to talk. Nothing more." I spread my arms wide in what I hoped was a gesture of goodwill. I accompanied the gesture with a smile, trying for guileless honesty rather than rakish good humor. I couldn't say if I succeeded.

"Vicenzu's pack of hounds didn't do all that to your face," she said. "They're punchers, not scratchers."

"Not particularly impressive punchers, at that," I said. "It was like being assaulted by children."

"Children you ran away from, as I recall," she said.

"Freakishly large children. And there were four of them." I wasn't making any points with that line. "Look, it isn't Vicenzu's bodyguards I want to talk to you about. It's about the...scratchers. And it affects you personally."

She tilted her head, thinking. I couldn't help but find it an adorable mannerism. "All right. You—what was your name again?"

"Cesar," I said. "Cesar the Bravo, at your service."

"Well, I don't know that I require your services, Cesar. Still, come upstairs. I don't want to discuss any of this business in the street. But watch yourself. I am more than capable of defending myself, should you get any ideas."

"Thank you for the warning. I have no desire to tangle with you. I've suffered enough for one day."

She raised an eyebrow. I'd stirred her curiosity. Good.

Maralla led the way inside. A wide hallway led back into the gloom, with doors on either side. A stairway commenced a few paces inside, dividing the hallway in half. I followed her up the stairs to the floor above. A narrow mezzanine overlooked the hall below. I could see a few of the doors opening off of it. The stairway switched back and Maralla continued up it to the top floor, where awaited her generous suite of apartments.

I couldn't help but contrast her spacious, clean, well-lit accommodation to my shipping crate of an abode. I took it all in with interest, like an estate auctioneer memorizing an inventory. The central living quarters occupied much of this upper floor, the walls a pale cream, a linear fresco of green vines and pale-yellow flowers striping them from the plastered ceiling to the hardwood floor. An open door let out onto a narrow balcony that offered her a southwest vista. Floor-length curtains of a deep green fabric covered most of the mullioned window to the east. Comfortably padded arm chairs grouped around a low, glossy oak table. An inviting bench for two, topped with a thick, quilted padding sat beneath the east window. A narrow marble hearth centered the northern wall. A half-dozen oil paintings filled the rest of the wall. An ornate carpet spread out before the hearth. Other doors led into other rooms, one presumably a sleeping chamber.

Maralla did not invite me to join her on the bench. She did not even invite me to sit. Instead, she strolled toward the fireplace—which showed no signs of having been used recently—and leaned against the marble. A kitten appeared from beneath the bench, sauntered over to Maralla, and rubbed up against her ankle for a moment before bounding away to pounce at something only it could see.

"Well, you're here," she said. "Now, tell me what you came here for, then go. Put some ointment on those scratches."

I paced a bit, continuing to admire the room and its fine furnishings while I gathered my thoughts.

"Maralla," I said, "I am here to keep an eye on you." I raised a hand, forestalling the question, comment, or objection I figured was rising to her lips. "Don't ask me who set me to the task. I won't tell you. Simply understand that your safety is my concern."

"Thank you, but I don't require your help," she said, straightening up. I thought she might toss her head disdainfully, but she merely stared at me. More prideful than haughty, I judged.

"I am certain you can fend for yourself in most circumstances," I said. "What you're facing now is not usual. For instance, I know what Vicenzu is up to, and he is not a man to be taken lightly."

Maralla's expression transitioned from prideful to mirthful instantaneously. She laughed.

"Vicenzu, dangerous? That self-absorbed cockscomb is

as dangerous as little Beppo," she said, pointing at the kitten, who was involved in a desperate battle against its own tail.

"Really?" I asked.

"Please, Cesar. Those were his bodyguards who roughed you up, not Vicenzu. And they weren't serious about it. They meant no real harm."

"Let's consider that a matter of perspective, Maralla. And allow me to point out that my perspective was rather closer to the flesh and bone of the matter. But, set Vicenzu aside for the moment. Are you familiar with the Venatores?"

Maralla stiffened. "Of course I am familiar with the Venatores. I maintain constant vigilance where those jackals are concerned. Why?"

"Because the Questor General of the Venatores met with Vicenzu today, right outside your front door, and the two of them agreed that Vicenzu would turn you over once he'd sold off the last house and no longer had need of your Talent."

"You lie!" Maralla said. She practically spat it. "You rotten liar. Vicenzu would never betray me. I don't know who put you up to this or why. But you won't turn me against my partner. Get out. Now."

"Maralla," I said. "Be reasonable about this. Why would I—"

"Get out!" she hissed. She flipped up an edge of the carpet with her toe and, with a kick, folded a section of it away from before the fireplace, revealing an elaborate, geometrical design painted upon the hardwood floor with some reddish pigment that appeared to have been impregnated with flecks of quartz or mica. I'd seen similar designs before, a pentacle within a ring. A summoning circle.

"Wait a moment," I said, raising both hands, palms up. "We're just having a conversation here."

Maralla wasn't listening. She stepped within the circle. She raised both arms, seemed to hesitate, then let one drop. Sweeping back her hair to reveal an ear, she reached up and detached a dangling earring. Muttering a torrent of incomprehensible syllables that were nonetheless irritatingly familiar, she dashed the earring to the floor. The bauble broke apart when it hit the floorboards, like an egg dropped in a mixing bowl.

And the egg hatched.

It hatched not, alas, a chick. Instead, from an expanding, roiling ball of sulfur-reeking, cinnamon-accented steam, a demon emerged. Thickly muscled legs supported a slender torso, which sprouted disproportionately muscular arms. An oval head with a wide-lipped mouth, no discernible nose, and bulbous, red-rimmed eyes with fiery orange irises, topped a slender, flexible neck. Its entire body possessed a greenish tint, and the skin carried the impression of scales. It wore nothing but an apron, a garment of uncertain purpose, suggesting something of the carpenter and something of the maid.

"See him out," Maralla told the demon. She pointed at me.

"Maralla, wait," I said. Uselessly.

The demon stumped on noiseless feet toward me. It held out its hands like a wrestler, thick, blunt, spatulate fingers spread.

I'd tussled with demons before. Never willingly, but such are the vicissitudes of a bravo's life. This particular specimen was less menacing than some I'd faced. It clearly did not derive from the same stock as did the war demons usually conjured up to kill and terrorize. But it nonetheless could toss me out on my ear if I wasn't careful. I cursed myself for not wearing my leather jack. I could use the protection if I had to tangle with this specimen.

I didn't want to, though. I was here to alert Maralla to the danger that faced her, keeping faith with my client, Fenetto, and earning my fee. Getting involved in a bloody affray in Maralla's sitting room wasn't going to help.

So, I left my steel sheathed. I backed toward the door. I tried again to talk sense.

"You don't have to believe me," I said. "Just keep your eyes open, Maralla."

I started to say more, but the demon moved faster than its bulk would suggest it had the capacity for. I dodged aside, but meaty fingers engulfed my forearm. I'm not a weakling, but the power with which the demon jerked me sideways and spun me toward the wall was irresistible.

I got a hand up in time to absorb some of the impact, but my head still smacked painfully against the wall beside the door. I sidestepped instinctively, and the paw reaching for my collar grasped only empty air, then slammed into the wall.

I spun, getting some space. But that only placed the demon between me and the door. And I'd begun to come around to Maralla's way of thinking: it was time for me to go.

"Vicenzu isn't some harmless grifter, Maralla," I said, without looking at her. I kept my eyes on the demon, which turned around and came at me, arms spread.

"It's too early to be drunk, Cesar. Go home and sober up," Maralla said.

I briefly reconsidered my commitment to continuing the contest empty-handed. A dagger might help me get through without further damage. Maybe. But I didn't have time to make the decision. I stutter-stepped, trying to confuse the demon as to which direction I'd move.

I failed. I pushed off my right foot, going low and left and losing my hat in the process. The demon wrapped an arm around my waist as I passed, hoisted me off the ground, then using my own momentum, drove me into the wall. I got both hands up, but was still stunned by the impact of my head against the door.

I blinked. The demon got the door open, while keeping me clamped tight against its side. Up close it smelled like an old iron brazier, with something reptilian overlaying it.

The demon toted me out the door and a few paces beyond, then I was rolling down the stairs, trying to refrain from breaking my neck. Falling down stairs is an unpleasant experience at the best of times. Being hurled down is worse. I don't recommend it. Add to the whirling and jarring descent the bulky hilts of sword and dagger digging into the body, and it becomes even more painfully bruising. The pommels and guards never strike in the same spot, ramming into ribs or hip or belly with each jolting impact against the hard stair. The only consistency is that each iteration hurts. I hit the landing still rolling, slammed against the wall, and lay dazed. I opened my eyes, let the world come back into focus, and saw the demon standing at the top of the stairs. It flicked a wrist, and my hat came spinning and floating down to land on my chest.

Without a word the demon left. I heard the door above close with finality.

Chapter 10

All of the recent beatings I'd suffered had taken a cumulative toll. I made an effort at convalescence in bed, listening to rain squalls pattering against the wall of my apartment and catching stray zephyrs as drafts of chill air wormed through the gaps in the aged, poorly-maintained building.

I imagined Maralla's rooms remained warm and quiet.

The throbbing in my head began to subside. I had experienced a bout of dizziness during my trip back to the Orine district and a few moments when even the dim sunlight filtering through thick gray clouds, fat with threatening rain, generated too much glare for my eyes to handle. During those moments, I stumbled along, navigating through a squint for yards at a time, and brooding; thinking vengefully that, just maybe, the Venatores had the right idea.

My bed seemed the logical destination. Yet after a few hours of attempting to find a comfortable position, willing myself to snatch some healing sleep, I decided on another recuperative method.

I rose, wincing at a temporary resurgence of generalized pain, then made my way to Giacomo's Wine Shop for a more immediately effective anodyne.

The ache dulled during the short walk from my apartment. The movement helped work out a degree of stiffness I'd not noticed set in while lying abed. But my variety of lacerations and contusions offered constant reminders of what this job I'd undertaken was costing me. So I was plenty sore, physically and mentally, by the time I joined the late afternoon drinkers in Giacomo's.

Bonfilia brought wine, and I flipped a soldo onto the table. I considered the state of my purse. Even after what I'd doled out to Donatello and the rest of my creditors, I was still in funds. Enough to leave town? Maybe. I could slink off, leave Herbieto to his own revenge. And let Primate Fenetto see to his own family complications. It was a Collegium matter, after all. Why did he have to mix up a poor bravo in the Collegium's internecine affairs? One hundred pistras might seem a substantial fee, but when I considered that my opposition consisted of demons and armored soldiers, it no longer appeared commensurate.

Who could blame me if I slipped out of Plenum during the night? With winter coming on, campaigning season had ended. So I couldn't sign on with a condottiere as I had a time or two in the past when events in Plenum had grown too dicey for me. But my purse might last me through to the summer in some backwater hamlet. After all, I wanted to get out of my increasingly intolerable apartment. Leaving Plenum would certainly accomplish that.

Giacomo's door opened. I didn't bother staring through the gloom to see who'd entered. I assumed the usual evening crowd was beginning to gather. I was more interested in my woes and my wine.

The sound of the wine shop's background noise of murmured conversation increasing in volume convinced me to—grudgingly—raise my head.

Maralla neared my table. She bent forward, burdened by the limping form she was supporting, a form ridiculously cumbersome for her to be handling unaided. Tasso Longarm had one long limb draped over her shoulder, leaning heavily on the witch. Blood dripped from the dangling fingers. He held his other arm clamped tightly against his ribs.

I overset my stool, jerking to my feet. My body protested against the abrupt motion, but I ignored it. I rushed around the table and assisted Maralla in maneuvering Tasso the last few paces. I got Tasso onto a stool. I called over my shoulder to Bonfilia, demanding wine, water, and clean rags.

The candlelight offered me a decent look at Tasso. His face was a mass of cuts and bruises that made mine appear in comparison as if I'd merely nicked myself shaving. His hands and forearms bore numerous gashes, suggesting he'd been warding off knife cuts barehanded. Along his ribs, where he continued to press one hand, a wide blotch of blood staining his already dirty shirt indicated that his warding had not been entirely successful.

I reached across the table, collected my cup of wine, and handed it to Tasso. Before he could engulf it within his massive, bloody hand, Maralla intercepted it. She held it to his lips solicitously and helped him drink. Her frank concern for the hired arm breaker—the widened eyes and parted lips—contrasted remarkably with the last glimpse I'd had of her: disdainful and outraged, mouth compressed, eyes mere slits through which she'd watched as her demon chucked me out.

Tasso drained the cup, then sighed. "I'm not getting paid enough for this, Cesar."

"I've been thinking the same," I said. "What happened?"

Bonfilia arrived, Giacomo huffing behind her. Between them they toted a pile of rags, of various degrees of cleanliness, a basin full of water—its steaming surface suggesting it had been sitting in a pot or kettle in the kitchen—and a brimming pitcher of wine.

I refilled Tasso's cup—my cup, really—from the pitcher, then signaled to Bonfilia for two more cups. If I didn't take action, Tasso would drink it all himself. I knew who'd be paying for it, and his name wasn't Tasso.

Maralla selected the cleanest rag, dipped it in the basin, and set to dabbing at the worst of the cuts. Tasso winced, but otherwise showed no reaction. He took another long pull at the wine.

"You have a report for me, or are you here to cadge free drinks?" I asked.

"Well, Cesar," he said, "I was keeping my watch. I saw that Vicenzu fellow approaching. Seemed a bit late for him. You said they usually go out late morning and are back early afternoon. I figured he was dropping by for a visit or something. I was curious. I must have made some noise shifting around for a better look, 'cause he turned and looked in my direction. Next thing I know, four bastards are rushing up the stairs. I went for 'em. Didn't want to get cornered, right? So, spread my arms and go for a diving tackle. Took a couple of 'em with me down to the street."

Tasso grinned at the memory, then grunted as the motion aggravated a few of his facial lacerations. He took another drink.

"Everybody got back up," he said. "I told them I thought that was enough fun for one day. But Vicenzu didn't agree. He told his boys he didn't want anyone watching Maralla, that he needed her all to himself for a couple more days. Said to send a message and that I was the message." Tasso drank again. "Then things got a little messy."

Maralla let slip a small chuckle. "Your friend here practices the art of understatement," she said. She was winding a strip of cloth about a cut on Tasso's forearm, on his non-drinking arm. "I overheard most of it from the roof. I've got a little herb garden going up there, and I was clipping some oregano. Tasso held his own, Cesar. For a moment or two, I thought he might actually win. But when I heard Vicenzu say not to be afraid of using knives, I figured differently. I ran downstairs, but they'd gone by the time I reached the street. Only Tasso was left. At first, I thought he was dead."

"Just taking a breather," Tasso said. "I wasn't sure what to do when I opened my eyes and saw her there, Cesar. She was trying to clean me up, some. But she wasn't supposed to know I was watching her. My mind kind of went blank. The only thing I could think of was to come see you. But I needed some help walking. And there was only one person around who could help. I hope I didn't screw up, Cesar."

"No, Tasso. You did fine," I said. "You gave her a glimpse of the true Vicenzu."

Bonfilia brought two more cups and filled them from the pitcher. I placed one before Maralla, whose hands were still occupied ministering to Tasso. She nodded her thanks.

"I'm afraid that I might owe you an apology, Cesar," Maralla said. "It is just possible that Vicenzu isn't the colorful-but-gentle soul I took him for."

"What, that loveable conman?" I asked. "Him and his hilarious troupe of comedy bodyguards?"

"I'm trying to apologize, Cesar," Maralla said. She tightened a bandage with a jerk that caused Tasso to spill a few drops of wine. "I can still change my mind. Maybe Vicenzu is simply a trifle overprotective. This incident doesn't necessarily mean you were telling the truth."

"What more do you want? There's no profit in my lying to you, Maralla. I know what you can do. You already had a demon toss me down a flight of stairs. Pissing you off isn't a smart move."

"I may have got a bit carried away. Sorry about that," Maralla said. She wasn't looking at me, still concentrated as she was on patching up Tasso. But I caught a flick of the eyes that suggested actual contrition. "More apologies. I'm not used to that, Cesar."

"Well, apology accepted. How could I not, when you deliver it so gracefully?" I took a drink, eyed her over the brim of the cup. Maralla appeared to be stifling a laugh.

"Do me a favor and keep that other earring attached to the lobe."

Maralla blew out a breath of frustration. She examined the latest bandage critically, then picked up her own cup. She grimaced at the taste. "Using the earring was a waste of a Vessel. Now I'll have to spend a full day or two englobing another demon. I hate that. It's tedious. I should have just used the circle. But at the time I doubted you'd have stayed in my apartment long enough for me to complete the summoning. I got flustered. Now I know you would have stood there all day, jabbering the entire time, trying to convince me of your story."

"You were up in her rooms, Cesar?" Tasso asked. He raised his bushy eyebrows.

"Yes," I said. "Right up to the point I was thrown out. Remember that bit I just said about a demon tossing me down stairs? Clean any filthy ideas from your mind."

Tasso grunted, then finished another cup of wine. One way to sluice the brain, I supposed.

I frowned down at my cup, grappling with the new set of circumstances. How would this affect the job? It would be tougher to keep from revealing my principal. But as much as I didn't want to annoy Maralla, the thought of irritating Fenetto concerned me more. Perhaps this was enough to convince Maralla to walk away. Leave her rooms behind and get out of Plenum for a while. That might do.

"Cesar."

I looked up to find someone else hovering by my table.

"Herbieto," I said. More complications. Why not? Everything else seemed to be falling apart. "Find an empty stool. Join the party."

Herbieto wore a neat, rust-colored ensemble, down to a matching hat. It was a clever bit of fashion, skillfully managing to appear at the height of style while at the same time not in the least catching the eye. Camouflage for the well-dressed man.

Herbieto glanced at my companions, clearly ill-at ease. I imagined he wanted a status update from me, some indication as to when he could expect to attend a duel between me and Vicenzu. But he could not bring himself to raise the subject before strangers. He dragged over a stool, probably to gain time to consider his words rather than any desire to add himself to the group.

I stood up as Herbieto sat down. I gestured with the cup in one hand, pausing to take a drink between utterances. "Herbieto, this is Maralla. She's a witch. And you remember Tasso, the fellow leaking blood as fast as he is sucking down wine. A bone breaker for hire, as you might recall. Maralla, Tasso, this is Herbieto, a successful milliner, and a client of mine. Interesting story: he's got a quarrel with our dear friend Vicenzu. Wants me to kill him."

The table was quiet as I spoke, though I watched both Maralla and Herbieto struggle to fight back ejaculations—mouths opening, lips compressing—as I spilled confidences like a drunk staggering about with a full goblet.

I sat down.

"A milliner," Tasso said. "What's that?" He sounded stronger for the rest, the bandaging, and the wine.

Herbieto wasn't listening. He and Maralla were sharing

a wary look.

"A, um, witch?" Herbieto asked.

"Why do you want Vicenzu killed?" Maralla asked.

"A milliner makes women's hats," I told Tasso, while refilling my empty cup from a pitcher that sadly ran dry much too soon.

I raised the pitcher over my head and summoned Bonfilia. This promised to be an expensive evening. But perhaps I might convince Herbieto to dip into his own purse. Maybe I should order a bottle of Senna ruby. It ought to appeal to Maralla's palate.

"Do you make Cesar's hats?" Tasso asked Herbieto, then laughed as if he'd cracked a real knee-slapper.

Herbieto spared him a brief, exasperated glance, then returned his attention to Maralla.

"Vicenzu killed my father," he said to her. "Indirectly, true. But he might as well have personally thrown the rocks that did the job." Herbieto's voice contained the bitter, choking note it had the first time I'd heard him discuss his father's death. Added to it was an air of suspicion.

"Vicenzu ran a land sale con on Herbieto's dad," I told a frowning Maralla. "Seeded some worthless hillside in the North and passed it off as a gold mine. Got the mark killed digging."

"Oh," Maralla said. "The prospector game." She squirmed, looked away for a moment into the gloom of the wine shop. "Well, misfortune does follow certain unwise choices."

"Are you saying my father's death was his own fault, witch?" Herbieto said. He blanched immediately after. He wasn't the sort to deliberately insult anyone; a natural gentleman, probably born polite, offering his mother a good day upon slipping free of the womb, and apologizing for any inconvenience. He wouldn't premeditatedly slight a woman—as that would be rude—and he decidedly wouldn't give willful offense to one who could conjure up demons, as that would be stupid.

"No, of course not," Maralla said. "That isn't what I meant. I'm saying that no one can foresee all outcomes. That many factors go into any given outcome. That fault is hard to ascertain, but that each of us must bear some degree of responsibility, however slight." She squirmed a bit as she spoke. I could only imagine the elaborate machinery of rationalization she was constructing in her mind to justify her work with Vicenzu, sitting here faced with one of his victims.

She picked up her cup, drank, then cleared her throat. "Also, I don't think I care for the term 'witch.'"

Herbieto doffed his hat, offered as much of a bow as he could from his seated position, and said "I beg your pardon, lady. Maralla, is it not?"

"Yes," Maralla said, and from that one word I could hear she'd been mollified by the gesture and its evident sincerity. "And you have my pardon, Herbieto." She returned her attention to Tasso, double-checking her work, until he grunted and pulled away.

"I think you've plugged all the leaks, miss," Tasso said. "Thank you. But if you keep your hands on me much more, my old lady is going to get pissed off. Don't ask me how she'll know. She just will."

Bonfilia arrived with reinforcements. She actually took

the trouble of topping off everyone's cup, exerting herself conspicuously before Maralla and Herbieto. Giacomo's Wine Shop seldom sees clientele of their quality. Usually I'm the class of the place, which emphasizes the point, I suppose.

"A pity Marteo isn't here," I said. "We'd have a quorum for a meeting." I pinched the bridge of my nose, squinted my eyes shut. Neither of my commissions was going well. I did not appear to be earning my fees. It was time to reconsider. Why not take a new approach? With both Herbieto and Maralla here, why not combine the two jobs? They were already linked anyway, with Vicenzu the common factor.

I raised my head, looked at Herbieto and Maralla in turn. "Maralla, you have to realize by now that I was on the level. Vicenzu is going to betray you to Azeglio. He is as much a danger to you as Azeglio. Herbieto, you need to consider Maralla an ally. Your enemy is her enemy, whether she recognizes it or not. That has to be an advantage for us."

Herbieto nodded. "I suppose so. A woman of her...talents...could be invaluable. I don't know exactly how. I mean, obviously I don't know how to go about this revenge business, or I wouldn't be paying you, Cesar. You are still working for me, right?"

"Of course I am," I said. "I accepted your coin. You're my client."

"One of your clients," Maralla said, offering me a significant look.

"Yes," I said. I picked up my cup and drank, not taking the bait. She'd not fish out the identity of my other client.

"The point is, your situations are related. Disposing of Vicenzu cleans up Herbieto's commission. And it goes some way to alleviate Maralla's immediate problem, the rest of the problem being Azeglio and his Venatores."

Herbieto tilted his head, like a quizzical dog. References to Azeglio and the Venatores meant nothing to him. I felt no urgent need to educate him. Why scare the man off? He might prove useful.

"So, what I propose," I continued, deriving inspiration from Giacomo's tongue-flensing wine, "is to turn Vicenzu against Azeglio."

"Brilliant," Maralla said. "How?"

"Patience," I said. "Plenum wasn't built in a day. I just now came up with the idea. Give me a little time to work out the details."

"Vicenzu doesn't know I saw what he did to Tasso," Maralla said. "As far as he knows, I'm still his partner."

Herbieto shifted on his stool, clearly still uncomfortable with the notion of sharing wine with an ally of the man who'd caused the death of his father. But he said nothing.

"I'm not his partner, Herbieto," Maralla said. "Not any longer. Not after what I witnessed tonight. Cesar tried to warn me. I did not listen. I should have." She sipped her wine and winced, still not acclimated to Giacomo's bargain vintages. "I hope everyone is happy, because that is the last time I'm going to apologize."

"That's enough abasement for me," I said.

"The slate is wiped clean," Herbieto said.

"What do I care?" Tasso said, reaching for the pitcher.

"Good," Maralla said. "So, I can return home tonight. Tomorrow, Vicenzu will collect me as usual. Then I get to work on him."

"And what work would that be?" I asked.

"As you said, I need to turn Vicenzu against Azeglio. Obviously, I'll have to reveal that I'm aware the Questor General is on my trail. But I don't have to explain how I know, or that I know Vicenzu plans to hand me over. I'll say I overheard something in the marketplace, someone inquiring about me. I heard the name Azeglio and put it together. Something like that."

"Fine, so far as it goes," I said. "The little lies are easy. What about the big lie? What do you tell Vicenzu that would convince him to oppose Azeglio? I mean, that's practically taking on the Collegium."

"That's the problem, isn't it? Vicenzu isn't suicidal. He wouldn't actively tackle Azeglio. I doubt he's a coward, but he is a man who carefully weighs up the risks." Maralla swirled her wine about within the cup, staring into it meditatively.

"So, give him a risk to weigh," Herbieto said. "Make him afraid of *not* taking down, um, Azeglio."

I raised an eyebrow. I'd not expected such deviousness from the milliner. But he was right. "Exactly. You heard more than the name Azeglio when you were out shopping, Maralla. You saw the man himself, talking to one of his subordinates. Azeglio was telling the Venatore to find out where Vicenzu lives. You don't know why. 'Whatever could the Venatores want with you, Vicenzu?' But he knows, of course. He knows that once he gives you up to Azeglio, Azeglio can add a feather to his cap by capturing a grifter who was working with a witch."

"Vicenzu is too close to completing this job," Maralla

said, nodding. "He's not just going to run. He's got four hired swords. If he can get Azeglio alone, surprise him..."

"Hey, Maralla," Tasso said, "you'd know this: do demons like to drink?"

"No," Maralla said. "In general, they are not interested in food or wine. I hear war demons have a taste for human flesh, but other than that... Why do you ask?"

"I was wondering why that one over there is in a wine shop," Tasso said, pointing.

My eyes darted in the direction he indicated. There, beneath a nearby table, crouched a squat, splay-footed demon, much like an anthropomorphic frog, dressed in a livery of dark red and hunter green. Its bulbous, amber eyes glittered in the candlelight as it stared directly at us.

"Venatore colors," I said. "That's one of Azeglio's demons."

The demon stirred, uncertainly. It apparently realized it had been spotted, but its orders had not covered such an eventuality. I decided to take advantage of its indecision. I rose from my stool and slid my rapier free of its sheath. I could hear the patrons of Giacomo's react. Stools clattered to the floor as people got to their feet, the sensible drinkers heading for the door, the curious hoping for a better vantage.

I advanced a step. I clearly did not face a war demon. But they were all dangerous to some degree or other. A well-placed thrust might—or might not—penetrate its thick, moist hide. The eyes seemed the likely target. Perhaps a threat to its vision might drive it off, or at least prevent it from tearing out my throat.

"Wait, Cesar," Maralla said.

I spared her a glance. Maralla had also risen to her feet. She was slipping free an earring from an earlobe. I recognized the bauble as the twin of the one from which she'd hatched the demon that chucked me unceremoniously down a flight of stairs that morning.

I waited. I'd been subjected to enough buffeting, bludgeoning, and bloodletting over the last couple of days. Why not let someone else handle the rough stuff this time?

The Venatore demon shuffled further back beneath the table. It seemed nervous, if demons could feel nervousness. I waggled the tip of my rapier at it, to keep it honest and give Maralla a chance to deploy her own captive demon.

Maralla let fly a string of syllables that must have left her tongue tired. I recognized not a single word, though I felt I ought to. Something flashed by, then smashed against the floor, breaking into fragments. A mist coiled up from the wreckage, adding its own unpleasant odors to those native to Giacomo's. Then from the mist rose a demonic form.

If the demon beneath the table was a frog, this one was a wolf. It stood on two legs, crouching. Two claw-tipped arms dangled above the floor. The head—at the back of which perched two triangular ears—elongated into a fanged snout. I saw no tail. The lean, angular body did not bear a furry coat, but in the dim light of Giacomo's I thought I saw a uniform growth of short, dense hair, enough that I'd consider it a pelt.

"Remove that," Maralla said to her conjuration. I could only assume she was pointing at the spying frog demon. I wasn't going to look behind me to check, being too intensely focused on the pair of demonic antagonists in front of me.

The sound of clattering stools and tramping feet suggested that a second round of Giacomo's customers was making for the door. The curious had decided the scene was not quite so fascinating after all. I can't say I blamed them.

The wolf demon took a bent-legged stride forward. It advanced low to the floor, snout snuffling, as if its eyesight was a secondary sense. The frog demon backed away beneath the table. I wondered what sort of conflict it suffered. What had it been instructed to do? Would it just turn and run?

The table flipped through the air as the frog demon erupted into action, springing upwards from its powerful legs. Giacomo's tables are not fashionable, lightweight examples of the carpenter's art. They are massive, old, and heavy; not intended to be easily moved around. The table hit the low ceiling, interrupting the ballistic arc that would have terminated in the teeth—or fangs—of the wolf demon. Instead it hit the floor, bounced once, then clattered to a stop, top down, in front of the wolf demon. Maralla's demon snarled, then dove over the table, clawed hands extended. The frog demon emitted a burbling croak of challenge, then sprang to meet the attack. It was a trifle slow. As the two demons collided in mid-air, the wolf demon hurled the frog demon off to one side and back. They hit the floor and rolled in a tangle of limbs, splintering stools, toppling tables, and flying candles. Clay cups slopped wine before falling to smash on the floor.

Candles guttered and went out, increasing the gloom that lent Giacomo's what charm it could claim.

The action grew hard to follow. It was from the noise almost as much as from the direction of travel of the billow of clay shards and fragments of wood that I realized the fray was rolling our way.

"Move!" I said. "Get back." I held the rapier before me, then added the main gauche. Perhaps I could fend off the demons if they got too close. Most likely I'd simply be rolled over, crushed beneath bodies that outmassed mine by a factor of two or three to one. But in the doing, I might redirect them with the gentle encouragement of two lengths of steel—right before getting snapped into bony fragments, much like Giacomo's furnishings.

The party moved. Maralla and Herbieto helped Tasso shuffle toward the rear of the wine shop. I tried to keep track of the brawl as it passed in and out of the range of the illumination of the ever-decreasing light sources.

A lantern hanging from a beam began a crazy, gyring swing as something dislodged in the battle struck it. A weak, passing beam from its erratic career showed me a glimpse of the battle, not two paces from me. I watched the wolf demon's jaws clamping down on the frog demon's arm. The view vanished in the gloom, but I heard the crunch, followed by a low croaking noise that rose to a sustained whine. When the light next caught the demons, it showed me their heels, as the wolf demon pursued the frog demon out the front door.

"Is everybody in one piece?" I asked over my shoulder, keeping a watch on the door in case one or both of the demons doubled back.

"Same number of pieces I came in here with," Tasso said. "Not that that's saying much."

Herbieto found a candle on its side that hadn't gone out. We regrouped around our table, scavenging what wine cups we could. I wondered if this was the last drink I'd have at Giacomo's. His place was trashed. He might hold that against me.

"I'm not sure Azeglio completely trusts Vicenzu," I said. It's possible my tone could have conveyed more dry sarcasm, but it would have required several attempts.

"You don't say," Maralla said. "But I doubt this means the deal is off. Azeglio is probably hedging his bets, trying to keep his own eyes on me in case Vicenzu fails to hold up his end of the bargain."

"How much do you think the demon overheard?" Herbieto asked.

A good question.

"It was sent to spy," Maralla said. "The safest assumption, then, is that it overheard everything."

"Meaning it heard our plan," I said.

"Yes, we'll have to discard that one," Maralla said, "and come up with a new one."

"Well, we probably shouldn't do that here," I said. "For all we know, once Azeglio gets the report, he might come here and grab you, deal or no deal." I didn't mention that I also wouldn't mind getting out before Giacomo poked his head back in.

"Where should we go?" Herbieto asked.

I found the "we" interesting. He could head back home. Why was he attaching himself to our little group?

"Obviously we can't go to my rooms," Maralla said.

"I know just the place," I said.

Chapter 11

Domenico was not pleased to see us.

"Anacleto, shut the door and bar it," Domenico said.

I was standing on the top step of the short stairway leading to the door of the Maestro's home and salle. Anacleto had answered my knock, asked us to wait, and summoned Domenico. One look at the group trailing me—Maralla at my elbow, Herbieto behind, supporting Tasso whose bandages were soaking up blood from wounds that had reopened during the walk—and Domenico's perpetual scowl had dug even deeper furrows into his forehead.

"Maestro?" Anacleto asked, raising his brow. While doubtless an excellent manservant, Anacleto's slender frame did not suggest any likelihood of him manhandling four people off the stoop and shutting the door in their faces. Not even when one was pale from loss of blood, one owned a millinery shop and looked the part, and one was a woman.

"Uncle Cesar!"

Valentina slipped into view from behind Domenico, squirmed past Anacleto, and dropped into a curtsy. She must have been practicing, preparing to return the bow I'd offered her last time we met. Unsurprisingly, she looked charming doing it, even graceful at her awkward age. She lifted her head and grinned, her eyes sparkling beneath her curls.

"Valentina," I said, "I would return your salute, but your father does not wish to grant us entry."

Domenico's scowl deepened. I realized that I was imposing, but he had agreed to work with me. So, some of the work followed him home. Was that so awful? Yes, that work did take the form of a bloody thug and the woman he'd been paid to keep an eye on, but if it were easy, it wouldn't be work.

My justifications might require some minor adjustments before I offered them for independent consideration.

"Daddy," said Valentina, "let Uncle Cesar in. And look, there is a lady with him. You can't leave a lady standing outside. It isn't genteel. And that poor man is hurt. See?"

"Let them in, Anacleto," Domenico said. "I need to renegotiate my fee with Cesar." He turned on his heel and stalked away.

Valentina commenced a flood of prattle that wouldn't cease, as far as I could tell, until she fell asleep. Maralla joined in shortly after setting foot within the salle, and within minutes, she and Valentina appeared to have been friends since the dawn of creation.

Valentina took Maralla by the hand and conducted her on a tour of the premises. I helped Herbieto and Anacleto with Tasso, getting the big man comfortable on a pile of blankets in a corner of the salle, where he'd not leak on the floor. Tasso seemed to improve once stationary, a bit of color returning to his face. He took his ease, gazing at the big, open room with its hardwood floors and high ceilings.

"Cleared all the furniture away for dancing, did he?"

Tasso asked. "You've got rich friends, Cesar."

"It's not a dance floor, Tasso," I said. "This is where I practice getting the pointed end of my sword past the sword of the man trying to do the same thing to me."

"I always wanted to study fencing," Herbieto said. "I never had the time. Too occupied with the business."

"Well, you're not in the shop right now," I said. I strode over to the rack of blunt practice blades and selected a pair. "Come on, let's begin your training."

Herbieto looked skeptical.

"Go on," Tasso said to Herbieto. "He's only a trained swordsman for hire. You can take him."

Herbieto shrugged, walked out to meet me in the center of the floor. I handed him a foil and demonstrated the approved grip. He wasn't precisely a natural, but he took instruction without balking. Soon enough I was walking him through the standard parries. After the day I'd had, resorting to the basics of my field felt like taking refuge. It was comforting.

"Giving lessons in my salle, with my equipment, are you, Cesar?" Domenico leaned against the doorway, arms folded.

"I'd hardly call it a lesson," I said.

"No? It looks like a lesson. Are you thinking of calling yourself Maestro, Cesar? Frankly, I don't think you're skilled enough. You certainly don't have the aptitude for teaching. But if you want to take up the calling, I'll have to charge you a rental fee for the foils, not to mention for the use of the space."

Domenico was in a mood, no question. I handed my practice sword to Herbieto and walked toward Domenico.

"Maestro," I said, "I know I'm imposing. I'm sorry. I realize that you signed on to keep a watch on Maralla, not to have her over to your home. But matters have changed. Abruptly and severely."

"And that is an excuse to bring matters here? Where my daughter lives?" Domenico straightened. He unfolded his arms and took a half-step forward, confronting me.

In another man I might have found it amusing. Domenico isn't a small man. In fact, he is taller than I am. But I easily outmass him and could toss him around like a child. That is, I could, were he not nearly as skilled in unarmed combat as he was with a rapier. One of the lessons I suffer from Domenico involves throws and grappling, with or without a sword in hand. It is a useful skill; little surprises an opponent prepared to duel sword-to-sword as much as finding his sword arm caught in an armlock, or getting thrown over a hip, landing face first on the ground. In our practices, I'm usually the one taking the fall.

So, I took Domenico's displeasure with the respect it deserved.

"May I tell you what happened, Maestro?"

Domenico considered, then grunted what I took for assent. I laid out the course of recent events. If I had expected any sympathy at my description of the lumps and lacerations I'd endured, I'd have been disappointed. Domenico showed no reaction. Luckily, I knew the man, so I didn't bother elaborating on that aspect. I did play up Maralla's contrition and the essential aid she'd provided. I figured that compassion for a woman was the best card in my hand.

"And so," Domenico said, once I'd wrapped up my recitation, "after destroying your primary haunt, Giacomo's, you bring your pack of demon bait to your secondary haunt. My livelihood is here, in this place. My daughter lives here. In this place. You need to clear out." Domenico's frown eased for a moment. "You can leave the wounded man. Tasso, right? He's not fit to travel further tonight."

I don't know if my face fell. I hope not. Maintaining an insouciant front is an important component of my career. I know that internally my organs felt as if they all plummeted into my boots. What was I supposed to do now? The thought of bringing Maralla and Herbieto to my rat's nest was too painful to contemplate.

"Daddy, you can't throw them out," Valentina said.

I hadn't noticed her arrive, having apparently terminated her guided tour here in the salle proper. Maralla stood close to her, almost protectively. I understood the impulse; there's something endearing about Valentina's childish ebullience that triggers an instinctual, almost paternalistic vigilance.

"Yes, Valentina, I can. This is my house, and these are not invited guests." Domenico turned his frown on his daughter. I'm not too proud to acknowledge that I was glad for the temporary reprieve.

"Maralla is too pretty to send away. It is getting dark, Daddy. You can't send a lady out into the night."

"She has an escort. Cesar can look after her. Besides, from what I hear, Maralla is capable of fending for herself if it comes down to it."

That last did not sound as if it carried much conviction.

Domenico is certainly gruff, but he is a gentleman. Whether or not a lady could attend to her own safety was not a consideration that Domenico would normally entertain. That he'd mentioned it meant he was weakening, devising arguments on the fly.

"She can handle herself," I said. "In fact, she'd be pretty handy to have around in the event that—oh, say someone tracked her here, returned to some secret Collegium base to report, then came back with a troop of Venatores, not realizing she'd already been kicked out into the night."

Now I was devising arguments on the fly.

Domenico grunted.

"Daddy, she is nice." Valentina was at Domenico's side now, tugging at one of his hands. "If she is in trouble we have to help her."

I watched Domenico's face as he gazed down at Valentina. Valentina had no memories of her mother. I had few of her myself; I'd only begun my lessons with Domenico—a few sessions for him to suss out my skill level—when the Bloody Froth had taken Gelica, still weak from giving birth. With the exception of hiring a series of wet-nurses, employed early on, Domenico had raised Valentina himself. He was blameless, yet I guessed he felt a certain guilt, seeing his daughter starving for a mother substitute, in whatever form that took.

"It is all right, Valentina," Maralla said. "I will find someplace to stay the night."

"You and Herbieto can spend the night at my place." I almost looked around to see who had said that. It couldn't have been me. But it was.

"Oh, I can't allow that," Domenico said. "That would

be inhumane. Fine, you can all spend the night here. But tomorrow you are gone."

"But not until after breakfast," Valentina said, then squealed. "Maralla, you can sleep in my room."

"Great," Herbieto said. "We've solved one problem."

I took his point. What was the next move? Azeglio had Maralla's scent. Perhaps I could help her get out of Plenum. But would that meet my obligation to Fenetto? And what about Herbieto? With Maralla out of the picture, would Vicenzu pack up and run as well? I couldn't very well face the man in a duel if he left town.

I smacked the tip of the practice weapon irritably on the floor.

"Careful, Cesar," Domenico said. "Those cost money."

Herbieto handed his to Domenico as if suddenly worried he might drop it and see it shatter, abruptly conscious he was a guest in another man's house and playing with his property.

Domenico took the foil with a nod and abruptly I was at ease, all problems washed away. I smiled and Domenico allowed one corner of his mouth to twitch. A moment later, we'd taken our positions, saluted, and fallen to.

I was aware from time to time that Maralla and Herbieto were in conversation, though their attention was divided. Domenico and I put on quite a show. During breaks between touches I caught snatches of talk indicating that they were doing what I should have been — trying to figure out what to do. I was content to leave them to it, focusing all my concentration on the bout with Domenico. A moment of distraction was all Domenico needed. There was a reason I paid him for lessons and not the other way around.

I surpassed myself. With the abuse I'd suffered, I didn't think I stood a chance. But I managed a touch. Out of ten.

"Did I hire the right man?" Herbieto asked when I slumped, panting, against the wall beside him.

"Even if he'd do it, you couldn't afford him," I said. "So, what did you two come up with while I was enjoying a free lesson?"

"Oh, that one will be entered on your account," Domenico said from where he was replacing the foils in the rack halfway across the chamber.

Good ears.

"We came up with several ideas," Maralla said. "All of them bad. I was thinking of visiting Vicenzu and conjuring up something fatal, but—"

"You know where he lives?" I asked.

"Certainly. He has a modest villa in the Broscine district, where Lucan Narrows enters Wolf Court, the one with the—"

"—dog and bear fountain, yes. I didn't realize you knew where he lived, that's all.

"He doesn't know it, but yes, I do. I sent a monkey demon to follow him home shortly after we began working together. I trusted him; he seemed so genuine, so transparent. It was us against the rubes, and he made me feel so good to be one of us and not one of the rubes. But I wanted to be smart, and I persuaded myself that knowing where he lives was all the insurance a smart girl like me needed. I'm apparently not as smart as I thought. Vicenzu is a master at this game. I was stupid to think I could play at his level."

"He's had a lot of years to perfect his play," Herbieto said, patting Maralla on the shoulder.

I cleared my throat. "So, you discarded the notion of having a demon tear Vicenzu to shreds."

"Yes. I'd need to be near to conjure one. I'm not sure I've the aptitude to summon a war demon. But I can bring up something nasty enough to do the job. However, Vicenzu does have his bodyguards. If they didn't stop me before I finished the summoning, they are probably sufficient to deal with whatever I produced. And, even if I did succeed, Herbieto would be cheated of his vengeance."

Here Maralla patted Herbieto on the knee.

Lots of patting going on.

"There's also Azeglio to consider," I said. "But honestly, I don't want to do any further considering. Why don't we take shameless advantage of the Maestro's hospitality, empty his larder, drink his wine, then sleep on the problem?"

"Only water for you, Cesar," Domenico said. "You're getting too slow."

Chapter 12

Domenico's house was less spacious than it appeared because the cavernous salle occupied the lion's share of the building. Maralla slept in Valentina's room. Herbieto bunked with Anacleto. I found myself on a pile of blankets and old cloaks atop the hardwood floor of the salle where I'd spent countless hours sweating under

Domenico's exacting tutelage. It felt strange, this convergence of an unusual activity with a familiar place. Falling asleep took some doing. Tasso's snoring didn't help.

Come the morning, I woke stiff and sore. While trying to stretch the worst of it out, I came to the conclusion that I had to act. Trying to devise some plan of action with this bunch had led to nothing, and that didn't promise to improve with more talk.

I cleaned myself up as best I could, frowning at my rumpled clothing. Anacleto offered me a hunk of buttered bread and a mug of steaming tea as I returned to the salle from the closet in which Domenico kept a chamber pot for his students. I munched at the bread and sipped the tea—vile beverage—hoping the nourishment would provide me some inspiration. Doing something made sense, but I had to figure out what that thing should be.

Back in the salle, I saw Valentina holding a practice sword that looked absurdly oversized in her child's grip. She faced Maralla and Herbieto—who stood with their backs to me—and was reciting the litany of basics I'd heard Domenico run through for beginning students innumerable times. She had it down pretty good, too, though some of the words she'd clearly picked up phonetically without comprehending the meaning. Still, I was impressed.

Domenico appeared once the scrape and clack of blade on blade commenced.

"What do you two think you are doing?" he asked.

"I'm teaching them, Daddy," Valentina said, moving between Domenico and her sparring students. "Lesson one: face your fear."

Domenico sighed, ran his hand through his thinning hair. "Fine. That's an excellent start, Valentina. Let's get those feet adjusted to the proper stance, shall we?"

"I'll sit this one out, if you don't mind," Tasso said to no one in particular.

The big man sat against the wall, still partially encased in blankets. He looked better, his face holding more color. I handed him my still-mostly-full mug of tea, then slipped out while Domenico worked at setting Herbieto's feet at right angles.

The morning air carried a chill. Scattered, high clouds suggested a clear, unusually cold day. At least I wasn't getting rained on.

My room waited for me not far from Domenico's salle. A short distance in space, an epic trek in quality. Most of the buildings in my immediate neighborhood appeared ready to topple over if you spoke harshly to them. They'd probably looked about the same a century back. Overdue for replacement, if you asked me. But the sheer number of floors, and the amount of individual accommodations the tenement owners could cram into those floors, meant it was easier to keep renting out rooms cheaply than to undertake the expense and effort of tearing the structures down and constructing more spacious, luxurious, and — presumably — profitable habitations.

It worked to my benefit, I suppose. I couldn't afford anything more spacious and luxurious. I still hated it though. My hatred renewed as I felt wood creak ominously beneath my feet as I climbed the stairs to my door. The door itself bowed in. It hadn't been hung properly to begin with and time had not improved its fit. I wiggled the key into what laughably passed for a lock, then put my shoulder against the door panel and shoved. The door gave way with its usual reluctance and welcomed me to the splendor of my abode.

Frankly, sleeping on the floor of the salle hadn't been much of a step down from the level of comfort to which I was accustomed. I checked for a fresh shirt, not needing to open the armoire, since it possessed only one remaining door. I decided what I wore would have to do. This job was death on clothing. The only one it seemed who'd profit from my labors would be Donatello.

At least I could don fresh socks. I sat on the floor and tugged off my boots. While I was down at floor level, I worked free the loose floorboard. Setting that aside, I reached into the space and pulled out a bag of oiled canvas. The bag bore evidence that the rats had been at it. But the little bastards still hadn't got through yet. Good.

After swapping old socks for new and thrusting my feet back within my boots, I opened the bag and removed what I referred to as my armor. That, of course, is an exaggeration. Atop a padded, quilted jack was layered a leather jerkin, with double thickness of leather in some spots and hardened, boiled leather in others. Not much use against a good, solid thrust, nor against an arquebus ball. But it could absorb the worst of a knife cut or blunt some of the force of a truncheon blow.

More important were the bits of metal—that had once imprisoned a demon—that I'd tucked into pockets sewn into the leather, the pockets positioned so that when I donned the armor the hammered-out metal would cover my throat as well as some of my favorite organs. Getting a large fragment of the dull-hued metal tapped out into a collar shape had been the hardest part. The result did not please the eye, which fact perhaps explained why I seldom wore it. But given the number of demons I'd encountered working the Herbieto and Fenetto jobs, I figured the time had come to prioritize safety over fashion sense.

I slipped the garment over my head and worked my arms into the sleeves. I tightened a couple of leather thongs, buckled a flap that folded up between my legs, then shifted and wriggled until everything settled into the least uncomfortable position. Draping my cloak in an artful fashion offered some concealment. I didn't want to appear openly prepared for battle, nor did I particularly care for the figure I cut in the lumpy, slapdash armor.

Nothing else in the room required my attention. So, happy to quit the place, I left, pulling the door shut behind me with a grating squeal of wood on wood. I set foot on the landing and looked down the stairway into the gaunt, upturned face of Ludivenco, the man from whom I rented my palace of decadent delights.

Ludivenco was a marionette of a man, all long, gangly limbs and fleshless, hawk-nosed face. He dressed no better than his typical tenant, wearing clothes I would have assigned to the ragpickers even at the lowest ebb of my purse.

"Cesar, you're two weeks overdue," Ludivenco said without greeting or preamble.

"Good morning to you, Ludivenco," I said. "Pleasant to get a glimpse of sun, is it not?"

"If it could reflect off the coin you give me, then yes,"

Ludivenco said.

I cordially detest Ludivenco. He makes the barest pretense of maintaining this place. He deigns on rare occasions to replace the odd brick, or perform a spot of half-assed tuckpointing. He does it himself, not spending a soldo on skilled workmen. Ludivenco is not, in any sense, a skilled workman. His skills, so far as I can ascertain, are limited to owning the building (which isn't a skill) and asking for money (which seems more an exercise in persistence than talent or expertise).

Some of the other tenants entertain the notion that Ludivenco is a wealthy miser. He could turn this place into a glamorous residence fit for the Sabatine district. But he prefers to horde every half-soldi. The clothes, these tenants insist, are simply emblematic of the miser.

I'm not so sure. My neighbors and fellow tenants are the wine-sodden and half-mad. Whores beyond their best years of productivity. Crippled soldiers. Artists who failed to reach their dreamed-of potential, earning wine money from painting frescoes that are a bare half-step above the product of children scribbling on the walls. Unemployed porters, charwomen, thieves, and beggars. It seemed to me that the rumors promulgated by crapulous pensioners and clapped-out drabs might be suspect.

More likely, Ludivenco was stuck with a building that he couldn't sell and that no one who could afford better wanted to live in. So he got what he could from those of us desperate enough to live here. And that was so little that his circumstances were probably little elevated above ours. The rent we paid simply didn't cover the expenses of repairs and improvements.

So, I had some sympathy for the man. That didn't mean I liked him.

"How much, bloodsucker?" I asked.

"Two pistras, five soldi," he answered immediately.

I untied the flap of my purse, turning side-on to Ludivenco while I did so. I fished out a single pistra and five soldi. I had enough to get current, even ahead. But frugality was a habit when it came to paying rent. And I wasn't certain how long I'd be in funds. The coin I'd received from Herbieto and Fenetto vanished like water in a salt flat.

"Here," I said, displaying the coin. "I'll try to get you the rest soon."

"That's a pistra shy, Cesar," Ludivenco said. "There are other people who could use your room. People who could pay rent on time."

I took a step downstairs, then another. Ludivenco's nose lowered, the tip dropping to track my progress toward him. There was little room for two. As I closed the distance, Ludivenco edged aside, pushing up against the wall side of the stairway.

"You'll get the rest," I said, brushing by him. The coins transferred from my hand to his. He made no further objection.

My desire to move out redoubled. Living like this had grown intolerable. But if I couldn't earn the final payment for the current jobs, especially the Fenetto job, where could I go?

My bitter mood lasted for about half the hike to Vicenzu's. A bravo either doesn't care about the future or he's optimistic. The despondent, the pessimistic, the fearful, and the doom-sayers all find other fields to work. Facing another man's blade, when he's got his heart set on seeing your life-blood, requires a positive attitude, a certainty of success. I'd figure this out. I'd collect the money.

Somehow.

The walk to the Broscine district took me through the Courts of the Ancients. The toppled, weed-grown majesty of the sprawling ruins still held the power to stir wonder in me, despite a lifetime spent in its vicinity. What must it have looked like in its glory, when all these buildings and columns stood whole and clean; when the vast paving stones lay unbroken and flat instead of fragmented and jutting at angles like a particularly bad set of teeth? (Those pavers that remained, that is. Most had vanished into construction projects long since.) What sort of men built this place? They must have been just like us, I supposed, but it was hard to believe.

I may have been alone in my musings. Despite the lack of paved streets, the Courts remained a convenient crossing of ways, and, as was typically the case, was crowded with Plenumites passing from one district to another. None of these people, occupied with their own affairs, appeared to be cognizant of the weight of ages the Courts of the Ancients exemplified.

Leaving the decayed glory behind, I continued on to the south east for another mile, then up the gentle slope of the Broscine Hill. It rose in easy rolls and terraces upon which sat detached houses and villas. The Broscine district was, for some reason, less desirable real estate for the well-heeled than the Sabatine. It looked nice enough to me.

Perhaps it was too far from the fashionable shops and bistros, too far from the Collegium, the true power center of Plenum. I don't know.

I found Lucan Narrows, in one of the older, more densely packed sections of the Broscine district where a modestly prosperous neighborhood of shop owners, artisans, and professionals lived and worked in three and four-story buildings set cheek-by-jowl. I followed the constricted, winding course of Lucan Narrows through the canyon of brick and brown stone walls to Wolf Court.

In the center of the shadowed, roughly hexagonal court a fountain burbled. A knee-high wall of gray stone encircled a sculpture depicting a rampant bear, brought to bay by a leaping, snarling hound. A decorative bit of vine work drooped over the bear's shoulder, and from the mouths of flowers blooming from the tips of the vines poured a continuous trickle of water. Apparently, this bit of statuary references some myth of the Ancients. I was never certain what, precisely, and didn't care enough to ask. Wolf Court is a nice place to visit during the worst of Plenum's summers, as it stays mostly cool and shaded except at high noon. That's good enough for me. I don't need to know what beastly crime the bear committed to so enrage the dog.

Off to my right, immediately before Lucan Narrows entered the pocket-sized plaza of Wolf Court, a break opened in the canyon wall of buildings. A gated-off pathway led to the door of a villa set at least a dozen paces back from the street. Through the wrought iron bars of the gate I could see rows of cypress trees lining the sides of the pathway. The treetops curved toward their opposites, the tips almost meeting to create a natural (though, doubtless artificially induced) archway shading the graveled path.

At first glance, a stealthy approach looked unfeasible. The gravel would crunch beneath my feet. One or more of Vicenzu's bodyguards could be stationed between a pair of trees, the narrow, columnar bodies just wide enough to offer concealment. Surely at least one of those human guard dogs was on duty, watching the gate from somewhere.

Perhaps I could find a way through the back. Climb a wall, clamber over the roof, drop down within the peristyle. I'd pulled off similar entries before. But I reminded myself that I wasn't here to infiltrate and kill anyone. I was here to talk. Alerting the bodyguards to my presence was fine, so long as they didn't beat me and toss me out on my ear. I had to gain an audience with Vicenzu.

The man should be home. Without Maralla, he must necessarily place his Hearth Demon scam on hiatus. Of course, he might be out looking for Maralla. I doubted it, though. Vicenzu struck me as the type more likely to have paid someone else to do the looking. He'd be at home, waiting. Scheming.

I drew a deep breath, held it, then let it slowly out. Enough standing around. I strode to the gate. There I made an ostentatious display of lifting the baldric from my shoulder. I hung it from one of the iron bars of the gate, the scabbarded rapier swinging freely, rapping against the bars, before hanging still. I worked loose the leather thong tying the sheath of my main gauche to my belt. Then I hung the dagger by the rapier, being sure to allow the wide guard to clatter against the bars.

A few people passing in or out of Lucan Narrows eyed me. I ignored them, though I did hope that my weapons would still be where they hung when I returned.

I waited a moment. A rustle of cypress branches revealed a hidden guard post. One of Vicenzu's men emerged. He strode down the path, gravel grating and shifting beneath his bootheels. As he emerged from the shadows, I recognized him as the broken-nosed, salt-and-pepper haired bodyguard who'd gotten in the first blow when Vicenzu had sicced the dogs on me. He recognized me as well.

"You," he said.

"Seen through my cunning disguise, have you?" I asked. "I'd like a word with Vicenzu. Is he available?"

"Not to you, he ain't," Bent Nose said. He eyed me, taking in the armor the cloak couldn't conceal. "Move on, or you'll get more of what you got last time."

I raised an eyebrow. I looked around, craning my neck.

"What? Just you?" I asked. I shouldn't have. I needed to see Vicenzu. Politeness might accomplish that. My usual bravado was unlikely to. The words slipped out before I could stop them.

Bent Nose swallowed, his Adam's apple bobbing. He cleared his throat. I saw his hands clench into fists. He too was laboring for control. He was, after all, expected to maintain a certain standard of professionalism. He couldn't leave his post to brawl in the streets simply because someone challenged his manhood.

"The stars must have aligned for you today," Bent Nose said. "I'm on duty. So you won't be swallowing your own teeth courtesy of Garon." He jabbed his thumb at his chest, apparently punctuating the fact that he was, in fact, that formidable character, Garon.

"We'll have to content ourselves with might-have-beens," I said.

Garon spat. "What do you want to see Master Vicenzu about?"

"Tell him Maralla would like a word."

"She with you?" Garon looked past me, his eyes shifting to see if Maralla was loitering somewhere behind me on Lucan Narrows.

I raised an eyebrow, gave him a moment to figure it out himself.

"Wait here," Garon said.

He turned and trudged up the path. As bidden, I waited, once again considering the approach I'd make to Vicenzu, what tone to adopt. And wondering if I'd get out of the villa alive.

Garon returned, with one his colleagues at his heels. He unlatched the gate.

"Go with Felpe," Garon said. "He'll take you to see Master Vicenzu."

"Keep an eye on my blades," I said. I unhooked them from where they hung on the gate and handed them to Garon. "Unsavory lot here in the Broscine. Can't be too cautious."

Garon took them, looked at them disdainfully, then let them drop onto the gravel path. Good enough. At least they'd be behind the gate.

Felpe looked like a farmhand, uncomfortable dressed in his city getup. He had a habit of raising one calloused, slablike hand, hooking a thumb in the collar of his doublet and hitching it up while shifting his thick neck. He managed that three times from the moment he spent eyeing me like a lump of horse dung he'd stepped in up to the moment we reached the front door of the villa. I knew he wasn't some hick straight from the fields. I'd observed him at work enough to respect his craft. I might run my mouth and belittle Vicenzu's bodyguards. It was expected of a bravo. But I wouldn't underestimate any of them.

The weathered grain of the ancient front door panel bore an oiled gloss. It might be old, but it was well maintained. That held true for the rest of the villa, at least as much of it as I saw. The place must have sat here for centuries, maybe longer in some earlier incarnation. Thick stone walls carried frescoes, both time-faded and more recent, displaying changing artistic tastes and styles. Lamps lit the passages. No windows pierced the exterior walls. I saw little furniture as Felpe led me past open doorways. The few pieces I saw looked expensive. Old, but solid.

The confidence game trade paid well, it seemed. Though I had a suspicion that Vicenzu wasn't the owner of the villa, merely a renter for the duration of his current gambit. He didn't strike me as the sort who'd keep a fixed abode, some definite location to which prior victims could track him.

Felpe came to a stop at an inner room. Light came from a mullioned window that gave a view of the atrium about which the villa was built. At a glance it appeared as if the gardening had been allowed to slip, plants beginning to run riot over the benches, decorative pergolas, and statues that adorned the atrium. I was more interested in the room itself, since it held Vicenzu.

He sat behind a desk, his feet—in calf-skin ankle boots—up on its surface in a relaxed, casual manner that I didn't buy for a moment. Vicenzu held a parchment in one hand and appeared to be absorbed in it. My reading lessons with Domenico had proceeded at least to the stage that I could tell Vicenzu was holding the document upside down.

Vicenzu wore the same outfit I'd first seen him in. That hat with the ostrich feather rested atop the desk. His red hair looked in need of a trim. I caught sight of a few strands of gray, as well as a small oval at the crown absent any strands at all. Vicenzu presented the picture of a worried man trying desperately to look at ease. He gave it a commendable effort, however.

"Ahh, Cesar the Builder," he said, looking up from his parchment after he'd given me enough time to notice how relaxed he was and how unimportant I was. "Or, whoever you are. What can I do for you, other than selling you a house? Please, make it quick, or I'll ask Felpe to gently escort you off the premises."

"You wished to send a message that Maralla was yours and not to be watched," I said. "Message received."

"That was you? I'm not sure what your game is, Cesar," Vicenzu said. He swung his legs down from the desk and rose. He placed his palms on the table and leaned forward. Even leaning he still looked down on me. "However, if you've got the message, you can take your game elsewhere and get out of mine. I'm willing to let the matter drop."

"Well, the problem is, Vicenzu, that Maralla also

received the message. And it concerned her."

Vicenzu straightened. His eyes narrowed. "You know where Maralla is?" he asked, snapping out the question. Then he cleared his throat, clearly afraid he'd revealed something to me.

He concealed it well. To succeed at his chosen career, he'd have to be an accomplished dissembler. But he was frightened. It wasn't hard to guess why. Vicenzu had made a deal with Azeglio. If he couldn't produce Maralla, he'd violate the agreement. Azeglio would not be pleased. The Questor General was not a man you wanted upset with you.

"I don't know where she is at the moment," I said. "But I can reach her. She'll want to hear from me, to get your response to her offer."

"Oh?" Vicenzu sat down again, though he left his feet on the floor this time. "She has an offer, does she?"

"Of course she has an offer. Use that gifted imagination of yours. Maralla knows you can't unload the rest of those properties without her to sell the Hearth Demon scam. Not unless you want to take a loss."

I looked around for a chair, found a small, low-backed settee, and dragged it near Vicenzu, the feet screeching over the stone floor before coming to a stop at the carpet atop which rested the desk. I sat and leaned forward, palms on my knees.

"Just between us, Vicenzu," I asked in a quiet, conspiratorial tone, "are you working from your own seed money, or did you take out a loan?"

The question struck home. For a moment his mask broke. He snarled at me. "That is none of your business,

Cesar." He mastered himself with admirable speed. "We are talking about Maralla. What is it she wants?"

Sitting and conversing with this man I intended to kill was an odd sensation. The relative civility of it was sheer artifice. And to add a further layer of dissociation, the very conversation was invention, a structure of lies I was building as I went along. It seemed so pointless. Why not get straight to the killing? I imagined it felt less strange to Vicenzu. He was used to duplicity, to sitting across a desk from a man he intended to bilk out of every last pistra and lying to his face, unconcerned with the consequences to his victim. I'm sure he was thinking how badly he'd like to set his dogs on me, see how many broken bones I would suffer before giving up Maralla's hiding place. But he had to assume I was telling the truth, that I didn't know where she was. The risk of her fleeing Plenum, leaving Vicenzu at the mercy of his creditors and, worse, Azeglio, was too great.

"Maralla is invested in this as well," I said, continuing to construct my house of lies and half-truths. "She doesn't want to walk away from the game if she doesn't have to. But the manner in which your boys handled the man I had observing the place...well, it made her uneasy. If she is to return, help you finish up, she has conditions. She wants certain assurances. Face it, Vicenzu, you scared your partner. Not a smart move."

Vicenzu drummed his fingers on the desk. He appeared to take no notice of my shot at his intelligence. "What sort of conditions?" he asked after a long moment. "What assurances?"

"There, I'm afraid, I can't help you," I said. "I was

merely to bring you the message and say that if you're willing to discuss it, she'll be willing to meet with you and lay out her terms. I'm to relay your answer. Not to her directly, but to a cut-out. Following me or trying to twist my arm until I reveal her location will just be an irritation to both of us."

"Did she at least tell you the place she wants to meet?" Vicenzu asked. The impatience showed beneath his calm demeanor, the control beginning to slip again.

I thought quickly. To buy myself a moment I said, "Yes, she told me the place she wants to meet. Certainly you realize how intelligent the woman is. After all, you selected her for your little confidence game." I layered enough scorn into my tone to rankle; get Vicenzu annoyed enough with me and he might fail to notice that I did not immediately provide an answer.

The moment was enough. While Vicenzu worked up a combined sneer and frown, I hatched an idea.

"Maralla said to meet her at Kertzel's." The idea made sense if Vicenzu thought of it from Maralla's notional perspective. It was a public place. One Vicenzu frequented. He was known there. He was unlikely to make a scene. And it would appeal to him since it was close. It was familiar; he'd feel he was on home ground.

I imagined I could see all these thoughts tumbling through his mind. He took on a distant look, then nodded. If he had a chance of getting Maralla back in the fold, he had to take it. And, perhaps even more urgently, he must take any opportunity to regain enough influence or control over the witch to be able to transfer her into Azeglio's clutches.

"Kertzel's," Vicenzu said. "This afternoon. The fourth hour." Vicenzu got to his feet. He poked a finger at me, leaning far across the desk to do so. I could see the bare patch of skin that interrupted the otherwise full coverage of his red locks catching the light from the window behind him. He tried to bore holes in my forehead with his eyes. The intimidating glare, my old friend. "But before you run off to deliver the message, errand boy, you need to hear this. You have been a source of irritation to me. I will endure it so long as I need to in order to achieve my goals. Once that time has passed, you will no longer enjoy my forbearance."

"Is that supposed to be a threat?" I asked. I stared fixedly at the bald patch.

"Yes. In deadly earnest." His gaze wavered, broke. He snatched up the ostrich plume hat from the desk and crammed it on his head.

"Good," I said. I stood up. Only a few feet of desktop separated us. I could lunge across it, slam his head against the surface, maybe cave in his skull before his guards could intervene. Maybe. But that wasn't the job. "I hope you keep your sword sharp," I said. "I'd hate to be killed by a blunt blade."

I started to leave, then turned back for the parting shot. "Come alone, Vicenzu. If Maralla sees you've brought your pack of hounds to Kertzel's, she's gone."

Chapter 13

I retrieved my blades from Garon, who appeared disinclined to return them. I smiled at him, showing as many teeth as I could, and told him this sounded like fine sport to me. Watching the gate at Vicenzu's villa was a one-man job, and perhaps Garon realized that. He lacked the support of the other three guard dogs. He returned my sword and main gauche, though with ill grace.

The fountain in Wolf Court gurgled behind me as I strolled down Lucan Narrows, reviewing my interview with Vicenzu. I thought I'd done all right. If I could set the stage properly, I figured I could fulfill the Herbieto commission by this evening. And that should at least remove one of the stumbling blocks hindering my fulfillment of the Fenetto commission.

Perhaps if I'd postponed my introspection and planning, I'd have been alert enough to notice my old friend, the Venatore sergeant Scar-beard. I suppose I should have guessed Azeglio would be keeping an eye on Vicenzu. Once Azeglio's spy demon had reported the meeting preceding the affray at Giacomo's, the Questor General would have grown even more concerned with Vicenzu's ability to uphold his end of the bargain. Stationing one of his men to observe Vicenzu was the obvious move.

So obvious I should have expected it. And I shouldn't have been wool-gathering as I wandered down the street.

"The Questor General would like a word with you," came that instantly recognizable voice from behind me.

I whirled, hands already in place to whip free my rapier. There in the middle of the street stood Scar-beard. He must have seen me walk past, then emerged from his vantage point. My guess was the barber's shop. An awning protected a couple of chairs from the worst of the elements, and a selection of razors, scissors, mirrors, and combs sat atop barrels or hung from the front of the storefront before which the barber had established his trade. The chairs offered a decent, if partially obscured, view of Vicenzu's gate. A healthy bribe to the barber could settle an observer in a chair indefinitely.

"Oh, it's you," I said, pretending to relax. I straightened, shifted my head as if working a kink out of my neck while looking around to see if Scar-beard was alone. I saw no one else in the blood red and dark green of the Venatores.

"Yes. Me," he said. His left hand gripped the rapier hanging from his baldric, his right on the hilt, mirroring my position. "My name is Bracceton. Before I joined the Venatores, I held a post as master of the hunt for a Prefect to the north of Plenum; doesn't matter who. Do you see this scar on my chin? A wild boar gave that to me. Escaped the dogs, disappointed the Prefect. I spent the next two days hunting that boar, alone. I killed it with a skinning knife. I don't like to let quarry slip away. Do you think I'd let a city boar like yourself escape Bracceton the Huntsman?"

The man had probably been rehearsing that speech from the moment he saw me enter Vicenzu's gate. He even managed to growl the last few words in what he must have thought a menacing fashion.

"That is a great story," I said. "I bet all the tavern whores love it."

Lucan Narrows emptied itself. Heads peered from

doorways or peeked from windows. But the pedestrians had yielded the cobblestones to Bracceton and me. There were no chance passersby to inadvertently jog our elbows or get in the way as both of us, with neatly timed—if accidental—synchronization swept swords from sheathes.

I assumed a fencer's stance without conscious thought, directing the tip of the rapier in a series of small circles to loosen up my wrist. I rocked back and forth, stretching the inner thighs. Bracceton shifted only slightly, his left leg moving back a mere few degrees. His stance kept his body facing me almost a full three-quarters. He kept his left hand before him, raised high. I noted the thick, iron reinforced gauntlet on that hand. Bracceton would use it to slap aside or grab my blade. With his own blade he wouldn't bother with the standard fare of parry and riposte; it would serve only to attack.

I shuffled back a couple of steps, drew my main gauche. I repositioned myself, somewhat approximating Bracceton's stance.

We'd apparently dispensed with conversation. No more posing, no more quips.

Bracceton began circling. Lucan Narrows wasn't the ideal location for circling. We all have our habits, however, and Bracceton's was, apparently, circling. I pivoted in place to match him. Once he'd brought himself within a step or so of the side of a building, I skipped forward and dropped into a deep lunge. It caught Bracceton by surprise, if not off guard. His gauntleted hand slapped at the driving steel as he simultaneously tried to hop back, out of range. He managed to push my blade off line, but hopping back failed to work out so well. He collided with the building behind him, ass first. The impact unbalanced him. Bracceton got one foot down all right, but the other slipped on a slick cobble and the bootheel caught against the wall of the building. The result threatened to drop him on his side, but he got his left hand down in time, leaving him in an off-balance crouch.

Instead of recovering to first position from my lunge, I shoved off of my back foot into a sort of deep stutter-step that brought me angling past Bracceton on my left as he fought to regain his footing. I flicked out with the main gauche as I went by and felt the parrying dagger catch flesh then slide free. I continued on a couple of paces, out of range of anything unexpected and unseen, straightening up with each step. Then I spun about.

Bracceton was on his feet again. A reddish stain was spreading through his beard where I'd slashed him. I'd not exactly matched the wound the wild boar had given Bracceton, but it wasn't a bad effort, considering I hadn't been able to see what I'd been cutting.

Bracceton spat a red-tinged froth. He snarled, resumed his stance. "You've drawn blood. My turn."

Snarling and spitting. Good; I'd made him angry. Fencing isn't a contest that favors the angry. If you can calculate and plan a few moves ahead you hold the advantage; if, that is, you can do so while engaging in nigh continuous, reflexive physical action, knowing that the cost of any error can be your life.

I spared a glance at my surroundings, checking the footing, watching for any rain puddles or other indications of ankle-catching gaps or slippery spots. The audience remained indoors, presumably riveted on the spectacle. I liked to think so anyway. A breeze carried the scents of Lucan Narrows swirling by me, the smells of people living in close proximity to each other, but without the worst of the effluvient reek I was accustomed to in the Orine district. I caught a whiff of fresh blood, as well as a breath of chill air, a reminder of the day's promised cold. I'd want to get inside soon if I worked up much of a sweat. But at the moment it felt good.

I smiled at Bracceton. Laughed.

He came at me. Droplets from his slashed cheek had splattered his teeth, lending his snarl a particularly ferocious aspect. He may have been angry, and was certainly over aggressive, but he retained a cunning in his attack. His initial, threatened attack was a cut at my head. I figured it for a feint and didn't commit to the parry, though I did raise my left elbow a trifle, prepared to bring up the main gauche to interpose in case I'd figured wrong.

I'd guessed correctly; Bracceton let his arm drop, turning the threatened cut into a low-line lunge. I parried octave, then riposted, extending the point to catch him in the throat. He'd closed the distance and wasn't slowing, threatening a corps-a-corps, so I had little to do but straighten my elbow. Bracceton interposed his gauntlet at the last moment. My blade bowed, dangerously. I shifted to my right, letting him lumber by, and easing the stress on the steel of my rapier. I lashed out again with the main gauche. If he continued to pass within range, I'd continue to cut him. I felt the edge part the cloth of his doublet and scrape along a rib. Bracceton emitted a noise that sounded as much yelp as grunt.

Again we turned and faced each other. I eyed the length

of my rapier, reassuring myself the steel hadn't flexed beyond its tolerance. It showed straight and true. Bracceton glanced down at his ribs, assessing the damage. This time I took the initiative, employing a cross over step to rapidly close the distance and thrust at the center of his chest. He parried with his sword, keeping his left arm clamped against his ribcage. Perhaps he was uncertain how badly he'd been hurt. The parry was competent, but no more. He did not riposte. I kept his blade engaged, flicking feints at his face and upper thighs.

The walls lining Lucan Narrows contained and amplified the sound of steel scraping on steel, the stamp of boot heels, and the grunts of pain and effort emitted by Bracceton as he labored to deflect strikes, real or merely threatened. His breathing grew heavier, chest heaving, and I watched his eyes widen at the burgeoning realization that this time the boar was going to win.

Time to finish it. I wasn't a cat and Bracceton wasn't a mouse. Besides, after the last couple of days, I wasn't in peak physical shape either; too bruised and battered.

I considered the closing gambit: a hard beat, a feint to the leg, bind the attempted parry with my main gauche while stepping in with a thrust to the heart. Should work if he didn't interpose that gauntlet. Anticipation rose within me, a swelling excitement that derived not from the thought of killing but from the thought of victory. It was the same feeling I experienced on those occasions that I knew I was about to best Domenico in the salle, or that I was only a move away from clearing the draughts board, idling away time playing at Giacomo's.

I rapped hard at Bracceton's blade with my own, the

two lengths of steel clacking loud but flat, like a clapper not ringing true within a bell. I supinated my wrist, commencing the feint—and checked the move when a voice barked from the direction of Wolf Court.

"Take that man. Alive, if possible."

I leapt back out of range of Bracceton's sword before turning my head to look. Even as I moved, I knew. Bracceton would survive. I'd been too slow. Disappointment swept through me, flushing away the glow of impending victory.

Neck craned far enough, I saw only what I expected: Questor General Azeglio and the remainder of his Venatores filling the constrained width of Lucan Narrows. And, up the side of a building, as if it had been built with projecting ledges at regular, convenient heights, scampered the frog demon I'd seen the day before—or one similar enough to be its twin. Perhaps Azeglio had assigned the demon to run messages from whoever was tasked to watch Vicenzu's house. If so—good plan.

I took to my heels.

Chapter 14

I was getting tired of running from the Venatores. What did they want with me now, anyway? Azeglio had—or, at least, thought he had—Vicenzu in his pocket. Even if he believed the claim I'd shouted about having Maralla secreted away, he had Vicenzu to work that problem. And I doubted he believed me, even if he recalled my statement.

Of course, I had killed a couple of his men. That would probably suffice for motivation.

There was never truly a good day for fleeing, but since I had to, today was about the best I could ask for, clear and cool. Though as I began sucking in deep lungfuls, I realized the day might be a trifle too cool, the chilly gulps of air paradoxically feeling as if they were burning my lungs.

Five Venatores came after me. A glance showed that, happily, they were not gaining ground, hampered as they were by halberds and breastplates. I did not have nearly that much weight to carry. Still, I had just fought a duel.

That thought reminded me to slow enough to sheath my blades. A man charging through the streets, weapons swinging in each hand—and one of those weapons bloody—tended to disturb the populace. That sort of thing made people likely to aid the body of uniformly attired men following in pursuit, the presumed representatives of justice and order. Which I suppose the Venatores were at that.

I did not want a repeat of the last time the Venatores had hunted me. That encounter had been too narrow an escape for my liking. I decided to change tactics. Instead of finding an isolated spot to hide from the pursuit, I'd lose it in a crowd. Simpler to do, now that I appeared more like a part of the crowd, my blades sheathed.

The ache in my lungs did not abate, and I began to develop a stitch in my side as I led the Venatores through turn after turn, splashing through the filth of cramped alleys and pelting down broader, cobbled streets. At each turn I demanded an additional burst of speed, trying to extend my lead.

At last, breaths coming in regular, heaving gasps, like waves pounding against a sea wall, I emerged from a paved way onto the dirt footpaths that crisscrossed the Court of the Ancients. Hundreds of people threaded along the beaten ways among toppled, weed-grown columns, and the stunted remains of once-great basilicas and palaces. I plunged into the crowd, then slowed to a walk, fighting to bring my breathing down to the more relaxed condition of the pedestrians surrounding me. I shifted from pathway to pathway at random, avoiding the temptation to look about for the Venatores. I was just another Plenumite, jostling along with the rest, taking a shortcut from the Sabatine Hill to the Vimine district, or trying to get from the Broscine to the Jacline without having to pass through the squalor of the Orine district. Nothing special to see here, merely another drop of water in the fountain.

It worked. I caught not a glimpse of the red and green livery, not a glimmer from the spiky tip of a halberd. I turned aside on a rising footpath that deposited me at the mouth of a paved way, and kept going. I took another couple of turns before pausing to get my bearings. That actually required a minute or two of casting about for familiar landmarks. But once I knew where I was, I headed for Domenico's.

At least Valentina was glad to see me.

"Where did you run off to?" Domenico asked. "You think I'm running a boarding house here? Someplace for you to stash your guests?"

"We need to coordinate, Cesar," Maralla said. "I cannot

form a plan without all of us here to contribute."

"I admit I'm happy to see you return," Herbieto said.

That was nice. But then he continued. "I thought you'd given up, left town while you still could."

I shook my head. "Faithless, the lot of you. Has Cesar the Bravo ever let anyone down, or left a friend in the lurch?"

"Would you like me to answer that?" Domenico asked. "Or was that purely rhetorical?"

"The point is," I said, "I've been hard at work—at the risk of my life, I might add—on setting up a final resolution with Vicenzu."

We were in the salle. Both Maralla and Herbieto were damp at the temples and holding practice foils. They hadn't been wasting time while I was out. I hoped Domenico would find a way to charge them for the lessons. Maybe he'd enroll them as pupils. A woman under Domenico's tutelage was uncommon, but it wasn't unheard of for an eccentric daughter of a wealthy house to take an active, sporting interest in the art of fencing.

I slumped down on a bench, weary legs extended.

"The risk of your life?" Valentina asked, coming over to sit beside me. "Are you hurt?"

"I am not, Valentina. Thank you for asking." I cast a look around at the rest—exempting Tasso, who was snoring steadily upon a pile of blankets in a corner—letting them know what I thought of their lack of concern. A wasted look, I'm afraid to say. "A certain sergeant of the Venatores by the name of Bracceton cannot say the same."

"Had a busy morning, have you?" Domenico asked. There was a touch of interest behind the bland, almost sarcastic tone of voice. There was also another note, annoyance, or perhaps disappointment. As if I'd interrupted something. The unwelcome guest at a party, the crawling spider in the bowl of olives.

"I'm a working man, Maestro," I said, ignoring the change I'd brought to the atmosphere of the salle. I'm sure they were all having a good time. Even Anacleto was there, leaning against a wall with a dusting rag forgotten in one hand, and in all my years studying with Domenico, Anacleto has shown no interest in observing the lessons his employer gave. It was time for them to get serious, get back on the job. "I keep busy." I straightened, stretched, rolled my neck. I didn't want to stiffen up after my recent exertions. Keeping loose might mean the difference between life and death later today.

I nodded toward Herbieto. "My client, here, hired me for a purpose. I brought the conclusion of that commission a step closer this morning."

Herbieto perked up. He walked over to stand near me, almost unconsciously rolling the foil in his hand through a series of parries. Domenico had been teaching, no question.

"Did you arrange the duel?" Herbieto asked.

"Not yet," I said. Herbieto's shoulders slumped. "But I've arranged for a meeting between Vicenzu and Maralla."

"How does that help either of us?" Maralla asked, coming to stand near where I was seated, bringing her almost shoulder to shoulder with Herbieto. "I'm not going to trap myself in Vicenzu's villa. I might as well cut my own wrists."

"Have a bit more faith in Cesar, people," I said. "I convinced Vicenzu to meet at Kertzel's Tea House this afternoon. It is a public place. Meaning—"

"Vicenzu cannot cage me for delivery to Azeglio," Maralla said.

"And you can issue a challenge," Herbieto said. "In front of witnesses. He cannot refuse."

"Not if he wants to stay in Plenum long enough to complete this con game the two of you have been talking about," Domenico said.

Herbieto and Maralla had apparently been chatting away like songbirds sharing a cage while I was gone. I didn't recall providing Domenico all the details regarding Maralla and Vicenzu.

"Having the three of you around does save me the effort of completing a thought," I said. "But, yes, you've got the gist of it. And, if I can convince Vicenzu to meet me immediately—say, by tomorrow morning—that puts an end to the Hearth Demon scam entirely. Tidies that up, Maralla, as well as removing any chance Vicenzu had left to turn you over to Azeglio."

"Assuming you kill Vicenzu," Domenico said.

"You too, Maestro?" I asked. "Think: if I lose a duel to this half-soldo grifter, it would reflect poorly upon you."

"This plan is fine," Maralla said. She was frowning at the practice sword in her hand, as if wondering how it had gotten there. "Fine so far as it goes. But the Questor General is still looking for me. Even with Vicenzu eliminated, the Venatores are still hunting."

"One problem at a time," I said. "We'll get to it. These problems are all connected, but we need to take them in order. First is Vicenzu. We need to focus on that problem."

"I thought you'd just done that," Herbieto said. He turned sideways, stepped into a shallow lunge. Not much flexibility in the man yet. "You have a plan, don't you?"

"*We* are making one," I said. "There has to be more of a plan than 'send Cesar the Bravo out, he'll take care of it.' This will require a group effort."

I saw Domenico frown at that. Herbieto turned back to face me. Maralla merely nodded.

"Vicenzu isn't the most trustworthy of men," I said, before Domenico could speak. "I'm thinking it would be advisable to have a few of us seated at Kertzel's, in case Vicenzu decides not to play this straight. Maralla has to be there, of course. That's the point of the meeting, after all. At least from Vicenzu's point of view. You'll want to be there, Herbieto, to hear the challenge. And, if I can impose on you a bit more, Maestro, you'd be invaluable." I continued on before Domenico could object. His mouth had been opening and shutting since I'd begun rattling this off. "Tasso, I'm afraid, won't be able to contribute. I believe Marteo would be willing to join us, but I imagine I'm not welcome at Giacomo's at the moment. I really don't have any other way to get in contact with him."

That all came out in a rush, by design. A tangle of voices followed, making it difficult to follow any individual strand.

Domenico's angry abnegation finally rose above the others.

"I am not one of you street-brawling bravos, Cesar," Domenico snapped. "Find someone else to guard your back. Doubtless that arm breaker you brought in to bleed on my floor has friends willing to mix it up for a few coins."

"Maestro," I said, "Vicenzu surrounds himself with the sort Tasso and his ilk aspire to be. Dealing with this level of competence requires more than a strong back and a dagger. I could use—*we* could use—your skill." Flattery is insidious. Even when you're fully aware of its presence, you cannot entirely avoid its manipulative effect.

"No," Domenico said. "I am out of that game. Permanently."

"Domenico," Maralla said, "I understand your reluctance, but—"

"I will not risk leaving Valentina without a father." The words came out low, strangled, barely above a whisper.

"All right," Maralla said. "You need say nothing more. Cesar, let it drop."

I nodded. I had to track down Marteo anyway. I could probably get word out at the same time that I was in the market to hire some muscle.

Valentina wormed into the arc of people standing about where I sat on the bench. She reached up, worked her little hand into Domenico's.

"Daddy," she said, "Maralla needs help. She is so nice. I would go, but I'm too little. Can't you go with Uncle Cesar?"

Domenico looked down at Valentina, then into Maralla's carefully neutral face. Valentina got her other hand up, fitting it into Maralla's. His instincts must be warring. I saw the moment that Domenico broke, that he yielded to his daughter's importuning, to her unspoken, unrecognized, need to please a mother surrogate.

I saw him squeeze her hand.

"As you wish," Domenico said.

That left me with only one matter to resolve: how to send a message to Marteo?

"Anacleto," I said, "may I have a word?"

Chapter 15

The Broscine Hill is, I believe, the least lofty of Plenum's prominences. And the least built over. Perhaps that is why Kertzel's could occupy such an expanse of it. A natural ledge in a westward facing flank of the hill had been flattened. Centuries ago, most likely. More recently the ledge was extended by excavating straight back into the side of the hill. Kertzel had built his Tea House here, a modest seeming frontage of yellow limestone and rose sandstone, though in fact it was larger than it appeared; Kertzel had delved into the hill, and the bulk of the Tea House structure—kitchen, storehouses, pantries—was underground. That left most of the expanse of the ledge itself free to fill with tables, potted trees and shrubs, reproductions of famed statues of the Ancients, and even a small fountain fed by some reservoir interred farther up the hillside. A waist-high paling of yellow-painted wrought iron fenced this expanse of patio, reached by a flight of ten steps climbing from the north side of Escaline Way.

Late morning saw the densest accumulation of customers enjoying tea and sticky pastries. But Kertzel's sustained a steady business through the early evening, before the impetus of Kertzel's patrons to indulge in the fashionable fad of tea drinking gave way to Plenumites' deeply ingrained habit of wine-guzzling.

At least half the tables were empty as I neared close enough to observe. That left, at a rough estimate, at least two score tea drinkers to serve as witnesses, reactive audience members, and cautionary social restraints.

The weather was cooperating. A rain sufficient to drive away customers would have put a crimp in my plans. Instead, intermittent bands of gray clouds drifted easily overhead, empty-bellied, having dumped their burdens on Spina before continuing inland. Clear blue afternoon sky graced Kertzel's in between the lowering striations.

We had arrived early; Domenico and Herbieto, a tightly strung Marteo, Maralla, and myself. Herbieto wanted to talk during the walk. I'd maneuvered him into a position next to Domenico, where the Maestro's fundamental taciturnity gradually shut off the flow of prattle. Marteo attempted to imbue his own silence with as much drama as his body language could achieve, his efforts mostly involving furtive, darting glances in between gradual, scanning head turns. Maralla busied herself with some bauble she turned over and over in her hands, muttering to herself while she did so. She wore the same outfit she'd arrived at Domenico's in yesterday, but by some feminine magic she managed to make it look not only fresh but somehow different.

I did not want us to arrive tired, but I did discourage dawdling. While it was possible that Vicenzu would honor his agreement to come unattended, I wouldn't have risked a half-soldo bet on it. I wanted to get my people salted among the tea-drinkers, ready to act if Vicenzu reneged on the deal and brought his guards along, secreting themselves in or around the Tea House, prepared to snatch Maralla.

"Marteo," I said, while we remained far enough away not to be individually identifiable, "go check it out." He'd be able to recognize Vicenzu's bodyguards, after his time watching Maralla's place.

It was exactly the sort of skulking Marteo lived for. He offered me a nod that he doubtless intended to freight with significance, then raised his hood over his head and slunk off.

The rest of us arranged ourselves as inconspicuously as possible outside a storefront that seemed to specialize in lace, combs, feathers, and sundry embroidered items. Herbieto took a professional interest in the store and scrutinized the merchandise with an expert eye. He engaged the proprietor in conversation, providing the rest of us loitering there with a false cover of legitimacy.

"I might be able to help Marteo," Maralla said, while she, Domenico, and I stood about, uncomfortably examining a rack of folding fans from Ihbar, or that at least mimicked the style. She tucked away the bit of filigree metal she'd been carrying since we left Domenico's. From the clutch in which she put the bauble, she retrieved a corked glass vial, a small ceramic pot, and an artist's paint brush. "Screen me, please."

Domenico and I stood shoulder to shoulder. Domenico managed to hook an edge of his cloak onto a corner of a shelf displaying a variety of combs fashioned from hardwoods, tortoise shell, silver, brass, or other materials

I couldn't immediately identify. Behind us, I could hear Maralla, on her knees, muttering. I strained my ears, imagining I could hear the noise made by grains of powder poured from the vial upon the tile floor of the store, the sound of the bristles of the paint brush applying pigments. Sheer delusion, of course. But it distracted me from a growing feeling of tension.

Herbieto continued his commercial chat. Whether he was acquiring a supplier of material for his millinery, or arranging to sell finished hats, I couldn't tell. It seemed to be going well, however. I experienced an oddly possessive sense of pleasure for him. Perhaps Herbieto would garner some good from his employment of Cesar the Bravo. Something other than consummation of vengeance, a more concrete acquisition than the gratification of watching me kill a man for him.

A familiar, unpleasant smell drifted up from Maralla's makeshift hidey-hole. Something skittered by my ankle, passing from behind me, then between me and Domenico. I glanced down, too late to make out what it was. Something small, scaled in laurel green, sped out of the shop and took to the air on spreading bat wings.

"There," Maralla said. I turned, offering a hand to help her rise, but she was already on her feet, dusting off her dress at the knees.

"Right," I said. "There." Other than sending some sort of bat-demon aloft I'm not sure what she'd accomplished. But I didn't need to know; Maralla was the witch. Certainly she'd conjured and deployed the thing with some purpose in mind.

But if she'd meant to assist Marteo, she'd taken too

long. I could see him returning. He didn't bother with any theatrics, no pausing before shop fronts, pretending to inspect the merchandise while in fact glancing about him. No attempt to slip from shadowed recess to potted plant. He merely slipped in with some closely-spaced pedestrian traffic and strolled our way. I assumed this degree of straightforward behavior indicated he'd observed something serious.

"Vicenzu brought all four of them," Marteo said, and lowered his hood. "One is sitting two tables to the left of the entry. Another is standing by the doorway to the Tea House proper, got a good patch of shadow from the hill to conceal him, but you can still make him out. Two more are opposite each other at tables on the east and west ends of the patio. Good lines of sight to Vicenzu, who has a table in the center. Also well-placed to control entry and egress. Professional."

Marteo sounded approving. Respectful, even.

"Then let's go perform a professional job of removing them," I said. There were other, less phlegmatic things I wished to say. However, to maintain morale, I merely thought them.

Carefully maintained landscaping provided a manicured forest of shrubs and dwarf trees climbing the steep incline up from the street to the Tea House ledge. The landscaping also provided cover for those at street level who did not wish to be observed creeping up to the patio.

At least the groomed topiary and trees did not smear my clothing to the same extent as had the grove at the Temple of Sighs. I hiked up the embankment, planting each boot carefully, and securing a grip on a tree or thick clump of roots before committing myself to each step. Beside me Marteo performed similar maneuvers. I imagine we received quizzical glances from passersby. But no one made inquiries, and soon we were high enough to go largely unnoticed; few people ever glance upwards.

Below us waited Maralla, escorted by Herbieto. A flutter of wings passed overhead, and I caught a scent that reminded me of both snakes and spoiled eggs. Maralla's bat-demon perched atop a dwarf cypress, the small tree swaying slightly as it accepted the weight. Another cautious move brought me almost level with it. Another shift up and I neared the base of the iron fencing.

Above me I heard Domenico's voice. "Excuse me, did you happen to see that—creature?" Domenico paused. "Right over the fence, down there."

I recognized Felpe's provincial face as he peered over the top of the pointed, canary-yellow palings. His gaze was over our heads, taking in the buildings across the street.

"I don't see anything," he said, sounding equally puzzled and annoyed.

"Look down," Domenico said. "It was down below, among the bushes."

Felpe leaned over the waist-high fence. I had a moment to see his eyes widen as he noticed the bat-demon. Then a startled instant of some mixture of alarm and recognition as he saw me and Marteo rising up. I reached, grabbed a fistful of doublet, and pulled. As Felpe toppled over the fence, Marteo slapped a palm over Felpe's mouth with one hand while plunging a dagger into his throat with the other.

I found Marteo's dagger to be uncomfortably close, though it was at least six inches from my hand. I jerked aside to avoid the jet of blood that emerged as Marteo yanked free the dagger.

The movement almost cost me my precarious balance on the steep embankment. But I kept my footing and my grip on Felpe. I deposited him behind a rank of topiary that I figured would keep him from sliding down to the street. Marteo, palm still over Felpe's mouth, stooped over him, dagger descending again.

The bat-demon swooped from its perch, winging around to the western side of the patio. Looking below, I saw those few pedestrians who had paused, eyes drawn by the motion of Felpe's killing, now follow the flight of the demon. Most of them quickly moved on. The presence of a demon in Plenum usually meant Collegium business. And when Plenumites encountered Collegium business, their instinct was to instantly tend to their own.

I hustled after the demon, as fast as the landscaping allowed. I hoped that would be fast enough. The other three bodyguards would focus on their assigned sectors and, naturally, Vicenzu. I'd never served as a bodyguard, but I guessed that from time to time they would check in with each other, to make sure security had not been compromised. How often that was, I didn't know. Kertzel's patio was spacious, but it didn't offer the vastness of Accordance Square outside the Collegium; one couldn't lose sight of a person within it. A casual glance in the right direction would show that Felpe had gone missing.

Spider webs broke across my thighs. Untrimmed branches slapped at my face. This side of the ledge hadn't received the recent grooming of the street facing frontage. Marteo scampered ahead of me, the folds of his oversized cloak somehow not snagging or catching on the foliage. Perhaps all that practice skulking served a practical purpose.

The bat-demon winged up to fence height, hovered a moment, then dropped back down. Next man spotted and marked. Marteo arrived in position below the demon a moment before I did, though I had put on a last burst of speed to close the gap.

I was in time to hear Domenico's voice again, employing the same gambit. A face appeared over the palings. I recognized the face, though I hadn't yet learned the name. I try not to forget the face of anyone involved in giving me a beating.

I wasn't yet in position. The guard was not within easy reach. I erupted upwards at the same time Marteo grabbed for him. The guard pulled back, spitting an expletive. And then he was coming forward again in an ungainly flop over the iron pickets of the fence. I caught a glimpse of Domenico, his position suggesting he'd hoisted the man bodily over the top.

There was no possibility that had gone unseen. Our half-baked plan to eliminate the bodyguards failed, not even surviving the midpoint.

The bodyguard emitted a yelp, then crashed headlong into a tangle of shrubbery. Marteo sprang after him, dagger flashing. Leaving Marteo to complete the dirty work, I reached up and got a hold on the fence. The paling was waist-high at the patio. From below it presented a rather more substantial obstacle. With a convulsive effort I vaulted up and over.

I landed in a crouch atop the travertine tiles of the patio. I'd narrowly avoided kicking over a chair with my bootheels as I descended. I'd come down between two empty tables, one of which had presumably accommodated the bodyguard currently enjoying Marteo's tender attention. Domenico was sprinting across the patio toward the bodyguard seated at the eastern end, following a path that required him to dodge the least number of tables, chairs, and tea drinkers.

A stir of something—interest, concern, alarm—began to affect the buzz of conversation and the clink of porcelain on porcelain. Given the abrupt vanishings and my equally abrupt advent, Domenico's charge could remain unnoticed.

I saw Vicenzu begin to rise from his chair, but ignored him. Assuming Domenico was competent to deal with the eastern bodyguard (a fairly safe assumption, I figured), that left the one near the entry to the hillside structure for me to handle. I shoved upward from my heels, rising from a crouch into a lurching stumble that became a sprint within a couple of paces.

Fast, but not fast enough. The fourth bodyguard emerged from his post in the shaded passage that led from the patio into the hillside: Garon, his bent nose unmistakable. His right hand crossed his body to reach for the hilt of his rapier.

I swerved around an occupied table, hipped aside a waiter who couldn't make up his mind whether to interpose himself or get out of the way, and thus committed to neither, and closed the distance in mere seconds. Too many seconds, however, to prevent Garon from clearing the scabbard. His rapier menaced me as I darted toward him.

My own hands remained empty as the gap between me and a sharpened length of steel narrowed. A serving table occupied a cleared space of the patio between the customers' tables and the side of the hill. It held a collection of tea cups, plates, and a large ceramic teapot, from the spout of which issued a plume of steam. I snatched the teapot up by the handle as I neared Garon's threat range.

Garon began to extend into a shallow lunge, then tried to abort the motion as he saw the heavy teapot commence its short ballistic arc that threatened to terminate in the center of his face. He managed to raise the rapier at the last moment, interposing the curving complexities of the guard between the incoming teapot and his nose. Ceramic cracked against metal, raining Garon in a shower of sharp-edged fragments and hot liquid.

Garon stepped back, wiped at his face with the sleeve of his left hand while sort of waving his rapier in my general direction with his right. I stepped around the fanning blade, grabbed his wrist with my left hand and tugged him toward me, meanwhile unloading a right hand that caught him directly in the center of his face. I could feel the cartilage of that already broken nose crunch beneath my fist. Garon stumbled back down the short passage leading into the hillside. His backside pushed open the door as he fell, rapier dropping from his fingers.

I caught a glimpse of the kitchen inside. Employees of the Tea House stared at Garon, stunned by the sudden intrusion. None made any immediate move to help him.

I trotted down the passage and stopped, bending to pick up the fallen sword. Garon looked up at me, face covered with hot tea, tiny clay shards, and the blood streaming from his nose or trickling from tiny cuts. He raised a hand, waved it.

"I'll sit this one out," he said.

I nodded. I didn't hand him his sword, however. I kept it, clutching the forte in my left hand as I trotted back to the patio. I had no particular reason to trust Garon. Why hand him back the sword he could use to stick in my back?

A band of clouds rolled overhead, shadowing the patio as it temporarily dimmed the sun. The temporary gloom seemed more appropriate for dark deeds. But it didn't last long.

Domenico had dealt with the fourth bodyguard. The man was clutching a bleeding swordhand, while Domenico, his own sword drawn, stood over him, angled to keep watch on him as well as, I supposed, everyone else on the patio.

The tea drinkers seemed to have adopted the role of audience. They'd noticed that the sudden onset of violence involved rather specific targets and was not directed randomly at Kertzel's guests in general. These were some of Plenum's monied and influential residents. In a word, jaded. Why not watch the show while enjoying an herbal concoction and a pastry filled with a fruit puree?

Vicenzu had resumed his seat, though he'd turned his chair to face me, focusing on the hill side of the patio rather than the street side. Coming up the stairs, unnoticed by Vicenzu, I saw Maralla, followed by Herbieto. The clouds passed as Maralla set foot upon the patio, leaving a stretch of blue sky to bathe the scene in sunlight again, at least until the next band arrived.

The players were assembled. I had an audience. Time to get the show started.

Chapter 16

"You—" Vicenzu said, then stopped. He seemed to be struggling for the right epithet to apply to me. He remained seated, though one hand was on the back of the chair, ready to help propel him to his feet.

Maralla and Herbieto took an empty table nearby. Vicenzu hadn't yet noticed the witch's arrival.

Herbieto appeared eager. He perched on the edge of his chair.

I could see Marteo's hooded face peering through the railings of the fence. His head shifted in a slow, constant side-to-side motion as he observed the scene.

"We did have an appointment," I said. I raised my voice enough to carry to all corners of the patio, allowing the audience to hear me declaim. "It pained me to think that you might break your word and bring attendants. However, others, less trusting than I, persuaded me to take precautions." I gestured vaguely toward Garon and the bodyguard at Domenico's feet. "I fear those who suggested a certain baseness in your character were proved correct. It saddens me to have to proclaim you both a liar and a coward."

Kertzel's patrons listened intently. Here was spice for their tea, something to discuss later when wine replaced herbal tinctures. I played to them, thinking this time I might come across as the sympathetic character, rather than the bully and villain of the piece.

"Who are you?" Vicenzu asked, raising his own voice now, adding a note of confusion. "Why do you come here and attack these men, then hurl insults at me?" His eyes darted, assessing, searching perhaps for exits, or aid.

"Come now, Vicenzu," I said, "don't compound your transgressions with further deception. You may fool those you cheat out of good, solid scudos for your overpriced houses, but you cannot fool the clear-eyed Plenumites gathered here at Kertzel's." I gestured at the onlookers, my wise, understanding friends, inviting them to take my side against this knave.

"This is too much," Vicenzu said. He stood up now, ran a hand through his shock of red hair, then retrieved his hat from the tabletop. "You are mad, coming here and hurling accusations at a stranger. I will not stay here and endure it."

"Your pretense of innocence is weak. Do you take these people for simpletons? You pretend not to know me, proclaim me a stranger," I said. "Yet this supposed stranger knows your name. And knows you would arrive here with bodyguards, despite your word to come alone."

"I don't know those men," Vicenzu said. "Why you and your ruffians attacked them, I don't know. But it has nothing to do with me."

The man Domenico was guarding grunted something.

Vicenzu shot him a look and he subsided.

"Nothing to do with Vicenzu, the confidence trickster?" I asked. "Nothing to do with Vicenzu, the cheat and liar? The man who has stolen from honest citizens, from those merely wishing to purchase a house. The man who has duped those innocents hoping to earn a fortune mining for gold?"

Vicenzu frowned at this last, either puzzled at how I'd known of his prospecting scam or merely trying to remember so far back. Herbieto tensed, trembling. I could see he wanted to leap to his feet and spit his fury at the man who'd led to his father's death.

"Let's not forget Vicenzu, betrayer of a woman's honor," Maralla said, getting to her feet.

I hoisted an eyebrow, then let it settle. It seemed unlikely anything untoward had occurred between Vicenzu and Maralla. She was merely adding another charge, helping push Vicenzu to the brink. Considering how she'd spent the last few weeks, another lie presented no great obstacle. And so what if she and Vicenzu had made the beast with two backs? Who was Cesar the Bravo to stand in moral judgment over anyone? Especially not concerning matters involving a woman's boudoir.

Vicenzu spun about upon hearing Maralla's voice, and a murmur passed through the patio audience, all of whom appeared enthralled with the unfolding drama. Quite a bonus for the price of a cup and a bun.

"Another stranger, is she?" asked one of the spectators, joining in the fun. His table companions laughed.

"Maralla," Vicenzu said. He'd taken a moment. I wondered what thoughts he'd had time to assemble.

"Vicenzu," Maralla said. Vicenzu didn't deny it. I'd won at least that point from the on-looking, de facto court.

"Maralla, come away with me," Vicenzu said. "Leave this farce behind. We can still complete our business."

"I know what business you wish to consummate," Maralla said. I gave her high marks for that one. The tea drinkers could assume a prurient meaning to her words, while Vicenzu would receive the message that Maralla knew of his arrangement with the Questor General.

"Look, Maralla," Vicenzu said, "whatever you've heard..." He stopped, tried again. "My business—our business—requires at times certain temporizing commitments that must be judiciously—forgotten. You know I would never betray you."

I felt the conversation drifting and grabbed the reins. "You have convicted yourself fully, Vicenzu. You are a liar, a scoundrel, a betrayer of women's honor, and a base coward."

That, I thought, was a succinct summation. Let Vicenzu try to weasel out of that one and still show his face in Plenum.

Vicenzu turned back to face me. His face had grown pale, contrasting distinctly with his red hair. I could see his hands tremble. Perhaps to control them he adjusted his hat, stroking the feather. As he did so, another length of leaden cloud rolled in overhead, throwing the patio once again into its chill shadow.

"I invite you to take those words back, Cesar," Vicenzu said. He adopted a stern, aggrieved tone. A victim, standing on his dignity. "This will be your only opportunity."

"That is convenient," I said. "I have no intention of withdrawing my words. In fact, I will add to them: that hat makes you look absurd. Or, rather, even more absurd than you already do without it."

Childish name-calling is often what tips my victims over the brink. It strikes at pride, undermining the sound, logical reasons for not risking life, and it can temporarily banish the fear that often hides behind the sound, logical reasoning. It worked here as well.

Vicenzu looked around him, his features twisted as anger fought with the calculating portion of his mind trying to work out an escape from this predicament. He found the only escape available, one that satisfied his anger. The escape I wanted him to take.

"I will cut your insolent, slanderous tongue from your lying mouth," he said, committing himself. "When and where?"

I had done it. Vicenzu had just challenged me, in front of witnesses. Killing him was now justified by law and custom. Obligatory, really.

"Why not here and now?" I said. "We can clear away a few tables, allow these good people to see justice done and the right prevail."

I heard murmurs of approval. The afternoon was just getting better and better for the tea sippers at Kertzel's. The scraping of chair legs on travertine indicated that volunteers were wasting no time in putting my suggestion to practice. I walked by Vicenzu, who eyed me as I passed. His mouth worked. He wanted to say something, or merely spit on me. Instead he swiveled his feet to keep me in sight.

Taller than I remembered. He'd have a significant reach advantage.

Herbieto sprang to his feet. He looked barely capable of suppressing his excitement, an admixture of anticipation and anxiety animating his face.

"Here," I said, handing him Garon's sword. "Hold onto this, will you?"

Herbieto took the sword, not even glancing at it.

"You did it, Cesar," he said. "I apologize for doubting you. You have earned every pistra coming to you."

"I haven't earned it yet," I said. "I mean, he might kill me. In which case, take three pistras from my purse before my body is hauled away. I won't have earned that retainer."

Herbieto looked taken aback. "Kill you? But, I thought—"

Maralla put a hand on his shoulder. "He is joking, Herbieto. I have seen it before, usually from soldiers before they march off to some situation they consider likely to be dangerous."

"She's right, Herbieto," I said, milking a sigh from the words. "A bit of a killjoy, perhaps, but right. Putting a sword through a man's heart is what I do. I doubt Vicenzu has so much as practiced his footwork in decades."

A dozen pairs of hands were busy creating an open square in the middle of the patio. I hoped they kept at it a bit longer. I prefer as much room as possible for a duel. Vicenzu was looking at me and Maralla, confusion on his face. After a moment, he too sighed, then began to stretch. I imagined he'd abruptly realized he was about to engage in a fight for his life and ought to begin taking it seriously.

"I suppose it would be wrong of me to ask you to make it hurt," Herbieto said. He was squeezing the blade of Garon's sword so hard I was glad to see him clutching it at the unsharpened portion of the forte, his thumb and forefinger pressed up against the outside of the quillons. "But it is hard to feel any mercy for the man who killed my father."

"Why don't you discuss it with him?" I asked. "You're not going to get another chance." I began limbering up. No point in going in cold. Even a tyro could get lucky. Besides, it offered a chance to display myself for Maralla without appearing to do so gratuitously. She hadn't shown a glimmer of interest in me. Not yet. Perhaps a virtuoso exhibition of swordsmanship would attract her.

Herbieto edged past me, stalking over toward Vicenzu, who was dropping into and recovering from a series of shallow lunges, empty hand extended, the pointer and middle fingers outthrust.

Domenico remained where I'd last seen him, though now the bodyguard he watched was seated, wounded hand clutched to his chest, elbow propped up on a table. Beside him sat Garon. The three men seemed engaged in a companionable enough conversation. Perhaps Domenico was offering lessons. Nothing like losing a fight to convince someone to brush up on his martial skills.

Marteo still peeked through the fence. I realized we'd need to get on with things quickly. The two bodies in the shrubbery would become a problem sooner or later. At the very least, the two living bodyguards would begin to resent the disposition of their comrades.

"Vicenzu," Herbieto said. The word came out choked.

He cleared his throat and tried again. "Vicenzu, when you feel the steel inside you and start bleeding, I want you to remember the name Horbet. Horbet the Milliner."

Vicenzu straightened up from a lunge and turned to face Herbieto. "Horbet the Milliner? I'm afraid I don't recognize the name. Nor you."

"My name is Herbieto." Herbieto was speaking clearly, all hesitancy gone. A cold anger provided the spine for each carefully enunciated word. "Now, Herbieto the Milliner. Horbet was the man you murdered with your prospecting scheme. Horbet was my father. You remember that name."

"I'll certainly remember yours," Vicenzu said, "once I dispose of this pest Cesar. Then I'll come pay you a visit, Herbieto the Milliner." He turned his back on Herbieto and resumed shadow fencing.

I gripped Herbieto by the bicep as he returned, his face red and furious. I gave his arm a squeeze.

"He'll remember," I said. "Your father's name will be the last word he hears."

Kertzel's patio now held an open square in its center. Sufficient, I figured, for the task. Time to earn the rest of the thirty pistras Herbieto owed me.

I stepped into the arena and drew my rapier. "It's time, Vicenzu. Any last words? Any final lies?"

"I would inquire what you want etched upon your tombstone, Cesar, but I assume you'll be tossed in a pauper's grave. So why bother?"

Vicenzu faced me, drew his rapier, and assumed a ready position. His chest rose and fell a touch more than normal, but he appeared composed enough. I couldn't tell if he truly was calm in the face of death, or if a lifetime of assuming one guise and character after another made acting unconcerned second nature.

The spectators grew expectant, mostly quiet, though I did hear a few wagers being offered and accepted. I wasn't the only one expecting to earn money from this fight.

With an audience, I was compelled to preserve the illusion of strict fairness. I left the main gauche sheathed. I took up my position opposite Vicenzu, wary, but not yet on guard.

"To be clear," I said, loudly enough to be heard in all corners of the patio, "this affair is not merely to first blood. Correct?"

Vicenzu grunted something.

"I didn't catch that," I said. "Can you repeat it, please?"

"Yes." He spat out the word, and I detected an edge of desperation in it, the desperation of a man down to his last toss of the dice.

I assured myself of a proper grip on the hilt, then saluted Vicenzu with the blade. He did not return the courtesy. I shrugged it off. I was about to kill him, after all. Why should he concern himself with protocol?

"Begin," I said.

Vicenzu shuffled forward a hesitant step, pressed his blade against mine. I could have ended the matter right there with a simple disengage and lunge, or perhaps even an aggressive glissade. But I felt Herbieto deserved a more prolonged revenge for his money. So, I merely tapped a ringing beat against his blade, feinted for his face to draw his guard, then thrust at his leading leg, pinking his thigh.

He stepped back, a cry as much startlement as pain

emerging from him.

"It's just a scratch," I said. "Don't whine about it like a babe needing to suckle." First blood within two seconds. I had worried Vicenzu would try to escape by claiming such a limitation on the duel. Then I would have had to ensure I didn't touch him until the killing stroke. A tricky prospect. Now, however, I could toy with him like a cat with a beetle until I'd determined that Herbieto had gotten his money's worth.

Vicenzu snarled, and came at me in a flurry. This is the most dangerous attack a trained swordsman can face from a novice; an avalanche of random blows from someone who'd abandoned all thought of defense. The parries and ripostes drilled into the expert by wearisome repetition are of lessened utility in such instances because they rely upon the assumption that the blows to be defended against are the rational, scientific strokes customarily delivered by a swordsman. This all goes out the window when facing the utterly unexpected, the absurd, the "why would you leave yourself open like that?" Usually a simple stop-thrust is sufficient to end the threat before the accumulating probability of danger achieves a certainty. Unfortunately for me, doing so would cut the duel short.

I retreated, trying to turn the ringing sequence of blocks and deflections into an exciting display of skill. To impress the crowd, of course, not merely for Maralla's eyes. I kept a smile on my face the entire time, but as I neared the edge of the makeshift arena, I began to think that perhaps Herbieto had received full value for his pistras. I made it look easy, but I'd turned the last couple of thrusts more by luck than skill.

If Vicenzu had no idea what part of me he was trying to skewer, how could I be expected to?

Enough. As my back foot felt a chair leg, I reached out with my gauntleted left hand and swatted aside a thrust directed at my face. I circled widely, backpedaling rapidly into the center of the arena. Vicenzu pivoted, and watched me go. He was panting, his chest heaving from the burst of exertion.

I patted at myself, pantomiming astonishment at finding no blood. The patio spectators laughed, some even applauding. They were enjoying the show. I imagined this event would increase Kertzel's already profitable business. "Pay for tea, watch a duel, gratis," people would say. And they'd return, with friends. Perhaps that degree of additional traffic might induce Kertzel to forgive the pair of corpses littering his shrubbery.

"I compliment you on your—energetic—style," I said. "Now, let's get down to it. I want you to remember salting a patch of mountainous ground with gold."

Vicenzu stood unmoving, listening. Probably grateful for the chance to catch his breath.

"I want you to remember Horbet," I continued, "a man from whom you conned not only money, but also his very life. I want you to understand that is why you are going to die today."

"I hate to disappoint the cowardly merchant who hired you, Cesar," Vicenzu said, managing a sneer in between indrawn breaths, "but I have little recollection of Horbet. The marks rather blend together into a single, homogenous chump after a while."

Herbieto emitted something between a growl and a

strangled scream. There may have been words blended in there somewhere, but I couldn't make them out.

I shrugged. "Just die, then," I said and closed the distance with a cross over step. Vicenzu's sneer disappeared as he saw me coming. I dropped into a deep lunge, thrusting at a point immediately above Vicenzu's right hip. He flailed a desperation parry in octave that came too late to save his skin, but in time to save his life. The point of my blade pierced cloth and about a half inch of good living before his blade knocked mine aside, opening a gash in his flank as it did so.

Had Vicenzu been an accomplished fencer, he could have extended into a riposte that likely would have impaled my right shoulder before I could recover. But the man was tired, terrified, and not much of a swordsman. I recovered, and immediately advanced, beating aside his blade, feinting at the wounded side, then puncturing a shallow hole in the meat of his right bicep.

Vicenzu stumbled back, barking profanities. "Garon, Phonsic, do something you faithless bastards," he called.

"Sorry, boss," called back the bodyguard Domenico was still watching. Phonsic, apparently.

"It's a duel," Garon shouted out, as if that explained his inaction. Which, in fact, it did. Vicenzu had voluntarily agreed to this fight. Garon's obligation to guard him terminated at that point. Vicenzu was on his own. I saw the resignation in Vicenzu's face as he realized the finality of it.

Then he nodded at me. "Come on then, let's get on with it." Something of his customary verve imbued the words.

I grinned at him. For a moment I could understand why

Maralla had agreed to work with him, had even liked him, unwilling to believe the worst of the man. Well, if he was ready to go down fighting, I'd oblige.

I'd toyed with him long enough. Time to end it, as painlessly as possible. I closed the distance, extended the blade of my rapier far enough to engage his, steel scraping on steel as I pressed, seeing if he'd resist or disengage. I felt the moment coming. The Tea House audience seemed to as well, the commentary and chatter ceasing as attention focused on the impending death. The only sounds I could hear were bootheels shuffling over the grit accumulated atop the travertine tiles, Vicenzu's heavy breathing, and the metallic sibilance of one sword blade gradually sliding along another.

The stillness broke. A shriek of twisting, wrenching iron preceded a full-throated bellow that partook as much of the lion as the bull.

Chapter 17

I slid rapidly out of the threat range of Vicenzu's sword before turning toward the source of the noise. Distraction had killed better swordsmen than I.

The roaring emerged from the throat of a massive war demon. It was finishing up the apparently minor task of uprooting and bending lengths of iron fencing on either side of the stairway leading to the patio. The entry being, it seemed, too narrow to accommodate the war demon's frame. I couldn't accurately measure it, as it remained partially concealed from my view across half the length of the patio and a couple of steps down. But I estimated it as standing roughly nine feet tall. It probably measured six feet across at the shoulders.

Big, then.

Scales of a mottled aubergine and ochre covered it from the top of its head to as far down its legs as I could see. The head looked like an amalgam of serpent and goat, coiling horns, abutting either side of the hairless skull, terminating in gleaming white, forward-pointing spikes. Muscle rippled and bulged beneath the scaled hide as the demon tossed aside a length of fence, letting it fly from hands that seemed sheathed in bone, or some cartilaginous growth overlaying the scales.

The flung iron fencing landed amidst the trees and shrubs. I heard it thresh through the foliage, followed by an exasperated oath from someone. Then I heard nothing but cries of alarm, overturned chairs, and other sounds associated with panic, as the patrons of Kertzel's Tea House abruptly realized that the show had taken a personally dangerous turn, and immediately thereafter discovered that exiting the place would prove impractical.

The war demon reached the patio, cracking the first travertine tile beneath an ebon hoof. Downward hooking spikes above the hoof emerged from the scaly hide on either side of the ankle. I revised my estimate of the war demon's height to ten feet.

As the war demon set hoof on travertine, men in familiar dark-red and hunter-green livery appeared along the fence of the street-facing side of the patio. One of these Venatores must have just avoided the wrenched-free length of iron paling the demon had chucked aside. It couldn't have been much fun climbing the embankment and pushing through the shrubbery while toting halberds. I hadn't enjoyed the climb myself, and I hadn't been burdened with a steel breastplate and a polearm. Yet I felt no sympathy.

I didn't see Bracceton among the Venatores. Perhaps he was recovering from the sword cuts I'd inflicted. It didn't appear that anyone from the ranks had been promoted to sergeant yet; the Venatore troopers present all bore the standard equipment, none carried a rapier instead of a halberd.

Then Azeglio appeared, emerging from behind the concealing bulk of the war demon. He wore his usual black. Teeth flashed white through a smirk of satisfaction.

I ground my teeth. Azeglio had scored a coup, no question. I thought I'd been a card up in the game, but it appeared that in fact I'd just lost.

I shot a glance at Maralla. She was sucking in deep, shuddering breaths, standing rigid, fists clenched tightly at her side. She appeared terrified. I couldn't blame her. Her worst fears seemed on the brink of becoming a horrifying reality.

Azeglio pushed his way past the war demon, which had stopped two paces into the patio. The Questor General displayed an indifference to the murderous bulk of muscle and destruction that bordered on contempt.

I heard a disbelieving bark of laughter behind me, then a cleared throat.

"Questor General," Vicenzu called, "I've come through with my end of the bargain, as you can see."

So, the grifter thought he saw his salvation, a way to

slip free. At least with his life. Though I guessed that even now Vicenzu was working the angles. He'd want more than merely saving his skin. He'd be trying to figure a way to leverage this turn of events to his advantage.

Azeglio had been surveying the crowd, taking in faces. His head jerked toward Vicenzu. His eyes narrowed as he saw me. He kept me in his gaze, I imagined, eyeing Vicenzu peripherally as the conman edged into view from behind me, where I'd been partially obscuring him from Azeglio.

"Ahh, you," Azeglio said. His voice held the purring quality of a satiated lion. "Vicenzu, right? I'm afraid you misapprehend the terms of our agreement."

From what I gathered, they both did. Wasn't Azeglio supposed to allow Vicenzu to finish up his Hearth Demon con before Vicenzu turned over Maralla?

"Possibly, Questor General," Vicenzu said. The wheedling, conciliatory tone he adopted ill-fit Vicenzu's customarily confident persona. "Perhaps I'm overzealous in my desire to please. We can discuss any alteration in terms later, at your convenience. But right now, allow me to turn over the witch to your custody."

I permitted myself another look at Maralla. She seemed to have gained control of her fear. She was breathing easily again, shifting from a stony look at Azeglio to a furious glare at Vicenzu. One delicate hand reached up to brush her hair back from over her ear.

"I will certainly take her into custody," Azeglio said, "but it won't be from your hands. Do not try to play your games with me, grifter. The witch is clearly not yours to dispose. You lost whatever ascendency you claimed to have possessed. The Venatores have not been blind to your activities, Vicenzu."

Over Azeglio's shoulder, a hint of motion caught my eye. Clambering up to squat atop the fence palings, next to one of the sections destroyed by the war demon, was Azeglio's frog demon. A busy spy, that demon.

Azeglio had neatly packaged his prizes. The Venatores lined the fence along the street side of the patio. The Broscine Hill bulked low and squat at the east side of the patio. The escarpment to the west was steep, thickly grown with decorative plants, and fenced off, while an upthrust, rocky prominence of the Broscine walled off any egress to the north. Tea House patrons were already beginning to bunch against the fence, weighing the risks of clambering down through the shrubbery against that of sticking around while the Venatores and a war demon apprehended a witch.

I couldn't say I blamed them. I'd gone up against war demons before and had little desire to repeat the experience. The rapier in my hand wasn't the ideal weapon. A dozen men with arquebuses, backed by another dozen with pikes, might be sufficient. Those I didn't keep lying around my room, however. Be a bit cramped, to say the least. I should have retrieved my cinquedea from the concealed space beneath the loose floorboard of my room. Its heavier, thicker blade might allow me to hack through the demon's hide. My rapier did possess a moderately sharp edge, but it lacked the heft to make the most efficient use of that edge. Not against armor, which the scaled skin of the war demon approximated.

Vicenzu edged past me, heading closer to Azeglio, perhaps hoping proximity would assist him in pleading his case.

"Clearly you are the master of the situation, Questor General," Vicenzu said. "I will aid you in whatever manner you deem best. Please consider me at your service."

A number of events then occurred more or less simultaneously, even as Azeglio's mouth twisted into a wry, supercilious smile.

Herbieto strode toward Vicenzu, the hilt of Garon's sword now in his hand, and gripped properly. He'd been paying attention to the lessons Domenico and I had given.

"You will not wriggle free of my vengeance, snake," Herbieto said, his voice taking on the impressive cadence I recalled it possessing after a few cups of wine at Giacomo's.

To my right, at the far left of Azeglio's line of Venatores, the soldier near the corner of the patio suddenly disappeared, pulled down into the shrubbery. I'd glimpsed a portion of a dark, hooded cloak and the flash of a dagger.

Maralla's arm whipped into motion. I understood what I was seeing, though it happened too fast for me to follow. She'd unhooked an earring and hurled it upon the hard, travertine tiles of the patio, where the bauble cracked open upon impact. A column of yellow-tinged mist coiled up from the ruins of the earring. A shape formed and congealed within the mist in the space of a couple heartbeats. It rose from a crouch, wisps of mist drifting away at the motion to dissipate above the patio. I recognized the wolf demon Maralla had conjured at Giacomo's. So, she had succeeded in preparing another receptacle while staying at Domenico's and had undertaken the effort to imprison a demon within it.

The Venatore war demon bellowed a challenge at the newcomer. Vicenzu shifted to face Herbieto. Domenico ran, leaped in the air and slid across a tabletop, headed for the fence, seemingly intent on facing down the soldiers and the unmoving frog demon on the other side by himself. Maralla had dropped to a crouch, beginning to sketch a circle on the travertine.

If none of my companions were willing to go down without a fight, they'd not find Cesar the Bravo hindmost.

"Questor General," I shouted, trying not to stare at the two demons squaring off against each other at an uncomfortably close distance from me. The wolf demon looked woefully outclassed, half the size of the war demon. But it came on, stiff-legged, with no sign of hesitation. "I have a grievance."

To ensure I had his attention, I strode forward, in the wake of the wolf demon, which brushed by Azeglio, picking up speed, and hurling itself at the throat of the war demon. I heard cries and the clashing of steel on steel all around, but couldn't afford to take my eyes from Azeglio. If the noise was Marteo ambushing another Venatore, or Domenico engaging multiple halberds over the iron palings, or Herbieto crossing swords with Vicenzu, or all of the above, I couldn't be bothered to check.

Azeglio did swivel his head, trying to take in all the activity. Well, he was a general of sorts. Either he decided events were comfortably in hand or there was nothing more he could do anyway, because he focused on me. Another smile shone from within his goatee. He did seem to enjoy his work.

"You have been a nuisance," he said, and drew his sword. A handsome bit of the sword maker's art, I couldn't help but notice.

"I was about to say the same of you," I said, and then burst into a skipping step that terminated in a deep lunge.

The move caught Azeglio unprepared. He jumped back, almost into the ambit of the furious combat of the two demons. Almost. It had been worth attempting.

Azeglio recovered in a heartbeat. He stomped forward, thrusting high at my right side. I parried in quarte, riposted. He was quick, parrying the riposte and trying to catch my blade in a bind. I stepped back, gaining a bit of room to work, and gestured at him to follow.

Before he could comply, a snarling, tumbling ball of muscle and short, rank-smelling pelt whirled between us. I jumped away, though not quickly enough. A clawed hand, extended from the somersaulting wolf demon—probably to break its fall or in an attempt to regain its balance—slashed across my chest. A steel-sharp nail tore through the leather as if it were no more than silk. The claw struck one of the makeshift armor plates within, the demon-proof material preventing the point from tearing open my vitals. But the power of the glancing blow still sufficed to spin me around.

I stumbled in a complete circle, but kept my feet. Even as I completed my round, the wolf demon was already flinging itself back into the fray, passing between me and Azeglio. I was afforded a moment to assess my condition—mercifully undamaged, thanks to my homemade armor—and to observe the proceedings.

A glance around showed most of the Tea House patrons clambering over the fence at the south and west ends of the patio, plunging into the bushes below, and slipping by the Venatores, who would probably have no inclination to stop them, even were they not busy with my companions. Hard to blame the tea-drinkers; the entertainment value of the martial display had just been replaced by a very real risk to life and limb.

I discovered I couldn't move much farther into the patio, lest I run afoul of the duel occurring at my back, Herbieto and Vicenzu going at it with gusto, if not a great deal of skill.

Only one Venatore remained visible on Marteo's side of the patio, and that one was probing the shrubbery with the end of his halberd. At the other side of the patio entry, Domenico was a blur, threatening each Venatore who tried to climb the fence while simultaneously fending off the slashes and thrusts of the other Venatores' halberds.

My glances around had allowed Azeglio to close. Nearer than I'd intended, in fact. I grabbed a handy chair and hurled it at him. He batted it aside, shifting a hip. I'd done no damage, but I'd bought myself time to move another step back. Someone trod on my heel. I heard Vicenzu curse.

I needed another venue for this fight. Azeglio flashed another of his triumphant smiles. I realized I'd love to smash out a few of those glittering teeth.

I planted a foot on a chair, then hopped from it atop a table. The tables cleared away for my disrupted duel with

Vicenzu provided wobbling, gap-surfaced footing. That presented an interesting challenge.

"Come on, Azeglio," I said, stepping back to grant him room to join me. "Don't you think you deserve a higher stage for your part of the drama?"

The table behind me shifted as it took my weight, the legs complaining as the table scraped a half-inch or so across the travertine before settling. Above, another band of clouds was passing. A stretch of clear sky followed, but behind it I saw a mass of black, threatening a deluge. The wolf demon was tangling gamely with the war demon, lasting longer than I'd anticipated, though already I saw steaming, orange-glowing rents in its flanks. I couldn't spare a glance at the other combats; Azeglio had accepted my invitation, hopping unhesitatingly up onto the unsteady plain of tabletops.

I came to meet him, hoping to catch him while he was still gaining his balance. I kicked a tea cup at him, nearly losing my own balance as the table tilted up a couple of degrees beneath me, before slamming back down on the tile. The tea cup glanced off of Azeglio's shin. His barked laugh cut off as I feinted a thrust at his face, then pronated my wrist, redirecting the blade toward his chest. He almost bought the feint, but managed to parry, shuffling back dangerously close to the edge of the table supporting him. Then he launched a series of thrusts and shallow lunges that sent me reeling back across the uncertain surface of our elevated piste.

Table legs protested as they grated over the tiles, shifting beneath my weight, some tipping, threatening to topple or dislodge me. I nearly dropped a leg through a gap between two tables, my left boot heel providing me just enough grip on the surface of the table behind to prevent me plunging through. I could feel the rear legs of that table rise. It was going to fall forward if I continued placing my weight where it was, hurling me onto my face beneath Azeglio's sword point. I leaned forward, placing my weight on my right foot, while catching in a bind a thrust aimed at my outside hip. That lifted my weight from the troublesome table and served to bring Azeglio's assault to a temporary halt.

"I'll be glad to see you dead," Azeglio said. "But I must admit you deliver entertaining table talk."

I scowled. The bravo is supposed to provide the banter.

Activity to my left drew a glance. Vicenzu and Herbieto were locked corps-a-corps, grunting, sweating, and swearing at each other. A half-full tea cup rested by my left foot. I scooted it across the tabletop with the edge of my boot. It shattered on the tile behind Vicenzu, where he stood wrestling with Herbieto. The grifter's foot slipped in the spilled tea, taking his right leg out beneath him. He went down on one knee, left hand out to prevent him falling farther.

It all happened in eyeblinks. Vicenzu raised his sword in a desperate attempt to interpose it between his body and Herbieto's sword. The attempt failed. Herbieto drove Garon's rapier down, over Vicenzu's guard, plunging the point into Vicenzu's neck immediately above the collarbone. The rapier slid through, several gore-dripping inches emerging from the back of the ruff Vicenzu wore with his doublet.

I wished I could have observed Herbieto's expression

as he realized he'd avenged his father, and had done so by his own hand. But Azeglio was unwilling to grant me that liberty. He was on me again. We crossed swords, fighting a tight, almost stationary duel, neither of us willing to further risk the treacherous footing of the tea house tabletops. Not immediately, at any rate.

We dueled in earnest then, Azeglio and I. I could not deny his skill. Despite the perilous footing of the battlefield, I found myself dropping into the familiar focus of fencing, thinking two or three moves ahead while still remaining alive to the immediate needs of the moment, responding to each flicker of Azeglio's blade with counters so deeply ingrained through repetition that they were practically instinctual. And at the same time, a detached part of me wondered at my involvement in this affair. I'd faced more than my share of duels. But never across a plain of adjacent tabletops, while demons, assassins, witch hunters, witches, and fencing masters battled around me. I felt a genuine grin stretching the skin over my cheeks, not merely the artificial smile I often employ to dismay my opponent.

I was enjoying myself. And I was pleased for Herbieto. On the other hand, Domenico and Marteo were likely not having much fun. And Maralla remained in danger, busy at her conjuring while demons savaged each other nearby. Better if I wrapped matters up with Azeglio before any of my companions took a serious hurt.

If, that is, Azeglio would cooperate. He was proving a better swordsman than I'd anticipated. Our duel expanded again, exigencies forcing us to roam. We ranged across the tabletop piste, leaping gaps, catching our balance as tables shifted or wobbled precariously, all the while engaging in a vigorous, scientific bout of thrust, parry, and riposte that I imagined might impress even Domenico, were he not too busily engaged fighting off Venatores to watch.

A croaking bellow drew my attention as well as Azeglio's, and we ceased our contest momentarily by some sort of unspoken agreement. The frog demon had leapt from its perch atop the iron pickets of the fence. It had judged its moment well, I saw. It now clung from the wolf demon's back, its jaws clamped down on one arm, its claws dug into the torso that already bore evidence of suffering numerous gashes and punctures.

Herbieto had joined Domenico in holding off the Venatores, though his aid consisted primarily of drawing the attention of one of the soldiers away from the true threat of Domenico's darting sword. None of the Venatores had yet tried to pass through the demon-obstructed gateway, restricting their efforts to either belaboring Domenico with halberds over the top of the palings, or attempting to clamber over the fence while Domenico was occupied. The demon battle remained largely confined to the gateway area, and the Venatores seemed to deem it the path of wisdom to avoid risking that approach. I could not blame them.

A howling rent the air. The war demon had gotten ahold of the wolf demon, hoisted it—and the frog demon clinging to its back—and pulled it close, onto the glittering points of its horns. The prongs gored deep, inflicting damage too great for the wolf demon to sustain in addition to its other wounds. As the howl continued, the wolf shape began to waver. Solid matter at the edges of the demon form flickered and whisked away in bits of orange-tinged smoke. Within moments, the wolf demon had dissipated, whether returned to the demon realm or destroyed entirely I couldn't say.

Nor did I have time to speculate. The destruction of the wolf demon left my small band now faced with two of the conjured entities, under the command of the Questor General. We were done for.

Azeglio beamed at me. The war demon emitted a triumphant roar. The frog demon bounded forward, leaping toward Herbieto.

As the frog demon hopped, a columnar spiral of smoke manifested before Maralla, from—I assumed—the conjuring circle she'd been employed in creating. A familiar-looking demon materialized. Whether it was the same one Maralla had summoned to chase me from her rooms, its sibling, or one of a myriad of an identical breed inhabiting the world of demons is a question for the Collegium. It reached out a hand to snag the frog demon in mid-spring.

From the frog demon emerged a startled *gawwwp* as it came to an abrupt stop at the height of its arc. Maralla's demon wrapped another hand around the frog demon's leg as the creature flopped to the patio, webbed fingers scrabbling on the travertine. Then, with a wrenching turn and a heel spin, Maralla's demon swung the frog demon along a half-circle trajectory that rose and fell as it went, terminating atop the pointed iron posts of the Tea House fence. The frog demon, punctured through in at least three spots, burst. The wet fragments underwent a rapid transformation, turning to steam and dissipating before striking the ground or any of the combatants.

Maralla's demon then shifted position to face the war demon. It seemed to me about as one-sided a contest as that faced by the wolf demon. Still, it meant I wasn't in immediate peril of being torn to bloody rags by a war demon. I was merely back to facing the point of Azeglio's sword. So, an improvement.

Azeglio's smile vanished. I offered one of my own to replace it.

I saluted. He snarled, kicked a saucer my way, then lunged. Our duel resumed in earnest, as, I could only assume, did that fought by Domenico, Herbieto, and the remaining Venatores. And, perhaps, Marteo. Wherever he'd gotten to.

The duel proceeded back and forth across the table tops. At length my luck—or balance—failed. A table tilted beneath me, dropping me on my back in the center of the patio where I'd fought Vicenzu. I slapped down my left hand as I fell, absorbing enough of the impact up through my arm that the fall failed to drive the breath from my body. And instead of cracking my skull open on the travertine, I merely suffered a blow that was likely to lead to a headache. If I lived.

I immediately rolled toward the tables, taking shelter from what I presumed would be Azeglio's descent, sword-point first. Chairs clattered and fell in my wake. I rolled to a stop against several chair legs, then rose to my feet, heaving tables up and away from me like a dog bursting through a flock of pigeons.

Azeglio retreated from a tumbling table, swearing. He

must have come close to skewering me while I was on the ground. I kicked aside a toppled chair and came on. A glance showed that Maralla's demon was getting the worst of the demonic affray, one arm hanging limp at its side. Herbieto had both hands wrapped around the haft of a halberd, standing inside the reach of the weapon's blade and point, and was engaged in a tug-of-war with the Venatore holding the other end. Domenico's sword blade showed red for most of its length, but the man himself was panting, beginning to move slowly as he engaged the only other Venatore I could see.

I saw nothing of Marteo. Of Maralla, I thought I caught a glimpse of her working beneath rows of tables, wisely getting beyond the immediate vicinity of the battling demons.

Then Azeglio occupied my attention fully. He threw a chair at me and followed up with his sword as I ducked the ungainly missile. I parried the thrust later than absolutely ideal, suffering a scratch along my right cheek in penalty. The insufferable smile of satisfaction Azeglio produced only added indignity to the stinging pain.

I gave ground, gradually, grudgingly, trying to ascertain a pattern in Azeglio's attacks or a weakness in his response to my reflexive ripostes. I found no obvious flaws in his art. I imagined that the Questor General must spend every moment not otherwise dedicated to hunting down witches in fencing practice. His style was classic, academically so. Now that we were off the table tops, and no longer hurling furniture at one another, he seemed even more comfortable, more self-assured.

To give him his due, he had good reason for his self-assurance. But he was facing Cesar the Bravo, a man trained as much by the harsh immediacy of street fighting as by the strict pedagogy of the fencing master.

A roar of triumph told my ears what I couldn't be bothered to observe with my eyes; the war demon had destroyed Maralla's demon. Time once again ran short.

Behind Azeglio, and sweeping towards me, came a wall of shadow. The threatening mass of rain clouds had come at last, pushing aside the stretch of blue sky. I marked the approaching crawl of relative darkness, observing the steady progress of an advancing line of heavy, black shadow. At the precise moment that shadow reached Azeglio's back, a heartbeat before the light abruptly dimmed, I moved, offering Azeglio an opening on a high line.

The *passato soto* is a risky maneuver. If it fails, it leaves the fencer attempting it temporarily at the mercy of an active opponent. As such, it is generally only attempted in circumstances that obscure the move, such as limited visibility. Thus, it is more commonly known by the suggestively ribald name of "the night thrust."

I had seen the wall of shade coming and was prepared for it. Azeglio was caught unaware. As the cloud dropped visibility to conditions nearing those of dusk, I also dropped, throwing my back leg far out behind me, my front knee bending as deeply as possible, while I bent forward at the waist. Meanwhile I stretched the fingers of my left hand wide, placing my palm on the hard solidity of the travertine tiles, supporting my suddenly unbalanced body. At the same time, I lunged, slipping underneath Azeglio's thrust passing overhead. My blade entered beneath the Questor General's short ribs, at a rising angle. The momentum from his own thrust carried him forward, burying my rapier even more deeply.

Azeglio emitted a gasping grunt. Looking up, I saw no smile on his face, only an expression of surprise. I pushed myself upright, levering the blade in more deeply as I rose. I caught his right arm with my left as I did, controlling his sword hand. No point in letting a dying man get in a final blow. And he was dying. My standing altered the angle of the blade inside his torso. I could feel the resistance within as the steel tore through muscle and organs, passing through them on the way to Azeglio's heart.

I looked into the Questor General's eyes, now wide with pain and fear. He moved his lips, trying to speak. But before he could utter whatever last thoughts were passing through his mind, two hands were on his cheeks, turning his head.

Maralla had, unnoticed, risen up from where she'd concealed herself beneath the tables. She forcefully swiveled Azeglio's head to face her.

"You failed to catch me, witch hunter," she hissed.

A groaning exhalation emerged from Azeglio. And, as if that final breath had been all that was keeping him upright, his body sagged. I allowed his dead weight to drag him free of my rapier, and the corpse of the Questor General thumped to the tiles of Kertzel's patio, his slack-featured face slipping from between Maralla's hands.

Only then did I turn to regard the war demon, belatedly realizing I should have been a trifle more concerned with it moments before. The great beast was shuffling toward us, its horned head casting side to side, as if searching for something. Its steps faltered, and the head turns grew erratic, uncertain.

"Step away from the body, Cesar," Maralla said, speaking quietly, but easily heard on the Tea House patio gone very quiet.

She didn't need to repeat the instruction. I backed away to the east while Maralla did likewise to the west. The war demon snuffled about a moment longer, then seemed to pick up Azeglio's scent, though I have doubts that any actual smelling was involved. The connections forged by a magus and a conjured demon were probably more involved and esoteric than mere odor. That was all beyond me, though. However it did so, the war demon moved to Azeglio's side, looming over the crumpled body. It stood still, as if awaiting instructions. Then the snuffling began again. The huge, ugly head tilted, like a confused dog.

And then the war demon faded away, dissolving in a swirling column of ochre dust shot through with tongues of yellow flame.

I watched its return to the demon realm, feeling two burgeoning emotions vying for supremacy within me: relief and triumph. I'd completed two jobs, somehow managing to fulfill both of my client's commissions at the same time. And I'd come through it all alive, which was nearly as astonishing. Assuming I could collect the rest of my fees, I could dispense with monetary concerns for a good year, perhaps more if I stopped spending like a bravo. I could patronize both Domenico and Donatello without fear of financial embarrassment. After a decent interval I could show my face in Giacomo's—shiny coin salves most wounds.

And I could move to someplace fit for human habitation.

Though, perhaps I ought to put it all off for a while. I'd publicly fought with men sworn to the Collegium. I'd killed the Questor General of the Venatores. It might behoove me to absent myself from Plenum for a season or two. I had the coin to afford a bit of travel. Something to think about, at any rate. Perhaps I could acquire a traveling companion.

What better traveling companion than Maralla? On that last thought, I glanced toward where I'd last seen her. She wasn't there. Looking around the patio, I found her in close conversation with Herbieto, who stood protectively near her.

Very near.

So that was the way of it. I shrugged, philosophically, then took in the rest of the aftermath of the Tea House battle. Domenico had taken a chair. He sat, panting, bloody rapier still clutched in one hand. He appeared unscathed. Of course. The man hadn't even taken a scratch. Across the fence that he'd held almost single-handedly, not a Venatore was visible. I did see Marteo, however. He rose from where he'd been stooping, a dripping dagger in one hand, a coin purse with cleanly severed leather ties in the other. Perhaps Domenico had enjoyed more aid in his battle than I'd known. Marteo's hood had fallen back, revealing his sallow, gaunt features. Marteo saw me looking his way. He winked, raised his hood, then disappeared down the embankment amongst the shrubbery.

The threatening cloud above began to deliver a

desultory scattering of fat, heavy raindrops. Time to go.

Chapter 18

I crossed the patio to where Domenico sat, my legs suddenly weary, my arms heavy. It took me two tries to sheathe my rapier. Nonetheless, I offered Domenico my hand, offering to help him rise.

Domenico stared at the hand for a moment, eyes narrowing scornfully. He rose smoothly to his feet, unaided.

"If you ever have children, Cesar," he said, "don't let them talk you into idiotic heroics." He shook his head. "Little girls. Cuteness is as deadly as sharpened steel."

"Well, Maestro, thank Valentina for the loan of her heroic father."

Domenico grunted. "The price of lessons is going up, Cesar. At least, it's going up for overdressed bravos." He offered me the slightest of nods—and, it was just possible, the hint of a smile—then headed toward the stair leading down from Kertzel's to the Escaline. At the point nearest to where Maralla and Herbieto stood, he paused. "If you two want to continue lessons at the salle, I'm offering an introductory rate. Fortune go with you."

Then he was gone.

I made my way over to the remaining pair, trying to keep my legs limber. After all, I still might need to flee from something in the aftermath of this escapade.

"Herbieto," I asked, "have I satisfactorily completed my commission?"

"That's unclear, Cesar," Herbieto said. A slight frown drew a divot between his eyebrows. "Ultimately, I had to do the work myself." He nodded at Garon's sword, which Garon had apparently not felt the need to recover; he and Phonsic having wisely taken to their heels at some point during the chaos.

I prepared to argue. While I could not dispute the fact that he'd run Vicenzu through, I was the one who publicly challenged Vicenzu and forced him to accept a duel. As per the contract. I'd done the work asked of me. How could I be penalized for the intrusion of Questor General Azeglio and a demon?

Perhaps Herbieto observed on my face the composition of my thesis. He produced a short bark of laughter before I could begin. "Come by the millinery, Cesar. I'll see you get the twenty-seven pistras you have coming to you. And worth every coin. If not for you I'd never have crossed swords with Vicenzu. Thank you. I feel as if I've set down a burden I've been carrying around for a long time. I feel lighter. Younger, even."

He reached out a hand. I grinned, extended my own, and we clasped forearms.

"I feel older," I said. "Five years ago, I'd have taken down Azeglio in two passes. But, time is inexorable. Like a tavern bill, eventually we all must pay. Speaking of which, we'd probably best leave Kertzel's before we end up paying for the corpses littering the premises."

"I suppose we should," Maralla said, sounding uncertain. "But I'm not yet sure where I'm going." She and Herbieto shared a look. They'd clearly been discussing something, but hadn't yet reached a resolution. Where would she go? Her role in Vicenzu's confidence game was at an end. Was it safe for her to return to her rooms? Perhaps, but that would depend upon Azeglio having failed to keep any records of his witch hunt. Maralla could do what she liked, but in her position, I'd not have relied upon such an assumption.

Clearly Herbieto wanted to offer her shelter with him. Just as clearly he was nervous to do so, perhaps thinking it presumptuous, perhaps simply too frightened of her rejecting the offer. I guessed Maralla felt it would be presumptuous of her to suggest it herself.

I readied myself to play matchmaker and raise the idea for them both. But the clearing of a throat behind me disrupted the attempt before it began.

I spun about on heel and toe. Then the hand I'd sent to my rapier hilt paused, hovering over the grip. Ascending the final stairs to the patio came my other client, Primate Aldus Fenetto, attired in full Collegium regalia. His henchman Klask followed close at his heels, one hand on the hilt of his own sword. Behind trooped a half-dozen men in Fenetto's regalia. And close on their heels trudged four demons, short-legged and long-armed, furred like apes, though no apes I'd ever seen bore pelts of shimmering blue and yellow, nor possessed elongated, trough-like heads.

What did Fenetto intend? It would not be the first time a client had turned on me, using me to achieve some goal and then treating me like a loose end to be cut off, like a workman hired to build a secret fortress, then buried beneath the cellar. Part of me wished that Domenico and Marteo had remained at Kertzel's a trifle longer.

Fenetto paused at the top of the stairs. His eyes swept past me, barely pausing before moving on to focus on Maralla. His customary expression of command and easy competence softened, his firm jaw developing a quiver. He swallowed. Twice. Then he regained control.

"Klask," he said over his shoulder, "collect the bodies."

Klask nodded. He descended a couple of steps. I could hear him issuing orders, though I couldn't make out the words. The liveried servants dispersed into the foliage, clambering over the escarpments, the demons following behind.

Fenetto approached me. I let my sword hand relax, allowing the arm to hang loosely at my side. It seemed he did not intend to employ the expedient of killing me and tossing my corpse into the Cloatus to avoid paying the remainder of my fee. Good.

He glanced behind me. Azeglio's body lay where it had fallen from the blade of my rapier. "Your methods are perhaps more straightforward than I entirely approve, Cesar," he said. "Effective, nonetheless. There lies the proof. I am in your debt."

"That's easily cleared up, Your Eminence," I said, holding out my hand, palm up.

Fenetto chuckled. "Klask will pay the remainder of your fee, once the work party clears away the...evidence." He paused. I saw his expression shift again, through tenderness and doubt, before settling on resolution. "Now, if you will excuse me, Cesar, there is something I'd like to do that I've put off long enough."

I shifted aside, pivoting as I did so in order to keep my eyes on the Primate as he crossed the patio to where

Maralla still stood with Herbieto.

What must it be like to face a daughter who remained unaware of your existence? Did Fenetto fear her reaction to learning the truth? Was he merely embarrassed? Ashamed? Did he harbor hopes of a grand reunion, of immediate acceptance? I couldn't say for sure. The problems the great and powerful bring upon themselves might be beyond the imagining of a lowly bravo. But I doubted it. The problem seemed human enough. I guessed he was experiencing the gamut of emotion, from fear to hope, filtered through a father's concern that he'd failed in his responsibilities, that he'd not done all he could for his child.

Fenetto cleared his throat, hesitated. But when he spoke, his confident, commanding persona came through clearly. He'd been a magus and a power in the Collegium for most of his life. Confidence—or at least the expression of confidence—must be second nature by now.

"Maralla," he said, "allow me to introduce myself. I am Primate Aldus Fenetto. And I am your father."

Maralla went momentarily limp, knees actually sagging, jaw opening. I had seldom seen such a reaction outside a playhouse. Herbieto's arms encircled her, supporting her for the couple of seconds it took Maralla to recover herself. She may not have her father's lifetime of Collegium politics to teach her, but from what I'd observed she possessed a native gift of poise and self-control. Such characteristics were probably essential to summoning and controlling demons.

"My father?" Maralla asked. Then she chuckled. "I suppose that does explain a few things. A magus. Of course."

Rustling and grunts of efforts indicated that Klask's work party was engaged in clearing the battlefield. I had to admire Fenetto's intelligence and initiative. He could earn the approval of the Inner Council—perhaps even the Predicant himself—by cleaning up the mess the Questor General had made. The semi-secret organization would remain semi-secret, the bodies quietly cleared away. The stories told by Kertzel's patrons would be contradictory and shy of essential details. In a city in which demonic activity was almost commonplace, interest in this tale would dissipate—merely one more anecdote, one more tile in the mosaic of life in Plenum buried within the larger picture. The entire incident would thus be soon swept beneath a rug. A new Questor General would be elected, the Venatore losses replaced. The Collegium would continue hunting down gifted women unwilling to join the Sorority. The status quo reestablished. All this due to Fenetto's quick, decisive action. Who would imagine that the Collegium's benefactor had acted solely to rescue his daughter from that same Venatore organization to whose aid he'd come?

That daughter was looking at him speculatively. "I want to thank you for looking after my mother all those years, Your Eminence," she said.

I could see Fenetto's body relax, as he released the tension he'd been carrying. He must have feared anger, recrimination, claims of abandonment.

"I did what I could to see that both of you were comfortable," Fenetto said. "I know I could have done more. I should have done more. I just don't know what.

And, please, Maralla—daughter—do not call me 'Eminence.' I would prefer 'Father.'"

"Father? I can do that," Maralla said. She smiled. "Father, I am not angry with you. When I grew old enough to ask questions, I was briefly angry. But Mother always spoke well of my absent father. She never truly lied about you. She never claimed to be a widow. But neither did she tell me the full truth. She said you were a good man and that you were doing what was best for us. And I believed her. We quarreled sometimes. What mother and daughter do not? But I always trusted her. So, if she said you were a good man, then you are."

Maralla looked down at the tile for a moment before she continued. "When she died I was furious with you—with the unknown you. But I realized that you loved her, and you must have loved me. I knew almost no one else who lived as comfortably as did Mother and I. You could have simply abandoned us, without a soldi. I admit it took me a day or two to get to that realization. Grief and anger are not conducive to clear thinking."

There might not have been a family resemblance, but I now felt certain they were related. Maralla had inherited her father's intellect. She considered a problem from all angles, thought through it.

I retrieved a fallen chair, planted it on the patio from where I could keep an eye on the stairs, as well as watching the newly united father and daughter as they conversed. I felt no shame at my obvious eavesdropping. I'd worked hard enough to bring about this meeting. I settled myself down on the seat, realizing only then how tired I was. I hoped the conversation did not last much longer, or I'd not be able to rise.

"Am I a good man? I don't know. I try to be," Fenetto said. "Though I was not with either of you, I did not abandon you. I ensured the estate received ample funds. And that I received regular reports on both your mother and you. I had my eye on a Red Hat, you see. I could not risk a scandal as I rose through the hierarchy. If I'd had my Red Hat, well, I could have snapped my fingers at the lot of them, visited as I wished. Even kept you here with me in Plenum, openly. But my rise has not been that rapid."

Fenetto looked about him, inspecting the patio and checking on Klask's progress. He seemed pleased, though he tapped the fingers of one hand against the knuckles of the other, suggesting a growing impatience.

"I believe a window to the Inner Council has opened, Maralla," Fenetto said. "I may soon be in a position to offer you protection. Councilor Fenetto, Elector Fenetto could keep the Venatores at bay permanently. I could even teach you myself, though I'm not sure what more of the science of Conjuration you have left to learn."

Maralla smiled. "That would be wonderful. I would like to become acquainted with my father, openly and without fear of being delivered to the Sorority. Yet, I hear a 'however' in your words."

Fenetto returned the smile. The two of them almost quivered with repressed joy. "The window may have opened, but I cannot crawl through it immediately. Gaining a seat on the Inner Council and donning the Red Hat will take some time, and is not a certainty. In the meantime, I wish to see you safe, somewhere away from the spying eyes of a renascent Venatore organization. A new Questor General will doubtless be appointed soon. And locating you would likely be a priority for him."

"Well, father, I am used to taking care of myself. I can keep my head down while I find some other way to support myself. In fact, I do have an offer of temporary lodgings." Maralla gestured toward Herbieto, who had hovered nearby, quiet and clearly nervous. "This is Herbieto, a respected merchant. He has graciously offered to allow me quarters, next to his mother's room, in his villa."

She may have embellished and whitewashed that somewhat. Already she felt the need to conceal from her father any suggestion of impropriety. There were layers of irony there I felt inadequate to grasp. And, while I'd never seen Herbieto's home, I doubted it qualified as a villa.

I failed to conceal a grin, though I didn't try hard.

Fenetto shifted to inspect Herbieto, though I doubted very much that the Primate hadn't already noted the man, wondering who he was, and of what his relationship to Maralla consisted.

"Your Eminence," Herbieto said, offering a slight bow.

"I'm sorry," I said to Fenetto, deciding I'd kept out of the conversation long enough. "I failed to introduce you. This is the milliner and accomplished duelist, Herbieto of the Flashing Blade."

"You do realize that I still hold the bulk of your payment, Cesar," Herbieto said.

"What? Have I oversold you?" I asked.

Maralla laughed, placing a hand on Herbieto's forearm as she did so.

"Clearly there are portions of the story I have not been apprised of," Fenetto said. "I keep an eye on you, daughter, but I do not spy on you. I would like to hear more of your exploits, Herbieto. You seem a man of...disparate accomplishments." He lifted a palm to forestall Herbieto's objection. "But, perhaps now isn't the best time. I am sure you can offer Maralla fitting accommodations in which to ride out events. However, might I suggest an alternative?"

Herbieto exchanged a look with Maralla. They both nodded. I expected they both felt a certain relief. While the two of them did seem absurdly attracted to each other—why a milliner, Maralla? Why not a bravo?—I guessed they both felt a certain trepidation at the thought of immediately moving into Herbieto's place. They'd both be eager to hear Fenetto's suggestion if it offered a temporary reprieve from such a precipitous act.

"You are both fond of wine, I presume," Fenetto said. "Do you care for Cellian? I happen to have a vineyard in one of my northern estates. It is far enough from Plenum—from the Collegium—to provide a high degree of safety from the new Questor General, whoever he might be. You can act as my factor and overseer while I play at politics. You are a merchant, Herbieto. Perhaps you can audit my accounts, see if my vintners are drinking up all the profit."

"And if they are, I will conjure a vengeance demon to chase them through the grapes," Maralla said. "I like your idea, father. But only if you come to visit soon. We have much to talk about."

Herbieto nodded. "I must speak with my mother and my employees first, and arrange for the business to run without me for a while." He looked at me. "And, I suppose I ought to visit my banker. I owe a debt."

"That you do," I said. "Don't think I'm offering a discount just because you pitched in to help."

"I wouldn't consider it, not even in jest."

"I too owe a debt," Fenetto said. "You've not been idle, have you, Cesar?"

"If a man wants to eat, he needs must work," I said. I flicked a finger ringingly against the knuckle bow of my rapier. "Each man to his own tools, Your Eminence."

Fenetto looked about him. He gestured toward the stairs. Behind Klask ranked the demons, their arms piled with corpses. "My tools seem to have completed their work," the magus said. "I think we have lingered here at this charming establishment long enough. I suggest we reconvene tonight at my manse. There I will direct Maralla and Herbieto to my northern estate, and Klask will pay you the remainder of your fee, Cesar."

I'd have preferred the coin right there and then, but declined to say so. Instead, I merely suggested to Herbieto that he bring along what he owed. I could at least save a trip.

I followed the others down the stairs from the Kertzel's patio. Herbieto and Maralla already looked like a couple. I wished them well, ignoring a twinge of jealousy. The world was full of women eager to encounter a bravo. Why begrudge the loss of one? Even one as charming, beautiful, and frighteningly talented as Maralla.

The important point was that I would be paid. I still supposed I ought to clear out of Plenum. Fenetto talked up a plausible future in which he'd rise within the episcopal hierarchy and secure the safety and anonymity of his daughter from the Collegium. But that notional shield—if it indeed came to pass—might not cover Fenetto's hired sword. Best not to rely overmuch on the gratitude of the wealthy and powerful. Once I crossed the city to my rented hovel, I would empty the concealed space beneath the loose floorboard of my few valuables, bundle them up, and bring them with me to Fenetto's, without a single look back. With a full purse, I could find a bed for the night, then leave the city behind me in the morning. For a while. Once I felt comfortable that no lingering questions remained regarding a certain bravo and a number of Venatore corpses, I'd return. And hire lodgings more suitable for a man of my station and wealth.

I followed the odd procession of demons, lackeys, magus, witch, and merchant wending down the Escaline. The street remained unusually free of traffic. Even in Plenum, people tend to remain indoors when a band of demons troops by, bearing corpses.

It would be good to get out of the city, enjoy some open country and a quieter existence for a season or two.

"Your Eminence," I said, pushing my way past the dawdling pair of Maralla and Herbieto, "why not break out another bottle of the Cellian this evening? I think you deserve a celebration. And I'm certain I've earned it."

The Bronze Helm;
or,
Unfinished Business

Spring traditionally commences the campaign season, with the weather beginning to warm. Warm is relative. I'm accustomed to a more southerly clime. This far north, the spring wasn't much better than a Plenum winter. And the rain hadn't eased significantly since the change of season. The condotta's bivouac, beyond the walls of our employer's castello, was a mire bedecked with mud-splattered canvas tents. While placing some time and distance between myself and certain concerns back home in Plenum, I shared one such overcrowded shelter with three other mercenaries.

At least, I *had* shared. That arrangement might have come to an end. A punctured goatskin of wine had become a point of contention between myself and my three large northern tent mates. I'd promised recompense, but my ready funds were insufficient to cover the debt, my purse sagging as empty and flaccid as the goatskin.

I left my arquebus in the tent, not wishing to subject the mechanisms to the rain and damp. I deemed it wise to take along the remainder of the tools of my trade; the time of my return—if ever—remained in doubt. Unless I could somehow scrounge up the requisite coin, I might well find myself taking an unauthorized leave of absence. The rapier hung from a baldric over my shoulder. The main gauche—the parrying dagger with its comfortingly broad, hand-covering guard—rode on my right hip. And the broad, sturdy cinquedea that I preferred if forced to wade into a battle, rested at the small of my back, horizontally.

Before I belted and slung the weapons, I briefly debated whether or not to shrug into the padded leather garment that served me as armor. It provided little enough protection in the sort of affray I'd likely face in this campaign. I was still working on wheedling a breastplate and helmet from the condotta's armorer. I concluded that the leather jack was better than nothing, placing something between my skin and the edge of a blade. And, perhaps more importantly, it provided protection that standard steel plate could not: defense against demons.

Sometime back, in my more customary role of paid bravo in the city of Plenum, I'd had occasion to scavenge the shattered remnants of a metallic egg fashioned from some hermetic material used to imprison a demon. Under the theory that if it could keep a demon in, it could keep one out, I'd shaped and flattened the fragments of the strange metal and fitted them into pockets sewn into my leather "armor." It has proved effective. I've pondered, over the years, why the magi of the Collegium do not have this otherworldly, dull gray metal fashioned into armor of a more conventional nature. It took me longer than it should have to divine the answer. Our lords and masters in the Collegium are our lords and masters precisely because they can conjure and command demons. If the rest of us, the ungifted masses, could furnish ourselves with protection against the more overt, blunt threat to life and limb that demons represent, then the power of the Collegium would diminish. Thus, so far as I know, I'm the only one possessed of armor that can—at least in certain vital spots—withstand a war demon's claws and teeth.

I can't say I approve of the appearance of the armor. My ham-fisted modifications turned a handsome, functional garment into something lumpy and inelegant. I've found, however, that an artfully draped cloak can mitigate the worst of it.

I was glad of the cloak—as well as of my wide brimmed hat—as I slogged away from the tent. The pigeon feather in the hat band drooped in the incessant drizzle, and a chill wind knifed through cloak, jack, and doublet. I directed my booted steps through glutinous mud toward the castello for no other reason than that the walls might shield me from the wind and allow me to scheme in relative comfort.

The extent of the grounds impressed me. As did the castello itself: a fretted, two-story rectangular box set within a triangle of towers, all constructed of contrasting bands of basalt and dolomite. Beautiful, in its way, though insufficient to impress someone inured to the glories of Plenum, used to seeing the ruins of the Ancients, the grand palazzos climbing the Sabatine Hill, and the dazzling edifices of the Collegium. Primarily from the outside, admittedly.

The expanse of open space inside the walls could have allowed for all manner of structures. The Prefect had, however, elected to keep it relatively empty, except for a few modest outbuildings. And except for one notable object. As if of their own volition, my feet carried me that way.

Several dozen yards from the entry, tucked into a corner where a guard tower swelled out from the south wall, squatted what appeared to be a massive helmet; a swelling, visored helm, a relic of the type of armor worn a century or two ago. If intended for use, it must have been made for a giant. As I neared, it became clear that the helm was as tall as I. Upon closer examination it appeared to be made of bronze. Perhaps, then, a sculpture of some sort, I guessed, watching drops bead and drip from the eye slit.

"Like the statue, do you lad?"

I turned toward the speaker. A man with a shovel and bucket—both items bearing clear, aromatic evidence of their utility in clearing the grounds of horse dung— sauntered my way. Here was a man content with—or resigned to—his lot and in no particular hurry. He looked to be in his declining years, lined of face and thin of hair, his clothing—a linen smock and woolen trousers, topped with a long coat of ochre-dyed fustian—patched and grubby, yet fundamentally sound.

"Like it? Well, it is unusual," I said. "Hardly in keeping with the classical tradition."

The man snorted. "That's Tranta for you, son. Goes its own way."

"So, tell me, what is this helm supposed to be? Some representation of family history?"

"Some would have you believe that," the man said. He leaned on his shovel, apparently glad of a chance for a break, though he did not appear to have been exerting himself. "If you ask most in the Prefecture, you'll hear that the helmet is a symbol that the Prefect is descended from giants. Some of the fools even believe it."

"Not you, though," I said.

The man spat. "Nonsense. I've lived too long to be that credulous. Long enough, in fact, that I know the truth, from my father. The helmet—and the story—only go back two or three generations."

"I'm listening," I said.

"The grandfather—or great grandfather—of the current prefect wanted a piece of monumental statuary. Why, I don't know. I'd make up something, if I were telling this properly over a flagon of wine. Don't matter, though. The point is, he had a new magus, sent up by the Collegium, and asked him to conjure up a demon to do the work."

I nodded. The Collegium dispatched a magus to most of the polities of the Faithful, of whatever political makeup. The hierarchical status of the magus sent was tied to the perceived importance of the polity. A minor prefecture like Tranta might warrant, say, a mere catechumen, while a major mercantile city-state might demand a Primate, or even a Red Hat. The local ruler gained the skills and knowledge of the magus, as well as the implied sanction of the Collegium, while the Collegium collected local intelligence and maintained its supremacy and authority. Everyone won.

"Problem was, the new magus wasn't up to task. Conjured up the demon all right, even got it started on the job." Here the horseshit shoveler paused to nod at the helm. "But after that, he lost control. Couldn't get the demon to finish up. Couldn't dismiss it either. He went back to Plenum in disgrace."

"Couldn't the Collegium have just sent up a more experienced magus to correct the situation?"

"I reckon so. Thing is, the people of Tranta are stiff-necked. No Prefect of Tranta has offered a magus a position in his household since. That's a point of pride to some. Others think it makes us backward—behind the times and out of touch, if you get my meaning."

A new voice joined our conversation. "I see someone who is behind in his work and won't find me backward in correcting his malingering."

I shifted my head to take in the new speaker: tall, erect, and self-possessed, with bristling black eyebrows above an aquiline nose. I had to give credit to his tailor, though the style would appear outdated on the streets in Plenum. A crimson half-cloak offered the black doublet with its oversized shoulder rolls some protection from the rain, though the knee-breeches and hose were suffering a gradual soaking. An extravagance of gold-thread livened up the somber black of his clothing. He wore no sword, though thick bands of gold adorned the steel of hilt and pommel of the rondel dagger at his hip. This was clearly a man of wealth and power.

"I beg your pardon, My Lord," the man with the shovel and bucket said. He bobbed an obeisance and made to get on with his business with more alacrity than his age suggested possible. He banged the shovel against the bucket, knocking the bucket from his grasp and spilling its steaming contents upon the flagstones. He dropped to his knees, scooping frantically. I couldn't blame him for being nonplussed, caught by the Lord Prefect, spilling prefecture secrets to a stranger.

"Calm yourself, Giovan," the Prefect said. "I am not angry with you. You've divulged nothing vital. And, if I am not mistaken, this man here is in my employ."

"Cesar, arquebusier, fourth squadron," I said, sweeping off my hat. "At your service, My Lord." A touch of politeness seldom hurts. And if you later need to employ insolence, the shock of the change in manner from obsequious to contumacious renders it that much more effective.

"The services of your condotta are welcome. And expensive," the Prefect said. "I am Alonz of Tranta, hereditary Prefect." He switched his attention to the shit shoveler, dismissing him with a grace and good humor that elevated him in my eyes somewhat above the position to which I inwardly assign prefects, aediles, and other assorted picayune administrators.

"My apologies, arquebusier Cesar, if my retainer soiled your boots," the Prefect said, his face impassive.

I checked. My boots, cuffed fashionably at mid-thigh, remained free of horse dung, though woefully caked with the mud of the encampment. He'd made me look. Another point for Prefect Alonz.

"Is the story true, My Lord?" I asked, for something to say, and gestured at the gargantuan helm.

"In essentials, yes."

"So Tranta is without a magus," I said. Whatever the local significance of that fact, it was of more interest to me that it meant the condotta was without the support a magus could provide. That was unsettling information.

"I keep up the family tradition, yes. Though"—and here the Prefect of Tranta relaxed his posture and scratched at the trim goatee on his chin—"I cannot help but feel it would be a comfort to have the Collegium, upon its own initiative, dispatch to us an adept, or even a deacon. That demon, summoned by my great-grandfather's inadequate magus, is still resident in the bowels of the castello, never having been properly dismissed. It would be a relief to have it gone. Once that was done, I'd feel as if I could break from tradition without any loss of face and Tranta could rejoin the modern world. However, I cannot send to the Collegium without it being seen as an affront to my fathers. You see my problem."

I nodded. "You'd like a demon removed, but family tradition won't let you beg the Collegium for the favor. You're hoping to get rid of the pesky thing some other way."

"Somewhat inelegantly put. Accurate enough, however. I would, in fact, pay a tidy sum for the task."

I perked up. "Precisely how much makes a sum tidy? If I like the figure, then I'm your man. You can consider this eyesore gone." I reached out and rapped my gloved knuckles against the brazen helm. It rang dully, sonorously.

Alonz lifted his impressively thick brows. Then he stated a number. It was, indeed, tidy.

"Why would you get rid of it? Adds charm and character, a great bit of local color."

Another voice added to our conversation.

"Cesar, allow me to introduce Severin, the envoy from Vitenza, nobly attempting to prevent our prefectures' dispute from requiring resolution by force of arms."

The envoy gazed at me coolly. He stood nearly as tall as Alonz, possessed of the slender, fencer's build that by rights I ought to have, given my chosen profession. He wore powder blue and silver, and bore a rapier at his side. His gray eyes suggested a touch of the north in his ancestry. Despite my fastidious attire, his long-limbed elegance contrasted markedly with my squat, thick-muscled stevedore's frame. I disliked him at once, primarily since his intrusion endangered my procurement of lucrative employment. I hadn't yet sealed the bargain with the Prefect.

After that single look, Severin appeared to dismiss me as beneath his notice. "Shall we resume negotiations tonight?" he asked, then left upon receiving Alonz's assent.

"Pompous blatherskite," Alonz muttered at Severin's retreating back. "Well, Cesar, consider yourself engaged. I'll let the staff know that you are authorized in the castello. I suggest you begin by searching the chapel. The demon has been known to make an appearance there. Without a resident magus, I'm afraid we've rather neglected the place, so I apologize in advance for any cobwebs you may encounter."

I nodded, already beginning to regret my impulsive offer. I needed an immediate re-inflation of my empty purse, true. But tackling a demon single-handed was foolhardy even by my standards. Having done so in the past, I, of all people, ought to know better.

On the other hand, I did owe a debt—payable in the morning—to a trio of grumpy northern mercenaries with whom I shared a tent. The balance of unpleasantness weighed in favor of doing the job now and getting it over with.

No more dithering. I turned my steps toward the castello, searching for the chapel.

I found the chapel on the east side of the castello. It appeared to be a later addition, a rectangular box of red brick with a clay-tiled roof angling down to the modest ground floor entrance. It was grander inside. The manner in which the ceiling rose toward the altarpiece at the back wall, where chapel met castello, created an illusion of spaciousness. The interior brick walls were faced with creamy marble, veined with green. Probably a rather nice chapel, when not neglected. No lamps or candles flickered within. Only the open door and two high windows in the north and south walls provided any illumination, and that only the half-light of the overcast, sodden day.

After allowing my eyes to adjust to the gloom, I entered. The conditions were not as woeful as Alonz had hinted. Some beadle or sacristan attended to the place often enough that my boots did not kick up a layer of dust, nor did I need to brush aside cobwebs. Still, it clearly had not seen regular use in recent memory. The fraught, foreboding atmosphere of cemeteries and the deserted, ruined fanes of the Ancients suffused the room, seeming to increase in intensity the farther in I went. An eerie place, the chapel.

I reached the elevated altar, eyes darting left and right for any sign of the demon's presence. I saw nothing. I found only the back wall and a door into the castello. I tried the door, discovering it to be locked or barred from the other side. Turning, I faced back the way I'd come. The light from the front door now seemed to flood the chapel. I actually squinted and glanced down to avoid what struck my eyes as an intolerable glare. As I did, I noted that the altar appeared a trifle askew, not set on the dais at precisely right angles to the back wall.

I crouched and examined the base of the altar. It was indeed askew. I could make out a mark in the floor showing where the altar sat when properly oriented. Someone, or some demon, had shifted the blocky rectangle of the altar: an artistic piece in glossy hardwoods and rosy-hued marble slabs. I set a shoulder against the edge of the altar and applied pressure. With only the slightest of grating sounds and minimal resistance, the altar shifted further, swiveling on a concealed pivot. Below, I could see the top of a stairway dropping down into darkness.

Darkness. I did not intend to grope through some nighted, subterranean passage until I blundered into the waiting arms of a demon. Alonz had said he would alert the staff that I was authorized to roam the castello. It was time to take advantage of my privileges.

I left the chapel, circled around the castello, and announced myself to the first menial I met. Borrowing a lantern required but a few moments. Getting its reservoir topped with oil and the wick lit required an absurdly longer period of heel-drumming and finger-tapping, due to some abstruse law governing the interaction of logistics, people, perceived urgency, and time.

At length I returned to the chapel and the gaping entrance to the mystery beneath. A stairway cut neatly from the bedrock led to a tunnel floor I could just make out at the limit of my lamplight. Cursing easily punctured wineskins, I began my descent. I noted, as my head crossed the floor level of the chapel, the gleaming metal of the concealed pivot; both the shaft connected to the corner of the altar and the socket sunk into the stone floor appeared formed of solid bronze.

The temperature dropped, seemingly in concert with each step downward. The chill of the grave. A squared off tunnel commenced at the bottom of the stairway, a geometrically precise hallway of naked stone as neat as an architect's ruled lines on paper. I held the lantern high in my left hand and off to one side as I traversed the passageway.

After perhaps fifty strides, an opening yawned to my right. The tunneler seemed to have intersected a natural cavern here. Throwing the light of my lantern within, I could see an irregular, low-roofed chamber containing heaps of rock and soil, dozens of individual mounds. I guessed the tunneler had taken advantage of this space to deposit all the material removed to form the tunnel. What I didn't see was any sign of a demon. I presumed the demon had dug the tunnel, though I could not be sure. It might have been the work of an earlier prefect of Tranta; some hidden escape route, the passage to a treasure vault, or even a secret underground reservoir intended for emergency use during a siege. But it had probably been demon-work.

Seeing nothing therein, I moved on down the tunnel. After only a few steps, I heard a throat-clearing behind me.

"I'm afraid that is as far as I can let you proceed," the

Vitenzan envoy, Severin, said. "At least you'll have this convenient, pre-dug grave. A grander tomb than you'd otherwise merit, I dare say."

A metallic click and a flickering cone of light accompanied these words. I turned about to see the envoy setting down a lantern, the hood of which he'd apparently just lifted. I crouched to set my lantern down as well, keeping my eyes on the envoy as I did so.

"You proceed directly to threats on my life," I said. "Don't you find that more than a trifle undiplomatic for an envoy?"

"I would indeed, if I were treating with anyone of importance, rather than disposing of mercenary scum much as I would scrape dung from my bootheel." Severin smiled as he spoke, as if his words were a joke between friends rather than a calculated insult. Then he let the smile vanish. "Of course, in all honesty, I'm not really here to treat with Alonz in good faith. Vitenza has no interest in a negotiated peace. I'm merely stalling for time while we hire a second condotta."

Severin drew his rapier, the motion casual. He glanced at it, as if surprised to see it there. I shrugged and drew mine.

"What does this have to do with mercenary scum like me?" I asked, matching Severin's disinterested tone.

The envoy placed his left hand behind his back, then tugged free the main gauche he'd sheathed there.

"Unless I miss my guess, Alonz has finally decided to do something about the family demon. I can't have that," Severin said. He planted his right foot, extended his left leg behind, and began rocking back and forth, loosening his muscles. "Should Tranta overcome its intransigence and accept a magus from the Collegium, Vitenza would lose its tactical advantage in the coming campaign. I'm sure I need not explain to a sellsword how useful a war demon is on the battlefield."

I tried not to shudder as memories of exactly that flitted about the back of my mind. I dismissed the unpleasant thought and instead drew my own main gauche.

"I'll try to leave your face unmarked," I said, "as a courtesy to such of your family as might wish to view your body."

The envoy grinned. His eyes sparkled in the lantern light. Then he launched himself at me in a ferociously explosive fleche. His hips and back scraped the right wall of the tunnel as he passed, rapier point darting at my left side and main gauche parrying the cross-body thrust I aimed at his hip. I deflected his rapier with my main gauche, steel ringing from the wide-bellied guard. The tip of his blade scored a shallow furrow through the leather of my jack, leaving the skin beneath unscathed.

I pivoted on my heel, then took a few steps back to regain the center point between the two lanterns. Severin carried on into shadows before slowing, turning around, and returning to our subterranean piste. He raised his sword in salute. I responded. It was not a statement of respect so much as an unconscious gesture drilled into me over endless hours in the salle training with my fencing master, Domenico.

Severin advanced cautiously, his approach more conventional this time. I extended my rapier, crossing blades, and applying tension to test his response. His sword yielded to pressure, so I attempted a sudden glissade, scraping my rapier down the length of his and forcing it aside before a thrust in octave. The envoy skipped back parrying the thrust with his dagger. His slashing riposte surprised me. I leapt back in turn, catching the blow ringingly on the forte of my dagger.

By unspoken consent, we reset for another passage. I eyed my opponent with a wary respect. He was good. Somewhat unconventional, without the predictability of the purely academic fencer. That suited me. My earliest martial academy was the gutters of Plenum. Fighting dirty was not second nature with me, but first.

I let him press me back, guarding myself from his lashing thrusts and the occasional lunge. I answered with the barest minimum of ripostes necessary to keep him from mounting some elaborate gambit. It was exacting work; he nearly caught me a time or two. The light dimmed as I passed out of the area illumined by both lanterns, our flickering steel catching only the beams of the envoy's lantern.

I continued to give ground. Once even with the lantern, I dropped to a crouch. I slipped the blade of my parrying dagger through the handle of the lantern. I snapped up from the crouch, flinging the lantern from the blade at Severin's face. He was fast, his reflexes sharper than most men I've faced. His rapier moved instinctively, parrying away the missile. In tierce, I believe. But I wasn't paying close attention to his defense. I followed the lantern with a deep lunge. Occupied with the lantern, Severin failed to employ his main gauche in time. My thrust caught him below the sternum and exited at the base of his skull.

His blades dropped from suddenly nerveless hands. His body followed. I stood, letting the weight of the corpse free my rapier. The envoy had failed to stop me. Yet he had served as an agent of delay. With a demon still to face, perhaps he still might succeed in his ultimate purpose. But he'd never know.

I wiped my rapier clean, then sheathed both weapons before retrieving my lantern. The tunnel continued on, regular and unvarying. I followed along for another minute, beginning to wonder if the oil reservoir would hold out.

The hallway took a sharp turn to the left. I peered around the corner. At the limit of my light, I could make out the dark rectangle of an opening, as if the tunnel ended at a doorway. I could see nothing else, but thought I heard a metallic clang. Then another.

I crept along the tunnel, which now began to warm with each step. The opening grew more distinct. I was unable to make out much beyond the opening from this distance other than an impression of space. The sounds grew louder. Worried that the light would announce my presence, I set the lantern down, then continued as noiselessly as possible to the doorway.

Beyond the doorway yawned a cavern. To my uneducated eye, it appeared of natural origin but seemed to have been excavated to provide additional room: certain of the walls showed tool marks and looked entirely too regular to be natural. The floor had been leveled and sat several feet below the level of the tunnel. A short stone stairway linked the two.

All this was illuminated not by the feeble light of my

lantern—that in truth reached little farther than the foot of the stairs—but by the bright, golden refulgence of a blazing furnace standing off-center toward the right of the cavern. A massive stone crucible hung suspended above the red-hot fire. Ingots and irregular metallic chunks formed a pyramid near the fire. Forms and molds, long-handled dippers, presses and clamps covered a work table on the opposite side. Before the furnace, hammering a block of glowing bronze upon an anvil, stood the demon, its back to me. It appeared squat, though that was illusory. I figured it for about seven feet tall. Its breadth of shoulder and the thickness of its prodigious, inhuman musculature seemed to diminish its height. I was not fooled. Demons come in a myriad of forms, and few of those forms mimic human proportions. Nothing more than a thick apron and a tool belt covered the demon's mottled red and yellow scales. I figured the apron served more as a convenient place to store additional tools than as any sort of protection. The demon's hide likely provided all the protection against sparks and heat that it truly required.

At widely-spaced intervals against the walls of the cavern rested sections of completed work. Here a lower leg, encased in a greave, there an arm, complete with vambrace, rerebrace, and pauldron. All intricate, masterfully detailed casting, sculpting, and bronze-smithing on a heroic scale. Perhaps two-thirds of the work was complete. The demon remained true to its task. I wondered if the demon had actually finished the statue before, perhaps multiple times, merely to melt it down and begin again, unable to return to the demon world until dismissed, compelled again and again to sculpt the grand figure it was summoned to create.

If it couldn't be dismissed, the only other way to send it home was to destroy it. That is, to cause so much damage to its physical form that it could no longer sustain itself and must involuntarily disincorporate, returning to the demon world. As far as I know, I couldn't actually destroy it in any permanent, mortal sense.

Could I damage it enough? My rapier would prove a poor tool against that scaled hide. Even if a solid thrust could penetrate it, I'd merely annoy it. I kept the blade honed to a fine edge. But the rapier simply wasn't weighted properly to allow me to hack deeply enough into the demon's body to cause a catastrophic injury. The cinquedea sheathed at my back might do. I'd had some luck with it against demons in the past. But I doubted I could count on more than a single blow, if that. I needed an advantage, some equalizer, or at least some temporarily distracting edge.

I gave the hellish atelier another close examination. An idea began to form, as the demon continued forming the bronze upon the anvil. I fixed in my memory the contents of the cavern and their positions. Then I slipped quietly away and retrieved my lantern. Once beyond any remote chance of being overheard, I trotted through the tunnel, toward the chapel.

The rain had let up. Cloud breaks allowed a few shafts of sunlight to pierce through, brightening my path from the castello back to the condotta's encampment. After a brief stop at the tent to fetch my arquebus and offer a few words of assurance to my tent mates, I made for the magazine. Within that thick-walled dugout, powder, shot, coils of slow match, a pair of cumbersome siege guns on limbers, and several score of stone cannon balls were stored at a respectful distance from the mercenaries' tents.

Alonz's authority did not extend to the condotta, and thus I could not rely upon his remit to requisition supplies for my mission. Instead, I relied upon the old soldier's standby: I lied. I pointed to the glimpse of blue sky and told the quartermaster and the pair of halberd-armed guards that I wished to take advantage of the weather window to practice loading and firing the arquebus.

Whether impressed by my zeal, utterly unconcerned whether or not I was stealing powder and shot to sell to the camp followers, or simply wanting to get back to his tankard of mulled ale out of the wind, the quartermaster swallowed my story. I returned to the castello, loaded down not only with my cumbersome firelock, but also a powder horn (and the half-dozen more I'd snatched when the quartermaster turned his back), a cloth bag of leaden balls, and a coil of slowmatch.

The envoy's body remained where I'd left it. The sounds of the demon beating out a bronze section of its colossal statue welcomed me back to its infernal workshop. I got to work as well, as quietly as I could, but with the din and clatter of hammer on metal, my fear of being overheard was minimal. Opening the lantern, I set the end of the slow match aglow and clamped it in the serpentine of the loaded arquebus. Then I peered into the cavern.

The demon held a curved plate of bronze in a pair of tongs, reheating it over the furnace. Its attention remained fixed. I waited, however, until the metal had reached a temperature high enough to satisfy the demon and it resumed its tapping and banging. I wanted the din to mask any inadvertent noise I might make.

I took a steadying breath. Taking on a demon single-handedly tries the nerves. If I lived through the event, I intended to buy a cask of wine. I might even share it with the other three arquebusiers in my tent—once I'd drunk my fill.

I crept down the stairs. The temperature soared as I neared the cavern floor. Sweat instantly began soaking my shirt and hose. The earth had been carefully scraped and pounded smooth, creating an exactingly level surface for the artisan to do its work. The monumental sections of the statue rested against the walls, providing concealment and shadows as I slipped along the wall to my right.

That brought me closer to the furnace and the demon than I'd ideally prefer. But my target lay that direction rather than more comfortably off to the left. Moving from shadow to shadow, casting frequent glances at the back of the demon in hopes that it wouldn't turn and notice me, I worked my way toward a towering section of the statue's torso: a swelling breastplate and backplate resting upon faulds and tassets. I couldn't help but admire the detailing of the piece, each over-sized curving band, every enormous rivet exactingly detailed. Close up, I could see the hollow between breast and back plate, but there was less space therein than had the demon truly been fabricating a gargantuan set of armor. It had used substantial quantities of bronze in the casting of the piece, the exterior finished with a jeweler's precision, but the interior left unfinished, the inside of the mass of bronze forming the breastplate a mere hand's-breadth from the inside of the backplate. Something this weight would require several men equipped with pulleys and tackle to shift, though doubtless the demon had moved it without assistance.

With enforced patience, I pried the cap from my powder horn, then wedged the powder horn between the section of statue and the rough stone wall of the cavern, placing the mouth of the horn in a concavity of the backplate, and lodging the pointed end securely against a rough section of stone wall. Then I repeated the action with all but one of the remaining powder horns, taking pains to ensure a snug fit. A protruding irregularity of the cavern wall prevented my placing the last powder horn. I emptied the cloth bag of arquebus balls, then refilled it with the powder from the final horn. Before I stuffed this firmly into position, I punctured a hole in it and ran a trickle of powder down a runnel in the cavern wall, linking each horn to the granular trail leading all the way to the floor.

I considered the slowmatch, still gradually eating itself in the serpentine of the arquebus. In addition to fearing that the demon would glance behind itself, I'd been constantly worried that the heavy gun would slip from where I'd leaned it and bang against wall, statue, and floor as it fell. But the ungainly length of iron and wood remained in position. I retrieved it, reviewing my plan. The slowmatch could serve as a fuse, if I removed it from the serpentine and placed it on the ground, resting the far end in the spill of powder. The timing, however, concerned me. I doubted I could rely upon the steady burn rate of the slow match and compliant behavior from the demon to combine for split-second accuracy. I'd have to employ a more direct expedient.

There was nothing more to do. Unless I meant to give this over as a stupid idea and make a run for it, it was time to act.

The demon slipped the hammer into a loop on its belt. It picked up the bronze sheet, which, as it turned, I recognized as part of a gorget. As the demon continued to turn, it couldn't help but notice me the instant it raised its eyes from inspecting its handiwork.

I stepped away from the statue torso and off to the right, bringing the thick butt of the arquebus to my shoulder and leaning into it. The demon raised its head, clearly focused on me now. I slipped my fingers around the long trigger lever, pointed the barrel at the demon, and squeezed my hand. The powder flashed, bright and sharp, adding the tang of burnt gunpowder to an atmosphere already redolent of fire and hot metal. A moment later the arquebus barked, slamming the butt against my shoulder and sending the heavy ball tumbling toward the demon.

The bronze sheet in the demon's hands deformed and leapt free from its grip, a hole punched through the metal. The demon jerked back and sideways. And then it straightened up to face me, its eyes blazing, its thin lips pulled back to expose a serried rank of fangs. I saw no evidence the arquebus shot had inflicted any damage, other than perhaps a slight discoloration on a single, reptilian scale. Whether the bronze plate had slowed the bullet enough that it no longer possessed sufficient force to penetrate the demon's hide or whether the demonic integument was of such thickness that the bullet would not have punctured it anyway, I'd never know.

The demon emitted a guttural growl. It shuffled toward me, picking up speed. I wanted very much to turn and flee, get to the tunnel and run for my life. Instead, I let it approach. Closer. Then a little closer. I saw more clearly than I ever wanted to the thick, yellow, gnarled claws like aged, filth-encrusted ivory, at the ends of the demon's powerful hands. Claws and hands that were moments away from rending and tearing me to shreds.

Close enough. I turned on my heel, brushing past the breast-and-backplate sculpture. As I passed, I leaned down, setting the glowing end of the slowmatch against the terminus of the trail of powder where it trickled into a ragged fan on the glossily smooth floor. The powder ignited, hissing and snapping as it climbed the trail toward the open powder horns.

I wanted to run. But I needed to keep the demon close on my heels, ensuring it passed before the massive hunk of sculpted bronze. So I fled as sedately as possible, feeling as if the hot breath of the demon was stirring the hairs on the back of my neck.

A narrowly spaced sequence of explosions was followed by the squeal of metal on stone. I spun about to watch the colossal section of statuary topple. The demon's thick neck swiveled as it sensed the danger. Its legs propelled it forward, trying to escape the falling mass. It failed. The bronze struck the demon, a monstrous hammer blow forcing it to the ground.

But the statue did not strike the demon in the head. Neither did the statue crush the demon's chest. The creature's desperate lunge slipped its upper half out of the way, and instead of being smashed beneath a ton of nearly solid bronze, it was pinned at the hips and legs.

And I'd spun about too soon. Too near. A massive fist wrapped about one of my ankles and yanked. The arquebus fell from my hand as I was jerked from my feet. I hopped, staggered, and managed to keep from falling, though I could not fight the arm pulling me inexorably toward the gnashing, snarling mouth. Despite the trauma caused by the battering its lower half had endured, the demon still retained the strength and vitality necessary to pull me toward my doom.

The demon hauled me within reach of its other hand. Clawed fingers slashed at my throat, raking through the tough leather of the jack, the stiff collar of which reached to my jawline. I felt a burning pain as the tips of those ragged, yellow nails gashed through the skin. But none of the bone-hard edges cut through to my carotid or jugular veins, stopped short by the unearthly strips of demon-proof metal sewn within the collar.

The shock of the pain nearly served to freeze me in place. But I'd been through too many close scrapes in the past. Instead, I took advantage of the demon's following moment of hesitancy, the creature either surprised that I remained alive or experiencing some other unpleasant sensation upon contact with the protective metal. I reached behind me, grasped the hilt of the cinquedea, and tugged it free of the sheath that belted it horizontally at the small of my back. The short blade, not much longer than the distance from my elbow to my fingertips, tapered from a wide base to a gleaming point: a fat-bottomed triangle, strong enough to punch through armor or hack an arm clean off at the shoulder.

The hand on my ankle let go, reaching up for another hold. I shifted my stance, not to get out of the way, but to set my feet. As the arm groped for a grip on my belt, I raised the cinquedea overhead. The demon's fingers found purchase in my belt, tightened. As I felt the tug hauling me down, toward its gnashing fangs and toward the open, cupped hand readied for another blow, I slashed down, letting the demon's own strength add to the force of the strike.

The edge of the cinquedea met the demon's neck. The resistance I felt was akin to that encountered hacking into a thick tree branch. I hammered the blade in deep, cleaving halfway through the demon's neck. The fingers at my belt relaxed their grip. A weird soughing noise came from the demon, partially from the half-severed neck, partially from the slack mouth. I could almost imagine the sound was a sigh of relief.

The damage I'd inflicted, it seemed, was too much to allow the demon to sustain its form in our world. It dissolved into a red-tinged mist, redolent of sulfur and cinnamon. And then it was gone.

I won't say it left behind no trace. Its presence was indelibly marked by the grand sections of bronze statue lining the cavern walls. An artist's legacy.

I sagged, my legs temporarily incapable of holding me upright. I twisted to lean against the toppled bronze torso and breathed deeply. I'd done it. Commission complete. I had a fat purse of soldi to collect. And I anticipated consuming an inordinate quantity of wine. Yes, I'd share with my tent mates. The money—and the wine—would assuage any ill-will. In fact, given what I knew of soldiers, this incident could initiate a relationship close to brotherhood by the end of this campaigning season. Assuming we lived that long.

But what then? Then, back to Plenum. Enough hiding. I couldn't live as had the prefects of Tranta, perpetually putting off dealing with a problem, unwilling to take the steps necessary to get on with life beyond circumscribed limits, bound by a combination of fear and pride.

No. Once I'd fulfilled my contract with the condotta, Cesar the Bravo would return to Plenum.

The Red Hat

I had thought I would miss Giacomo's Wine Shop. It turned out that clean tables, copious lighting, prompt and courteous service—not to mention exceptionally good wine—vaporized any wistful longing I might have harbored for Giacomo's dim, dingy cellar and the throat-scouring near-vinegar he sold.

Plenum itself seemed to agree with my assessment of Trattoria Baccho, a hillside drinking establishment in a newly fashionable section of the Vimine district. A district I now called home, though my new place was admittedly a few twists and turns of Plenum's warren of streets away from the trendy area. Close enough though that I could consider Trattoria Baccho my new watering hole. It catered to more than me that evening; as I said, the city at large agreed this was the place to be. The diners and revelers patronizing the place that night included a party that occupied three tables and threatened to conquer more as the tipplers engaged jovially with neighboring parties, absorbing them into their own celebration.

And then the joviality took a less social turn, as it so easily can when the wine swillers swagger around with rapiers. A member of the larger group took affront at something said at a neighboring table. He was young, dark-haired (the norm in Plenum, of course), trim, and well into his cups. He surged to his feet, his low-backed chair (no cheap three-legged stools at Baccho's) toppling to the tiled floor. His hand went to the hilt of the sword hanging from a baldric faced in red silk. The rest of his attire matched the expense and showy style of the baldric. I'd like to have taken a moment to memorize the ensemble for later discussion with my tailor, Donatello: the slashed sleeves of the doublet, the padding at the thighs, etc. But I was already moving from my seat at a table-for-one in the corner.

I'd determined to adopt Baccho's as my own. Drunken brawls were fine for Giacomo's, but this wasn't Giacomo's. I was in a new place in my life and intended to keep that place unspoiled.

The man at the other table stood also. He had a few years on the offended youth—clearly a few more years of good living. Though dressed nearly as fashionably as the young man, he did not carry a sword. That lack did not seem to deter the youth, who ignored the placating gestures of the older man and drew his blade in a dramatically deliberate manner.

"Pardon me," I said, approaching the youth from his left side and drawing his attention away from the object of his wrath. "If you're going to commit murder, do you mind taking it outside? Some of us are trying to drink in here."

The hilt of my own rapier was already loosely cupped in my palm. I'd given myself enough space to draw if necessary, but I figured I'd start in a non-threatening manner. That notion lasted about a heartbeat.

The youth was not a picture of grace as he shifted to face me, but the steel in his hand appeared steady enough as he directed the point toward me.

"If you're going to pick a fight, Guellmo, I'm pleased to

see you at least have the courage to do so with an armed man." The words—each distinct and carefully pronounced in the fashion of a man endeavoring to demonstrate that he was not inebriated—emerged from a member of the party to which the youth—Guellmo, it seemed—belonged. This statement was met with approving, even sycophantic, chuckles from those about him.

I sighed and slid my rapier from its sheath. It seemed I was the armed man referred to.

I'd wanted to ensure the civility and peace of the establishment by shifting the impending violence outside, thus maintaining the atmosphere and making points with the management. Spilling blood inside was likely to achieve the opposite result.

So, I wouldn't spill any blood.

Guellmo did not share my pacific intentions. He attacked, the thrust coming in smooth and quick for a man who'd consumed an entire vineyard's worth of grape. But his line was off, arrowing for the middle ribs of my left side. I parried in quarte, bending my knees a trifle to compensate for his sloppy approach. The parry pushed his blade off line. Instead of responding with an almost instinctual riposte, I caught his blade in a bind, straightening my knees as I did. A darting half-step forward terminated the bind with a pinprick to his wrist as his rapier was at the apex of its compelled spiral. He let go of the hilt.

I should have stopped there, but I had an audience. I tried something I'd seen my fencing master Domenico perform once on a cocky tyro he'd been instructing. The trick was possible only because Guellmo was using a rapier with a traditional hilt, rather than the increasingly popular cup hilt. The quillon block guarded the hand with knuckle bow, rings, curving transverse bars, and other such convolutions that provided a graceful beauty as well as protection. As his rapier described a short arc through the air, I inserted the point of my own between side ring and knuckle bow, capturing the weapon and sliding it down the length of my blade, the two meeting with a musical chime.

A momentary silence fell. I tensed, waiting for Guellmo's friends to come to their feet and make their displeasure known in an overwhelming and brutal manner. Instead, cheers, laughter, and applause broke the silence.

The voice that had praised Guellmo for choosing a target other than an unarmed man rose above the clamor.

"There, you see, that is a bravo. Exactly the sort of man we need. Did you see that move? Not even Fienze's blade Ruggo could do that."

I picked the speaker out from the crowd. Young, as most of them were. If anything even more expensively dressed than Guellmo, who had stepped back and was nursing the nick on his wrist as if I'd severed his hand. The speaker was sleek, content, and well-fed, an incipient double chin beginning to develop, hinting at the corpulence he'd achieve if he maintained his sybaritic lifestyle. There was something about his clothing, something suggestive of the Collegium: a hint of clerical robing in the cut of his doublet, an evocative geometrical severity in the shape of his hat. A shade of crimson, identical to that of Guellmo's baldric and other fashion accents, predominated in the speaker's attire. In fact, I realized I could distinguish the core members of the party by that red hue.

The speaker went on, as if I were not there hearing him discuss me like a racing horse he considered purchasing. "Wasn't I just saying we needed a hired blade of our own? A man who will pick a quarrel for a purse full of pistras?"

Pistras? Back in my more destitute days (which, to be honest, until recently had been most of them) I'd once engineered a duel for a handful of copper soldi to pay off my bar tab to Giacomo.

No one argued with the speaker. Instead, I saw only nods of agreement. The speaker was clearly the hub of the group, the one whose opinion ruled. He deigned to address me directly.

"You, what is your name?"

I doffed my cap, and sketched a bow. "Cesar the Bravo."

"Well, Cesar, come sit. Have a glass with me."

I did. And so I met Primate Emalio Orzi, in Plenum with his retinue to push his candidacy for an open Councilor's seat, thus acquiring his Red Hat. The last thing I wanted to do was become involved again with the machinations of the Collegium. But the Collegium was the power in Plenum, the ultimate authority throughout most of the lands of the Faithful. Keeping clear of the Collegium might be a desirable goal, but it was hard to achieve in practice.

Emalio Orzi was young for a Primate. Notably so. But the Orzi family was immensely wealthy, a trading power entrenched in a port city to the southeast of Plenum.

Money can accelerate the advance of a career. And it seemed the Orzi hoped to push Emalio's to the penultimate rung, one step below the summit currently occupied by the Predicant.

There were rivals for the Red Hat vacancy. But only one seemed to matter: Primate Lorenz Fienze. The Fienze did not possess the same degree of wealth as the Orzi. But Lorenz had worked his way up steadily through the Collegium and was favored by the establishment. He was older, more experienced, and had had the years to develop connections that young Emalio lacked. And, it seemed, Lorenz Fienze had Ruggo, a bravo newly in from Ihbar, where he'd made a name for himself.

The wine flowed freely and at Emalio's expense. Somehow, without ever actually agreeing to anything, I found myself attached to the Orzi entourage, along with Guellmo and the rest of the young bucks carousing through Plenum, causing trouble and antagonizing the Fienze adherents while waiting for the Collegium to reach a decision.

The next morning, wishing I'd restrained myself somewhat (but free wine is free wine), I considered what I'd gotten myself into. At least I had comfortable surroundings for pondering and nursing a throbbing head. My days of living in a dilapidated one-room, rat-infested tenement in the Orine district were behind me. I'd parlayed a job into sufficient scudos to purchase an entire house of my own in the Vimine. Modest, perhaps, to those who inhabited villas on the Sabatine, but to me it was luxury.

A leisurely lunch at Madina's food stall purged any

lingering effects of the night before. By the time I finished, I'd resolved to learn more about Lorenz Fienze and his band of followers. I wasn't happy being assigned a side without any say in the matter. But if I must indeed become an Orzi partisan, I figured it was the path of wisdom to scout the opposition, see what I'd gotten myself into.

The afternoon I spent asking questions and wearing down my boot heels. By that evening, interminable hill climbs and descents brought me to the Broscine district where Lorenz Fienze entertained his band of well-wishers in an establishment known more for the commercially available charms of its women than for its wine. It also lay about as far from the Collegium as possible while still remaining within the bounds of Plenum proper. The Fienze adherents were partial to wearing yellow, but otherwise appeared much like the Orzi crowd. Perhaps trending a bit older, with subtle aspects of dress suggesting less affluence. As a gutter-born orphan, such distinctions had meant little to me, but they were now useful crumbs of knowledge for a bravo with the occasional need to navigate the treacherous shoals of the social hierarchy. Not to mention a bravo with an expensive penchant for dressing in the height of fashion, when in funds.

I found myself an unobtrusive table from which to observe, tucked away near a staircase in a shadowed corner of the ground floor of the establishment. The place was a repurposed structure of the Ancients, its weathered concrete and chipped marble patched with mortared stone. Lorenz Fienze did nothing to hide his status as Primate, openly wearing his Collegium robes. The staff showed no fear of him, nor any unusual deference, suggesting he frequented the house. He looked much like I imagined Emalio Orzi would in about a decade. That is, corpulent. While the Fienze clan could not boast the wealth of the Orzi, they seemed to have profited from Lorenz's position in the Collegium. Wine flowed freely, women drank glass for glass with the yellow-clad men. I observed more than one pairing slip away to climb the stairs. There awaited private rooms on the upper floor built of brick, plastered with ochre and cream stucco.

Only one man in yellow kept to himself, nursing a glass of the mediocre house red. Hooded eyes above a sharp prow of a nose regarded the festivities with a barely concealed contempt. He watched, silent and motionless as a bird of prey. When I did see him move, it was with the smooth, rapid grace of a striking viper.

A gentleman entered the common room. From the dust layering his five-years-out-of-fashion clothing (a ruff that broad, seriously?) he was no Plenumite. Some country gentleman from the provinces in the city on rare business, I guessed. The scabbard of the sword at his side caught on the edges of table tops and threatened to become wedged between chair legs. He looked about himself with frank curiosity and a touch of bewilderment. His awkward passage from door to bar brought him past the quiet man in yellow. The chape of his errant scabbard clattered against a chair adjacent to the man in yellow. Somewhat startled by the noise, the country gentleman started, his abrupt turn causing the scabbard to strike the knee of the man in yellow.

The man in yellow uncoiled. He was on his feet, hand

on the hilt of his rapier in an eyeblink.

"Ruggo," snapped Primate Lorenz Fienze, in the tone of one used to being obeyed. Then the tone softened, and in a half chuckle Fienze said, "Oh, as you will."

Ruggo stepped toward the country gentleman, who was stammering apologies and backpedaling toward the bar. Ruggo looked every inch the bravo. He was tall, lean, broad of shoulder, and narrow of waist. Tight hose above half boots displayed powerful calves. In short, he was my opposite. I'm built more like the ideal of a wrestler than a swordsman: low to the ground, thick chested, and muscled like a laborer rather than a fencer. Such is life.

"You, hayseed. You smell like the back end of a horse," Ruggo said. His accent placed him as Ihbarian.

"I'm sorry, sir. It was an accident. Please, let me buy you a cup of wine to make amends."

"You carry a sword, hayseed. That means there is only one way to make amends."

What happened next was not pretty. The Ihbarian style of fencing is florid, more space-consuming than that of Plenum, which emphasizes economy of movement. Had Ruggo faced an opponent with more than a rudimentary familiarity with the sword, I might have found it instructive. Instead all I learned was that Ruggo was a bully and a sadist. He toyed with the hapless gentleman before running the sweating, exhausted, and terrified man through the heart.

I must have let some of my disdain show. A Fienze adherent—to judge from the yellow silk panels of his doublet—descended from the upper floor near the end of Ruggo's display of butchery and stopped beside my table as I grunted something uncomplimentary beneath my breath.

"Uncivilized, these Ihbarians. Half-heathen, if you ask me," he said. "But, at least he's on our side." He blinked at me, then said, "I beg your pardon. I assumed you were with Primate Fienze."

Perhaps I could still remain unobtrusive. "You have my pardon. In fact, sit with me, share a flagon, and tell me about the Primate."

It did not work. The Primate himself noticed the advent of my new friend and waved him over, genially inviting him to describe his amatory adventure upstairs. And, with a broad, universal generosity he hadn't shown to the poor country gentleman, he insisted I join the group to partake in the next flagon.

A description of a night of drinking is substantially less entertaining than the night itself. To summarize: Lorenz Fienze, though a genial host, was also calculating. With armed factions roaming Plenum, each supporting opposing candidates for the Red Hat vacancy, he felt less than secure. Accidents happen. Bodies appeared every morning in Plenum's alleys or drifted heavily along the Cloatus until they sank. That sort of occurrence had increased in the past couple of weeks as the competing parties encountered each other in the streets. Once he'd discovered my profession, it wasn't long until I received an offer of employment.

The idea of earning two paydays from this contest for a seat on the Council appealed to me more and more, the increasing appeal linked to each additional glass I consumed.

When I sobered up the next morning, the pain I endured came as much from the realization of the danger I'd put myself in as from the hangover. What had I been thinking? Whoever won, I'd also be on the losing side. The members of the Collegium are our lords spiritual. Most are also magi, capable of summoning entities from the demon realm, thus making them practically our lords temporal as well. Angering anyone in the Collegium is an excellent way to find yourself facing a slavering, ten-foot-tall demon.

Leaving town suggested itself. But I'd only recently bought this house. The idea of abandoning it did not appeal. What then? Pick one side and inform the chosen Primate that I'd act as a double agent? Play both sides against each other? To what end?

Thinking hurt too much. I left home, shuffling bleary-eyed toward Madina's. A platter of olives, hard cheese, and bread helped some. The clay cup of a sweet, northern vintage might have helped more, but I barely had a chance to wet my lips before the seat next to me was occupied.

"Cesar."

Reluctantly I shifted my attention from the wine to the newcomer. He clearly knew me. Unfortunately, I knew him as well. He did a better job of hiding his membership in the Collegium than did young Orzi. The recently elevated Councilor Fenetto had more experience with discretion and a character predisposed to it. Taking a job for him was what had enabled me to purchase my new house, and I supposed I should be pleased to see him. Yet there were reasons beyond the mere social gulf between a Red Hat Arch-magus and a sellsword bravo that discouraged our meeting. We shared secrets that neither of us wished to come to light. Fenetto's approaching me publically, incognito or not, indicated the gravity of his motive.

I lifted my cup. "Congratulations on your Red Hat." The courtesy provided a good excuse for me to take the drink his arrival had preempted.

"Thank you, Cesar," Fenetto said. He ordered a cup of his own, tasted, and frowned. His palazzo on the Sabatine boasted a top-notch wine cellar, and his country estate possessed a fine vineyard. Madina's offerings could hardly be expected to rise to his standards.

He set down the cup, pushing it from him with a finger. "I need your help, Cesar. No, that's incorrect. The Collegium needs help, and it occurred to me that you might be the man to provide it."

Again, allow me to summarize. Councilor Fenetto had not approached me entirely of his own initiative. The directive to act came from the highest level. The Predicant himself disliked both major candidates for the open Council seat. He also disliked the disruptions, the street brawls, and back-alley knifings that accompanied the contest. He had declared that the disturbances must cease. Fenetto had taken it upon himself to hire me as the tool to see the Predicant's will done.

I'd have liked very much to say no. I was already in too deep and floundering about, trying not to drown in the fecal matter I'd thoughtlessly waded into. Adding yet a third client did not immediately appear wise. But I owed Fenetto. And the more I sat considering the matter, the more I saw the offer as a lifeline. Angering either Orzi or

Fienze put me on the bad side of a Collegium magus. What better way to avoid the ire of the Collegium than to serve the will of the Predicant, the very embodiment of the Collegium?

"Fine, your Eminence," I said. "What did you have in mind?"

Fenetto rose from the food stall chair and waved at a figure pacing the cobbles of the street. This one wore Collegium robes. The young man with an older man's serious expression approached as rapidly as dignity would allow. Fenetto introduced the Catechumen Sergiano Tritano. As a catechumen his position in the Collegium hierarchy was low. But if Fenetto trusted him, I'd best assume he was gifted and competent.

"This isn't a problem we can solve with quiet diplomacy and face-saving mitigants," Fenetto said. "We can't employ a blunt force solution either. The Predicant believes deploying soldiers would be a sign of weakness. You, Cesar, are the stiletto through the visor rather than the mace to the skull. Catechumen Tritano can provide that mace if absolutely necessary, if you can arrange for the blow to be struck discreetly."

Tritano allowed a supercilious smile to disturb his gravitas. He raised a chain of heavy brass links, partially concealed by the half-cloak fastened over his robes. At the end of it hung an ovoid of some dense, leaden material, artfully fashioned of loops, swirls, and arabesques. I recognized it. Or, rather, I recognized the sort of thing it was: a prison or containment vessel bottling up a demon. I'd encountered such before. In fact, I had a notion that I knew something about the material these devices were composed of that remained unsuspected (or at least held secret) by the Collegium. But that's another matter.

"This vessel cages a War Demon," Tritano said. His smile vanished when I nodded, unperturbed.

"Nasty sort of grenado, I know," I said. "Toss it into the midst of a fray, and out boils a mountain of muscle, fang, and claw. Fine, I can see how you're the bludgeon to the back of the head, Sergiano."

I turned dismissively from the catechumen to the Red Hat in mufti. "Now, Fenetto, about payment..."

The rest of the day I spent shuttling between the Orzi and Fienze camps. A certain wheedling charm is requisite in the best bravos. Convincing people to show up at a certain place at a certain time is often useful in orchestrating a duel. My plan required priming the pump with suggestions to a few of the minor hangers-on of each faction, then steering some conversations in the desired direction. But by that evening, both the Orzi and the Fienze entourages were filtering through the streets of Plenum to attend what I'd insinuated was a monumental party thrown by a wine importer eager to curry favor with the soon-to-be-elected Red Hat; a party featuring flowing hogsheads of noble vintage, women of negotiable virtue representing all lands of the Faithful, and—in some tellings—even the highlights from a comic opera.

South of the Sabatine district opens a flat plain upon which the Ancients had built a vast, oval racetrack. Most of it was now an open market, catering to the servants who stocked the kitchens of the palazzos and villas that marched up the sides of the Sabatine. But at one end rose the decaying remains of a structure of indeterminate purpose. It functioned now as a storage depot for grain, olives, and other produce. What it was originally, who could say? It showed evidence of dating back to the days of the Ancients, but like so many of Plenum's buildings it had, over the course of generations, been added on to, partially demolished, rebuilt, and remodeled in the varying architectural styles of a thousand years.

I'd taken shameless advantage of Councilor Fenetto's authority and wealth. Cressets lining the walls of the cavernous space illuminated trestle tables loaded with viands, arrays of goblets, and bunged hogsheads: the bait to my trap.

I escorted Lorenz Fienze's bunch there first. He strode amiably beside me, the remnant rosy glow of a bibulous lunch still visible in the fading twilight. Ruggo the Ihbarian stalked along at the rear. When I glanced back, I caught him turning and frowning, not liking something about the situation. I led the way in, thrusting back the doors and loudly declaiming that the feast was laid.

The others piled in behind me, swarming into the place, eager for yet another party. Primate Fienze blinked at me.

"I see the food. I even, praise be, see the wine. But where are the servitors? Where are the women?"

"An excellent question, My Lord. May I suggest you set your partisans to pouring the wine and dishing up the food while I go investigate?"

I think the notion of watching some of his good-for-nothing relations do some actual work tickled Fienze, and he put my plan into motion at once. I made for the exit. Ruggo met me as I started to slip out.

"I'll come with you," he said. "I don't like the smell of

this."

"Know what, Ruggo? Neither do I. Maybe I ought to stay behind, watch the Primate's back while you go see what's going on."

Ruggo frowned, swiveled to take a look at his employer, who was cheerfully ordering a gorgeously attired hanger-on to knock the bung from a cask. Ruggo looked back at me, then shook his head.

"No. That's my meal ticket. You'll not be snaking it from under me, Cesar."

"Ruggo, you wound me. Fine. I'll track down the catering staff myself."

I left. I nodded to Catechumen Tritano, hunkered down in a shadowed alcove, of which the exterior of the warehouse possessed an abundance. I doubted I'd be able to see him by the time I returned as night was fast enveloping the city.

Orzi's entourage carried lit torches as I led them from the designated rendezvous. The young swells swaggered, laughed, and swore as they passed through the streets, the exuberance of youth and comradeship rendering them princes of the city, lords of the night. Invulnerable and invincible. The dwindling traffic gave them wide berth. Few honest folks remained on the cobbles after the sun went down. Night was the abode of large, armed parties, thieves, whores, assassins, and bravos.

I tried to spot Tritano as we neared the warehouse, but failed. Light beckoned beneath the wide double doors and beneath the cracks.

I slowed as we drew close. Primate Orzi gave me a questioning glance, his face in the torchlight a picture of youth and happiness.

"I need to bleed the demon," I said in answer to his unspoken query. "Barge on in, My Lord. They are expecting you."

I slipped away into the darkness. Once out of sight I sprinted, making for a corner of the building from which I could observe the entry. With the assuredness of a man accustomed to belonging wherever he set foot, Orzi thrust open the doors and strode through without pause, his retinue continuing to jest and laugh as they pushed in after him.

Catechumen Tritano rose from his shadow as the rearmost man in red barged through the doors. The magus removed the orb—the demon prison—from over his head, then tossed it like a grenado, chain and all, deep into the suddenly silent warehouse. He spoke a word I could not hear, and probably wouldn't have understood if I had. Then he pulled the doors closed.

I moved, clambering up the rough, irregular stones of the building. I worked my way above the door, and there I crouched. Not, I'd like to think, like a gargoyle, but rather as one of the heroic statues of the Ancients that are still discovered from time to time when the foundation of a new house is dug.

The narrow ledge upon which I perched allowed me sufficient space to twist and shift without falling off. I squirmed about and found a spot in the wall where the mortar had crumbled and fallen free from between two stones. Leaning my head against the stones enabled me to place one eye to the gap and observe the carnage inside the warehouse.

The Fienze and Orzi hadn't truly begun their set-to. I could see only one man in red down. Ruggo stood over him, bloodied sword in hand. The two factions were focused on the advent of the monster in their midst, rather than on each other. The War Demon towered above the two retinues, a behemoth of horn and claw, it scales glistening the color of congealing blood in the light of the cressets. It bellowed, and waded into the drawn swords, indifferent to faction, favoring neither side.

Some stood in shock, unmoving as claws ripped open throats, as hands as broad as shovels hurled men with bone-breaking force against the walls. Other men panicked, overturning tables in their flight. Food and wine mingled in the air with the spray of blood. Swords struck the War Demon's hide and glanced harmlessly off, points slipped off or dug in so little that the demon did not appear to notice.

The two Primates slipped behind overturned tables, out of my view. Ruggo followed their example in taking cover, but only after—with a casual malice—pausing to stick the point of his rapier into Guellmo's back as the Orzi adherent flailed wildly at the War Demon.

The War Demon required less than a minute to wipe out half of its helpless victims. The initial opposition of the bravest turned into a rout, and the demon commenced stalking the survivors. A few of these recalled their mutual enmity, attacking each other as they fled: running, leaping over or crawling under tables, jumping overturned hogsheads of wine, desperately dodging and ducking the claws and snapping tusks of the War Demon. An ugly free-for-all with the winner predetermined.

But then a spiral of green and gold smoke arose beside the table behind which one of the Primates had taken refuge. The two were both magi. Fienze, I assumed, possessed bona fide Arch-magus talent. And even though Orzi had been considered for the open Council seat due to his family's wealth, he couldn't have made it as far as he had in the Collegium without possessing some legitimate skill of his own. I was not surprised then, when the glittering particles of green and gold cohered, and where the smoke had been there now crouched a stocky, ape-like demon with four arms. Its thick, shaggy fur was a muddy ochre color, brightened by a ruff of bone-like spikes around its throat, the color of aged ivory.

With a shriek, it threw itself at the War Demon. The two thrashed and battered at each other, biting and tearing, providing the still-living men a temporary respite.

One of the doors below me scraped open, drawing my attention away from the carnage. Two men—one in yellow and one in red—burst forth, engaged in frenzied combat complicated by fearful glances back inside. Neither noticed Catechumen Tritano standing before them. I hadn't either. He may have looked mature and serious, but apparently he was enough of a young idiot to want to watch the mayhem inside through a gap in the doors instead of finding a safe place to await the outcome.

He went down, catching a sword thrust through the throat. Then all three were down, the others tripping over his body and getting tangled in his Collegium robes. The two others thrashed, cursed, punched, and stabbed. Then both fell silent, unmoving.

I considered jumping down and running. The plan had

required Catechumen Tritano to release the War Demon. It had also relied on him to imprison it again or dismiss it back to the demon realm once it had done its bloody work. I wasn't prepared to tackle a demon. I'd not worn the unique armor that provided me some protection against demons, and I was armed only with rapier and main gauche, having left my sturdy, broad-bladed cinqueada at home. I'd have been unconvincing to either side had I led them to a party while dressed for battle.

Flight recommended itself as the safest course. But I'd agreed to take the job for Councilor Fenetto. And I couldn't help but feel this mess was partially my fault; I had gotten involved with both rivals. Also, disappointing the Predicant seemed a poor choice. The factor that tipped the balance, that kept me crouched over the doors, was the presence of the two Primates, one of whom had already summoned a demon of his own. Two might be capable of defeating the War Demon. Or, at the least, of damaging it.

From the screams inside, it wasn't much of a hope. The War Demon must have been back to his hunt, or had found a way to take on the ape-demon while continuing his slaughter. The bellowing and smashing I heard suggested the latter possibility, sounding like a bull charging through a weakened fence at a challenger. That notion offered the distant possibility of the demons clearing up the problem themselves, through mutual destruction. I'd witnessed more than one such encounter. They tended to be this noisy. And hard on the furniture.

With a spark of optimism kindled, I turned back to look in time to see the War Demon using the ape-demon as a cudgel, splattering a pair of Fienze adherents against the wall and shattering another cresset in the process, igniting the ape-demon's fur. The ape-demon began to dissolve, becoming again a diffuse mass of green and gold smoke that blinked into nothingness.

The ape-demon, however, had provided enough time for another summoning. A squatting, four-legged thing with an outsized head—something like a reptilian bulldog, its pebbled skin a glossy, ruby-studded turquoise green—sprang up, sinking fangs the length of cutlasses into the shoulder of the War Demon. That, however, was the extent of its success. With its free arm the War Demon tore loose the bulldog and exuberantly battered it into non-existence—braining Emalio Orzi in the process when the Primate made a break for the doors.

I shook my head. So much for optimism. But I'd already determined my course. Watching the War Demon's final mopping up would do nothing but weaken my resolve. So I faced the other way and prepared.

Moving gingerly to retain my balance, I slid free both rapier and parrying dagger, reversing my grip on each hilt. It was awkward; neither blade was meant to be held in such a fashion. But I had few advantages and figured I'd best make full use of what little I had.

The sounds of combat diminished, then ceased. Only dwindling moans and whimpers reached my ears. Then a chuffing and grunting preceded an unsteady shuffling of feet.

The War Demon emerging from the massacre limped heavily. One massive, scaled arm hung at an awkward angle, thick black blood trickling down the purple integument that gleamed eggplant dark, backlit by the increasingly bright firelight. A hornlike fringe ran about the base of a head that merged without a noticeable neck into shoulders nigh twice as broad as those of my own stevedore-like frame. I couldn't accurately judge its height from above, but my one-eyed view of the slaughter in the warehouse provided an estimate of nine or ten feet tall.

The smart thing to do would be to let it limp away. Let the Collegium clean up the mess. The magi would deal with it before it could do more than demolish a house or a shop or two, maybe kill a score or so of innocents. Plenumites were used to demons. The beings were nigh ubiquitous in the city: constructing monuments, running errands, delivering messages, and otherwise serving the members of the Collegium. True, the commonly utilized variety here in the city were not War Demons, but people would know to get out of the way. So I knew I ought to stay put, do the smart thing.

As usual, I did not do the smart thing.

I dropped from my perch, utilizing my weight and the fall to drive my blades through scales and thick hide I probably wouldn't have been able to pierce with strength alone. The main gauche sank to the clamshell guard. The rapier penetrated about half its length, then began to bend as I slipped down the broad back, rough scallop-edged scales abrading the fabric of my doublet. The rapier showed no inclination of sliding free of the deep wound, so I released my grip on the hilt before the steel blade reached the limit of its flexibility and snapped. A rapier is hardly a needle or a whip, but compared to, say, a cinqueada or a storta, it's slender. It is designed to flex and bend, but it is not meant to support the weight of a grown man. I couldn't afford to break it; a good sword is expensive.

I snapped my right hand over to grab my left wrist, and lifted my knees before my boots could touch the ground, throwing my entire body weight onto the short blade of the parrying dagger. The War Demon hide was thick and the muscle beneath incredibly dense, yet it wasn't stone or teakwood. The edge of the dagger began to draw raggedly down through the shoulder and into the back, hauled earthward inexorably by my weight.

The War Demon's confused whuffling had stopped at my advent. Now it bellowed, sounds I interpreted as pain and fury. It began circling, trying with its good arm to slap its tormentor off of its back. I hung on grimly, inching downward as yellow claws the length of boar tusks scraped against scales close enough to do further damage to my attire.

And then I fell a hand-span, my knees striking the cobbles with enough force to bruise even through my high-topped boots. Where the War Demon had roared and spun, I saw only an amorphous purple cloud swirling about me, shot through with crimson and emerald, scintillant in the light of the fire that seemed destined to engulf the warehouse and all evidence of what had transpired within.

As the cloud dispersed, returning the essence of the War Demon back to the demon realm, I squinted into the firelight. A dark form emerged from the roiling orange and yellow inferno. The furor of the flames consuming the fuel began to increase, starting to rival in volume that which had been produced by the now utterly vanished

War Demon. The scent of roasting flesh reached my nostrils at about the same time the dark form resolved into Ruggo, the yellow sleeves of his doublet scorched, smoke drifting up from singed hair. But his sword was in his hand, the blade dark to the quillon block with blood.

He did not seem to notice me, his cold, killer's eyes now wide and staring at nothing. I scrambled to my feet and scooped up my fallen rapier. I got my boots planted as Ruggo ran by and was in pursuit an instant later. Ruggo was a witness, a loose end that needed to be tied off. Also, I strongly disliked him. He was a stain on the already blotched and murky reputation of bravos.

We ran into the night. Plenum at night is best navigated by bats, not men. The blaze at the warehouse provided some visibility for awhile as we dashed through the empty stalls of the open-air market. Ruggo's yellow clothing was some help as it caught what stray light sources were available once we'd passed beyond the reach of the illumination cast by the conflagration. I almost lost him a couple times, finding him again only by the sound of his drumming boot heels on the treacherous footing of the worn cobblestones.

When Ruggo noticed me following him, I couldn't say. But my guess was that it was a moment before I heard his running footsteps slow. He didn't strike me as the type to run from a fight, rather the type to instigate one. By unspoken agreement we came to a halt in a narrow, oval piazza centered on a fountain—some sort of nymph disporting with a dolphin whose mouth spit forth a steady, musical stream of water into a stone basin. This was visible due to the ranks of flambeaux lining the exterior wall of a tavern or inn. If we were where I thought we were, it was both: an establishment catering to Northern mercenaries searching for work. They'd be inside swilling beer, singing songs, and—with atrocious grammar and limited vocabulary—propositioning the serving girls.

Ruggo turned to face me as I exited an alley that debouched into the piazza. He frowned. Then grunted.

"Cesar, of course," he said. "I knew something stank."

"You need to work on your banter," I said. "Try, 'Cesar, it is fortuitous we meet at this fountain, so that I may wash away your stench.' Show some flair, man."

I shook out my sword arm and rolled my dagger wrist as I spoke, moving slowly about the piazza to test the footing and give myself a chance to recover my breath after all that running.

Ruggo did likewise, not bothering to reply. Either he was saving his breath or he truly wasn't up to verbal fencing.

He was, however, up to the physical form. He came at me without salute or preamble, leaping in from an angle, his back to the tavern wall, the torchlight in my eyes. I gave ground rapidly, circling the fountain, parrying half-seen thrusts instinctively, and trying to widen the distance between us in the hope that any attacks that got through my half-blind defense could do little more than scratch.

The arcing retreat removed the glare from my eyes. I'd escaped with nothing more than a torn sleeve and graze on the left forearm. With some opponents, this might lead to a pause as each man considered his next few moves, studied the terrain, and evaluated options. Ruggo paused only to draw his own parrying dagger—little more than a poniard with curving quillons and a single loop—and came on again. He feinted to my right, then curled around to my left with a looping thrust to quarte that should have appeared awkward, but from Ruggo seemed merely flamboyant and dynamic. I edged it aside with the main gauche, hearing the foible ring against the curving clamshell guard. His leading leg was exposed and I flicked a thrust at the knee. But the leg was no longer there and for good measure he beat aside my blade with his dagger as he twirled away only to return from another angle.

The pattern—if that can be called a pattern—for the duel was thus set. Ruggo attacked relentlessly and never from the same angle twice. I countered steadily, riposting automatically, awaiting my opportunity. We circled the fountain twice. I imagine we drew spectators from the inn, probably wagering on the outcome. But I could not spare a glance and did not wish to risk the torchlight dazzling my vision.

The man would not stand still. He seldom came at me straight on, and when his motion suggested he would, it was almost always a feint. My breath began to come in ragged gasps. My already damaged doublet suffered more slashes from narrowly avoided blows.

Feigning a stumble wasn't hard; I was close to the point of exhaustion already. I'd backed close to the low wall of the fountain, driven back by a flurry of thrusts from both of Ruggo's blades. I allowed my back leg to bend a fraction more than it should, let the toe of my boot drift along the spray-dampened cobbles. I went down on one hand, holding myself off the ground with the guard of the main gauche. Had I found myself in that position unintentionally, Ruggo would have skewered me where I stood. Instead, I was up and moving a fraction of a second before his lunge could strike. His momentum carried him forward toward the fountain, while I scooted by and pirouetted to face him. Forced to turn to face me in response to my ploy, he yielded the initiative, at least for the moment. The pivot placed his back against the thigh-high rim of the fountain, limiting his options.

I did not give him the time to shift laterally. I came on, straight on, our stances mirrored, rapiers facing parrying daggers. I dropped the point of my main gauche, as if the fatigue was beginning to tell, inviting a rapier thrust. He responded to the weakness. As Ruggo's rapier flicked toward my heart, my left wrist turned, catching the foible and lifting, redirecting it above my left shoulder. At the same time, I extended my rear leg and lunged, shifting my line below the guard of his parrying dagger, and drove eight inches of steel into his chest at a rising angle, just beneath his sternum.

The cobbles rang as Ruggo's weapons dropped from suddenly nerveless hands, the sound muffling the explosive exhalation of one of his final breaths.

"For that poor country gentleman, you graceless butcher," I said. Then I recovered from the lunge, stepping forward and straightening up. The motion punched the point of my rapier entirely through Ruggo's body. The corpse sagged into me, and I held it momentarily upright, the spreading blood soaking into my doublet and completing its ruination. This night's work was proving hard on my wardrobe. A good chunk of what Fenetto had promised to pay would pass straight through to Donatello.

I considered the inn. Those who'd wagered on the winning duelist might stand me a drink with their winnings. But no. An evening without wine would do me no harm. And home beckoned.

END

www.ingramcontent.com/pod-product-compliance
Lightning Source LLC
Chambersburg PA
CBHW060939030726
47503CB00003B/660